D0262416

THE RISE OF THE
IRON MOON

By Stephen Hunt

The Court of the Air
The Kingdom Beyond the Waves
The Rise of the Iron Moon

THE RISE OF
THE IRON MOON

STEPHEN HUNT

HARPER
Voyager

Harper*Voyager*
HarperCollins*Publishers*
77–85 Fulham Palace Road,
Hammersmith, London W6 8JB

www.voyager-books.co.uk

Published by Harper*Voyager*
An imprint of HarperCollins*Publishers* 2009
1

Copyright © Stephen Hunt 2009

Stephen Hunt asserts the moral right to
be identified as the author of this work

A catalogue record for this book
is available from the British Library

ISBN 978 0 00 723222 2

This novel is entirely a work of fiction.
The names, characters and incidents portrayed in it are
the work of the author's imagination. Any resemblance to
actual persons, living or dead, events or localities is
entirely coincidental.

Typeset in Sabon by Palimpsest Book Production Limited,
Grangemouth, Stirlingshire

Printed and bound in Great Britain by
Clays Ltd, St Ives plc

All rights reserved. No part of this publication may be
reproduced, stored in a retrieval system, or transmitted,
in any form or by any means, electronic, mechanical,
photocopying, recording or otherwise, without the prior
permission of the publishers.

Mixed Sources
Product group from well-managed
forests and other controlled sources
www.fsc.org Cert no. SW-COC-1806
© 1996 Forest Stewardship Council
FSC

FSC is a non-profit international organisation established
to promote the responsible management of the world's forests.
Products carrying the FSC label are independently certified
to assure consumers that they come from forests that are managed
to meet the social, economic and ecological needs
of present and future generations.

Find out more about HarperCollins and the environment at
www.harpercollins.co.uk/green

'Every child comes with the message that God is not yet discouraged of man.'

Rabindranath Tagore

MORAY COUNCIL LIBRARIES & INFO.SERVICES	
20 26 58 37	
Askews	
F	

CHAPTER ONE

Purity Drake tried to struggle as the long needle of the syringe sank towards her arm, but the leather straps on the restraining table were binding her down too tight.

'Try not to move,' ordered the civil service surgeon operating the blood machine. 'We really do need to take a clean sample this time.' He looked across at the official from the Royal Breeding House. 'She can talk, can't she?'

'Oh yes,' said the breeder. 'Her family madness comes and goes, but when she's not fitting, she's actually quite well-spoken, for one of them.'

Talk? Surely that was a hypothetical question right now. Purity wanted to swear and scream, but the restraining table was fitted with a rubber sphere that inserted itself in the prisoner's mouth. After all, the civil service's surgeons didn't want their deliberations on bloodwork and which pedigree lines to crossbreed to be interrupted by abuse. She thrashed and tried to yell as the needle sank into her arm with a flare of pain, the glass tube of the syringe slowly turning crimson. She had been feeling faint enough before, on short rations for waking up the guards with her nightmares and

1

her cries – and her rations really hadn't been that generous to start with.

'We're under a lot of pressure to give this one a clean bill of health,' said the breeder.

The Greenhall surgeon shrugged and tapped the transaction-engine drum rotating in the steam-driven blood machine. 'I can only give you back what the machine says. How you choose to act on that information is up to you.'

'Come on,' pleaded the breeder. 'You know how thin on the ground we are for fertile females. She's just turned sixteen, we can't afford to let—'

The surgeon tapped the vial of blood, making sure every last drop cleared into the siphon on his machine. 'I can see precisely how thin on the ground you are. This family's history of lunacy would never have been allowed to breed down another generation in the old days.'

'Beggars can't be choosers. She's the last one of her house; we can't afford to let an entire royalist bloodline die out. Not now.'

The surgeon absently rubbed Purity's black hair as if she was a cat. 'Ah yes. The invasion.'

Ah yes. The invasion. Purity's eyes welled with tears at the memory of it; the carnage in the Jackelian capital and the charnel house that the Royal Breeding House had been turned into by the invading troops. The choice her mother had been forced to make by the foreign soldiers from Quatérshift, between Purity and her half-brother. Which of the royalist prisoners was to be allowed to survive. No choice at all, you always went with a fertile female; they were almost guaranteed to be forced to have children, to continue the family line. Purity tried to close the memory off. Her mother and brother being marched into the Gideon's Collar, the chack-chack-chack of the Quatérshiftians' notorious killing machine, each report a bolt through the neck.

'Pity about her madness, then,' sighed the surgeon. 'She's pretty enough, all things considered. Very unusual to see eyes this pale and blue. Green used to be the most common colour for the royalists' eyes, you know. A little piece of trivia. I collect them.'

Behind them, the blood machine began to rattle as a tape spool printed out its results.

'Is she fit to be taken to stud?' asked the breeder.

Purity struggled at the terrible thought of it, trying to break her bonds. Let her still be sick, with whatever illness was stopping them from treating her like a prize mare in season, even the fever of the family madness that had gripped her so tightly.

The surgeon shook his head, confused. 'No, it's another partial match for her. Less distinct than last time. Very odd. I can't even confirm her identity against her house records, let alone declare her clean for your use.'

'Your machine isn't working,' spat the breeder.

'It was working well enough for the duke's son I had in before,' said the surgeon. 'And I wager it'll be working fine enough for the children I have in tomorrow.' He rubbed the wound on Purity's arm with a swab, a brief sting of alcohol. 'What's going on in inside you, eh? Your precious royal blood. We'll do it the hard way, then. I'll get her sample sent over to the department and they'll check her bloodwork for diseases and the like. We don't want the next prince to have six fingers, now do we?'

The breeder snorted. 'We'll need another massacre over here before the likes of her would be used to sire a prince. The royal family are mad enough already from inbreeding without throwing this one into the mix. No, any children we squeeze out of her will only be used to diversify the royal breeding pool around the edges. Hopefully we'll be able to screen the worst of the lunacy out of her children if we can find her a suitable stud.'

Looking out through bars across the window, the surgeon folded the test results into his pockets. They were old-fashioned at the Royal Breeding House. No cursewalls laid by sorcerers. Just thirty feet of granite, the parapet patrolled by redcoats, their rifles slung over their shoulders and their shakos oiled against the rain.

The arm holding Purity's gag in place rose with a squeaking of metal, and the breeder unlocked her restraints. 'Thank the nice gentleman from Greenhall, then. It can't be pleasant for a gentleman such as he, coming all the way out here to the fortress to see the likes of you.'

Purity rubbed her arm, pulling the featureless brown house-issue shawl back over her wound. 'Thank you, sir, for taking the time to test me.'

It was a litany, really, like the oaths to parliament they made the royalist prisoners parrot in the brainwashing that passed for a school at the breeding house. The real farewell she invoked in her mind involved the needle on the machine and the surgeon from the civil service's stinking Department of Blood loosing his footing. Purity tried not to scowl. Keep your face neutral, a mask. That was the way you got through each day. She watched the breeder ring the bell-pull for someone from her dormitory to come and take her away.

Wiggling her cold toes on the flagstones, Purity stared enviously at the plain brown shoes on the Greenhall man's feet. Even a man's shoes like these would do, any shoes. Something to keep out the chill of the Royal Breeding House's stone floors.

'Take her back to her hall,' the breeder ordered the young girl who turned up at the door – another royalist prisoner.

'I missed the dinner call for the test,' Purity complained.

'Back to your dormitory,' snapped the breeder.

'We didn't get much,' hissed the girl who had been sent to escort Purity, closing the door to the surgeon's office. 'All of Dorm Seven's going hungry thanks to you.'

'It's the last day of short rations,' pointed out Purity, but she could hear the paucity of the excuse even as it escaped her lips.

The dreams, the dreams of her madness. Purity had always suffered them, but they had grown so much more intense last month, as if the flaming firmament accompanying the brief passage of Ashby's Comet across their skies had set fire to her mind. Now the thousand-year comet had sped past for another millennia-long circuit of the heavens, but its mortal effects remained – while she could get through most nights again without visions, without waking up the guards with her puking, there was still a gnawing raw emptiness in her gut.

Still, things could be worse. After the invaders from the Kingdom of Jackals' eastern neighbour – that most perfidious of nations, Quatérshift – had broken into the breeding house and slaughtered half of the royalists a few years back, things had nudged a little to the better. The shortage of those of noble descent meant that parliament's stooges couldn't go as hard on the royalist prisoners as they once had. Why, when Purity had been ten, a punishment like short rations – shorties – would have meant going hungry for a month, not a week. There was a rumour that those held prisoner at the palace were even served watered-down beer for supper now, the iron in the drink good for warding off flu and fever. Purity didn't believe it, though. Perhaps she'd bump into one of the royal family to ask the next time the palace grounds needed sweeping. Purity had known Queen Charlotte fairly well when the monarch had been a prisoner of the Royal Breeding House, though there was always the inverse snobbery of the house

5

to contend with. While the rest of the kingdom loathed the imprisoned royal family with a passion in proportion to their inherited rank – *bottles for a baron, eggs for an earl* rang the cry of the stall holders in palace square on stoning day – the blueblood prisoners of the breeding house wore their ancient titles like badges of courage. Which was bad news for Purity Drake. Her ancestors had barely qualified as knighted squires when they had found themselves on the losing side of the ancient Jackelian civil war. Add to that the fact that Purity was a mongrel – the mysterious identity of her father the result of an unplanned liaison forbidden by parliament's breeding programme – and it wasn't much of an exaggeration to say that there were guards patrolling the breeding house with more status than her among the royalist prisoners.

The hard shove in the small of her back as they got to Dorm Seven was a frankly unnecessary reminder of her position. Purity's heart sank as she saw the line of dorm mates waiting for her return. Emily was at their head, the self-appointed duchess of their dorm by virtue of her rank and her bulk. She had Purity's shoes, looted from her mother's few possessions after the massacre. They were faded and scuffed, but everyone knew whose shoes they were. Only the strong prospered in the breeding house. The rest made do with bare feet.

'It's the last day we're on shorties,' said Emily, 'and we don't want you shouting the odds tonight and bringing the guards down here again. We want to eat from full plates next week.'

'I won't wake the guards,' promised Purity. 'My nightmares have nearly passed now.'

'I was hoping the surgeon would have twigged that you're not one of us,' said Emily. 'That it was all a big mistake you being in the house at all.'

'Mongrel peasant,' called someone at the back. 'Half-caste guard's daughter!'

As Emily stood aside, Purity saw that the inmates of Dorm Seven had rolled the hard hemp blankets off their bunk beds and her heart sank in wretchedness.

'The word of your sort doesn't mean much to us, you understand.' Emily pointed to their bunks lined up against the damp wall. 'Time to walk the line, peasant.'

There were too many of them to fight back, and Purity knew it would only make things worse. The governor of the breeding house knew where collective punishment led: it led to the royalist prisoners keeping order among themselves – that was rather the point of it.

'Walk the line. Walk the line,' the chant began.

Purity sank to her knees and began to crawl under the line of bunks. A member of Dorm Seven stood at every gap and laid into her with knotted sheets as she emerged into the open, a few seconds of lashing pain before she dragged herself under the cover of the next bunk. Purity almost made it as far as the sixteenth bunk this time before the blackness of oblivion overtook her.

Kyorin leapt down the steps, the tranquillizer dart shattering above his head on the tavern sign swinging in the alley's draught.

Damn this foul complex of garbage-littered rookeries. Middlesteel was confusing enough a city to those born and bred to its smog-ridden lanes, let alone to a visitor and his companion. A companion who seemed to be far fitter than Kyorin, far better able to leave their pursuers behind him.

The dart's near miss gave Kyorin a second wind. His legs pumped harder and he nearly caught up with his companion, leaping over a couple of empty barrels tossed out of a jinn house, the smell of rancid water assaulting his nostrils. Kyorin was about to wheeze something but an outburst of crude drinking songs from the tavern behind them put him off. His companion redoubled his own efforts to escape, as if realizing that if Kyorin could catch up with him, then their pursuers – who lived for the hunt and the kill – would be close behind.

Steps led down to a wider street, just behind the course of the great river Gambleflowers. His comrade cut left in front of him and Kyorin followed. They really should have split up; Kyorin could have sprinted off in the opposite direction, hoping that the pursuit would only go after one of them, but he sensed that this would be death for him. Of course, Kyorin didn't want to die, but he also suspected that of the two of them, it was he who had the best chance of making contact with those who could help their cause. This fast-footed ally of his was desert-born, wild, simple and able – unlike Kyorin – to put up a fight worthy of the name. Neither of them knew the other, but that was the way with a rebel cell structure, compartmentalized to minimize infiltration and betrayal. That they were both in the capital city of the Kingdom of Jackals and on the run from those that hunted them was commonality of cause enough.

The sound of pounding feet down the stairs behind him made Kyorin's eyes dance about for an escape route off the street – disgustingly well-lit by the iron gas lamps rising out of the gutter. There! A passage, the smell of river water strong on the wind.

Kyorin sprinted away down the pathway, his companion taking another turn ahead. So many scents in Middlesteel – puddles of rain, wet grass in the parks, the river's pollution – nothing at all like the odours back home. The silence of the docks was broken by the beat of machines from a tannery on the other side of the river. Kyorin could sense the stench of death, of rotting animal skins, even from this side of the water. Curse his luck. The great sage had to have chosen *him* to come to this city, this Middlesteel, this capital of the strange, rain-soaked nation of Jackals. But no other rebel had been in the right place to pose as a loyal servant joining the party scouting Jackals. And now someone or something had given Kyorin away. Was it the fact that he had allowed a stow-away to join their party, the desert nomad who seemed so eager to abandon his slow, unfit ally, now that their ruse had been rumbled? Had the fool forgotten to use his masking stick to disguise his scent? Perhaps Kyorin could ask his hunters what had given them away, before the monsters devoured him.

Out in the open, the nomad raced away, disappearing into the docks – past silent cranes and bundles of pulley ropes lying on the cobbles. Kyorin was about to follow after him, when a bright light shone in his face, destroying, as was intended, his night vision.

'Aye, aye. What's all this, then?'

Blinking away the dots of light dancing in front of his eyes, Kyorin saw it was a policeman. A *crusher*, as the locals called the enforcers of their law, his black uniform illuminated by the backspill from a bull's-eye lamp. The crusher rested a hand on his belt, heavy with a police cutlass, a leather holster and a hulking cudgel.

'You just off a boat, then?'

Taken for a foreigner. Well, that was true enough.

'I have to get away,' said Kyorin, 'There—'

'Like your mate who bolted off?' said the crusher. 'Them that runs away from a warehouse past midnight normally have their pockets full of something that doesn't belong to them, in my experience.'

It was dark enough that the policeman hadn't noticed that Kyorin was managing to talk without moving his lips.

'Please, you must help me—' Kyorin's plea was interrupted by a scream from the docks, the nomad breaking cover, a flaming comet with his clothes and body on fire. Not yet dead, Kyorin's companion launched himself into the river, dousing the flames – but of course, the desert-born could not swim, and as he realized that he had traded a death by fire for a death by water, the wounds of his incineration overcame him. The corpse swept past them face-down on the fast-moving currents. The river took everything, in Middlesteel.

'Bloody Nora,' said the policeman, his hand sweeping down towards his pistol as his lamp shone along the dock front. 'You lads been nicking oil?'

Kyorin's companion had put up a fight, then – enough of a fight that *they* hadn't taken him alive with a paralysing dart, but burnt him to the ground with a lethal-force weapon. From behind the crates a couple of dark shapes shifted just out of sight, hissing in frustration that they hadn't been able to feed on their first victim. An eerie clicking sounded out of sight of Kyorin and the policeman, rising and falling in a rattlesnake rhythm.

'Just how many of you are there out thieving tonight?' asked the policeman, annoyed that one of the gangs of the flash mob had chosen his beat for their night's pilfering. He rested his lamp on a pulley block and aimed his pistol down the dock towards the crates. 'Out you come, you toe-rags. Step lively now.' His spare hand unclipped a Barnaby Blow from his belt. He flicked the trigger on the bronzed canister of compressed air and a banshee whistle split the night. Other whistles sounded as nearby crushers converged on the position of an officer in need.

10

The hunters' lethal-force weapon would be recharging. Kyorin only had seconds left.

'No you don't, my old son.' The policeman's pistol swung towards Kyorin and he pointed to a pair of iron manacles he had laid next to the lamp. 'You slip those on, nice and easy, like.'

'Run, you fool,' Kyorin pleaded to the policeman. 'You can't—'

'Hey!' The Middlesteel constable had finally noticed that Kyorin was speaking without his lips moving. 'How—?'

The bolt of fire leapt out from the other end of the docks, striking the crusher on his chest. The black patent leather belt that crossed his tunic shredded as the uniform became a conflagration, the silver belt buckle bearing the arms of the Middlesteel police flying past Kyorin's face, tiny drops of molten metal splattering his brown hair.

Kyorin caught the burning police officer's body as he fell back, just enough life left in him to help Kyorin escape – to serve and protect, as the crusher's oath demanded. Resting his hand above the policeman's fluttering eyes, ignoring the smell of burning flesh – so repellent to a plant-eater – Kyorin made the connection to the crusher's forehead with his hand. *Swim. How to Swim? I must know!* Kyorin was flooded by images – visions that seemed to last hours rather than the solitary second that was passing: the chemical reek of the public baths along Brocroft Street, a stream in a small flint-walled village in Lightshire, fishing rods laid down in the grass while the policeman and his friends launched themselves into the water. The images grew angular and sharp, the constable's brain shutting down as the fatal burns worked their way through the beautiful system of cooperating organs that was his body.

Letting the dead policeman drop, Kyorin sprinted towards

the river and launched himself into its cold, enveloping cover as the howls of his pursuers echoed around the docks. Holding his breath, Kyorin kicked under the surface, using his new-found swimming skills, allowing the current to sweep him away as the water boiled where the hunters' recharged weapon furiously steamed the river's surface. But the waters were deep and wide and the sky too dark for the hunters' killing lances of fire to find his heart this night. With the weapon drained, a hail of darts broke the surface, spiralling past Kyorin like stones dropped in the water. Their final act of desperation became a brief flash of elation for Kyorin. He had escaped! As he swam, his hand checked the carefully wrapped bulge in his pocket where the book was, brought from the stationer's cart on Burberry Corner with a coin so realistic the shop-keeper would never realize it had been perfectly counterfeited for the expeditionary party. Back home, that book would have been a death sentence. But here in Middlesteel, well, here it might just be a chance for life.

Kyorin let the currents carry him after the corpse of his compatriot, the poor dead desert nomad, leaving hungry mouths behind on the docks; mouths that would now be considering how best to evade the call of compressed air whistles converging on their position on the docks.

The river took everything, in Middlesteel.

Warder Twelve looked at the new boy, hiding his deep reservations about the quality and judgement of the lad. Why, wondered Warder Twelve, when analysts in the great transaction-engine chambers did not live up to their potential, did the Court of the Air's ruling council always judge that their next career move should be across to the spheres of the aerial city where the Court held its prisoners? Surely the dangerous breed that the Court of the Air removed from circulation in the Kingdom of Jackals warranted more respect than the bored attitude of this new greenhorn. A greenhorn who judged – quite rightly – that duty minding the cells was something of a demotion from modelling the plays and flows of their civilization in the great transaction-engine chambers.

'So, these colours,' said the boy, tapping the card slotted above the armoured cell door. 'They indicate the potential of the prisoner to make trouble?'

'Aye,' said the warden, 'and the care you need to take when interacting with the prisoner. The likelihood they might escape.'

'Escape?' The lad laughed. 'There has never been an escape from the Court of the Air. Not once in five hundred years.'

Warder Twelve winced. This young buck didn't see all the work that went into keeping things that way: the effort, the foiled escapes – many of them just mind games to keep hope alive in the prisoners, to keep their wickedness and ingenuity flowing in streams the Court could control and curtail. It was the curse of being a warder. Nobody noticed when you did your job well; nobody thanked you for decades of trouble-free internment. But let just one rascal escape, why then the rest of the aerial city would be complaining for months about how many staff it took to man the cells, how they did nothing but sit around and play cards out on the prison spheres.

'This is a green-ten,' said the warder, laying a hand on the cell door. 'Green is the lowest level of threat and ten is the lowest level of prisoner intelligence.'

'Ah,' said the lad. 'A politician, then.'

The warder opened a small slot in the door, a slit of one-way glass revealing a man in a faded waistcoat sitting by a desk before a sheaf of papers, reaching over to dip his metal stylus in a pot of ink. Writing memoirs that nobody would ever read – well, nobody except the Court's alienists, as the surgeons of the mind perfected their understanding of the criminal soul.

'Crimes against democracy. This flash fellow used to represent a district down in Middlesteel, until he started using his street gangs to intimidate voters on election day. We disappeared him after he made contact with the flash mob to arrange to have two of his opponents poisoned.'

'He hardly seems worth the effort,' said the boy.

'You think so?' The warder shook his head. Underestimating an opponent. Shocking. Hadn't his tutors knocked *any* sense into him when he had first been apprenticed into the Court of the Air's service?

The lad fingered the red lever to the left of the door, a wax seal protecting the metal switch, proving it was unbroken and had never been used. 'Decompression throw for the cell?'

'Yes.' Warder Twelve pointed to a bigger lever at the end of the corridor. 'That one up there will flush the whole level, in case there's a mass breakout attempt. Back in the control room we can blow the entire aerosphere and disconnect all corridors into the rest of the city if it cuts up really rough across here.'

'Have you ever had to blow a cell?'

'On my watch?' said the warder. 'Once, seven years back. The science pirate Krook. He had decrypted the transaction-engine lock on his cell and was working on the last of his door bolts. He was a master of mesmerism and had hypnotized the warder walking his level. We killed Krook from upstairs. He left us no choice in the matter.'

The lad nodded. Explosive decompression, a couple of seconds choking in the slipstream of the troposphere, then unconsciousness long before the impact of a mile-high fall from the dizzying height of the Court's levitating city removed his mischief from the face of the world. A fitting fate for an enemy of the state.

The lad looked up at the card above the next armoured door. It was purple, with the numeral *one* stencilled across it. 'That's the first time I've seen that colour over here.'

'A P1. So, you've a taste for the strong stuff?' noted the warder. 'Do you really want to see who's inside this cell?'

'I—' he hesitated. 'I think so.'

Warder Twelve laid his hand on the viewing slit. 'Then gaze upon *Timlar Preston*!'

Timlar Preston? But this was just a man, not an ogre. Old and thin, in a cell wallpapered by white sheets, every inch thickly pencilled with formulae and diagrams. He was standing pushed up against a wall – so close you'd think he was trying to draw warmth from the riveted metal, his pencil scratching in ever smaller circles, the writing increasingly tiny now there was hardly any space on the papers left. He turned around to gaze at the viewing slit, a flash of wild eyes and wispy silver hair, then returned to his scribbling.

'He can see us?' asked the lad. 'I was told that the door's cursewalls allowed one-way viewing only?'

'He always knows when we're watching him,' said Warder Twelve. 'Don't ask me how. There's a touch of the fey about him, if you ask me.'

The greenhorn gazed into the cell again. Timlar Preston didn't seem like much, certainly not the man who had nearly destroyed the Kingdom of Jackals during the Two-Year War, the *Great War*, the foreigner whose weapons had propelled the hell of conflict deep into the Jackelian counties. He was from Quatérshift, that much you could see, a dirty shiftie, no honest, round jowls of the Jackelian yeoman for this one; no honest fat from a diet of roast beef, beer and jinn. Thin, wiry, with a proud nose that lent him an hauteur distinctly lacking in his mad scratchings.

'You still think you have what it takes to keep such as he away from our shores?' asked Warder Twelve.

The lad held his tongue. Inside the cell, Timlar Preston was turning in a circle, waving his pencil. Conducting an imaginary symphony of madness.

'You want to keep him dancing for us, rather than inventing bloody great devices of war for the shifties to use against your fellow Jackelians? Men like him aren't controlled by this—' the warden slapped the transaction-engine drum turning on the armoured lock. 'They are controlled up here!' He tapped his skull. 'Walking the cells with a toxin club swinging from your hand won't be your vocation in the prison spheres, any more than tapping the ivories on your key-writer was your job when you worked over in analysis. Getting into the minds of people like Timlar Preston, that's the task for you and me. We drug his food once a week; change his pencil for one slightly fatter, slightly longer, a different shade. To keep him off balance, you see? Then we take his sketches, the ones we can understand, and change some of the formulae. Forgery section uses his handwriting to do it for us. Just enough to keep him wondering if it was he who wrote the maths or one of us. Just enough to keep him wondering if he's going mad. And while he's doing that, he's not trying to break the hex we've got laid around his cell. He's not thinking of creating weapons that could lay waste to our country.'

Timlar Preston's mad dance in the centre of the cell had ended, the genius arriving at the other side of the viewing slit in three long, low strides. His shriek was relayed by the voicebox next to the cell door, the piece of paper he had been writing pushed up against the viewing slit, full of spirals, a procession of seashell-like geometries drafted with insane precision. 'They're coming! They're coming!'

The lad looked at Warder Twelve. 'What is he talking about?'

'Something new,' said Warder Twelve. 'He's been ranting about it for days. He's due for the old sleepy soup and a few mind games at the end of this week. When we search his cell, we'll probably find the notes on whatever his latest obsession is.'

'I can hear him!' Preston yelled. 'Talking to me. Telling me what to do. What we need to do to survive.'

Warden Twelve flicked the sound off the voicebox and closed the viewing slit. 'Back to the lifting room; the next level down is where we keep the prisoners with special powers – all the fey ones, the sorcerers and witches. You're going to *love* them.'

They walked away, oblivious to the muffled banging on the other side of the cell door. Timlar Preston howling and throwing his papers around the cell.

Commodore Black looked over at his friend Coppertracks. It would take someone very used to steammen ways to tell that the scientist was nervous. But then, the commodore had lived with the steamman under the roof of Tock House for long enough that he could read the patterns of energy that danced under his iron friend's transparent crystal skull like other men could read furrows in a brow or the nervous drum of fingers on a desk. And it took a lot to make one of the metal creatures nervous.

The patter of polite applause from the direction of the stage indicated that the previous presentation in front of the massed ranks of the Royal Society was going well. Well for the presenter, but not so well for Coppertracks' chances of

17

extracting the full financial and intellectual backing of the society if they squandered their time and resources on too many of his rivals' proposed projects. It was a competitive business, this society of ideas, mused the commodore – as if the Kingdom of Jackals only had so much deck space for what its people thought about, and the pondering of one belief – one truth – left less room for any others to thrive.

'You are sure you have all of my slides in the correct order?' asked Coppertracks.

'You know that I do,' said the commodore. 'Haven't I practised enough on your blessed magic lantern back at the house? You keep your attention on the audience, I shall give your scientist friends a visual display of your genius that would put to shame the lantern operators of the theatres along Lump Street.'

'There is really no need for you to assist me, dear mammal,' said Coppertracks. 'I could have brought one of my mubodies to operate the projection apparatus.'

Commodore Black nodded, but didn't point out that having one of the steamman's metal drones capering about the stage would only serve to remind the mainly warm-blooded races sitting in the auditorium that Coppertracks was a slipthinker – his genius so large he had to distribute his consciousness among multiple iron bodies. Back home in the Steammen Free State, they treated Coppertracks as royalty. Here in the Kingdom of Jackals, he was just a metal clever clogs who constantly reminded the members of the Royal Society how dim most of them were in comparison.

'Now,' said Coppertracks, rubbing nervously at his metal hull, polishing it to a high, gleaming sheen, 'where is Molly softbody? She must have picked up that slide I changed by now.'

'I have,' said a voice behind them. It was Molly Templar,

the third member of the trio that shared the comforts inside Tock House's walls. Molly was sweating slightly under her long red hair – she had obviously been straining to get to the presentation in time. 'It turned out the chemist finishing off your last slide was one of the more persistent devotees of my writing. He wouldn't hand over the damn thing until I had signed at least two of my novels for him.' She produced a little glass square, chemically etched with one of the steamman's images.

Molly peered round the curtain to see how well the current presenter's talk was going, then ducked back and lifted a copy of the *Middlesteel Illustrated News* out of her coat pocket, passing it to Coppertracks. 'Read the cover story. It's a pity your presentation isn't proposing a superior design for airship engines. The merchant marine has grounded all its flights – apparently dust from the wake of Ashby's Comet has fouled the fleet's motors. While they're being checked and cleaned out on the airship fields, the cost of narrowboat berths and stagecoach tickets is rising in every county.'

Coppertracks showed the commodore the newspaper's cover illustration, a swarthy canal boat owner with a long queue of Jackelian citizenry alongside his narrowboat and his oversized cupped hands full of coins. The speech bubble read: '*A ride, good damsons and sirs? I think I may yet take you for a ride.*'

'Lucky then, that the three of us have no mortal plans for travelling beyond the capital,' said the commodore. 'Let them jack their prices up to a guinea a ticket. We can warm ourselves by the fire in Tock House and wait for winter to come while Coppertracks tinkers with his science, you pen your novels, and I take my well-earned rest from the trials and tribulations fate has sent nipping at my heels.'

One of the society administrators slipped behind the crimson curtain. 'Aliquot Coppertracks, you are on, sir. If you don't mind keeping your presentation to ten minutes, with five for questions, we are running a little behind at the moment.'

'Ten minutes, lad?' interjected the commodore. 'If we can't make the members of your fine society see the bright fury of Coppertracks' brilliance in half that time, then they haven't half the wits they were born with.'

The administrator moved aside so that the commodore and Molly could pass by to the table where their magic lantern was burning oil in front of an array of mirrors. Coppertracks rolled carefully to the lectern, staring out at the sea of faces – sombre stovepipe hats and conservative dress the order of the day among the race of man. A few thinkers of the Kingdom of Jackals' other races were present too: steammen, graspers, a handful of lashlites – lizard-winged sages whose adherence to their aural teachings had driven them to seek wider learning when the sagas of their gods had been mastered and exhausted.

Coppertracks motioned to the commodore to project the first slide onto the white screen behind him, when a buzz of excitement arose from the audience, interrupting the start of the steamman's presentation. Molly nudged the commodore.

Commodore Black looked around to see the source of the commotion and groaned. It was *him*. Making a fashionably flamboyant late entrance – no doubt perfectly timed to put Coppertracks off. Behind the lectern, the energy swirl under Coppertracks' crystal skull had turned spiky. The steamman equivalent of a back arching as he recognized the face of his rowdy adversary. For every academic paper Coppertracks published, Lord Rooksby could be sure to make it into the journals with a contrary view. While Coppertracks shared his metal race's methodical, steady brilliance – progress cautiously but steadily advanced over a lifetime of many centuries – Lord Rooksby was the exemplar of the race of man's short-burn approach to science. Erratic leaps of faith and intuitive gambling that sometimes paid off, but often floundered with a heavy landing. Of *course* Lord Rooksby would be here at the Royal Society meeting. He couldn't resist the opportunity for a little mischief at the expense of his steamman rival. Rooksby believed that Jackals did best when it was the hand of mankind that ruled it, and that the place of steammen, graspers, craynarbians, lashlites and the other creatures of the nation was walking two steps well behind his race's polished calf-leather boots.

'Don't mind me,' said Lord Rooksby, sweeping back his velvet-lined cloak with a flourish. The two women he had brought along sat down on either side of him and looked up adoringly at the slim, elfin-chested scientist, as if his every aristocratic word contained a new insight into the nature of the universe. 'No, really, don't look at me. I am fascinated to hear what we're being asked to support this year.'

At this, his escort broke into giggles and he rested his polished boots up on the seat in front, prompting an angry glance back from its occupant.

'Go on, man,' whispered the commodore, willing his friend to ignore the most persistent of his scientific antagonists.

Coppertracks began. 'I am before you, seeking your indulgence to reveal the findings of my latest research. Research that has been aided by my fellows back in the Steammen Free State.'

That drew a murmur of appreciation from the assembled scientists. If King Steam was backing Coppertracks' endeavours, then there was as like to be something of note to be heard here this day. The people of the Steammen Free State held to their secrets fast, and getting direct aid from the monarch of the kingdom of the metal was often like pulling teeth.

'As you may be aware,' said Coppertracks, 'the home of my people in the mountains of the Mechancian Spine is both cold and high, constructed at an altitude beyond that of any Jackelian city.'

'A geography lesson,' interrupted Lord Rooksby, his voice carrying from the back of the hall. 'Capital stuff.'

'A *geography*,' explained Coppertracks, 'which means the procession of the stars and bodies celestial above us can be viewed without hindrance, without the smogs and rains of Jackals. A geography most conducive to astronomical obser-vation, which is why—' Coppertracks paused to wave his iron hands excitedly, 'King Steam sponsored the construction of a new observatory in my homeland, equipped with the latest astronomical apparatus, some of which I myself had the honour of designing.'

Commodore Black grinned to himself and nudged Molly back. So, the old steamer had made good use of his visit to the Free State last summer after all. Lord Rooksby was frowning in his seat. This wasn't the way things were meant to be going at all. It was all running far too smoothly for his adversary.

'This apparatus has allowed my people to peer deeper into the celestial void than ever before,' said Coppertracks. 'To observe the celestial bodies that accompany our own world's procession around the sun at greater clarities than previously thought possible.'

That drew a few dark mutters from the crowd. Coppertracks was taking the side of the radical argument that said that the Earth orbited the sun, rather than the sun and other bodies paying due homage to their home by orbiting the Earth at the centre of all things.

'Not decided, not decided,' groused a few dissenters.

'Well,' called out Lord Rooksby. 'It appears you've already

got the support of your great King Steam, so what do you need the aid of *mere* softbodies like us for?'

'Dear mammal,' said Coppertracks, raising the amplification on his voicebox, 'I am here, among other things, to share the wonders of the universe with you. For instance, many of us have speculated that the number of celestial bodies that share our world's procession around the sun is uncommonly high at forty-six. This new apparatus will help us discover—'

'Discover what?' boomed Lord Rooksby. 'Are we mere astrologers now, or noble leaders of science? Have you, sir, uncovered any new comets with which to unsettle the great unwashed masses?'

This drew a peal of laughter from the crowd. Ashby's Comet just two months gone, had left a trail of broken-in windows and broken-up riots when various factions in the capital had sought to make mischief out of the auguries of ill fortune said to arrive with the crimson harbinger of doom.

Lord Rooksby nodded sagely, as if he exposed a great truth this day. 'If I wish my fortune to be read in the stars, I have a gypsy caravan that calls at my house in the shires each summer. Maybe the gypsies can sharpen your wits while they sharpen my knives, old steamer!'

'This *is* science,' protested Coppertracks. 'Science of the deepest sort. There is much our neighbouring celestial bodies have to teach us about our own home.' He motioned to the commodore and the hulking u-boatman advanced to the next slide, an image of a fiery red circle captured bright against the darkness of the face of night.

'Behold, Celibra, a world – I believe – of inferno temperatures. This is a celestial body fixed at a distance from the sun almost identical to that of our own world, yet in composition and temperament it seems to be radically different from the systems of life we are familiar with here on Earth, a world that is almost certainly uninhabitable.' The next slide in the rotation clicked forward. 'Now this is an image of our moon: observe the tinges of green we have picked up beneath the cloud cover – could it be that the lunar surface has forests as dense as any found in the jungles of Liongeli?'

'Cheese!' laughed Lord Rooksby. 'Obviously it is nothing but green gas rising from the finest cheese.'

There was more laughter from the audience.

The commodore shook his head in annoyance. Coppertracks was leading the audience in too fast – ploughing ahead at ramming speed. He should have been revealing his findings at a rate of knots the scientists' conservative bent could more readily absorb and adjust to. The crowd were not, for the main, steammen who could share new information between themselves with a joining of cables and the implicit trust that came from such networking. They were minds of slow meat that needed wheedling and convincing.

'Let us gaze next, my colleagues in science, towards our world's nearest neighbour in the dark, cold void: Kaliban.'

The red world came onto the screen, the light from the magic lantern catching the swirl of smoke from mumbleweed pipes as several of the assembly lit up. Coppertracks waved an iron hand at the screen. 'Long linked in song and saga to various gods of war, instead, in reality we find a dead, dry world of crimson dunes and – perhaps – something else.'

The commodore advanced to the next slide, a high-magnification view of the celestial body.

'The shooting stars lighting up our skies of late have not all been debris from the tail of Ashby's Comet. I have traced some of the rocky projectiles back to what I think must be volcanic eruptions on the surface of Kaliban. And see what else I discovered during my explorations. Observe the fine splintering of lines you can see across the celestial sphere's surface. I have analysed the geometry of these lines and come to the conclusion that they are artificial in nature.'

A hush fell over the crowd.

'Yes, artificial. I believe these lines are a series of canals, vaster and far more sophisticated than the waterways of our own Jackals. A universal transport system that may once have rivalled the timetables of the merchant marine of the Royal Aerostatical Navy in its ability to transport cargoes and people around their world.'

'Poppycock,' said Lord Rooksby. 'You see a splintering of rock fissures and detect the hand of intelligence behind it! I have never heard such arrant nonsense. It is well known that you share the roof of your home with an author of celestial fiction, one Molly Templar, whom I see has accompanied you here tonight. I believe you have spent too much time pondering her last tome of facile writings rather than upon serious scientific investigations.'

Molly made to leap up from their projecting lantern, but the commodore pulled her back.

'I'm going to go up there and shove my last tome of facile writings down his smug, grinning—'

'Leave him be, lass,' whispered the commodore. 'Or at least, let's be leaving the long-haired popinjay until later. A fight in here is what he wants, anything to embarrass our old steamer in front of his fellow scientists.'

She saw enough reason in the commodore's words to shrug off his hands and sit down.

'Nonsense is it?' retorted Coppertracks, pointing an iron hand at Lord Rooksby. 'Then by my cogs, how do you explain this?' Commodore Black advanced to the next slide, an amorphous grey mass whose peripheries were tinged with red.

'Sir, I do not even know what that unsightly mess you have so kindly brought before us is.'

'That is because you do not have access to the transaction engines of the Steammen Free State,' said Coppertracks. 'Some of the most advanced thinking engines of their kind in the world. When the geometries and shadow lines are resolved and cleaned using the power of our transaction engines, we see instead . . .'

The commodore shook his head. That was a terrible mistake, reminding the Jackelian audience that their civil service's great engine rooms beneath Greenhall had a rival high in the mountains of Mechancia – a rival with steam-driven thinking machines that made their own transaction engines look like wind-up toys sold over the counter at Gattie and Pierce.

'. . . this!'

The commodore advanced to the next slide, the image of a stone-carved face filling the screen, a scale written across it indicating that the face was three hundred miles across in width, four hundred from neck to skullcap.

Coppertracks continued over the hush of the crowd. 'This incredible carving is clearly humanoid – the features of the race of man, or something close to it. An artefact on a scale more massive than any we have attempted here on Earth.'

'Clearly, sir,' shouted Lord Rooksby, 'you have taken leave of your senses. Give me but a lump of coal from your boiler's furnace and I will whittle you a shape as pleasing to the eye with my penknife.' Another member of the audience lifted a piece of coke from the boiler bin of the steamman sitting next to him and tossed it towards Lord Rooksby. The aristocratic scientist seized it and raised it towards the ceiling. 'Behold, damsons and gentlemen of the Royal Society – I give you the miraculous face of the great Pharaoh of Kaliban. Give me but a hundred years of erosion, a real-box camera and the poorly written plot of a penny dreadful, and I shall carve for you an entirely new branch of science – and for my next trick I will find you the face of the Man on the moon and send an airship to converse with the ice angels of the coldtime.'

The crowd followed Lord Rooksby's lead and began to bray Coppertracks down in annoyance.

'You fools,' cried Coppertracks, pointing to the image on the screen. 'Can you not see the evidence before your eyes? There was once life on Kaliban, life capable of constructing canal works and carving vast effigies from their mountains.'

'Celestial fiction, sir,' hooted Lord Rooksby, sensing that now was the time to steer events towards the projects favoured by his own lickspittles. 'This is pure celestial fiction.'

'Life!' called Coppertracks, beseeching the massed ranks of the Royal Society. 'Life that might be able to converse with us, if we would but make the effort.'

A low wailing echoed about the assembly chamber now, Coppertracks struggling to be heard over the eerie heckling. 'My proposal is to build a colossal transmitter capable of receiving and generating vibrations across the void. We have already seen that the vicinity of our sun is blessed with an uncommonly large quantity of celestial bodies, many that would appear to be candidates for bearing life.'

The commodore dropped the next slide down in front of the assembly, but it was too late, the scientists had become a mob. A piece of coal was thrown towards the screen, an explosion of black soot impacting the image of Coppertracks' proposed large-scale transmitter schematics.

'Give him the shoulder,' someone hissed.

'Ah, no,' wheezed the commodore behind his magic lantern. 'Not the high shoulder. Not poor Coppertracks.' He glanced around the room, trying to see who would do it first.

Would they?

It was too late. The mob of scientists had eagerly taken up

the cry and at the other end of the hall the first boffin was already being boosted onto the shoulders of a colleague. Across the seats, the smaller, lighter members of the Royal Society were mounting the shoulders of their fellows, pointing and shaking their fists angrily at the steamman presenter. The energy under Coppertracks' skull fizzed in disappointment and shame. In all the years of his long scientific career in Jackals he had never been given the high shoulder before. All scientists stood on the shoulders of giants when they undertook their solemn investigations, but now they were doing it to *him*, standing on the shoulders of those more worthy than the steamman, looking beyond his work. Coppertracks' proposal had not even been judged valuable enough to come under the gaze of his colleagues' scrutiny.

Commodore Black glanced furiously up towards the smirking Lord Rooksby, who was now pretending to pay attention to his two blonde dollymops rather than enjoying the moment of his adversary's discomfort.

By Lord Tridentscale's beard, thought the commodore, it didn't take too much to work out who had prepared the others in the assembly to arrange this ritual howling down of his friend. Well, two could play at ambushes. The commodore's eyes narrowed. There were a lot of dark lanes in the capital where an alley cat of Lord Rooksby's reputation could run into a masked thug and come away from the fisticuffs with a few lumps and bruises and the silk shirt ripped off his blessed back.

Coppertracks was collecting his papers and speaking notes, gathering them up before the light hail of garbage being tossed in his direction grew into a storm. Commodore Black swept up the slides into the pocket of his greatcoat then sprinted up onto the stage with Molly and helped hustle the steamman off.

'This is an outrage,' spluttered Coppertracks, his voicebox a-tremble. 'I show them hard scientific proof and they dare to throw coal at me! I should call on the Steamo Loas and ask Zaka of the Cylinders to shake the walls of this assembly down upon them.'

'Let the spirits of your blessed ancestors rest in peace,' said the commodore. 'Those rascals and stuffed shirts are not worth the oil you'd need to shed to call your gods down. You've got all the discoveries of your people's new observatory to take up your time, and you secured that without this crew of scoundrels' help.'

'Let's get off the stage,' said Molly, ducking a projectile, 'Quick.'

They disappeared behind the curtain, a soggy ham roll bouncing off the back of the commodore's naval greatcoat.

'I simply don't believe it,' said Coppertracks. 'If I had not seen the evidence of their disgraceful misbehaviour with my own vision plate . . . '

Commodore Black led the two of them along a corridor and to the exit, ignoring the jeers of the crowd from the other side of the curtain. The commodore closed the door to the stage, cutting off the din of the mob. 'Ah, your science is a fine thing indeed, but for all your years living in Jackals, your understanding of the nature of a hall full of your rivals is still a little shaky.'

The Royal Society organizer came up to them, leading the next presenter who was pushing a handcart stacked high with chemical spheres. 'Well, that went, umm, well.'

Commodore Black smiled at the organizer, then slapped the chemist on the back of his tweed waistcoat. 'Hear them cheering, lad? We've warmed them up for you good and proper. But no thanks now, we must be on our way.'

Molly didn't look as if she was finding it as easy to put

on a brave face. 'All that time you spent putting your presentation together, old steamer, I'm so sorry.'

'It is not beholden upon you to apologize for those louts' behaviour,' said Coppertracks. 'The Jackelian Royal Society is obviously not the institution it once was.'

'I'm going to wait here for Lord Rooksby to leave,' growled Molly, 'and when he stumbles out into the street with those two dollymops he had hanging off his arm, they can watch me break his fingers and—'

'I really would not see you sink to the level of that softbody scoundrel on my account,' interrupted Coppertracks. 'And I believe the police still have a caution outstanding against your citizen record from your altercation with the last poor author you believed was plagiarizing your work. Please, let us retreat without creating any more gossip for the news sheets.'

Outside, the thick, marble-clad walls of the society's headquarters muffled the noise of the harsh reception they had been given. There was a lone hansom cab waiting up the street, a single dark horse clicking its hooves in boredom. Commodore Black waved his swagger stick towards the cabbie and the driver flicked the reins to start the two-wheeled carriage rattling forward.

Coppertracks' twin treads carried him towards the lane, every movement of his polished silver plates heavy with dejection. The commodore didn't add to the steamman's woes by referring to the proving tower Coppertracks had already constructed inside the orchard back at Tock House. That had already diverted enough of the coins from their finances without any degree of success being returned in the steamman's direction.

A thin slick of rain had fallen during the presentation, the drizzle still tinged crimson even now, weeks after Ashby's Comet had passed through the wet Jackelian skies. Also braving the day's showers was a Broken Circle cultist labouring under the weight of a wooden placard proclaiming the final hours of the world. He was from a splinter group of the mainstream church that believed the cycle of existence could be broken, a belief that, in the commodore's humble opinion, rather went against the central thrust of their church-without-gods. There had been many more of his ilk parading the streets as the comet passed; but they had thankfully grown scarce when, as usual, the world had not ended. What did they do, the commodore wondered, in the years between centennial celebrations, the years that were dry of comets and dark signs in the sky? Why, they bothered him and his friends, of course. As usual, the cultist seemed curiously attracted by the pull of Molly's gravity.

'It's not too late,' cried the would-be prophet, his beard tinged crimson from standing in the rain too long.

'It is for you, lad,' said Commodore Black. 'Your boat sailed from port a long time ago, I think.'

The madman ignored the aging u-boat officer and reserved his spittle for Molly. It was as if he understood there was something special about her. 'The portents, are you blind to the portents in the heavens? A rain of blood on the blessed land of Jackals, our green hills and valleys soaked with it. It is the age of the Broken Circle.'

'The comet's gone, old timer,' Molly said kindly. 'It passed us by.'

Commodore Black muttered a sailor's curse and waved his cane – a spring-loaded swordstick concealed inside, in the event this lunatic turned violent – motioning their hansom cab to make haste.

'Gone?' moaned the cultist, as if the news was a revelation to him. 'It is gone? No. It will come back to us. Make a furnace of destruction of Jackals and all who live in our land. We must meditate now for salvation. Come with me and meditate in my lodgings, lady. Come meditate with me before the world ends.'

'I hardly think so,' said Coppertracks. 'Ashby's Comet is heading towards the sun, I have been following its passage with my own telescope from the top of Tock House.'

'The portents!' wailed the cultist, trying to infect them with the deep despair he obviously felt. 'The Broken Circle.'

'I am afraid it is your logic that is broken,' explained Coppertracks. 'In my experience, the great pattern of existence carries a substantial weight with it. More than enough to survive a few knocks and jolts of celestial mechanics. Now be a good mammal and run along, I rather fear your proximity to us is putting off the driver of the licensed carriage we have hailed.'

Molly watched the man shamble off, his wooden placard swaying above his shoulders, and she smiled as she noticed the sudden distractions that seemed to engage everyone else walking along the street as the cultist approached them.

'In the desert,' noted Molly, 'there are nomads who believe people like him are holy, connected to a deeper truth through their affliction.'

'And in the lanes of Middlesteel there are people like me who believe he has been connecting with a pint too many and an ounce of mumbleweed smoked on the top of it,' said the commodore. 'Don't you go paying any attention to his ramblings, lass.'

With the placard waver now sermonizing his beliefs further down the street, the hansom cab pulled up before them. Commodore Black opened the door and Molly stepped around a pile of manure that a previous cab's horse had deposited on the cobbles.

It was then that the vision struck Molly's skull, entering it like a spear. The layers of the capital peeled back to be replaced by a white, featureless vista. Of her friends from Tock House there was no sign. Breaking the dimensionless purity, the only landmark in this strange new realm was a brilliantly glowing sphere hovering above the ground. It was the size of a bathysphere, with a single silver eye sitting on its top. Molly picked herself up off her knees, her skin tingling with the familiar presence of the thing. The Hexmachina! Sometime saviour of the Kingdom of Jackals – of the entire world.

'Operator,' said the Hexmachina, a gentle child's face forming across its surface. 'You can hear my words?'

'Yes,' said Molly, stumbling through the white void, trying to reach the safety of the Hexmachina. Of course she could hear its words. She could wield the machine like a god-slaying sword if she could only get close enough to pilot it.

'This realm is not real,' warned the Hexmachina, sensing her intentions. 'You cannot pilot me here. This is a construct, a simulation I am using to communicate with your mind.'

Molly stopped trying to navigate the featureless realm. 'Where are you, then? Are you still riding the currents of magma under the earth?'

'No. I am fleeing, operator,' said the Hexmachina, the child's face assuming a look of desperation. 'My lover the Earth is trying to protect me, but her warmth and the life of our world is no longer enough. Her powers are being subverted and with them the powers that I can draw upon in turn. I need you . . .'

Already giddy in the dimensionless white space, Molly was left reeling by the unsettling implications of the Hexmachina's plea for help. This was the machine that had once helped her defeat a slavering army of mad demon revolutionaries and their allies from the nation of Quatérshift. What could possibly overwhelm something as powerful as the Hexmachina?

'Are the ancient enemy trying to breach the walls of the world again?'

The Hexmachina's voice carried as an echo across the space. 'No, Molly, this threat is not something that I was designed to defend against. My pursuers are operating firmly across our level of reality, and they know the fabric of the world as well as I do myself. This is a force manipulating the channels of earthflow, sabotaging the leylines, turning my own techniques and cunning against me. They are masters at it.'

'But you must be close,' pleaded Molly, 'I can see you, hear you. Rise to the surface and I can pilot you. Together we can—'

'No, I am far from your location. I created a channel between us within your mind, Molly, before we took our leave of each other after the last war. When you were the only operator left alive in Jackals.'

'There are others born with the gift now, operators other than me?'

Hovering above the shiny material of the sphere, the child's face nodded in confirmation. 'Hundreds have passed through their age of puberty in the years that have passed, those who share the blood of your distant kin. But while the blood of those that can pilot me is carried by a new generation, they may soon not have a craft left to direct.'

The white expanse trembled, distortions washing through it like waves. Molly fell over. As she picked herself up, she saw that the facsimile of the Hexmachina was being absorbed slowly into the ground, the featureless white plain that bore their weight becoming an albino quicksand.

'Stay back,' shouted the Hexmachina as Molly ran towards the god-machine. 'The purpose of this mental construct is to allow us to communicate without your position being traced. Do not touch my avatar's skin, or my attackers will be able to mark your position.'

'What is happening to you?'

'I am being frozen,' cried the Hexmachina, its female voice growing fainter. 'Sealed within the heart of the Earth inside a tomb of modified diamond-lattice carbons. I have never seen the building blocks of matter being manipulated so adroitly, my own powers leeched, vampirized, to strengthen the bonds of my captivity.'

'But you must be able to escape,' pleaded Molly. 'In the name of the Circle, you're *the* Hexmachina. Who has the might to trap you?'

'Locusts, despoilers. What are they, indeed? It is almost as if they understand the principles of my construction, but that would mean . . . no, no it cannot be . . .'

'Please!' Molly tried to scrabble around the featureless floor, searching for a way to stop the Hexmachina from disappearing.

'You must stop them, Molly, my beautiful young operator,' whispered the child's face, rising up the side of the Hexmachina's hull as the god-machine was submerged. 'You alone, this time. I cannot help you in this struggle. Seek out the scheme of defence: together you may be able to save Jackals.'

'I haven't seen Oliver Brooks for years,' said Molly. 'Not since he started wearing that stupid hood and scaring the constabulary out in the shires.'

The child's face, the Hexmachina's body, had almost disappeared. 'You – this – the comet, it is the—'

With a snap reality returned and Molly found herself lying in the gutter in the shadow of the hansom cab, Commodore Black splashing crimson-tinged rainwater over her face.

'Ah, lass, I told you that you've been working too hard on your novels, too much time spent crouching over a writing table, knocking around the dusty corridors of Tock House with the likes of Coppertracks and myself, rather than accepting the invitations of those gentlemen callers whose cards pile up unanswered in our hall.'

Blood was running down Molly's face, her nose leaking a stream of it. 'The Hood-o'the-marsh, Oliver Brooks.'

'That dark fey lad?' The commodore helped lift Molly to her feet, passing her across to Coppertracks, the steamman already inside the carriage. 'Let's not talk of that wicked lad, Molly Templar. We're well shot of him. Oliver's good for a tale of highwaymanship in one of your penny dreadfuls, but let's not have him hiding out in the warmth of Tock House again. No, one outlaw on the run from the cruel House of Guardians is enough sheltering under our fine roof.'

'I fear you have struck your head, Molly softbody,' said Coppertracks. 'One of your fastblood fevers, perhaps? Shall I send for a doctor of medicine?'

Molly shook her head. The fever was in her veins, blood that still fizzed with the tiny symbiote machines of the Hexmachina. The Kingdom of Jackals was threatened once more.

But threatened by what?

Opening the curtains wide enough to see the drops of red rain rolling down the windows, the woman gripped the thread-bare fabric nervously and tutted in disgust. She hated the bleeding stuff, filthy red rain that would stain your dress – the normal variety was bad enough. Rain, bringing the risk of fevers and time spent off the job. Time not earning money. And here it was again. Rain that might wake up her mark if it drummed down too hard on the roof above. She glanced back inside the bedroom. Thank the Circle, he was still snoring. Down in the lane outside a figure moved from the shadows and crossed to her side of the street, stepping over a gutter quickly filling with a torrent from the crimson downpour. There weren't many people out late enough to witness what the two of them were about to do, which was just peachy by her. She slipped out of the bedroom and into the corridor, stepping lightly so the floorboards wouldn't squeak.

She always murdered her victims on her second visit, the first being a sizing-up – so to speak – of the mark's valuables. Although in this instance there almost hadn't been a second visit from her; the Circle knows, the absence of anything of value and the dilapidated state of the apartment had given the lie to all the tales she had heard about the apartment's owner from the tavern's drinkers. That her mark came from a wealthy upland family, that they had purchased him a commission in the regiments down on the southern border. That he was some sort of war hero. Connor of Cassarabia, that's what the others called him, half-jokingly, as he drank himself into oblivion. The great Duncan bloody Connor getting bladdered in the corner of their jinn house every night.

Well, all that family money had to have gone somewhere. Yes, she had nearly dismissed her scheme of murder when the bailiffs had arrived during her first visit to the hero's home, banging on the door of the lodgings and shouting through the letterbox about the unpaid bills at the butcher's, the tailor's, the vintner's. She had been witness to enough similar scenes from her own life to know that the embrace of the debtors' prison – the dreaded sponging house – wasn't too far off for this so-called war hero. But *then* she had seen the ex-soldier hide his little travel case, the hard leather shell not much of a treasure chest, but never kept too far away from him when he was at home. There had to be valuables inside the case, she could feel it with every iota of her street-sharp senses. A man with a suitcase, living alone and half-mad, he was almost begging to be robbed and murdered.

A gust of rain blew in from outside as she opened the front door. Her thug glanced up the empty stairs. 'He asleep then?'

'Five pints of jinn and an hour biting the pillow with me, what do you think?'

The thug pulled a garrotte out of his heavily patched coat, a thin, rusty hang of wire between two wooden handles. 'I think you should find that suitcase you were so full of yourself about.'

'It's in the cupboard in his bedroom.'

'Right,' whispered the thug, taking his not inconsiderable bulk up the stairs. 'After I've done him, I'll take him down to the waters of the Gambleflowers and toss him in. By the time the river crabs and eels have had their meal, his own mother wouldn't know him – or want to.'

She felt a little shiver of excitement. The murder was always exciting, that little tug of power over life and death. It was a power she lacked in almost every other area of her life. Swinging open the bedroom door, there was enough light from the oil lamp's dwindling reservoir to see her thug moving across to the ex-soldier's bed. She levered open the cupboard and, finding the suitcase, lifted it out and placed it on the floor. It certainly felt heavy enough. Family silver? Gold gewgaws looted from one of the battlefields down south? Enough to keep her from the company of the other working girls down in the jinn house for a good few months, hopefully.

Her man was about to slip the wire around the uplander's neck and send him along the Circle when she opened the suitcase. And saw what was inside. And screamed.

Duncan Connor was up and out of the thug's grasp far

quicker than anyone with five pints of jinn sloshing around their body had a right to be. Her thug kept a long knife for the difficult ones, the ones who wouldn't go quickly, but the ex-soldier's sheet was off the bed, turned into a matador's cloak, concealing him from her man's blade, before becoming a whip, wrapping around the thug's arm, yanking him off balance and into the ex-soldier's reach. There was a crack as a kick shattered the thug's kneecap and a louder snap as the collapsing man's neck was twisted at an angle his spine could not survive – at least, not while still attached to his head.

Duncan Connor rose up from the floor as a breeze from the corridor outside lifted the papers pinned across the wall. The lassie was gone. She wouldn't be surfacing at the old tavern on the street corner again, but then Middlesteel had a thousand more taverns like it scattered across its rookeries in the shadows of its pneumatic towers, and a thousand more like her, no doubt, too.

Lifting the suitcase up carefully, the lid still open, Duncan Connor placed it on top of the mattress of his bed. 'I'm sorry you had to see that wee barney. Are you all right?'

<*I think so. Who was that woman?*>

'Nobody you need to worry about.' He turned the suitcase away from the direction of the thug's corpse, hiding the sight of his dead would-be assassin.

<*It's nighttime, isn't it? I should away and sleep some more.*>

'Aye, you should.' He shut the suitcase gently and placed it back inside the cupboard, making sure to hide it properly under the threadbare blankets this time.

Duncan Connor looked at the corpse. No doubt the thug would be known to the Middlesteel constabulary, his blood code turning on the drums of their transaction engines, a

39

Ham Yard arrest record linked to his citizen file. But if he involved the police in this hubbub, one of them would only leak the tale to the news sheets and Connor of Cassarabia's name would be linked to yet another horror. It was hard enough finding work as it was, and he had the promise of a little job coming his way from the circus that might vanish if he was dragged along to listen to a coroner pontificate and call witnesses from the jinn house. No, the wee waters of the Gambleflowers would do for this one.

The river took everything, in Middlesteel.

Kyorin departed the perfumery shop along Penny Street leaving an assistant looking in surprise at the silver coin in her hand – not because she had seen through the counterfeit, but wondering how someone as dishevelled as Kyorin actually had the money to buy an expensive bottle of scent for his beloved in the first place. The last couple of days hadn't been kind to Kyorin, harried and hunted across the streets and slums of Middlesteel by the monsters, staying only in cheap, anonymous dosshouses. He stopped in an alley and squeezed the scent bulb, spraying his clothes and exposed skin, even his hair. Watching the carts and carriages rattle past and praying that the stench of this perfume would be enough to mask him from his hunters for a while.

One of the residual thoughts of the policeman whose mind he had joined with floated up unbidden. <*You smell like a whore's handkerchief.*>

'Shut up,' Kyorin muttered. 'When I want your advice, I'll ask for it.' He had grown uncharacteristically cantankerous with hunger and desperation.

A vagrant stumbled past, his clothes so frayed and ancient they were almost black. He stopped when he saw Kyorin slumped against the wall, muttering to himself. Taking him for one of Middlesteel's own, obviously. Two friends together, living low on Jinn Lane.

'Penny for an old soldier? Fought at the Battle of Clawfoot Moor, I did.'

'What's a soldier?' asked Kyorin.

Laughing, the vagrant raised a bottle of cheap grain whisky to his lips and stumbled deeper into the rookeries.

The dead policeman's residual pattern jumped out unbidden again. <*Lying old rascal.*>

There it was. Soldier, like a keeper of the peace – <*I was a bloody crusher.*> – but they acted in rituals of mass aggression between societies, formalized right down to the different colours of the tunics the opposing sides wore to mark their allegiance. <*War, it's called bloody war.*> Ah, Clawfoot Moor was the final battle of the Kingdom of Jackals' civil war between its monarchy and parliament, some six hundred years before. Kyorin's hunters would appreciate this, although he could thank all that was holy that they were not here to do so. The vagrant's memory was so raddled the only battle he could dredge up for his beggary was something he had been taught long ago in school.

So many voices in his mind. Too many voices. Kyorin rubbed his head frantically. 'I just wanted to learn to swim.'

'I can swim,' the vagrant called out from further down the alley.

Kyorin had to focus. Two days of adrenaline-fuelled near escapes, low on sleep, nearly out of counterfeit currency to exchange for fruit from the sellers who wandered the streets of the capital with their trays. He pulled out the book from his pocket, the pages still damp from his escape down the River Gambleflowers. *Velocities and Trajectories of Science* by Timlar Preston. It had originally been written in Quatérshiftian, then translated into Jackelian; not that the language it was written in would have mattered to Kyorin. There was enough detail in the book that he could model the mind of the individual who had written it, feel its uniqueness. Resting his palm on the pages, he reached out.

<Timlar, can you hear me?>

Far above in the holding spheres of the Court of the Air, Kyorin sensed one of the cells of the aerial city filled with a screech of recognition, the noise muffled from the warders patrolling outside by riveted armour and pulsing curse walls. <You have been gone for so long, what happened to you?>

<I haven't been able to contact you. It hasn't been easy for me,> Kyorin was burning up, running a fever from too much time exposed to the near constant drizzle of the Kingdom of Jackals' capital city. <The things I told you about have been hunting me, the masters' servants. My scent is unique in this city and they are nipping at my heels. I can sense them getting closer, even as we speak.>

<I'm not going mad, am I? You aren't a figment of my id, you're real?>

<You'll find that out soon enough,> said Kyorin. <I wish I were a figment of your imagination, Timlar, I truly do; that all I have warned you about was a fiction.>

<I thought you might be my own genius, broken free of my imprisonment up here. Coming to remind me of who I was, what I once achieved . . .>

<You have a little more to achieve yet, I think,> said Kyorin.

<I am very nearly finished,> said Timlar Preston.

Kyorin received an image of the Quatérshiftian prisoner brandishing his pencil like a sword, ready to sketch out the few missing pieces of the mechanics he needed for his device.

<The help you have given me, it is amazing. Concepts that I could never—>

<Merely knowing something is possible, that is often enough

to begin the journey,> said Kyorin. <And you had been working along the right lines long before I contacted you.>

<I still have not find a way to stabilize the wave front, though. That is where we always failed back in Quatérshift, we always lost focus during the test firings . . .>

Kyorin listened and began to fill in the gaps. Thank the stars it was he who had survived the masters' hunters, rather than his ignorant desert-born friend swept away by the river. Half an hour later Kyorin was finished, the voice of the man held captive by the Court of the Air fading as the power of Kyorin's weakened body began to wane.

<That's everything I need. But how will you get me out of here?> Timlar Preston's anxiety was almost overwhelming. <No one has ever escaped from the Court of the Air.>

<I don't know. I will find a way. I must, or we are all finished.>

<I never wanted to use my skills for war, you know,> sobbed Preston. <I nearly became a priest of the Child of Light, once, taking vows for the seminary. I was a pacifist, but the revolutionary government took my wife hostage, my three children. They said I was to dedicate my work to serving the Committee of War or we would all be banished to an organized community.>

<You deserve better than what happened to you,> said Kyorin.

<No, the devices I built were used to slaughter countless thousands of innocents during the Two-Year War,> said Preston. <Children no different from mine, who just happened to have been born inside the Kingdom of Jackals' borders. I do deserve this. I sacrificed my principles for a mean, personal thing. And what good has it done me? My family have no doubt starved on a widow's pension during my years as a prisoner. Even before the Court of the Air's agents seized me,

43

Quatérshift's streets were full of soldiers' wives begging in the streets for food, their children in their laps, babies' arms as thin as shoelaces. The gratitude of our glorious revolution. I helped murder thousands of Jackelians in the Two-Year War and what has happened to my dreams, my nation, my family, as I rot away up here?>

<Your designs must be used as you once intended,> said Kyorin. <And if you once killed thousands, you can now save millions. I must go, we have been in communication with each other for too long. Your mind was not born to safely receive my thoughts over such a duration.>

Far above, Kyorin sensed the Quatérshiftian prisoner finally lying down exhausted on his bunk, left to wonder if the voice in his head was indeed his madness snapped free.

Kyorin rested the book down by his side and glanced miserably towards the strip of sky above the alley. He couldn't see the Court of the Air from the ground, so high was the aerial city's station. Wrapped in clouds generated by its steam-driven transaction engines as they modelled the ebb and flow of Jackelian society, in as perfect a simulation as such primitive technology allowed. 'I'll get you out, my new friend. I must, or we are all dead.'

The chequerboard hull of a Royal Aerostatical Navy airship went past, a brief thrum from its engine and then it was gone. For a moment, Kyorin thought its shadow had remained, but it was the shadow of the vagrant looming large above him.

'I'll trade you.'

'Trade me what?' asked Kyorin.

The vagrant pulled out a book from his own jacket pocket, in a better state than the clothes from which it had emerged. 'Lifted this from the stationer's stall at the Guardian Fairfax atmospheric. Finished it now.' He pointed at Kyorin's damp book. 'You finished with that?'

'Yes,' sighed Kyorin. 'I believe I have.'

Kyorin received the book from the vagrant and passed up his own. A sudden suspicion struck him as he saw how the vagrant was looking at the cover of his new book. 'You can't read, can you?'

'No, squire. But there's plenty on the streets around here that can, and they read them for me – Old Man Pew, Barking Billy. The words don't make sense to my eyes, see. Got the reading sickness.' The vagrant sipped another swig from his upland firewater. 'This book any good?'

'It's a philosophical treatise on velocity science and its practical applications as related to gunnery and celestial mechanics. Royal Society Press edition as translated from the original Quatérshiftian.'

Belching, the vagrant felt the smog-damp wall of the alley for support. 'Sweet as a nut.'

Kyorin glanced down at the cover of his new book. *The Moon Pirates of Trell* by Molly Templar. There was a lurid illustration on the front: three explorers in pith helmets clutching lethal-force weapons as they stepped out of a crashed high-altitude airship onto a desert-like moon. Now this was really very promising.

In the road outside the alley a hansom cab had collided with a brewer's wagon and an argument was about to boil over into violence. The crushers would be here any minute. Time to be off before the first police arrived.

As Kyorin walked past the vagrant he quickly stooped down and laid his palm flat on the man's forehead. The vagrant yelled at the terrible flare of burning in his skull as his brain reworked itself into a new pattern.

'Ask Old Man Pew to teach you to read,' said Kyorin. 'I don't think you'll have problems interpreting written words any more.'

45

Groaning, the vagrant reached for his bottle, trying to gulp the pain away. With an obscene gargle he spat the whisky down onto the mud.

Kyorin smiled, disappearing into the labyrinth of the rookeries. 'Unfortunately, intoxicants will no longer taste quite as appealing as they did to you before your healing.'

There was a Pentshire moon outside the farmer's window. Round. Full. Easily enough light for the farmer to see by as the squire's thug took his hand and raised it slowly up in front of his face.

'Now, imagine your fingers are voters,' said the thug. He gave the farmer's fingers a little wiggle.

'Pay attention!' hissed one of the other two men pinning down the farmer's body. 'This is important.'

'Nice, fat, plump little voters. Contented,' explained the ringleader. 'They know who to vote for. They know who owns the tenancy on their farms and crofts. But—' his voice turned ugly '—now someone else comes along to stand for parliament, and look, they're all confused.' He wiggled the farmer's fingers in a sad little dance.

'Someone who's not been paid off to throw the election for you in your rotten little borough,' spat the farmer, spots of blood from his smashed face landing on his bedroom floor as he spoke.

'That's a terrible accusation to make,' said the ringleader. 'You see, when the voters are confused, they just need straightening out.'

The ringleader took one of the farmer's fingers and pushed it back, the snap of bone nearly making him faint.

'That's a lot of work for us,' observed one of the thugs behind him, hissing the words into his ear. 'And the Circle knows, you've kept us busy enough this year already, organizing every labourer whose ear you could grab to pour your poison into their thick heads, setting up a damn tenants' union.'

Another finger snapped and the farmer desperately tried to stop himself screaming so he didn't wake up the others in the farmhouse, trying to keep his family out of this.

'And you wouldn't like parliament,' added the second of the thugs behind him. 'All those long airship trips down to Middlesteel, and the prices in the capital are diabolical.'

A third finger snapped and all the farmer could think of was how he was going to walk the shirehorse and the plough across his fields next week in this mangled state.

'Don't get me wrong, now,' continued the ringleader, 'but I just can't see you sitting in the House of Guardians. They're carriage folk, mostly, and there's you with no carriage at all – why, I wager you wouldn't even know which spoon to pick up from the table to use for your soup. You would just embarrass us all if you got elected.'

The ringleader made to break the farmer's last finger, but then shook his head as if changing his mind. 'And here's something I bet you haven't considered. If you're down in Middlesteel, hobnobbing with all the quality and listening to all those boring bills being read in parliament, then who's going to be looking after your family?'

The farmer's heart leapt. Even *they* wouldn't? A fourth thug emerged into the room with the farmer's son struggling in his grip, one hand covering the boy's mouth, the other clutching a pheasant-skinning knife.

'Please!' the farmer begged.

'What, you thought we were joking?' said the ringleader. 'Thought we'd come a-visiting your home at night for a bit of sport, did you?'

'Please!'

The shadows in the room were growing longer, thicker. Like mist. But no one noticed. The farmer was struggling desperately under the weight of the thugs holding him down, the others were too giddy with the excitement of the kill.

'*Shut up*, you've got another two lads, you're not even going to miss one of them.'

'You can't do this!'

'I feel your pain,' laughed the ringleader.

'And I feel your evil,' hissed another voice, as the thug holding the farmer's son stumbled back into the shadows of the room. They were both enveloped and disappeared, a second before the grip holding the farmer fast seemed to slip away and he was free.

The farmer backed away as the ringleader and the remaining thug glanced hastily around at the shadows of the room, hundreds of them, swelling and moving like the surf on the sea. Solid. Black. Laughter seemed to bubble out of those shadows, but there was no happiness in it. It was a pit to hell opened in that room, the echo of a fallen soul rising out of the depths. But where was his lad, and where was the thug who had been holding him?

Twisting a knife around in his hand, the ringleader seemed to be trying to locate the sound of the terrible laughter. There was an explosion of light from one corner, blinding the farmer, then a series of wet slaps. As the dots cleared from the farmer's eyes, he realized the only other person left in the room was the ringleader, the shadows twisting and circling around him.

'You've carried your squire's message for him this night,' laughed a dark voice. 'I have one for you to take back to him.'

There was a snap-snap-snap of light – like the powder flash on a camera – the shadows and the light merging to become

48

an angular figure striking at the gang's ringleader. The farmer turned his head to avoid the shower of splintering glass as the thug was forced to leave by the window.

The room seemed to return to normal, the intense light diminishing to a sparkle on the handle of a pistol – one of a pair – holstered on a figure wearing a jet-black riding coat, his face covered with a dark executioner's hood.

'My son?' trembled the farmer, looking mesmerized at the three corpses lying on the floor of his bedroom.

'Back in his room,' said the figure. 'A child's mind is a very flexible thing. He'll remember nothing of this night.'

'Dear Circle,' said the farmer, 'what have you done, man? There's three dead here. The squire has the county constabulary in his pocket, they'll—'

'The county magistrate is due a visit from me, as, I believe, is the squire.'

'You can't interfere with justice!'

The terrible laughter returned to the room. 'They only know about the law; *I* shall explain what justice is.'

'You're him, aren't you. The one they talk about.'

'Look out of the window,' said the hooded figure. 'What do you see?'

The farmer stood in front of his shattered window. There was the gang's ringleader, crawling across the glass on a broken leg, moaning, trying to reach his horse. And a dense fog was forming – seeping out of the woods, fingers of it probing along the ground like the legs of a curious spider. It was a *marsh* fog. The farmer looked around, but the three corpses had disappeared.

Vanished too was the Hood-o'the-marsh. Only the broken window remained as evidence that the farmer hadn't dreamt the whole break-in.

*   *   *

49

Walking into the woods, the Hood-o'the-marsh allowed himself a smile, shouts from the squire's mansion echoing behind him as the great house's retainers spilled into the night, waving their blunderbusses and birding rifles. Someone was yelling to douse the lanterns, more of a hindrance than help on a nighttime pursuit. Not that it would do them any good, any more than cavalry redcoats would be able to help the bloody figure of a county magistrate in a dressing gown, stumbling towards town and the garrison. *He* owned the night. Not much of a recompense for losing the ability to sleep, to dream.

Which was why the silhouette of the woman waiting at the top of the hill took him by surprise. Nobody could sneak up on him. Nobody. Not since he had found . . . both pistols were suddenly in his hands as he advanced, treading silently towards the woman. After all these years, could it really be her?

'Mother, is that you?'

There was no answer. He could feel nothing from her, as if she had no weight on the world. No evil. No goodness either. And there was only one person – if you could call her a person – who had ever registered on the Hood's senses like that.

'Mother, if—'

'I am not the Lady of the Lights,' said the silhouette. 'But perhaps you should recognize me anyway, Oliver Brooks?'

He moved closer. There was just enough moonlight to see that the silhouette was wearing what looked like leather armour covered by bronze chainmail – archaic, the very picture of a warrior maiden from the cheap woodcuts of a child's novel.

'Enough of this.' Oliver pointed his two pistols at her but they vanished from his hands, reappearing in her own. The light reflecting from the pistols became twin suns, blinding him. As the light dwindled he saw that the pistols had changed form, one becoming a trident, the other an oblong shield with the crude face of a lion cast on it. The lion of Jackals.

Oliver gaped. 'They're mine.'

'No,' said the woman. 'They are *mine*. As are you, Hood-o'the-marsh.'

'You *are* an Observer then,' said Oliver.

'No, I'm not one of them,' said the woman. 'I'm a local girl. Did you never wonder where those two pistols of yours, so carefully passed down the ages from master to master, actually came from? It is my work you are about, Oliver Brooks.'

'Is it, indeed?' said Oliver. 'Then return those two pistols and I'll be about it once more.'

'Time enough for that,' said the woman. 'There are more important matters to attend to than corrupt guardians and local magistrates. Have you not felt the wrongness in our land?'

Oliver gazed down at his empty hands. She knew that he had.

'There is an ache in my bones,' continued the woman, 'and I fear what it augurs.'

'Your bones?'

'The bones of the land, Oliver Brooks of the race of man,' said the woman. 'The bones of the Kingdom of Jackals.'

'Jackals is a country, not a person,' said Oliver. 'It's my country.'

'You are half-right,' said the woman. 'Jackals is an idea, a dream of freedom that is dreamt by all those who live in the forests and glades of this green land. That is why you can dream no longer, Hood-o'the-marsh. Your job is to protect those who do dream, those who still believe in me.'

51

'Are you certain that you're not an Observer?' said Oliver. 'You surely sound like one to my thick ears.'

'I'm not one of the grand system's angels, I have already told you that. I'm the god of details. I'm the rustle of the wind in the oaks, the splash of a stone rolling into a loch, the mountains that stood against the glaciers and the spirit that won't be crushed.'

'Why are you here?' asked Oliver.

'Do you not remember the tales of battle your uncle told you sitting around the fire grate of Seventy Star Hall?' said the woman. 'Of a time when Jackals would be threatened and of what would arise once again from a circle of ancient standing stones?'

'He told me a lot of things about the war,' said Oliver. And so his uncle had. The mud-drenched fields of the east, Jackelian troops in trenches, wiping the smoke of battle from their gas masks' visors. The visions they sometimes saw in the sky, the product of chemical leakage through their suits or a by-product of the earthflow particles and mage-war. Lions running through the sky. Strange angels clashing in the heavens. 'Are the first kings really about to return from their slumber? There's no danger of war between Jackals and the Commonshare now. Quatérshift can barely feed its own people, let alone mount another invasion.'

'No, the threat is not from the east this time.'

'Where, then? Cassarabia? The regiments saw off the last bandit army that came up from the desert. The caliph fears the high fleet and the wrath of the Royal Aerostatical Navy too much to make a more direct intervention.'

'There is an old saying in the Jackelian regiments,' said the woman. 'It is always the bullet you don't see that gets you.'

'I repeat my question: are the first kings about to return?'

'Right idea,' said the woman. 'Wrong gender. You are the

key, Oliver. You will need to reunite with the scheme of offence to defeat that which is coming.'

'You mean Molly Templar?' Oliver laughed. 'You're a little out of touch. Molly is a famous author now, her celestial fiction the toast of the publishing houses along Dock Street. If you want someone to fill five pages in a penny dreadful with a story of derring-do, then she's definitely your woman. But this—' Oliver gestured around the woods '—running around the night, getting shot at. I don't think so. Not anymore.'

'Her path is still bound to yours,' said the woman. 'I need both of you together again, though far more than the pair of you will be required for the conflict that is bearing down upon us. Even together, the two of you are not enough to defeat that which you will face . . .'

'Yes, the enemy. I was hoping you could be a little less obscure on the nature of the enemy, given how you're definitely not an Observer, but the goddess of details and all that.'

A fog was rising around the warrior woman's body, a marsh mist. An hour ago Oliver would have said it was one of his mists, but now he knew better. The mist belonged to the land. It was the Kingdom of Jackals'.

'You are the key, Oliver; you will know when the time comes. Remember, you wear my favours, young man. Wear them proudly.'

With a burst of light, the familiar, comforting weight of the two pistols was back in his hands. The mist had enveloped the warrior woman, returning her essence to the soil of their land.

CHAPTER TWO

Purity Drake bent down to pick up the empty brown beer bottle, recently rolled under the tall iron railings of the palace following a chance impact with one of the many pairs of shoes exiting from Guardian Fairfax atmospheric station – the gates to the underground transport system hidden just out of sight, but not so far away that the grit and soot from the vast stacks that kept the atmospherics' tunnels under vacuum didn't rain down on the palace grounds day and night. Endless supplies of soot that constantly needed sweeping from the flagstones in front of the palace's faded marble façade.

But what shoes there *were* in the crowds outside. Polished knee boots the season's fashion for the men; patterned red leather with shiny copper buckles and heel ribbons for the ladies. Shiny patent dress boots for the soldiers barracked in the capital, so swish under their cherry-red cavalry trousers. And big hobnailed affairs – toe-armoured for protection, cushion-heeled for comfort – for the workaday crushers patrolling the royal precinct. All serving only to remind Purity of the dirty naked feet at the other end of her grimy, stockingless legs. She wiggled her bare toes sadly, then stood up and dropped the empty bottle in her rubbish sack.

Purity's mind drifted to the daydream – her favourite daydream. One day some young girl going to school, a rich mill-owner's daughter, would notice a small hole in her perfect, fashionable shoes, and her mother would arch an immaculate eyebrow in disgust and pull the shoes off, leading her daughter at once to the nearest cobbler for a fresh pair. The discarded shoes would land near enough to the railing for Purity to reach out and lift, lift towards her, the beautiful pair of—

There was a loud, a meaningful cough. One of Purity's two political police handlers had noticed she had stopped working. He nodded contemptuously towards the wire-haired brush – almost as tall as Purity after her sixteen years of the Royal Breeding House's meagre diet. Gruel and bread, with meat served on Circleday only. She didn't complain. Who would care to listen? Picking up the brush again, Purity quietly wiped the dirt off her drab grey shawl and went back to sweeping the flagstones. It was a mixed blessing, the duty of cleaning the palace grounds. It freed her from the captivity and tedium of the Royal Breeding House, true, and the exercise and fresh air were welcome. But this close to the main gates it would not take much for any bored passing republicans to notice the golden crown sewn onto her clothes. Republicans who would not mind that it wasn't a stoning day and that Purity Drake wasn't the queen. The types who would take it into their thick skulls that she made a perfect target for a bit of impromptu sport.

Purity glanced out of the railings towards the other side of the palace square. There had been a shoe shop in the line of merchants opposite at one point. Thank the Circle, that concern had shut down last year. Those bowed windows filled with tiered rows of boots and shoes stitched by the hands of a master cobbler had been so tantalizing – no cheap manu-factory offcuts there.

One of the politicals shoved Purity hard in her back, breaking her reverie and nearly sending her sprawling. 'I said, get to work, girl. Showers come back, I don't want to be standing out here getting soaked.'

As if the pair wouldn't stand in an alcove and watch her work from the dry. Purity didn't voice that thought, of course. Young Pushy was handy with his fists, one of the political police's officers who believed there weren't many subversive tendencies against the Kingdom of Jackals' perfect democracy that couldn't be beaten out of a recalcitrant with an iron bar. His older partner had cruel, careful eyes and liked to sit and watch Purity with his toad-like gaze whilst smoking a large mumbleweed pipe. The violence of youth tempered with the older hand of experience. Except that Officer Toad didn't seem too inclined to do much tempering at the best of times. Purity looked at the older officer and he merely nodded in confirma-tion of his younger colleague's orders, as if Purity should know better than to try to slack off while they were on watch.

'Hey,' called a voice from the other side of the railings. 'She's half your size.'

Purity cringed. It was a real policeman – a crusher walking the palace beat outside, wearing a neat black uniform rather than her two guards' forest green. Hadn't the officer seen the golden crown sewn onto her dress, or had he allowed the animosity between the crushers and the political police to overcome the citizens' usual prejudice against the nobility? Maybe he had a daughter her age, but either way, the well-meaning policeman didn't know these two as well as she did, and he wasn't helping her situation.

'What did you say?' spat Officer Pushy.

The crusher leant against the railings. 'I said it must be a hard duty for you, pushing around a right little villain like her.'

'Sod off, Wooden Top,' said the Toad. 'Find some anglers to arrest.'

Purity winced. Anglers were one of the lowest rungs of the ladder in the capital's criminal ecosystem, using modified poles to lift women's unmentionables and other laundry off the drying lines hanging suspended high above the narrow streets of the slum neighbourhoods. Catching anglers was a job given to cadets at Ham Yard.

Outside the railings, the policeman pushed his pillbox cap – oak-lined to take a good knock or two – back up his scalp. 'You two are fine shoving around children, but you wouldn't last two minutes on the beat against the flash mob down in Whineside.'

'This 'un,' said Pushy, 'this 'un is a stinking royalist, and you treat *them* like you'd treat your hound.'

Pushy went to strike Purity in the face and she flinched, but suddenly there was a snap as reality dislocated and the political officer's hand vanished, becoming a green-scaled fist. The courtyard was gone, replaced by a long and windy shale beach. *No, not again.* Another one of her visions. The madness that ran down her family line.

Purity was ducking the fist, moving fast under the weight of heavy armour, a trident in her right hand sweeping down to hook a beast off its feet, the shield in her other hand smashing into its snarling face, rendering it dead or unconscious. As always, her madness came like a dream, she was trapped as an observer in her own body. Where was she? All down the beach, warriors dressed like Purity were dancing a ballet of death. Their foe was coming out of the ocean:

57

seven-foot tall humanoids covered in scales, dripping with seaweed, heads shaped like a bishop's mitre. Crocodile teeth in wide, snarling grins. Her warriors were shouting insults at the sea creatures, gill-necks from one of the ocean kingdoms. Their language sounded like Jackelian, but incredibly archaic. How long ago was this?

Purity's movements and those of the woman she was dreaming – or was it the other way around? – were fused together perfectly. One of the sea beasts raised a pipe with a series of metallic bulbs at its end, and Purity's shield flared with blue energy, deflecting a hail of spearheads driven by compressed air. By the Circle, Purity could feel the power, the raw power of the earth throbbing beneath her feet. Drawing it into her body. This must be what being a worldsinger was like, the sorcery of the earth charging her veins. The earth of the kingdom, the holy dirt these sea beasts wished to claim as their own.

Muscled arms wrapped around Purity's waist, crushing her bones beneath her mail armour. She shoved her trident back into the beast's gut, reversing it to swing its triple prongs down towards the winded invader. Then she stumbled. A momentary disconnection between the past and the present, the dreamer and the dream.

'Who am I?'

The sea beast snarled, revealing its white fangs, and spat something at her in a language full of whistles and guttural stops, a language that was made to carry underwater. Purity didn't need a translator to know it was a curse of the deepest kind. The gill-neck reached for a razor-sharp blade strapped to its forearm and she squeezed the trigger on the trident, a stream of energy shooting from its prongs and burning a hole in the beast's chest. The beast was still shuddering its last breath when she whirled the trident around, releasing a whip of energy across a line of the corpse's kin wading out of the sea and trying to break through the warriors defending her beautiful white cliffs.

'I am Elizica, Elizica of the Jackeni. Drive them back! Drive the gill-necks back into the water!'

Snap.

'Into the water, into the water.'

The Toad was dragging her off the prone form of Officer Pushy. 'Stop it, you mad little cow. You'll put his brains across the floor, you will.'

Outside the railings the policeman was laughing. 'She can take a slap and give one back.'

'I'll see you get a flogging for this, you little—'

Purity stopped struggling, the terrible realization of what she had done sinking in. The sudden strangeness of modern Middlesteel replaced the vision of the ancient battle at the beach. The knock of the atmospheric station's steam engines in the distance, the shadows of the pneumatic towers lengthening as the sun emerged from behind heavy rain clouds. She'd struck a political officer, struck him down unconscious by the looks of it. What would they do to her now? How much was her rare, wild, mad royal blood worth to parliament after such a vicious assault?

'You'll pay for this, you—' The Toad was bending down over his colleague, touching two fingers to the man's neck. 'He's dead! Oh, jigger my soul, how am I going to explain this one to the colonel? He's dead.'

'But I only knocked him to the ground, how can he be bloody dead?'

The Toad drew his pistol from his holster, slipping a crystal charge into its breech. 'You broke his nose, drove the bone right back into his head. It's a murder trial for you now, girl, no two ways about it.'

A trial! Purity looked at Officer Pushy desperately, as if she could will the dead guard back to life with the seeming ease that she had brained him. She couldn't even remember doing it. A death. A trial. The state always turned a blind eye to deaths inside the Royal Breeding House – but only among the royalists. One more or one less in the breeding pool was just natural wastage. But a guard, not even a redcoat, but an officer, an agent of the political police? Purity had been eleven when they took Jeffers away, the wild boy, a duke's son who'd knifed a soldier on the ramparts as he tried to escape from the breeding house one night. They didn't allow much reading material in the Royal Breeding House, but they had allowed the copy of the *Middlesteel Illustrated News* that had carried the front-page cartoon of Jeffers being hanged outside Bonegate, the crowds howling their rage at the royalist murderer. Would Purity's end be any more dignified when they dragged her to the scaffold and slipped a noose around her neck? She didn't even have the customary coin to bribe the guards to jump on her legs and pull her feet to make it quick for her.

The Toad licked his lips nervously. The man's position wasn't that different from hers now. Justifying this calamity, on his damn watch, back to his masters in the state was going to be no small matter.

'I want his boots,' sobbed Purity.

'What?' the Toad levelled his pistol at Purity, unsure if he needed it. Was she the girl they pushed around at the Royal Breeding House or was she the young wolf who had just killed his colleague?

'I'm going to bloody swing for this,' said Purity. 'At least let them kill me wearing his boots. I can pad them out with paper and cloth; they'll fit me fine, you'll see.'

'You're mad,' growled the Toad. 'Mad as a bloody biscuit.

When they take you to the scaffold they'll be putting you out of your misery.'

Toad-face needed her alive to bear the punishment for this; the man wasn't going to shoot her now. Purity knelt to untie the dead guard's laces, but the voice in her skull returned, the woman's voice she had heard on the beach. *Bare feet are conscious of the land. They feel the bones of Jackals, connect with the blood of the world. You will know when the time is right for shoes.*

'The blood of the world.'

'Get away from his boots, you babbling nutter. You're not even fit to touch him.' The Toad grabbed a bunch of hair at the back of Purity's head and yanked her to her feet.

She let him have the hair. Ignoring the pain, she seized his wrist and rotated the arm so he had to fall to his knees, kicking the pistol out of his other hand with her rigid toes. 'The bones of Jackals.'

'My bloody bones!' the Toad screamed as his arm stretched close to breaking point.

Purity released her grip and spun around on the ball of her left foot, smashing the Toad's face with her right sole. Bare, calloused, Purity's foot was every bit as tough as shoe leather. Catching the falling body she rammed the Toad against the palace railing, jamming his head between two bars. It was like watching one of the crude plays the children in her dorm put on for each other back in the Royal Breeding House. Although here she was the audience and the actor both – but with every movement her actions felt more and more like her own volition, not the ancient thing whispering in her mind. She even knew why she had rammed the Toad's head through the railing, stepping back, running at him – a human vaulting horse. A quick jump. Her hands dug into the metal between the palace railings' sharpened ornamental spikes, hauling her weight up.

61

Purity saw the crusher with his pistol drawn below, the old constable stunned by the murderously quick turn of events on the other side of the palace gates. 'Gentle as you like, girl, back onto the ground with you.'

Purity's shared, knowing vision noted the gun's clockwork firing mechanism, the hammer cocked back behind the crystal charge, its fluid explosive sloshing around inside the shell, the curve of her arc down at him and the insignificant chance his ball might miss at such close range.

'Please don't!' The voice distracted the crusher. A vagrant, his clothes dirty and torn, his mind probably too raddled to do anything but be drawn closer to the centre of the action rather than scatter and run like all the other panicked citizens in the square were presently doing.

Drawing his club from his belt, the crusher waved the cosh at the vagrant's face while his pistol stayed firmly pointed up towards Purity. 'Back to the jinn house with you, you damn drunken fool, or you'll know the why of it from me.'

'I have not been drinking,' insisted the vagrant. 'Can you not see this child is pure? Is this how you honour your sages?'

'No, this is how we do it at Ham Yard.' The crusher swung the cosh towards the vagrant's head and the thing inside Purity's skull told her to leap. She did, the policeman catching the movement out of the corner of his eye and triggering the hammer on his pistol. As a storm of smoke blew out of the pistol, Purity felt as if she was frozen in amber within the air. The ball exited the barrel with a crack of broken crystal. The vagrant had raised both of his hands – not to ward off the cosh, though – a wheel of air detonated out of his outstretched fingers. Followed by another and another, the policeman slapped off his feet and falling into the railings, Purity rolling in the air with the backdraft of the strange energy force, pushed out of the path of the ball. She landed down on the square's flagstones as nimble as a cat. This was a vagrant? If so, he was the sort who must have studied the sorcery of the worldsong at some point; he had surely mastered the magic of the leylines. Purity heard redcoats shouting from the palace grounds behind, running towards the sound of the pistol shot.

'Come,' called the vagrant, beckoning Purity to follow him.

No time to slide the unconscious policeman's boots off, not that they would have fitted her. Pity, a crusher walking the beat every day would have some pair of boots.

'Other keepers of your law are approaching, they will come after you.'

He had that right. Purity Drake on the run from the Royal Breeding House, a political officer lying dead in her wake. They were going to keep on coming after her until they had her kicking at the end of a gallows rope. She looked at her odd saviour. There was something wrong with the vagrant's face, as if the proportions were out of balance, the hair too stiff, like feathers on a bird. The voice in her skull was undecided about him, but Purity was out of options.

'Thank you for saving me,' Purity wheezed as the pair of them fled into the side lanes.

'I have done you no great favour, I fear,' said the vagrant. He was fast on his feet for someone living on the street; Purity was having trouble keeping up. 'You should leave my presence, there are people pursuing me far more dangerous than the keepers of your law.'

'I doubt that,' said Purity. 'Hey!' She had just realized how unnatural the vagrant she was running with actually was. 'You're speaking without moving your lips. Am I on the skip with a theatre act?'

He slowed down, his eyes blinking. 'No, I am not one of your city's stage players; I am a visitor. I have travelled down to your kingdom from the north.'

A foreigner, she should have guessed. Perhaps she could slip out of the country with him, back to his land. Jackals was never going to be safe for her again. By tomorrow, her blood code sigils would be printed on an arrest warrant hanging in every police station from Middlesteel to the border. The full horror of the future she had opened up for herself dawned on her.

'They couldn't see it,' said the foreigner. They had fled deep enough into the tenements to catch their breath briefly.

She looked at him quizzically.

'Your purity. You walk with the power of your land.'

She gazed down at her bare feet, standing in a puddle of stagnant rainwater in the rookery alley. 'I walk with no shoes, sir, and that's just what they call me. They call me Purity.'

'I am called Kyorin.'

'You're a strange one, Kyorin, but with the way things have been going for me lately, I'm not much of a one to talk. Do all your country's people speak by throwing their voices like a stage act?'

'Not all of them,' said Kyorin. 'The ones who are coming after me would be more interested in eating me than conversing with me.'

'Circle be damned, you say?' Purity looked at her saviour's oddly angled face. From the north, the far north perhaps? The polar barbarians were said to practise cannibalism, but this queer fish didn't even have a beard, let alone a fur-shafted axe with him.

'It is true,' insisted Kyorin.

'Well, Jackals is full of refugees. You're one kind, Kyorin, and now I'm another. A royalist on the run, like old King Reuben hiding in the forest from parliament's rebel redcoats.'

Kyorin bent down to examine Purity's feet. 'Your connection to the land, it is consuming for one so young. Have you yet experienced the visions of a sage?'

What was the point of lying to this vagrant, this shambling exiled witch doctor? Whatever arts of the worldsong he held to, he had the measure of her, all right. 'I thought it was madness. Everyone in the house did.'

'And so it is,' smiled Kyorin. 'But it is a glorious sort of madness. You are a conduit for the soul of your land, nourished by the leylines. It is no wonder I felt myself drawn to your presence. I can feel the power within you, it is very strong.'

'You are a witch doctor then?' said Purity. 'What you did to that crusher who was going to put a bullet in me . . .'

'I am not permitted to take life,' said Kyorin. 'It is not my people's way. I merely disorientated your keeper of laws to prevent a worse crime being committed.'

'Best you don't try that line on a magistrate here,' said Purity. 'You'd get a boat to the colonies or the rope for helping me escape.'

In the far distance there was a whistle from a policeman's Barnaby Blow. A pickpocket diving into the rookeries to escape justice, or were the police on their trail again? Time to be moving on. Purity looked about the narrow passage, branching out into shadowy lanes that didn't even have old-style oil-fed lamps, let alone the new-style gas ones. Not a place to be hiding after dark. What did Purity know of Middlesteel's geography? Depressingly little. Only what she had seen of the capital while being marched around on a handful of routes by her guards. Hiding inside the Royal

Breeding House, that she could do. The other children had taken enough lumps out of her hide that there weren't many nooks and crannies in the old fortress on the outskirts of the capital that she didn't know like the back of her hand.

'Do you have any money?' asked Purity.

Kyorin took out a bag-like pocket book and jangled it. 'I had more yesterday, but I lack the means to replicate additional Jackelian tokens of exchange now.'

'Well, I've got a five-hundred-year-old act of parliament that forbids me to hold property and chattels in my name, so you're looking pretty flush to me. My mother told me once that if I ever needed a safe place to stay, the flop houses in the east of the city don't ask too many questions.'

Kyorin sniffed at the wind. 'The keepers of your law are coming after us. We should leave here.'

'That's a handy nose.'

'It is the hunters from my land that we must fear. Come . . .'

The two of them fled deeper into the heart of Middlesteel.

Harry Stave pulled out a handkerchief from his trouser pocket and wiped the pinprick of blood away from his finger, the transaction engine drum on the blood machine in the doorway rattling on a set of loose bearings as his identity was successfully matched to the record on the shop's files. The Old Mechomancery Shop along Knocking Yard, where Middlesteel's secrets were hoarded and sold, although very few of Dred Land's customers were aware that the shop was a station house for the Court of the Air. Its proprietor a *whistler*, in the parlance of the great game the various intelligence agencies of the continent's states played against each other.

If Harry's two companions – so traditional in their long-tailed coats and stovepipe hats, tailored in black and starched to perfection – were surprised by the appearance of the shambling, mute steamman that greeted them as the door opened, they did not show it. Harry smiled, the two crows stepping inside behind him, laconic and hardly taken aback by this obviously human-milled automaton, an expensive toy in comparison to the creatures of the metal that came down from the mountains of the Steammen Free State. A form of labour that was never going to take off, not while the race of man lounged unemployed in vast numbers across the capital's slum districts, breeding and fighting and breeding some more.

They were good, Harry's two crows, the Court of the Air's finest, their presence underlying how unsettled things had become upstairs. Not even fazed when Dred Lands appeared, his silvered face-mask riveted with gold pins covering his terrible wounds; opening up the basement entrance to the duke's hole and taking them down to the concealed rooms underneath his shop. But what was on the table now was enough to pierce even their laconic detachment.

'It's a beauty, isn't it, Harry?' said Dred Lands. 'My informer came up trumps when she fished that floater out of the river.'

'You're as good as my word, old stick,' said Harry. 'I told the Advocate General when she gave me the nod for this job. It'll be Dred that comes up with the goods first. And you haven't disappointed, no you haven't.'

'Not really my area of expertise,' said Dred, indicating his primitive iron drones moving about behind the steam-fogged glass of his underground orchard room. 'But you don't have to be a butcher to appreciate a nice piece of roast beef on Circleday.'

'Don't you worry about butchers,' said Harry. 'I brought my own.'

'Sharp tailoring,' said Dred, moving aside as Harry's two crows got to work. 'Very sharp.'

Running his hands over the wet corpse, the shorter of the two agents murmured in appreciation, pushing at the skin and the bones like a doctor trying to diagnose an inflamed chest.

'Worth the trip down?' asked Harry.

'Yes, indeed,' said the shorter of the two crows. He unbuttoned his coat and pulled it open, revealing dozens of tools fastened to the lining with straps – bone saws, scalpels, hammers that could crack open ribs.

Harry shook his head. 'Not here. We'll take him back upstairs and do it properly.'

Dred nodded in thanks to Harry. As he might. Dred's iron drones would have been scrubbing for days to remove the blood if the two crows had gone for a full dissection down in his bolthole.

'Then I am done here.' The crow looked at his companion. 'Mister Shearer?'

'Thank you, Mister Cutter.' The second crow ran his hands along the body a couple of inches above the burnt flesh. He hummed an incantation to the worldsong, the air crackling with energy, vortexes of dancing witch-light snapping in and out of existence above the body.

'What about his mind?' asked Harry. 'Can you go for a reading? His last memories?'

'No,' said the crow, through the gritted teeth of concentration. 'Not even I can do that. He's been cold for far too long. One thing I can tell you, though, his death was not an accident. There is an aura of great distress imprinted across the residue of his soul.'

Harry hadn't been expecting anything else. 'How far off the map are we, then?'

'Let me show you,' said the crow. 'Mister Cutter . . .'

'Mister Shearer?'

'Cleaning fluid, seven strength.'

The other crow reached into his coat and pulled out a bottle, a line of sigils printed in transaction engine code the only markings on its label. Taking the bottle and carefully pouring it onto the corpse's face, the crow rubbed the cheek gently with a cloth. As he rubbed, the pink skin changed colour, the dye running off, revealing a light powder blue underneath.

'Bloody Circle,' said Dred Lands, peering in for a closer look. 'A blue man!'

'And not from the cold of the river, eh, Mister Cutter?'

'Certainly not, Mister Shearer. He's been painted to fit in with the people of Jackals. All very theatrical.'

'Not from the race of man?' asked Harry.

'No, nor from any of our ancestral tree's offshoots,' said the crow. 'His muscles and skeletal groupings bear no relation at all to craynarbian or grasper physiology.'

'From one of the other continents, then?' said Harry. 'Lots of odd creatures and races out down Thar-way. And our colonists have only explored a small part of Concorzia.'

Lifting the lips of the blue man and running a finger down the teeth, the crow indicated the stubby molars. 'Look, flat. No edges to the teeth, no canines at all. This creature is a plant eater. I can sense more than one stomach inside his belly, maybe as many as five, all interconnected. He wouldn't have been able to nibble so much as a ham roll for lunch without becoming violently sick from indigestion.'

'A plant eater,' murmured Dred Lands, looking down at the corpse. 'I knew there was a reason why he was bleeding green blood when my informant brought him down here.'

Mister Cutter ran his hand fondly through the dead

creature's hair. 'Yes. A plant eater. I think he would have been non-violent by nature. Peaceful.'

Harry lifted up the blackened sleeve of the corpse's jacket. 'Burnt up, then drowned. If it was peace he wanted, he should have buggered off out of Jackals.'

'You know more about this than you let on when you tipped me off, don't you?' said the owner of the Old Mechomancery Shop.

'Ask no questions and be told no lies.'

'Harry, I'm the chief whistler in the capital, I need to know what's going on here!'

'Someone has been sniffing around, and not one of the usual suspects, either,' explained Harry. 'One of the Greenhall engine-room men on our payroll found something nasty turning on their drums, not a natural information daemon evolved from legacy code like they're used to dealing with. Rummaging around the Board of the Admiralty's drums it was, but it didn't know we had a sentry on the Court of the Air's own back-door watching it breaking in. The daemon erased itself when our man tried to isolate it for examination.'

'If they got that far into our transaction engines, then they're sharp,' said Dred Lands. 'Very sharp indeed. You know how many checks a punch card goes through before it's injected into the Greenhall engine rooms. And the Admiralty drums are the most secure in the whole civil service. Which makes it doubly unlikely that our dead friend here is an agent of the Commonshare's Committee of Public Security.'

'Plenty starving across the border in Quatérshift eating grass soup these days,' snorted Harry. 'But you're right, this one is no shiftie agent.'

Harry didn't mention the headaches the Order of Worldsingers were experiencing in Jackals, all those little acts of sorcery going wrong, misfiring with unexpected results. He could feel it himself, the change in the earth. Like a bird following the magnetic paths of navigation to the wrong destination. Geopathic stress was what the Court's experts called it. The world was turning, always turning. But where were they going to end up? Maybe there would be more answers when the three of them returned to the Court of the Air and really got to work on the corpse.

'Bundle him up.' Harry indicated the strange body. His two crows did as they were bid.

'But are you for the good or the worse, that's the question?' whispered Harry.

And more to the point, who in the Kingdom of Jackals wanted the blue man dead in the first place?

Purity returned from the vendor with a handful of apples and a couple of pears, and Kyorin nodded his approval at the girl's selection.

'You'll need to eat more than fruit if we're going to keep on walking across the city all day again. There's an eel-seller over there and his jelly looked fresh . . .'

'My digestion is not very steady where fish are involved,' said Kyorin. 'Let's eat while we walk. It's important we keep moving.'

'If these people from your kingdom are after you, why stay in the capital? I'm getting tired of diving into the crowds every time I see a crusher. I think there's still enough money left in your pocketbook for a couple of berths on a narrow-boat up north. We could travel back to your land.'

'I would not be welcome in my home,' said Kyorin. 'I am a slave and I have slipped the collar of my masters.'

'A slave!' exclaimed Purity, spitting out pieces of apple. 'I thought you were a prince, a noble in exile with assassins

71

on your trail to ensure you couldn't return home to reclaim your throne.'

Kyorin devoured his pear, even finishing off the core and pips. 'Nothing so grand or romantic, I fear. Of the two of us, you are the one with a royal birthright. At the very best, I could only be considered a revolutionary . . . to those who pursue me I am a mere piece of disobedient chattel, to be destroyed for my treasonous inclinations.'

'More reason to be off and out of Middlesteel.'

Stopping in the shadow of a shop window, Kyorin pulled out a waxy white stick and, as he had done so many times before, rubbed his exposed skin with it. Face, neck, hands. 'My hunters are creatures called *slats*, they track by scent. Luckily for me, they prefer to hunt at night— they are eyeless and see using the noise they project from their throats. There are so many people here, so many strong smells. Even without the cover of my masking stick, your capital is the safest place for me to hide.'

'You sure you're come down from the north, not up from the south? I'd love to go south. They say that the caliph has given sanctuary to Jackelian royalists in the past to tweak parliament's nose.'

'You may use my remaining tokens of exchange to book a passage to this nation by yourself,' said Kyorin. 'It would be best if you headed as far away from the north as you can. You should travel south, travel there and keep on going.'

'And how long would you survive in Middlesteel alone with no coins?' asked Purity. 'You need me to buy things for you. I've seen you covering your mouth when you talk to people, so they can't see how you speak without moving your lips. Everyone thinks you're lying to them.'

'Quite the opposite, young sage. I carry the seed of truth within me.'

'Along with half a kilo of pear seeds. It's the truth I'd like from you myself,' said Purity. 'What are you really doing here? You're not just on the run from these hunters, are you?'

'I escaped here to see if your people would be able to help overthrow the masters' rule. My people are called the Kal, and we have been subject to occupation by the masters for so long we have almost forgotten that there was a time when we were not slaves. Our culture is suppressed; if we are even caught teaching our young to read we are executed. We hoped that the people of the Kingdom of Jackals might help free us from this yoke.'

'We don't do that,' said Purity. 'It's the Jackelians' oldest law, dating from long before parliament made the kings hostage. No empire, no interference with our neighbours' concerns. We can act only in defence of the realm, never in aggression.'

'I rather approve of that law,' said Kyorin. 'But I am afraid my mission to your land will soon become an irrelevancy. My masters will be at your borders shortly and from what I have seen during my travels here, your nation will not be able to withstand their might.'

'You are mistaken, sir,' Purity protested. 'Jackals is the strongest nation on the continent. There is no one who has attacked us who has not lived to rue the day.'

'I wish I was mistaken,' sighed Kyorin. 'But I know better, as I believe do you. Your bare feet feel the power of your land throbbing; can you not feel the sickness spreading underneath you?'

'I—' Purity hesitated. This runaway slave had the measure of her. That was exactly how it felt, like a wrongness in the earth, spreading inexorably slowly beneath the bones of the land; the woman's voice in her skull, her strange madness, whispering to her of the disorder in the land.

'What you feel is no illusion,' explained Kyorin. 'The beastly slats that pursue me may need flesh to dine on, but my masters need life itself. Their machines will drink the life from your land. At first your worldsingers will notice small failings of their sorceries as the leylines grow weaker, then your people will grow listless and uneasy as the connection with the soul of your home dwindles, and then, when enough of your power has been made theirs, your strength weakened, then will my masters' slave armies appear. Legion upon legion of slats. Some of you will be made slaves in turn, some of you will be farmed for your flesh, the majority of your population will be culled down to a manageable number.'

'That will not stand,' insisted Purity.

'You are a sage,' said Kyorin. 'You are a living conduit for your land and she is screaming her rage through your mouth. But your rage will not be enough, just as it was not enough for my people when we faced the masters' fury.'

'But there must be a way to fight your masters,' said Purity.

'Perhaps, but it is not to be found here. There is one among my people who can help, one of the last of our great sages to evade capture. He was meant to send me word of how to defeat our masters; this I was to pass on to your people. But the party travelling to me across the wastes with his secrets was betrayed and ambushed. Only one rebel survived, a desert-born nomad. He escaped to your kingdom alongside me, but I suspect my simple friend was lax with the use of his masking stick. The hunters caught up with us and murdered him.'

'If you have a way of stopping your masters, why has this great sage of yours not used it in your own land to free your people?'

'The same thought occurred to me,' said Kyorin. 'Possibly such a weapon will not work for our people. Perhaps its deployment was judged too late to be of use to us now. Activating it will almost undoubtedly involve the use of violence that is not permitted to my people. Or the whole tale may just have been a fiction by my own side to encourage me to infiltrate the expeditionary force to your kingdom in the hope that powerful allies could be found here.'

'Allies don't come more powerful than the Jackelian navy,' said Purity.

Kyorin smiled. 'It will take more than your airships to lift the oppression of the masters from the Kal, or to stop them claiming your nation as their territory.'

'What is your kingdom called?'

Kyorin sang a long musical string of words that lasted for a minute.

'But what do we call your land here in Jackals? Where would I find it on a map?'

'I believe it would translate as *Green Vines of the Kal: Clean Waters of the Kal*.'

That wasn't what Purity had asked, but if he didn't want to tell her . . .

Kyorin started on the other pear, eating it carefully and consuming all the fruit. 'It is not a description that has applied to my home for a long time. The masters have sucked my land dry. What used to be lakes are now dust bowls swirling with mists of stinging chemicals and our once endless forests have become salt wastes and deserts.'

'It can't be worse than the smogs here. Have you ever smelt a Middlesteel peculiar when the winds don't clear away the smoke?'

'It is far worse. The masters are very adept at dealing

with the miasma and filth of their slaves' labours. It is said that long ago they changed the pattern of their bodies to cope with the waste that they generated. Then they introduced schemes to transmute their detritus. But after a while, even their tinkering with their bodies was not enough and when my land itself had had enough of their presence, it tried to restore the balance of the ecos by sending ages of ice and heat. But the masters controlled even the land's attempts to fight back, pumping chemicals and machines into the air to stop the ecos from cleaning their corruption from her skin. Fixing our land in a state of living death. Then the masters settled in for the long haul, feeding on the static corpse of my nation until there were no more resources left to convert, no mines left full, no soil fit for growing food, until even the animalcules flowing under the earth and the magnetic energies that pump through the land's veins had been exhausted.'

'I was hoping I might find sanctuary in your home,' sighed Purity. 'Now I'm glad we're not going back there.'

'I never said I wasn't going to return home,' said Kyorin. 'But the time is not yet right. I need the help of a friend I have made here to return to my land. And I still hope to find allies among your people. Those with the wit and the will to survive the journey with me to meet the great sage and join our last effort against the masters. If I cannot bring the mountain to the Kingdom of Jackals, it seems I must bring the Jackelians to the mountain.'

Purity felt disorientated. There was an empty barrel by one of the market stalls and she used it as a seat. Was it Kyorin's tale, or was it the light and the space of the capital's streets? Even in a crowded market, the sense of freedom from the familiar corridors of the Royal Breeding House was dizzying, overwhelming at times. She knew Kyorin's story was the truth, the part of her that throbbed with the land, the whispering voice of her madness, told her so.

'You could stay here with me.'

Kyorin squeezed her hand in reassurance. 'It is not my wish to return home. You don't know how beautiful your land is, with fresh water running through the centre of your capital, sparkling and alive with the creatures of the river. Clouds that swell with falling rain you can walk in without it burning off your skin. Parks of trees and lawns you can actually stroll across, blades of grass you can feel between your fingers – all this we know only in memory. But if your kingdom is to be spared the fate of my home, I fear the journey must be made.'

There was something about his tone of voice. A warning note rose from the ancient voice whispering through her soul. 'You've never met this great sage of yours, have you? You're not even sure he's not just a rumour, an old slave legend invented to keep a spark of hope alive.'

'You are learning to listen to your powers,' said Kyorin. 'That's good. One day soon your intuition may be all you have to keep you alive. You are correct. I am city-born; my cell in the freedom movement was attached to the maintenance of the masters' great devices of geomancy. Only a few nomads in the salt wastes can truly count themselves free of the yoke my people wear, and it is they who carry the word of the great sage.' He kicked the ground with a boot. 'I fear I make a poor sage. The few powers I have are amplified massively here, thanks to the vitality of your land. Back home I could not cast even a basic shield of protection. If I could have performed such feats, my family would have been culled and I would never have been apprenticed as an engineer.'

Purity was about to ask Kyorin more about his life, but

he sniffed the air and cursed in his singsong tongue. 'The slats hunting us are drawing closer. We must pay a boatman to row us down the river again and reach a different district of your city.'

'What about that perfume stick of yours?'

'It is running low and the masters will have sent their most proficient pack of hunting slats after me. I fear my pursuers may now be tracking me by the scent of the masking stick itself. But even they have not yet mastered the art of following a scent across water.'

Their lives weren't so different, Purity mused as they sprinted off towards the embankment of the River Gambleflowers. Both born as prisoners to the rulers of their land. Both slipped their chains. And both of them due to be swiftly executed if they fell back into either of their masters' clasp. Two kingdoms to save, but they could barely even preserve their own lives.

Molly wiped the dust off the bottle of red wine – a Quatérshiftian vintage brought over from before the revolution and the execution of the Sun King – a rare treat and just the thing to cheer up Commodore Black. While the rest of Middlesteel was celebrating Smoking Prester Charles Night by building bonfires and letting off fireworks, the commodore was moping around Tock House, resolutely refusing to celebrate the foiling of the notorious rebel's ancient attempt to blow up parliament with his underground cache of compressed-oil explosives.

'Ah, Molly,' the commodore had wheezed. 'You cannot expect me to celebrate my own ancestor's betrayal into the hands of those grasping bureaucrats and shopkeepers that rule us. Leave me alone this evening and you raise a glass to those rascals in the House of Guardians with your writer friends down on Dock Street. Don't expect me to go out carousing with you tonight.'

'Perhaps you could look upon it as a celebration of royalist bravery?' Molly had slyly suggested.

'The bravery of a mortal failed fool. Have you seen what our neighbours are building on the green outside our own gates to rub my face in it?'

She had. The ritual of Smoking Prester Charles. A bonfire platform topped by a straw figure covered in a silk gauze screen – a cheap effigy of the glass dome into which parliament's soldiers had pushed the captured rebel five hundred years ago before burning chemically treated wood to fill the man-sized bottle with poison gases. As humane a method of public execution as any, she supposed. Centuries on, Smoking Prester Charles Night had become an excuse for a little fun in the capital, rather than the pretext parliament had needed to disinherit the losing side of the civil war of their remaining lands. Had the political police known about Prester Charles' plot, and perhaps even encouraged it? Probably, but that wasn't going to get in Molly's way of a night's much needed diversion from the worries the Hexmachina's final fraught warning had filled her with.

She examined the faded label on her bottle. Perhaps the wine would lift the commodore's spirits a little; he disliked the massive cellar levels and relied on Molly to ferret out the surplus bottles racked outside of their pantry. She walked up the stairs in search of the old u-boat man. There were eight storeys in Tock House, not counting the basement levels. Molly had once investigated getting a lifting room added onto the outside of the tower-like structure, but the architect she had wheedled into inspecting the building had sadly shaken his head, tapping the walls. Seven feet thick, built after the Jackelian civil war in an age of paranoia. A layer of innocent red brick concealed hard-cast concrete layered with rubber-cell shock absorption sheets. The mansion was a disguised Martello tower, a veritable fortress masquerading as a folly. Masons weren't going to be knocking through to build additions to *this* place. Not without the assistance of a volley from the Jackelian Artillery Company.

Finding the commodore's rooms empty, Molly continued up the stairs to the highest level of Tock House and sure enough, the old u-boat skipper's complaints could be heard coming from the chamber that housed the tower's clock mechanism and Coppertracks' laboratory. But that was odd . . . None of the oil lamps in the corridor was lit. . .

She found Commodore Black in a room at the back, tugging on the handle of a winch with the help of three of Coppertracks' diminutive mu-bodies. As the commodore and the drones heaved, the two halves of the dome above were creaking apart, revealing a cloudless, starry night. Molly buttoned up her tweed jacket tightly. No wonder it was so cold and dark up here, their steamman housemate was planning another series of observations on his telescope. Along with the oil lamps, the pipes that carried Tock House's warming waters from the boiler downstairs were turned off across the top floor.

'Ah, this is no night for your peerings and proddings about the firmament, Aliquot,' said the commodore.

Alongside the submariner, Coppertracks' drones raised cyclopean eyes to the heavens, extending them telescope-like to their maximum length, as if they might help the intelligence that inhabited their bodies in his endeavours of astronomy. 'I believe our position at the top of Tavistead Hill will isolate us well enough from the firework displays this night,' said Coppertracks.

80

'The commodore might have a point, you know,' said Molly. 'Fireworks or no, they're getting ready for a bonfire on the green opposite. When the smoke from that starts to fill the sky, you're not going to be able to see much tonight.'

'Then let us make haste,' said Coppertracks. 'If I were to abandon my work every time you softbodies held a celebration in the capital, I would spend more of the year playing chess against Jared here than I would in achieving anything of scientific merit.'

Commodore Black finished winching open the dome and eyed the bottle of red wine clutched in Molly's hand. 'Now there's a friend on a cold night like this. Not many of those left downstairs, nor any more likely to come our way. The ingenuity of those that owned the vineyards crushed like their own grapes in the monstrous killing machines the revolution has raised in Quatérshift.'

Molly watched Coppertracks extend the tubing of his telescope to its maximum length, a clockwork-driven engine doing the heavy lifting. 'I thought with the new observatory in the Free State at your service, you'd be using your telescope less now?'

'So I had planned,' said Coppertracks. 'But last night I experienced a disturbing dream, a visitation from the Steamo Loas, urging me to seek the pattern of the stars in the toss of the Gear-gi-ju cogs.'

'Say you did not,' said the commodore. 'Throwing your blessed cogs like dice and shedding oil you can ill afford at your age, murmuring like a gypsy seer.'

'My people ignore the advice of the Steamo Loas at our peril, dear mammal,' said Coppertracks. 'Of course I performed the ritual of Gear-gi-ju at the Loas' urging.'

Molly had an uneasy feeling about this. After her own

81

communion with the Hexmachina a couple of days ago, a fruitless search for any sign of where her old ally in high adventure, Oliver Brooks, might be now had turned up nothing more than a trail of tall stories in the penny dreadfuls and almost-as-fictional accounts from the lurid crime pages of the capital's news sheets. The warning from the Hexmachina seemed like a dream. At least, Molly deeply hoped it had all been a bad dream.

'And what did the pattern of your mortal tossed cogs reveal?' asked the commodore.

'The Eye of Eridgius,' said Coppertracks. 'The ancient astronomers' name for Ashby's Comet.'

'Is that all? And we are well shot of that, then. Off past the sun, you said. A fare-thee-well until the comet returns in a thousand years' time.'

Coppertracks' telescope swept along the sky, fixing on the position where the comet should be, the steamman's mubodies setting up a table to take notes of their master's observations. Coppertracks raised an iron finger to tap his transparent skull in perplexity. 'This is most irregular.'

Molly moved out of the way of one of his scuttling drones. 'What is it, old steamer?'

'Ashby's Comet has disappeared!'

'Maybe that wicked flying star has finally burnt itself out?' said the commodore.

'That's not how the mechanics of a comet work,' chided Coppertracks. He returned to the telescope, placing his vision plate on the rim of the device, swivelling the assembly's axis across different portions of the heavens. 'It is not one of your night's fireworks. Where have you gone to, now, you erratic little—' Coppertracks emitted a startled fizz of static from his voicebox. 'This cannot – this is impossible!'

Coppertracks abandoned the telescope, his diminutive drones already rolling out large tracts of paper on the table behind their master, pencils in their hands, scrawling at a frantic pace – filling the cream vellum emptiness with calculations and equations. Molly pressed her right eye to the telescope. Against the inky canvas sat a tiny crimson dot so small it might as well have been a fleck of brick dust blown off Tock House's walls.

'You've located it again, then?' said Molly. 'The comet looks so small now.'

'It should be far smaller,' said Coppertracks from the table, the fire under his skull-top pulsing with the energies of his vast intellect. 'And more to the point, the comet should be in a totally different quadrant of the sky.'

'Those calculations you received from King Steam's new observatory must have been off by a margin, then,' said the commodore. 'Sure and it's happened to me often enough, plotting a course underwater with only the stars and the maths on an old transaction engine to see my u-boat through the straits of the ocean. That's a shame, but these celestial games of yours seem a complex and deep matter, everything so far away in the darkness with only a polished lens and a length of copper to peer out at them.'

'King Steam himself assisted in my initial calculations,' said Coppertracks, irate at the commodore's lack of faith in his people's infallibility.

'He's young metal.'

'His body might be young, dear mammal, but his mind is the latest incarnation of a long line of ancient wisdom. King Steam does not make mistakes, and neither do I.'

The sinking feeling in Molly's gut was getting worse. 'It's coming back towards us, isn't it?'

Lifting the equation-filled paper from the hands of a mu-body, Coppertracks scanned the maths, and then nodded. 'Yes, you are quite on the mark. Ashby's Comet is returning. Given its present size and position, there is only one explanation that fits the mechanics of the situation. Ashby's Comet must have used the gravity well of Kaliban to slingshot around the celestial body of the red planet, and, as you say, come back towards us.'

Molly tried to keep the panic out of her voice. 'Returning towards us to ram into the Earth?'

'No,' said Coppertracks, 'my calculations suggest the comet will not collide with us, but pass near enough by that it will be captured by the gravity of our world. I believe, dear mammal, that we are soon to have an extra moon sitting in our sky.'

'Please, now,' wheezed the commodore, his breath misting in the cold air of the chamber. 'This is a huge great comet in the heavens we are speaking of, not a billiard ball knocked around across our table of velvet downstairs.'

'I do believe you are closer to the truth than you realize,' said Coppertracks. 'Ashby's Comet must have impacted with another minor celestial body after it passed us by, its trajectory nudged into the gravitational pull of Kaliban and set on a new course back towards us. A billiard table is exactly what our celestial bodies' dance of orbits and velocities have become.'

'Is that it, then?' said the commodore. 'A cruel chance meeting of vast stones in the heavens and now we are to have a new moon.'

'How long?' asked Molly. 'How long before Ashby's Comet returns to our skies?'

'My estimation at this point would be in the order of five days.'

Five days! The Broken Circle cultists would have a field day when the comet they believed augured the end of all times returned and set up permanent residence in the heavens.

CHAPTER THREE

The force commander looked out across the plains of Catosia: green fields irrigated by aqueducts that ran out from the city behind her like spokes on a wheel. All except the sparring fields, of course, which were dust, rock, trenches and cover. No olive groves or rows of corn there. That was where the civilized cities of the Catosian League settled their differences using free companies such as hers. Professional fighters and citizen soldiers with a taste for it who would flourish their drug-swollen muscles – so large in some cases that their war jackets could barely contain their flesh – before commencing the ritual of battle. Fighting in front of the judges from the nearest city both sides could agree as neutral in whatever dispute had sparked the fight. That was the way the civilized people of Catosia made war. Unlike, of course, the other nations of the continent. The fat, complacent Jackelians, who relied on their cowardly monopoly of airships and fin bombs to preserve their freedoms, or Kikkosico to the southeast, with the god-emperor's shiny legions trampling across the pampas.

Which made it all the more painful to the force commander

that her sparring fields lay empty. No judges in purple togas. No audience behind the observer wall, cheering their city-state's women into battle from the relative safety of angled viewing slits. Instead, the city-state of Sathens' towering walls were reconfiguring for a full siege; the pneumatic pumps hissing as her battlements raised themselves to full combat height. Seven-inch thick steel plating gliding up and into position, clanking as the walls moved forward to create buffer cavities that began to fill with sand-like compounds piped up from the underground silos ringing the city. The streets of the city were being reshaped in the opposite direction, tall towers sliding down into underground holds, doors and windows disappearing behind blast plates as the lower rise buildings rotated to present a blank face to their thoroughfares.

Inside the Catosian city, a state of change had infected the population too. After the people of Sathens had taken in the survivors from the city of Unarta, the normally turbulent currents of their city's anarchy had converged into a single focused stream of purpose. Survival. Survival against the terrible horde their neighbour's survivors had nicknamed the *Army of Shadows*. Every voter of Sathens had filed past the crystal head of the goddess their city state had been named for, filed past long into the night, dropping in their pebbles. White for war. Black for peace. When the sun rose over the central square, the crystal goddess had stood proudly as a mass of shimmering white in the sunrise. Not a mere sparring war against civilized neighbours, where the citizens would go unhurt and the city's infrastructure would be spared. Total war. Absolute war. The sort of war barbarian nations such as the Kingdom of Jackals and Quatérshift still foolishly practised against each other. The sort of war that nobody had been unwise enough to wage against any city-state of the Catosian League in a long, long time. *Leave your sword at home or your corpse in Catosia* was the adage that was often directed towards foreigners.

Jackelians might look down on the Catosian League because they treated war with the codification of a duel, but that was only between the city-states. For foreign barbarians, the Catosians practised a different sort of war altogether. Even the *men* would fight, those who weren't guarding the children in the city vaults. Ever since the population had voted, the drinking water of Sathens had run crimson with the holiest and rarest of their drugs, the Blood of Forman Thawnight. Some of their men had refused to drink it – the philosopher scientists, so ethereal and haughty in their starched white robes. Their contribution to the war effort would be in tending to the automatics, they had argued, in converting the cogs and artful clockwork mechanisms of their mechanical servants to a war footing. But their wives had known better. They had dragged their menfolk to the drinking basins and plunged their faces under the water until they could breathe no longer and were forced to sup the drug-filled waters. And where the men had no wives, the warrior maidens of the free company had broken down doors and performed the same rites on the trembling virgin lads.

Now the Catosian law that all men must walk clean-shaven save in time of war was showing its worth. Within days of drinking the Blood of Forman Thawnight, the men of the city had sprouted beards that would have made a polar barbarian proud. Sathens' nights had been filled with the sound of its men screeching their newfound rage at the stars. The mornings found adrenaline-twitching husbands begging their wives to pass on the skills of the women's mandatory daily war practice.

The force commander extended her brass telescope to its maximum length and was about to raise it to her eyes when one of the philosopher scientists barged forward and offered her a heavy double-tubed binocular set. 'Use these. Gas compression lens. Triple the range of that old piece of brass.'

'You have been busy,' said the force commander, approvingly.

'A toy!' shouted one of the scientist's fellows. Then he proudly pointed to his ranks of automatics shining like steammen knights in front of the city's walls, jangling with maces, spears, and ammunition bins. 'Does he expect you to toss his binoculars towards the enemy's helmets and brain them? I took four of my own servants and built them into a cannon, a cannon that walks! What is that piece of optics compared to my genius?'

The two males looked as if they were about to start wrestling over the matter, but a company leader stepped forward and as she drew her sword, both men hurriedly stepped back into the ranks.

'The enemy had better come soon,' whispered the force commander's aide. 'Trying to keep any semblance of discipline among these damned males...'

'Be careful what you wish for.'

'The city of Unarta was not expecting an attack,' said the aide. 'There is no element of surprise here. Our city is reordered for war, as are our people. Even my little husband will fight today.'

'What else can we expect from filthy barbarians?' said the force commander. 'A declaration spear shoved into the sparring field and five days of feasting with the opposition free company first? Well, we shall have the measure of these foreign dogs soon enough.'

There was a rifle shot below as one of the free company officers punished a fighter trying to break the order of the line. Another male overcome with the berserker fury of his drugs a little too early.

'Save it for the enemy,' muttered the force commander.

Yes, the enemy. Unarta's survivors had been hysterical. Men, of course. No warrior woman would willingly abandon her city. *Carry me to victory or carry me home on my shield.* The end had come shockingly fast, but there was one thing Unarta's survivors agreed on. The cloud. The hideous crimson cloud gathering overhead and a darkness like night falling during the high heat of the day. Something terrible was coming out of the north. But what was the Army of Shadows? The far north was just a wide wilderness, worthless ice plains and glaciers left over from the age of the coldtime. It had been centuries since any lord of the north had emerged capable of uniting the polar barbarians' feuding tribes.

A flaming cloud was rolling forward, shadows lengthening across their olive groves. The force commander rolled a wheel on the side of her binoculars, a hiss escaping from the instrument as its amplification was pushed beyond its safety parameters. At last, she saw the enemy; saw what the hundreds of thousands of corpses now rotting at Unarta had seen before they died.

The Army of Shadows was like nothing any Catosian city-state had ever faced before. The force commander experienced a feeling she had never known before. *Fear.*

She slammed her rifle against her shield and the drumming was taken up across the thousands formed up in front of the wall and the thousands more manning the ramparts. Anything to smother the feeling of dread rising in her stomach. Did her fighters realize they were now drumming their own march into the gates of hell?

CHAPTER FOUR

Molly saw Commodore Black opening the door to Tock House just as she was struggling up the main staircase with a wooden crate full of periodicals, news sheets and journals. The old u-boatman rushed over to pick the box out of his friend's arms. With his bulk and strength he lifted it up easily before she caught him remembering to put on a show, pretending to puff and struggle.

'Have you been laying in reading material for Coppertracks, lass? The old steamer is off in the woods again, tinkering with his tower – his genius is occupied enough for now, I think. No need for these.'

'These news sheets aren't for his distraction, Jared,' replied Molly. 'I need to track down Oliver Brooks. Coppertracks can find patterns in the information, things too subtle for me to notice. Somewhere in here is the clue to where I can find Oliver.'

'Good luck to you, then, for our old steamer isn't noticing much these days except his tower and his dreams of conversing with the man in the moon.'

Molly looked towards the house's orchard. The tip of the

91

lashed-together tower was just visible over the trees. 'He wants to prove the Royal Society wrong.'

'He wants revenge,' said Commodore Black. 'That's what his boiler heart desires now, and that's not an emotion that sits well with a blessed steamman.'

And that was equally true of another creature of the metal Molly was well acquainted with. She thought of the Hexmachina's final plea to her before it was frozen in the centre of the earth. It seemed so much like a dream now, she was half-doubting her own memory of the vision. Perhaps she *had* been working too hard of late?

Molly left the commodore and walked over towards the orchard. She had always loved the peace of the apple and pear trees, left to run slightly wild in their grounds. In the summer months, Molly would take an old collapsible card table from the cellar of the house and set it up in a glade alongside the ruins of an overgrown gazebo. There she would lay her writing paper and pencil down on the green felt top, watching the butterflies flit over the lilacs while she imagined tales of terror to stir the hearts – and pocketbooks – of the penny dreadful readers. Now, of course, she had the presence of Coppertracks' tower of science for company, a small Porterbrook-model portable steam engine chugging away beside the ever-lengthening pyramid of lashed together girders, crystals and cables.

Molly could tell that Coppertracks was agitated, his mu-bodies falling over themselves to keep the tower running smoothly as his attention darted between his drones and the task at hand. One of the drones held a cluster of cylinders to its cyclopean eye, taking a reading from the sun, while Coppertracks seemed more interested in a large sheet of calculations resting on her card table, still out from her morning writing session. As Molly got closer, she saw there was also a map of the stars open before him – she even recognized a few of the constellations.

'What's the matter, old steamer?' Molly called.

'The matter? Why, everything is the matter, Molly softbody. Reality is not as it should be.' Coppertracks' caterpillar tracks ground at the grass in frustration. 'I have been checking the declination of my tower's transmissions to our closest neighbour in the heavens, Kaliban, and I have been missing the red planet by at least two degrees.'

Molly stared up at the dish at the top of the tower, a polished silver shield like a giant's porridge bowl turned on its side. 'Maybe the rain last night knocked your dish out of kilter? It sounded like it was becoming quite a squall from my bedroom.'

'That is what I had assumed too, but my mu-bodies have checked and rechecked the tower and my apparatus has not shifted by an inch. It is transmitting at exactly the same angle as it has always been, yet now my signals are passing by Kaliban and falling away into the void.'

'Then if your tower hasn't moved, the logical conclusion to draw would be that it is either the Earth or Kaliban that has shifted.'

'Precisely, but as we both know, that is impossible. Celestial bodies do not jiggle around their orbits like fidgeting young children swapping desks in a classroom.'

'Very odd,' said Molly. A puzzle fit for one of her celestial fiction novels, certainly.

'It gets worse,' said Coppertracks. He indicated the constellation of the Windmill on his astronomy charts. 'I have been checking the position of the stars from my observations the other night against the official charts and something is terribly wrong. While some of our stars are precisely where they should be, others have changed station, a couple of stars have vanished entirely, and I have even found a new star appeared as if from nowhere.'

'Surely not? You always told me—'

'Yes, I know,' said Coppertracks 'and I still hold to my people's belief that the stars are celestial bodies similar to our own sun, but viewed from the vantage point of an incredible distance. Huge cosmic kilns many times larger than our own world, able to circulate heat with an efficiency that makes my own boiler heart look like a toy.' Coppertracks tapped his charts. 'But measuring against the astronomical record, the face of night above us has been transformed in a manner that should be impossible. Conventional science can offer *no* explanation for this. We might as well subscribe to the teachings of the old Quatérshiftian religion and assume that Furnace-breath Nick is flying through the sky on his demon steed, snuffing out the candles of the Child of Light and firing up his own wax lights in their stead.'

Now Molly saw why Coppertracks was close to despair. Entire stars disappearing, while their neighbours twisted across the firmament to settle in new positions. It made even the problem of a new moon appearing in the sky appear like a mere distraction in the cosmic ordering of things. What if their sun should just disappear? It would be as if the boiler were turned off at Tock House in the dead of winter. No heat, no light. An eternal winter of such ferocity would make the coldtime look like a picnic in Goldhair Park on a balmy summer afternoon. The world would die, as would every creature that swam, walked, flew or crawled across its surface.

'So what are you going to do about it?' asked Molly. 'Does King Steam know about this?'

'I am certain he does,' said Coppertracks, distractedly. 'With our new array tracking Ashby's Comet, King Steam's astronomers would have to possess defective vision plates not to have noticed this.'

Coppertracks' mu-bodies began shinning up the tower, recalibrating the transmission dish and showering Molly with flecks of paint and dust from the girders as they scrambled about on high.

'You're continuing with your work on the tower?' Molly was flabbergasted.

'Dear mammal, the forward momentum of science must not be swayed off-course by an as-yet-undiagnosed disorder in celestial mechanics. I must press on with my transmissions.'

Above their heads, the dish was ratcheted around to a new setting.

'Even if you find someone on one of the other celestial spheres with a level of engineering as advanced as ours and willing to converse with you, what in the name of the Circle would you say to them now?'

Coppertracks stopped for a second, as if this thought – of all the thousands he was capable of processing in parallel in his impressive mind – had only just occurred to him. 'Say? In this instance, I believe I would say *hello*.'

Pulling the lid off two drum-like chemical batteries, Coppertracks' drones observed the mixture bubbling inside and pronounced themselves satisfied. It was always dangerous, using wild energy, the power electric, but nothing else would do for throwing a pulse across the heavens. Luckily for the inhabitants of Tock House, scanning the heavens for a reply didn't require a discharge, or their orchard would soon resemble Lady Amazement's Lightning Gardens down at Makeworth Park. As distant as Molly's neighbours were behind the ground's high walls, Tock House had already seen a number of petitions circulating in the village as a result of Coppertracks' unorthodox scientific interests.

A spectral moaning along the iron girders warned Molly that the pulse of exotic waves Coppertracks intended to direct towards Kaliban was about to be released. She moved back beyond her card table as emerald energy lit the girders, sparks raining down over the ruined gazebo. With a bacon-like sizzle the dish vibrated at the top of the tower, a couple of holding pins blowing out, followed by a dying whine as the apparatus powered down. Coppertracks' mu-bodies were back over the tower instantly, like ants on a picnic basket, checking it for signs of damage and resetting it to its receiving configuration.

'Excellent,' said Coppertracks, checking the signal readings on a bank of dials at the foot of the tower. 'A clean send with very little leakage this time. Tight and focused. Each time we do this, it gets easier to calibrate the tower for an optimal transmission.'

Molly took a step back – the line of crystals running up the far side of the tower was starting to vibrate, the grass under her feet trembling with the force of it. Dials twitched violently across the board on Coppertracks' instrument bank. 'I think that might have been a pulse too far, old steamer. Should we start running and take cover now?'

Coppertracks' stacks whistled in excitement as he momentarily lost control of his boiler function. 'By the beard of Zaka of the Cylinders, that is no feedback loop! It's a signal. Molly softbody, someone is answering my communication!'

His mu-bodies rushed to the tower from wherever they were standing in the glade in a fury of coordinated action, the steamman desperate that this message should not be lost. For all his practice in sending transmissions over the past year, he was a virgin at the art of receiving anything other than the occasional internal test.

'This is odd,' said Coppertracks, checking his equipment bank.

To Molly the whole thing felt odd. She was actually present at the receipt of the first communication from another celestial body within their solar system. Who would believe that she hadn't just invented the whole tale for publicity? 'What is it?'

'This can't be a reply to my communication, it's the same message repeating on a loop, over and over.'

'A loop?' said Molly. 'Who would want to put a message on a loop?'

'The logical inference would be someone who needs assistance, possibly someone who has long been deactivate and unable to switch their transmission off.'

'How long do you think it will take you to translate it?'

'No time at all,' said Coppertracks. 'The message is in binary mathematics and transmitted using something similar to crystalgrid code, dashes and dots that any station operator in the capital could understand. It carries a table key at the front based on the periodic table with the translation of their language.'

Molly hardly dared to ask the next question. 'And it says . . .?'

'*They are coming*,' said Coppertracks. 'That is all it says. Over and over again. *They are coming*.'

The steamman and Molly stared up at the Kingdom of Jackals' grey cloudy sky, Molly imagining that she could see Kaliban as it appeared in the images from King Steam's observatory. Plains of red sand and barren mountains. Vast dead valleys. A world that now conclusively harboured enough life to send them a message. Possibly their last.

A tear welled in Molly's eye. 'Hello.'

Molly saw Commodore Black fiddling with the rusty lock to the roof of Tock House, but Coppertracks was nowhere to be seen in his laboratory.

'Where's the old steamer gone now?'

'Have you checked the orchard, lass?' asked the commodore.

Molly looked at her crates of periodicals, news sheets and journals, hardly touched, despite her protestations to Coppertracks about the Hexmachina's warning. Did the steamman still believe her vision of the ancient god-machine was a result of stress and fever? 'That was the first place I checked, but he wasn't there.'

'Then perhaps he has finally had a bellyful of that message of his, repeating over and over again like a parrot trapped in a cage.'

It was a mystery, right enough, yet as much as the steamman analysed the message for hidden patterns or deeper clues, there appeared to be no other information forthcoming from the signal. Molly sighed. 'I dare say he's gone to the crystalgrid station to transmit word to King Steam of his lack of progress.'

'There'll be no progress in this mortal matter,' said the commodore. 'His tower of science has found nothing but a message in a bottle, cast off by some poor wretch. The Circle knows how long that signal has been rattling around up there. I found as many when I was master and commander of my beautiful u-boat. Bottles lying on the seabed, their paper washed of blessed meaning by the waters and the ages and the changes in language. Half of them from bored sailors tossing away sheets of their diaries in empty rum bottles for a jape.'

'Coppertracks is certain the message originates from Kaliban.'

The commodore shrugged. 'Well, we're never going to know.'

Molly rattled one of the crates, frustrated at the lack of progress. 'Then what good are these newspapers to me? I can't use them to help me find Oliver Brooks. Meanwhile stars are disappearing, a comet is heading back towards us to take up residence as a new moon, and I'm not even sure if the warning I got from the Hexmachina wasn't just the result of a slip on the curb and a bump on my head.'

'The first of those questions I can answer for you.' The commodore waved a page torn from a news sheet in front of her. An advertisement.

For your delectation, a circus of the extreme – the famous troupe of Dennehy's Divers – will be launching from Goldhair Park. Cannons, rocketry and sail riders, in a dumbfounding display of daring unrivalled in the realm. Discover why Jackelia still rules supreme over our dignified skies.

Molly read the small print. 'That's today. You'll never get to the park in time. The streets will be packed.'

'Aye, as will the park. But I have no intention of paying tuppence for a chance to be jostled, have my pocket picked, and get hot rocket ash falling in my eyes if the wind changes course.' He pulled open the door to the stairs to their roof. 'Not when I have a fine view of proceedings from afar for free.'

Free, the commodore's favourite price. Molly followed him up the small winding stairs to the house's battlements. The top door opened with a squeak, and Molly emerged from between the two smoke stacks of their furnace room to stand by Tock House's balustrade.

'I have heard of these mad boys of Dennehy's Circus and I have always wanted to see them.'

Molly looked out. Below Tavistead Hill, the gardens and trees of Goldhair Park could just be seen as a splash of green far beyond in the centre of the capital. Sail riders were a mad breed at the best of times, taking to the air with their silk sails and kite frames. Any jack cloudie in the Royal Aerostatical Navy would tell you jumping from a wrecked airship was not something you did lightly. If the sail folded, failed to open or you landed badly, you were dead. Then add to that risk by being shot out from a cannon or having yourself strapped to an oversized firework to reach the giddying heights they sailed down from – well, that was plain madness. No wonder Goldhair Park was packing them in; Middlesteel's crowds were thronging the park to see men and women die in front of their eyes. The only reason Dennehy's Circus didn't put on more performances in a year was it took that long to gather enough performers suitably desperate and down on their luck to mount such a spectacle.

A signal rocket rose to explode in a cloud of yellow smoke, a dim cry of encouragement from the distant crowd barely perceptible out on the brow of Tavistead Hill. Molly and the commodore could hear the next sound, though; the faint boom of cantilevered cannons accompanied by the sight of the human cannonballs moving almost too fast to track. But the show wasn't over yet. Coordinated plumes of rocket smoke carrying a second wave of sail riders followed shortly after the cannon fire. Slowly to Molly's eyes – but no doubt at an incredible velocity to the sail riders concerned – multicoloured spears of rocket smoke passed from view into the clouds above the capital.

'We'll see them come down on their sails soon enough,' said the commodore. 'And it's a sight that wasn't always so blessed welcome to me. Have I told you of how the Quatérshiftian men-o'-war used to winch sail riders behind their frigates, higher than any crow's nest, searching for the trails and periscopes of my privateer's u-boats?'

'Many times,' said Molly. She stretched on her toes for a better look. What kind of formations and high-altitude stunts would the sail riders put on for the crowds below? Commodore Black took a brass telescope from his coat pocket and pulled it open.

But the next sound Molly heard wasn't the soft susurration of the distant crowd as sail riders emerged from the clouds; it was the scraping of Coppertracks' treads as the steamman came up the stairs to the tower roof.

'I have news,' announced the steamman, his voicebox trembling with excitement. 'The observatory in Mechancia has communicated its findings back to me.'

'News about the disturbance in the heavens?' said Molly. 'How do your people explain new stars appearing while others are snuffed off your charts?'

'King Steam's scholars have devised a theory,' said Coppertracks. 'To formulate it, they consulted copies of pre-Camlantean texts so ancient there are none among you fast bloods who still have the knowledge of their translation. The theory suggests there is a cloud drifting through the celestial void, composed of a dark substance that is the antithesis of the very fabric of our universe. King Steam's scholars believe that if this cloud has been clearing in some places while thickening in others it would lead to the effect we have been observing: some stars vanishing while new ones appear to be born in the sky.'

Molly realized she had been holding her breath and let the air escape from her lungs. The sun and its life-giving warmth was safe, and perhaps her vision of the Hexmachina just a trick of a tired and overtaxed mind. Yes, that was it. What had she been thinking of? Molly laughed out loud. She had ridden the god-machine, joined with it once to cast down the dark gods trying to scuttle back into their world. Felt its incredible power. Of course nothing could seal up the Hexmachina like a ship inside a bottle.

Her relief was interrupted by a distant buzz of excitement from Goldhair Park. The sail riders were returning to the capital – but not in a coordinated display of multicoloured silks. Dozens of blackened bodies were plummeting from the sky, smudged smoke trails spiralling behind them.

'Their sails haven't opened,' shouted Molly. 'None of their sails have worked.'

The commodore put aside his telescope to take in the terrible scene with his own eyes. 'Ah, those poor brave lads and lasses. They're finished.'

The crowd's distant noise grew louder. Molly could imagine the astonishment among the ticket holders in Goldhair Park turning to screams as the corpses of the circus entertainers impacted among the watchers, at speeds fatal for the sail riders as well as any below they slammed into.

Coppertracks rocked on his treads, the energy in his transparent skull calculating the odds of so many sails failing to open at once. 'There is only one explanation: the cannon charges must have been overfilled by the circus, the riders killed by the velocity of their launch, fired too high into the firmament to breathe without a mask.'

'Then riddle me this, old steamer.' The commodore pointed to the second wave of sail riders – the rocket-launched entertainers – now returning through the clouds. Unlike the human cannonballs, their sails had successfully deployed, but their silks were burning up between their plywood frames. 'Did they fly too close to the sun?'

The second wave of performers was spiralling down, their silks an inferno. Even at their distance from the display, the three friends on the top of Tock House could see this was enough to finally panic the crowd into a complete stampede, a ripple that became a violent surge as the sightseers abandoned their once fought-over places for the relative safety of the streets outside the park.

'I simply do not understand,' said Coppertracks. 'I have never seen the like before. There are geysers of volcanic debris from the Fire Sea that erupt into the sky and could burn sail riders like this, but the flues of the Fire Sea lie many hundreds of miles north of us.'

Flaming masses were striking the capital now, some of the smoke trails lost among the pneumatic towers of Sun Gate. All ability to control their landing had vanished – a rain of dead circus men and women striking Middlesteel's streets. Finally, the sky was filled with the gentle fall of a thousand smouldering silk threads as the entertainers vanished out of sight. All save one, a tri-sail rider hanging limp as his main-sail was tugged by a side-draught while the glider's tail-sails crackled into nothingness; a side-draught that was dragging the contraption high above the streets of the capital and towards Tavistead Hill. Towards Tock House!

The dot grew larger and larger in the sky. Embers from the disappearing tail-sail finally ignited one of the mainsails and the rider frame began losing height rapidly, falling out of the wind's clasp above the capital. Down below, Coppertracks' mu-bodies were running out from the house, crunching the gravel of the path, swinging buckets of sand unhooked from the fire point of their boiler room. If the sail rider managed to avoid being impaled on the tip of the steamman's tower of science, then he was going to come down hard in their orchard. The three owners of Tock House were fast after Coppertracks' drones, joining the little iron goblins converging on the likely landing point.

Down to a single sail now, the flaming craft swung across the clearing where Coppertracks' celestial signalling apparatus stood spearing up towards the clouds. Then the rig blew into the line of pear trees, wrapping itself around the canopy of branches, burning silk billowing into dozens of pieces across the tree line. Where sheets of flaming material blew across the grass, the friends quickly extinguished them. Splintering,

103

the main frame of the sail-rider rig folded in two, the limp mass of the rider swaying to a sudden halt, left hanging upside down from a tangled snarl of harness belts and sail pulleys.

Commodore Black pulled out a knife and shimmied up the tree to cut the pilot loose, Molly and Coppertracks waiting underneath to catch the body in the canvas rain cover they had pulled off the glade's small Porterbrook steam engine.

'The sail rider's a lad and he's taken some burns,' shouted the commodore.

'Is he alive?' Molly called up.

'He can count his lucky stars, but I believe the fellow is.' The commodore was sawing his way through the nest of ropes. 'His lucky stars and the fact that for all its bright rainbow colours, this sail frame is an old RAN chute. I can smell the retardant chemicals from his blessed burning silk, like bad eggs. Treated to exit a cannonshot-riddled airship when needs demand.'

With a final slice and a warning shout, the commodore cut the pilot free to flop down into their canvas. Molly pulled off a black leather glove from the pilot's hand and felt the wrist for a pulse. Yes, he was still alive, but in what shape was anyone's guess. 'Send for the doctor and make sure she turns up half-sober.'

'One of my mu-bodies is already on its way into the village,' said Coppertracks.

Molly rolled the pilot over. What she had first taken for part of the sail frame caught up on his back clearly wasn't. 'Look, a travel case! Why in the name of the Circle would you sail-jump with the weight of a travel case tied to your back?' She tried to open the case but it was locked. Damned heavy too.

Commodore Black landed down on the grass next to the pilot. 'A queer thing to do, but it saved his life. The weight of that case would have kept him at a lower altitude than the rest of his circus friends. Whatever ignited the others' sails only singed his poor head a little.'

Molly glanced up towards the firmament. Only the flat grey clouds of Middlesteel hung over the capital, but this carnage was no accident. The mystery of the disappearing stars might have been solved, but something else was deeply awry up in the heavens. The Jackelians were used to being masters of the sky. Their airships ruled the vaults of the firmament without peer or equal; a monopoly of aerial destruction that had long preserved their ancient kingdom from her many enemies.

But it appeared it was a monopoly no longer.

CHAPTER FIVE

I t took a lot to recall the Jackelian parliament from its summer recess. The honourable members of the House of Guardians didn't collect much of a stipend from the state for their troubles, but at least they could usually rely on the long days of hunting, shooting and fishing on their estates. Estates that the members of the present Leveller government often lacked, so the grumbles went, hence their eagerness to recall parliament at the drop of a hat. The guardians' resentment at the interruption of their amusements was slowly bubbling over while the speaker of the house's lictors assembled the bones of King Reuben, his ancient skeleton dangling from a seven-foot staff of heavy Jackelian oak.

'Get a move on,' shouted one of the guardians, a ripple of agreement running across the benches.

'Order!' hissed the speaker.

With King Reuben's bones at last wired together correctly, the lictors formed a column, the master whip Beatrice Swoop at their head, and set off to march the last true king's remains around the floor of the house for the prescribed three circuits.

'Parliament shall not sit,' chanted the lictors, speaking for the bones.

'Says who?' roared the guardians, getting into the swing of the opening ceremony at last.

'Parliament will never sit again, by the force of my army,' recited the lictors, dangling the king's bones menacingly as they stamped across the wooden tiles.

All the guardians rose to their feet, pointing angrily at the bones of the once absolute monarch, slamming their canes on the benches in lieu of the heavy debating sticks that stood racked below. 'King of the Jackelians by our command, not king of Jackals. By the force of *our* army.'

'Ohhhhh,' moaned the master whip, running out of the chamber with the dead king's bones, the final customary call a lonely echo down the corridors outside. 'Sod this for a game of soldiers.'

'Parliament's writ runs supreme,' announced the speaker. 'Parliament is hereby declared open in a session most extraordinary. I call upon First Guardian Benjamin Carl to make the opening address.'

From the cabinet bench the first guardian pushed the wheels of his bath chair forward, occupying the podium of oratory. Carl tutted to himself. In the old days, the bones of King Reuben would have been borne through the streets of Middlesteel. Then the citizens of the capital would have tossed rotten fruit at them, a purse bearer from the treasury at Greenhall walking behind the skeleton with a bag full of copper pennies for any urchin who managed to detach the king's skull from the staff. But the expense of the public holiday and the disruption to commerce had led to the parade's abandonment some thirty years earlier. They were a modern people now, after all.

Carl cleared his throat. 'I have come before you many times

over the last few years and asked for changes to the laws of Jackals that have been considered radical by many of my honourable colleagues and some editors of Dock Street.' He gave a little nod to the public gallery, packed with pensmen from the news sheets. 'So who am I to deviate from the front page editorial that the *Middlesteel Illustrated News* has no doubt already laid out on their composition board? I shall even raise the ante for their editors a little. It is my terrible duty to ask you today for the passing of perhaps the most radical bill of them all. As radical as the threat this land of ours now finds itself faced with. We must repeal, at least temporarily, the Statute of Splendid Detachment.'

'No, NO,' howled the opposition benches – worryingly, the cry appeared to be taken up by many members on Carl's own side of the house as well.

'There are reports circulating which cannot have escaped the attention of my honourable colleagues assembled here today, reports that have been carried back from our trading houses in the Catosian League. Reports that I can sadly confirm. Almost all of the Catosian city-states have now fallen.'

From the facing benches, the opposition leader Guardian Hoggstone came to his feet. 'The policy of splendid detachment has served this house well for seven hundred years. The study of history is a litany of conflicts raging into war across the continent and ever shall it be so. Are we to act as policemen to the world? You will find it an ungrateful business, sir. We have no mutual assistance pact with the Catosian League. Indeed, who in the anarchy is there to sign a treaty with? Where each citizen speaks for him or herself, with not a government worthy of the name. We would go into their land as liberators and be shot at as occupiers within the week, mark me well on this matter.'

Carl continued. 'We know of no nation to the north capable

of defeating Catosia. An expeditionary force would allow us to gather information on the invaders and—'

'And it would cause the Jackelian people to become embroiled with every foreign intrigue and border dispute on the continent,' roared Hoggstone. 'A little bit of splendid detachment when it suits one is similar to one's daughter declaring she is merely a little bit pregnant for the afternoon. And I have read the developments in today's news sheets as well as you.' He flourished a copy of the morning's *Illustrated*. 'Quatérshift has now been invaded from the north by the polar barbarians, this Army of Shadows the refugees speak of. Would you have us come to the shifties' aid too, send our redcoats outside of our borders to help protect the ancient enemy, *compatriot*?'

'Come to order, damsons and gentlemen, please,' yelled the speaker as the house descended into uproar.

'Carl by name, and Carlist by nature,' yelled a guardian from the Heartlander party.

The master whip's lictors slapped their coshes menacingly into their palms, trying to bring the frenzied politicians into line. Uncowed, the guardians hooted their rage and threw the remains of their lunch at the enforcers of the chamber's law. It usually paid to have a pocket stuffed with apple cores and half-eaten pies in parliament.

It was time for the First Guardian to play his trump card. 'There is a related matter which I have the grave duty of bringing to the attention of the house. Despite my honourable colleagues supposedly partaking of the many joys of the season's recess, you will no doubt be gratified to hear I already have a tray filled to the brim with complaints from the guardians assembled here today vigorously protesting against the grounding of the aerostat fleet of the merchant marine. The announcement that Admiralty House issued – that all airships had been grounded for maintenance checks following the crash of the *RAN Amethyst* due to engines clogged with the dust-ridden rain left in the wake of Ashby's Comet – was falsified by cabinet order. By *my* order.'

Now the house really descended into chaos. They had been lied to, the First Guardian dared do this to *them*, the elected representatives of the people! A guardian from the Roarer party vaulted the opposition rail and tried to strike Carl across the head with her cane; but the lictors were all over her with their clubs, a tattoo of brutality drummed across her body until the politician slumped into unconsciousness.

'Banned from sitting in the house for a week,' pronounced the speaker from his perch, as the body was dragged to the infirmary by two footmen.

Carl grimaced. It would take twice as long as that for her wounds to heal. He looked at the pensmen and illustrators scribbling frantically in the gallery above. By the Circle, they would have their fun with this day. His voice rose above the bedlam. 'My order was not issued lightly, but to avoid mass panic while parliament was being recalled. The *RAN Amethyst* was never grounded, it was posted missing. Along with sixteen airships of the merchant marine that disappeared in a single evening. Yesterday, as those of you who were in attendance at Goldhair Park will have noticed, dead circus performers rained down from the sky. I think it is safe to assume that they were not killed by a noxious cloud of vapours widely adrift from the Fire Sea as the penny sheets have been speculating.'

'You are saying these events are connected?' asked Hoggstone, the leader of the opposition's face returning to a more normal shade now he realized how deeply his beloved Kingdom of Jackals stood threatened. Hoggstone's Purist party members took his lead and fell quiet by his side.

'I don't believe in coincidences,' said Carl. 'The Catosian League has collapsed. The north of Quatérshift has been invaded. Our airships are being plucked from the sky without a trace like pigeons devoured by hawks. The order of worldsingers is reporting a consistent failure of its most basic sorceries. It is as if our strength, the strength of our great people, is being slowly sapped away by a fever. And who can this state of affairs suit? We have always feared a foreign nation would one day threaten the Jackelians' sovereign rule over our proud skies. That day has now arrived, and while it may be advancing towards us from the north, I doubt if the Army of Shadows comes in the guise of any barbarian horde.'

'But polar barbarians have been sighted on the move by my own clipper captains,' a backbencher called out.

'No doubt fleeing south from the same forces that are occupying Catosia,' said Carl. 'It may be that the Army of Shadows are from one of the continents on the other side of the polar darks. Quadgan, possibly; a crossing over the ice pack passage is still possible this late in the year. What is certain, however, is that if we meekly await our fate within our borders, we cede a vital strategic advantage to the invaders. Our duty to the people is clear! We must act to preserve the kingdom, even if that means intervening in the affairs of our neighbours.'

'A twelve-month repeal of the Statute of Splendid Detachment,' boomed Hoggstone, waving a fist at the members of his own party. 'And I'll take a debating stick to the skull of any man-jack among you that dares to vote against it.'

'I thank the leader of the opposition for rising above narrow party interests. You should know I have already ordered the high fleet to be concentrated at Shadowclock,' said the First Guardian. 'While the Board of War is now mobilizing every regiment of the New Pattern Army, ready to receive our instructions.'

'That's the style, sir,' said Hoggstone. 'Taking a Jackelian merchantman by surprise on her bow is one thing; let's see how these sneaky damn foreign devils like a dozen squadrons of RAN frigates up 'em.'

Gripped by the moment, the mass assemblage of guardians howled their approval. The vote was a foregone conclusion now. Benjamin Carl looked at their faces. Contorted by rage. Haunted by fear. Shown their own weakness, where an hour before they had still laboured under the illusion that their nation was unassailable. Thinking the unthinkable. A foreign war, not a war of defence within the Kingdom of Jackals' acres, but a true war of aggression.

But a war against who? Who were the Army of Shadows?

Duncan Connor looked up from his bed, alerted by the smell of the commodore's seadrinker broth, which Molly was trying hard not to spill as she opened the door to the room.

'Your bruises are fading,' said Molly, putting the food down to take a good look at the sail rider they had pulled from his burning rig in their garden.

Duncan touched his lumpen cheeks. 'I think you're just trying to make me feel better.' He picked up that morning's copy of the *Illustrated*. 'Aye and thank you for all of this, I've stayed in worse hotels. Far worse, in fact.'

Molly pointed to the line drawing on the front of the newspaper. A portly Jackelian, the cartoonist's everyman, old John Gloater, standing on an outline of the realm and shaking a blunderbuss at a giant, sly-looking polar barbarian from the Army of Shadows while a mob of miniature politicians pushed and shoved the large-bellied yeoman across the border. *''Pon my word,'* announced the speech bubble from the Jackelian's mouth, '*this splendid detachment is a right sharp business.*'

'Interesting times,' said Molly.

'It seems our army commanders are showing a taste for original thinking the medal-heavy numpties singularly failed to demonstrate when I was in service in the regiments.'

'A soldier? I thought you might have been a jack cloudie,' said Molly. 'Your sail-rider chute . . .'

'From an old friend in the navy,' said Duncan. 'I served in the Corps of Rocketeers, until myself and the general staff over at House Guards had a wee philosophical difference of opinion over the development of the rocket as a weapon of war. A consideration for you, if you ever fall foul of a recruiting party – never put yourself on the side against tradition, tradition always wins out in the regiments.'

'I believe I'm a little too respectable to be press-ganged now,' said Molly. She didn't elaborate on how things might have gone for her a few years back, though.

'Broth again?'

Molly laid the bowl down on the bedside next to the travel case – the one he had woken up shouting for when he first regained consciousness. Did it hold his campaign medals? Something about Duncan's manner told Molly he would have pawned those off a long time ago. Anybody desperate enough to strap themselves to a rocket would have gone through a lot of trips to the pawnshop first. 'The commodore swears by it.'

'Aye well, you won't find me complaining. As I said yesterday, I'm afraid I'm rather between trades now that the army doesn't require my soldiering and the Circus of the Extreme has no doubt gone bankrupt.'

'You've not remembered any more about your sail jump?'

'Nothing you could make a penny sheet tale out of, I'm

afraid, lassie. The force of the rocket launch concussed me during the ride up. And things happened awful fast after that. I remember seeing shapes moving in the clouds. Very big shapes. Then there was just waves of flaming pilots plummeting past me. A wall of fire above me that set my own sail rig ablaze.'

'Aerostats?' said Molly.

Duncan shook his head. 'I've flown on enough RAN airships as regimental steerage to recognize the hull of a man-o'-war running in the clouds alongside me, and the shapes I saw didn't look much like one of our bonnie ladies of the air. Not the underbelly of a skrayper, either. All you ever see of one of them is a half-transparent tentacle coming down from the sky to tear you apart.'

'Well, I'll tease a tale out of you for your board somehow,' said Molly. 'That is, if the Army of Shadows manages to forgo looting all the stationers in the capital that are willing to take my work.'

Molly left the sail rider to his broth.

As she shut the door to his room, Duncan tapped his travel case thoughtfully.

<I like her.>

'Aye, so do I,' said Duncan. 'All three of Tock House's owners appear to be fine wee people. We were owed a turn of good fortune and I believe we'll be safe enough laying away here awhile.'

<I'm afraid of these polar barbarians. You won't let the Army of Shadows get me?>

'Don't be a daftie, I'm always going to be here to protect you,' said Duncan. 'This hubbub may be an opportunity. When the regiments start running short of cannon fodder and are down to bairns who don't know one end of a dirk from another, the recruiting sergeants might not be so fussy about letting the likes of me hold a commission again.'

<I don't care for war.>

'Nobody ever does,' said Duncan. 'Nobody ever does. But work is work.'

Molly blinked the sleep out of her eyes, the owl's cry fading away. Woken again. She normally slept so soundly too, but then, the birds had been chattering uncommonly loudly since the news of the fall of Catosia – each dawn chorus a panicked explosion of robins and starlings. Now, even the nocturnal birds had become infected with the fear of what was coming down from the north. But this night there was something else in the air, the sense of something familiar. Something was— no, it couldn't be? Molly swung her feet out of bed and padded over to the window, pulling the curtain back an inch. Down among the trees, was that a shadow of moonlight and clouds, or . . .?

'Please don't be alarmed.'

Molly spun around. To see . . . not who she had been expecting! A thin and scrawny young girl, as much a raga- muffin as Molly had been when she was a poorhouse urchin cleaning the heating stacks in the capital's great pneumatic towers. Accompanied by a man who might have been her father in his dishevelled lack of means. Molly kept a compact purse gun in her sideboard, but these two odd intruders were between her and the expensive little Locke's Lady Pattern.

'How did you get past the front door? Molly hissed.

'I spoke to your lock,' said the man.

'There's seven drums turning on my front door's transac- tion engine,' said Molly. She should know, she had upgraded the cipher on the engine herself. 'That must have been quite a conversation.'

'For Circle's sake, Kyorin, you're frightening her,' announced the ragamuffin. 'I told you we'd be better waiting for daylight hours to come visiting.'

'Would that we still possessed the luxury of a lost night, Purity, our time is running short,' said Kyorin.

'Listen to Purity's advice next time,' advised Molly. 'If I scream for help there are three others inside the house.'

'There is no need for that. I intend no harm towards you; quite the opposite, I have come to warn you.' Kyorin drew out a copy of Molly's novel from the pocket of his frayed jacket.

'Oh, please! Not another one of my readers who belongs in an asylum. This is completely the wrong way to get me to write a dedication in your bloody book.'

'I have come to warn you, to enlist your help as a person of influence with the vision to appreciate your people's predicament. But I believe you have already been warned, you have a . . . talent for the soul of machines, you are – ah, now I see, you are a hybrid – your blood bubbles with sub-cellular level machinery.'

Molly stiffened. Who was this madman? 'I really don't know what you are talking about.'

'There is no need for deceit. You must not think of me as an enemy,' insisted Kyorin. 'I can feel the imprint of your land's sentinel machine upon you. We share an enemy, you and I, Molly Templar of the Torley Street Press. An enemy who I fear has already neutralized the sentinel machine you act as a symbiote for.'

'Torley Street Press are only my publisher,' said Molly, 'and who are you to know of the Hexmachina?'

'He's a slave and a witch doctor,' blurted out Purity. 'On the run from the polar barbarians. He should have a beard, I know.'

116

'Yes he should,' said Molly, looking more closely at the ragamuffin. And the girl should have stolen a shawl from a washing line to hide the shadow mark where the golden crown of a royalist prisoner had so obviously been ripped off her cleaner's pinny.

'I know of your sentinel machine because my people once created similar devices. But they were not nearly enough to protect us from the masters' fury.'

'You're talking about the people who have frozen the Hexmachina within the earth? I had been hoping that it was all only a bad dream. Who has the power to imprison the Hexmachina . . . ?'

'It is no dream. My masters' craft is great. I can show you, if you allow me to join with your mind. I carry a forbidden memory, a seed of truth passed down from mind to mind, from generation to generation. That is why I am here, to try to stop the fate of my land being visited upon yours.'

Molly touched her neck nervously.

'He means well,' said Purity. 'He does. He saved my life.'

Molly nodded towards her dirty pinny. 'He picked the lock on the gates of the Royal Breeding House too?'

'I will not hurt you,' said Kyorin. 'I sense that your brain is already evolved for a similar form of communication. Your land's sentinel machine has used the structure of your mind to join with you before.'

For the seed of truth? Molly winced. The truth was a mutable thing, it moved and flexed with the eye of its beholder. But she had to know, after the Hexmachina's last garbled warning and the polar barbarians' deadly incursion from the north. The Army of Shadows. She had to know.

'Show me,' whispered Molly.

'Clear your mind,' instructed Kyorin, reaching out with his hands. His fingers felt warm on Molly's forehead, warmer still as the vision began to rise inside her mind. It was as if each of her eyes was showing her a different sight, the dark familiarity of her room at Tock House overlaid with something alien, at first smoke-thin, but the image growing clearer as she focused in on it.

It was a room, a large chamber made of a glowing substance Molly could not put a name to. A council was about to begin, illuminated by an emerald light falling through cathedral-sized windows that should have been covered in ocean, but were submerged no longer – waves of green sludge lapping against the lower panes instead. She could hear the noise of the surf in the vision, a repugnant polluted gargle as each thick wave sloshed against the glass.

Around the crescent table sat rubbery-skinned albino creatures, octopus-like, but with very humanoid eyes and very humanoid fingers branching out at the end of their tentacles, the pallid limbs flickering across machines built into their table. Communicating with distant functionaries while they waited for the council to start. This was a most peculiar vision. Molly could actually interact with it, push her mind towards areas of the image and gain knowledge of what she was looking at.

Molly was about to try to divine just what these strange creatures were, when a truly giant member of the species rose into the chamber through an opening in the floor.

'The emperor's council is in session.'

Molly concentrated on what was being said, trying to banish the image of her bedroom that underlay this strange sight. Hear the words; hear her vision's translation of them.

'The Department of Nourishment will open this session of the council with their report.'

One of the creatures leant forward to speak into a box on the desk, its beak warbling. Others were watching this scene, the session broadcast to a select group of rulers who could not be present, sent out like a punch card message coded and carried across the Jackelian crystalgrid. 'Oceanic evaporation has increased by six per cent since the last reporting of my department, four per cent higher than the predictions we had been supplied with by the Department of Adaptation.'

Another of the creatures stiffened at so public a rebuke.

'Our remaining plankton farms at the south pole are now reporting ninety per cent harvest failure, despite the successful seeding of the latest heat-resistant strains.'

'Then your new strains of plankton were obviously not nearly heat resistant enough,' hooted the council member who had been singled out for criticism a moment earlier.

Sharp beaks clicked angrily at each other, but Molly's vision lacked the means to translate so quickly.

'There is another way,' announced one of the creatures. There was something about this one. Molly probed and got back the answer. This creature was the source of the secret recording of these events, the one who had passed it on to hands that would have been regarded as outlaws by the others within this chamber. 'We can make a truce with the faction of the healers. They have a plan to regenerate the heart of the world, to inject the core with modified bacteria to begin to clean the atmosphere, to—'

'For shame,' hissed the giant bull creature whose entry had started the meeting. 'Do we have a hundred generations of life left to us to wait for such a wild scheme to bear fruit? Our land is dying *now*. To hear such defeatist anti-science sentiments from one of our own council. Our people strive to master base nature, not surrender to it. Would you invite disease back into our world as well? Would you take the cells of predators from our zoo's refrigerated vaults and release extinct killers back into the land? Would you turn off our sky control and allow superweather systems to ravage the surface without check?'

'You can see about you what wonders our industry has wrought,' argued the dissenter. 'When land temperatures climbed burningly hot we adapted our bodies to live under our oceans, but now even the seas our grandparents swam in, the seas we have farmed for centuries, have dwindled to a barren desert with a shrinking lake at its centre. This chamber once rested secure on the seabed and now look at it.' The dissenter raised a tentacle to point at the ceiling. 'The walls of our sanctuary hum with the buzz of insects swarming over stagnant water. How shall we adapt our bodies to survive next? Will we become sand serpents wriggling through the wastes of the dunes? Is that the fate you wish for the children of our mighty civilization, to hunt rodents through the deserts we ourselves have wrought, only dimly remembering that they were once masters of machines and the keepers of ancient wisdom?'

'There is food enough,' said the giant bull. 'You know of what I speak. Food enough to last our people for the handful of generations we require to lay the plans to reach our final sanctuary.' As the creature tapped the desk in front of him, the image of a blue sphere flickered into view, bands of white clouds swirling above seas and green landmasses.

Molly focused in closer on the rotating globe. A verdant, ocean-covered celestial sphere. Green fields. Oh sweet Circle! Catosia hadn't fallen to a horde of polar barbarians. Quatérshift hadn't been invaded by the bear-pulled sleds of any northern warlord. These invaders were from one of the celestial spheres neighbouring the Earth – a devastated dead world of sand and dunes. Dunes . . . all the images of Kaliban produced by Coppertracks' observatory rose up at once. *Kaliban.* As if confirming her epiphany, the vision running across her mind shifted to a scene of black cones lifting away from the endless wastes on beams of light, great shell-like vessels to cross the celestial darks and burrow into the poles of their new home – the valuable polar territories, always the last land to heat up and lose its life-giving moisture while the world's bounties were depleted. Locusts and despoilers, indeed.

Molly's vision started to shift onto something new, but the scene fragmented before it fully formed, broken by Purity's scream as the window looking out at Tock House's inner courtyard shattered, the dark shape that had been pressing its face to the pane judging its prey located.

Something black and heavily muscled swung through the gap. Molly stared dumbly at the creature for a second, frozen by the splintering of the vision that had been filling her head and paralysed by the shock of the brute's sudden appearance. Taller than a man by a head, the bipedal creature appeared both rangily thin and densely muscular at the same time, moving across the floor with the deadly predatory grace of a flicked whip. The intruder's skin was dark and oily, covered in chitin-like plates and glistening like a blood-wet blade, the slyly darting skull a flat, shockingly eyeless oblong of bone, a fanged mouth leering under a cluster of nostril slits. It moved on all fours like the killer apes Molly had idled afternoons away watching in Middlesteel Zoo, but quicker, long talons on its fingers clicking on the floor where they briefly gashed the wood. The womb mages of Cassarabia were said to be masters of growing horrors inside the wombs of their slaves, and if they had captured a demon and crossbred it with a mantis and a bat – then spiced the mix with the instincts of a shark given legs – something like this thing might have puddled out of some poor unfortunate's thighs in the caliph's slave pens.

Purity was retreating to the far side of the bedroom but the intruder wasn't after the ragamuffin – it flung itself at

Kyorin, lashing at a shield of energy cast by the traveller,
invisible save where the beast's claws struck, sparks flying off.
Molly dived for her sideboard and her purse gun as Kyorin
and the beast rolled across the floor.

Molly was pulling her pepperbox-shaped pistol out of the
drawer when two other eyeless fanged faces appeared hissing
at the broken window, one of them poking its own big black
pistol through into the room. The realization that these things
hunted in packs struck Molly like a lead cosh as she fumbled
for a crystal charge to prime her gun. Don't feel the fear, don't
feel the – a shadow lengthened across the room and the two
beasts clinging to Tock House's wall disappeared with a wet
slap.

'About bloody time.' Molly snapped the purse gun shut
and shot Kyorin's attacker in the back, dead in its spine. Its
head turned slowly towards her and she saw the blood running
down the thing's fangs. Green blood.

Kyorin had stopped struggling; his shield broken under the
storm of claw strikes. With a yell of anger, Purity grabbed a
poker from the room's cold fireplace and ran at the beast.
The creature didn't even look around at the girl as it batted
her and sent her flying across the floor. Molly broke her pistol,
ejected the shattered charge and reached for another shell. On
the creature's back a bubbling froth of blood had congealed
as hard as stone, closing the wound. A purse pistol was no
thunder-lizard gun, but even so – she had just shot this thing
square in its spine. No street thief in Middlesteel could have
taken such a shot and survived. The creature turned the eyeless
plate of its skull towards her and raised its hand, wagging a
finger disapprovingly – the scalpel-sharp talon flashing in the
half-light, a coughing rasp laughing mockingly at her. Circle
on a stick, the damn thing was sentient. How lethal did that
make it?

In the corner Purity pulled herself to her feet. She was a game young bird, tougher than she looked, obviously. Molly squeezed the trigger and her pistol's clockwork mechanism struck the fresh charge, but there was no explosion. Misfire! No time to clear it. Arms outstretched, the creature leapt at her, an arc of death springing across the bedroom. Only to meet a wall of flesh as the taut bare-chested form of Duncan Connor slammed the beast off balance. It rolled over and brought both its long muscled arms up, fingers twitching like miniature sabres, marking the location of its new prey with a series of sonar clicks out of its throat. Duncan charged first, roaring his anger and scooping a knife-long shard of broken glass from the floor. Springing forward, the beast tried to regain the advantage of the fight, but it wasn't used to this. Prey ran, prey begged for life, it didn't attack first.

The ex-soldier drove a foot down into the creature's knee, ducking under its sweeping claws and seized the beast from behind. There was a quick flash of glass as Duncan slashed the creature's throat. The beast stumbled forward, the sudden fountain of blood slowing almost immediately as it congealed rock-hard. But whether it was healed enough to resume its attack was left to conjecture as Commodore Black kicked open the bedroom door.

'Hello, my bucko.'

The multi-barrelled deck-sweeper that had once graced the conning tower of the commodore's u-boat jolted with an eruption like a cannon and the creature was shredded and thrown across the room, flailing onto Molly's bed. The beast tried to move, spitting out a few guttural words in a language Molly didn't recognize – but then the words' meaning formed in her mind like an echo of the alien tongue. It was counting, reeling off a line of numbers before growing still. How could she possibly understand what this terrible creature was saying, and what did the sequence of numbers mean?

'That's a blessed ugly thing you've let into the house to disturb my sleep this night, Molly Templar.'

Molly waved her diminutive purse pistol at the commodore by way of thanks and looked over at Kyorin, his body half-concealed by the kneeling form of his ragamuffin companion. Tiny sparks of the vision from Molly's joining with the foreigner flickered in her mind as she bent down beside them both.

'Please,' Purity begged, tugging at Kyorin's sleeves. 'Don't leave me. You'll be fine, you'll see.'

Molly ran a hand along the claw gashes marking Kyorin's chest. It was a miracle he was breathing at all.

'I should have been able to save him,' cried Purity. 'I killed a political officer when I didn't even mean to. So why couldn't I save him from the slat when it smashed the window?'

Slat? An ugly name for equally ugly creatures. 'You tried,' said Molly. 'But that thing on my bed isn't from the race of man. If it weren't for my two friends here, everyone in the house would be dead right now.'

Kyorin's eyes flickered open, glancing at Purity then sliding over towards Molly. Kyorin and Molly exchanged a glance – both of them knew he wasn't going to make it.

'You – must – travel to meet – the – great sage.'

'Your home,' said Molly. 'You mean Kaliban, don't you?'

'Our joining – has – left – a mark on you. My brothers – and – sisters – will know you – now.'

'Sweet Circle, fellow, I only write about travelling to the moon. I don't actually own any airship that's capable of making the flight!'

Kyorin coughed out a stream of green blood from his mouth as he forced a smile. 'You can't travel – to – Kaliban by dirigible. There – is only – one who – can help – you get there. He is – a – prisoner of – your – watchers in the air.'

The commodore shouldered the weight of his monstrously large gun. 'Ah, no. You don't mean who I think, do you? You can't ask Molly to trust those rascals in the Court of the Air.'

'Yes – your – Court. The man is – called – Timlar Preston.'

Kyorin's back arched as his body began to convulse from the damage done to him.

'Kyorin,' Purity sobbed. 'Use your power, use it to heal your body.'

'I have no – power. Only – what I borrow – from your land. Home is – so far – away.' Kyorin groaned as the pain grew too much, clutching the arms of the two women by his side. 'The – face. The face. Set my – people free.'

'What face?' Molly asked.

Kyorin's hand stretched out to feel the tears rolling down the ragamuffin's cheeks. 'Purity – Drake.' The air expelled from Kyorin's lungs.

Kyorin's arm slumped down and he moved no more.

By the door Duncan Connor twisted the dial for the bedroom's gas lamps, bright yellow light flickering into life and casting the two corpses into sharp relief. 'Aye, and I used to believe garrison duty along the southern frontier was dangerous.'

Molly closed the traveller's eyelids with her hand and as she drew it back she saw the pink dye staining her fingers. Reaching into her nightdress she withdrew a tissue and rubbed at Kyorin's face, revealing his real blue skin underneath the paint – as bright as the cobalt waves of a cove. 'Good grief, he's blue! A blue man.'

'Aye, he's painted his skin to be able to walk among us,' said Duncan. 'He would have caused quite a stir if he hadn't.'

'I never knew,' said Purity. 'All this time with him and I never knew.'

'Come on now, lass,' said the commodore, moving Purity's shocked form away from the corpse. 'It's no good you crying here. Your friend has moved along the Circle and that's the way of it.' Commodore Black choked back his surprise as he had a good look at the ragamuffin for the first time in the gaslight and saw her pinny with the golden crown so obviously ripped from it. Two royalists hiding under Tock House's roof now, then, the commodore and Purity both, and a monster lying dead in Molly's bed. Molly had experienced better nights. They all had.

A voice called up from the small quadrangle at the centre of Tock House. Molly carefully poked her head out of the broken window. Coppertracks stood surrounded by mubodies, his diminutive drones clutching everything from pitchforks to a blunderbuss. They were prodding at the dead bodies of two more slats; brothers to the beast lying blasted apart in her room.

'I have never seen such a strange-looking creature,' the steamman's voicebox carried up at its maximum volume. 'Molly softbody, are you and the others safe?'

'Quite,' answered Molly. 'Come on up, old steamer. Those things down there look dead enough and we could do with your help in here. And you—' she turned from the window and announced to the air '—you took your damn time getting here.'

A figure stepped out of the shadows behind her four-poster bed. 'Please, there were two of them and they took a lot of killing.'

'According to the penny dreadfuls, the Hood-o'the-marsh has had a lot of practice recently.'

'Few who didn't deserve it,' said Oliver Brooks. The two guns at his side flashed their approval with a wicked patina.

'Oh, this is a bad turn,' said the commodore. 'We're in the eye of the storm, now, if you've come back to us, lad.'

'Not in the eye yet,' said Oliver. 'The storm is sweeping towards us from the north this time. I'll take that as a thank you for killing those two monsters outside.' He pointed to Kyorin's corpse. 'Was your blue-skinned friend really serious about Kaliban? And what did he mean when he said the *face*?'

'He was serious enough to give his life bringing us the warning. And he was talking about his face,' said Molly. 'Or one very like it. How about it, Jared, you helped me and Coppertracks present to the Royal Society, doesn't his face look familiar to you? Think about the slides...'

Commodore Black sucked in his breath. 'You're right, lass. No wonder his mug looks familiar. His face is the face on Kaliban, the mortal great carving from the observatory slides.'

'You wanted to know who on Kaliban was signalling to Coppertracks,' said Molly. 'The message in a bottle we heard. It was Kyorin's people. I think they're slaves, a subject race, and their masters are the ones toppling Catosian city-states and taking over Quatérshift.'

'Kaliban!' said Duncan Connor, the meaning of Molly's words finally dawning on him. 'You're saying yon fellow and his ugly kelpie both travelled here from another celestial sphere? Surely this is whimsy?'

'You served in the New Pattern Army,' said Molly. 'Have you ever heard of a horde of polar barbarians capable of over-running a Catosian force defending their own gates?'

Duncan sighed. 'No. If it weren't for the Royal Aerostatical Navy protecting us, we'd probably be a member of the Catosian League ourselves. There is no lord of the north with barbarians enough to storm one of the league's fortress cities.'

'But you can't be travelling to Kaliban, lass,' said the

127

commodore. 'These creatures might have the skill of crossing the void, but we surely don't. It's too dangerous.'

'I'll go with you,' spat Purity. 'However dangerous the journey is. If it means paying back the jiggers that killed Kyorin.'

Duncan shook his head. 'Listen to the commodore's words. Even if you're right, the battle will be here in Jackals. Whoever this Army of Shadows are and whatever land they hail from, their forces are almost at our borders. The high fleet of the RAN is preparing to sail, the regiments are mobilizing. War is upon us and it will be fought here on our doorstep.'

Molly thought of the mighty Hexmachina, trapped in the centre of the world like a fly in amber. Even the power to slay gods was not enough to deal with the invaders. 'No, I don't think we can fight them and win using airships and rifles. What Kyorin showed me in his vision was hideous. The invaders' rulers are ancient, masters of a very old science that has bent all of creation to its will, every other race fit only to serve as their slaves or their sustenance.' She pulled a blanket off her bed, covering up the slippery black muscles of the beast lying slaughtered there. 'This slat is one of the masters' *own* children, twisted into the perfect killing machine by their womb mages. These masters have no care for their own seed, let alone other races' lives. And there are entire armies of these things moving around in Catosia.'

'I feel the pressure of their evil, growing stronger each day,' said Oliver. 'Like a headache. To the north. Running to the east now, too, in Quatérshift.'

'Can we call these slats evil?' asked Molly. 'Beasts like this are only what they were bred to be. But their masters, they've made their choice, and they've chosen our world as their new home. The knowledge of defeating them lies in their old land. Kyorin's masters have consumed it and discarded it like an old apple core, but somewhere among the ruins of Kaliban the answer to stopping the invasion is to be found. That's what he came to tell us.'

'Talking of travelling to Kaliban might make a grand tale for your new fashion in novels,' said the commodore. 'But how are you going to get there? Will you have these monsters give you a berth on one of their terrible ships of the void?'

'No,' said Molly. 'It's a one-way trip for them here. They're fired across the celestial darks in shells that ride beams of light.'

'Shells,' said Duncan, a realization dawning on him. 'Shells. Timlar Preston, that was the man our blue friend mentioned. You ken who Timlar Preston is, don't you? He's a damn shiftie scientist.'

'Cannons,' said Oliver. 'Very big ones from the Two-Year War. The war Timlar Preston nearly won for Quatérshift.'

'It simply can't be done, lassie,' said Duncan. 'Trust me, I've been fired out of cannons and I've ridden up on rockets with my sail rig and anything that could lift you that far and fast would kill you. You can't travel to Kaliban shot out of a great cannon shell – the physical shock of it will pulp your wee body into jam.'

'Quite correct,' announced Coppertracks, rolling into the room, his train of mu-bodies clambering nervously around the bedroom. How long had the steamman been listening there? 'But King Steam has something that could see you there safely.'

'Now don't you be encouraging Molly in her damn fool scheme,' begged the commodore. 'Tossing messages at Kaliban with your mad tower of science is one thing. Shooting our good friends out into the wicked night is quite another. Save your travels to the moon for your novels, Molly.'

A wave of bile rose in Molly's throat and she yelped, nearly falling onto the bed on top of the cold, wicked thing lying there. Oliver caught her and steadied her back to her feet. 'I sensed something flaring inside your mind. Are you all right?'

'My mind.' Molly felt quite nauseous. She glanced angrily at Kyorin's corpse. So many voices, the cries of the dead, the memories of those that had passed into the beyond. 'I do believe this runaway slave dumped everything he had into my skull when he heard the slats at the window. Sweet Circle, it feels like a million thoughts and memories welling up inside me.'

Molly wanted to kick the slave's corpse. Kyorin had done what he believed necessary for the survival of both their races, gambling that the ancient machine life that swam through Molly's veins was powerful enough to absorb the full exchange of their intimate mental sharing.

'He wouldn't have hurt you,' Purity protested. 'It was not his way.'

Molly gritted her teeth. A little knowledge was meant to be a dangerous thing, but how about an entire fallen civilization's store of knowledge floating inside her skull? That remained to be seen. 'Remind me of that again, girl, when I'm sitting in the barrel of the cannon your friend wanted us to build.'

'How are you going to get Timlar Preston out of the wicked Court of the Air's hands?' asked the commodore. 'Ask them nicely?'

'Leave that to me,' said Oliver. 'I know an agent who isn't going to have too much of a choice about helping us.'

'Take a long spoon to sup with those devils, lad! You don't have to be doing this,' insisted the commodore.

'Yes we do,' said Molly.

But even as she said the words she knew how mad they sounded. How desperate was their last hope. All she had to do was free Timlar Preston from the Court of the Air's clutches; and having held him a prisoner for so many years, the Court must be convinced the mad genius was still a deadly threat to the kingdom. Then she had to convince the Jackelian authorities, distracted by the danger of imminent invasion, to help Preston build the mightiest cannon the race of man had ever constructed to fire her at Kaliban. When the government asked why, she would have no answer save the slim hope that a dying runaway slave's last words might bear fruit on a dead world which had already been conquered, spoiled and discarded by the enemy. And all this coming from a celebrated author of celestial fiction.

Damn. Molly would be lucky to avoid being dragged off to an asylum.

Harry Stave's boots echoed down the corridor of the Court of the Air's prison sphere. Behind him, Oliver Brooks pushed the handcart with a body on it – the passenger lying horizontal, his face hidden by a bulbous rubber mask regulating the timed release of sleeping gas.

'You could help me push the cart, Harry.'

'And how believable would that look?' asked the agent of the Court. 'Besides, it would be an inversion of the natural order of things. Some are born to push, others are born to lead.'

'Old times,' muttered Oliver.

'If only,' said Harry. 'I think I preferred the old days. In fact, right now, I preferred last year.'

'You'll be telling me next that you'd have helped me for "old times' sake",' said Oliver.

'Who knows? But on balance, I would say the blackmail helps. It always helps.'

'I might not fully understand the hollow replica of the Kingdom of Jackals you've got turning on the transaction-engine drums of your little metropolis in the clouds,' said Oliver, 'but I know the basics well enough to recognize that such a model only functions when all the variables are known. How broken is that thing right now?'

'Broken enough for me to let a scrote like you walk around the Court of the Air.'

'I thought that was what the Court wanted,' said Oliver. 'Me up here. Your people have been trying to catch me for years now.'

'Unknown variables,' sighed Harry, looking across at where his old friend's brace of pistols lay concealed within their double shoulder holster. 'And the Hood-o'the-marsh is one of the biggest of them all.'

'Your people have been trying to catch the wind with their fingers, Harry. You could toss me into one of your cells right now – you know what would happen next. One day someone in your armoury would open the vault where you'd locked away my guns and they wouldn't be there. They'd be in the hands of someone else wearing a hood and leading your agents a merry dance across the face of Jackals.'

Harry was about to reply when the door of the lifting room at the end of the corridor slid open, revealing a warder doing his hourly cell check.

The warder looked quizzically at the trolley, the cell number hooked around the front just as regulations required. 'What's Timlar Preston doing out of his cell? He's not due to be put under for a room sweep until the end of the week?'

'What does it look like?' said Harry. 'I'm a wolftaker, he's a wolf. I'm *taking* him.'

'I know who you are, Mister high-and-mighty Wolf Twelve. What I haven't seen are any release from custody papers for Timlar Preston.'

'Special orders,' said Harry. 'He's about to get time off for good behaviour.'

'You've got to be having a bloody laugh—' the guard's protests were interrupted by a klaxon, an urgent, intense burst of sound from the other end of the prison sphere.

'Proximity alarm,' announced Harry for Oliver's benefit. Not their prison break discovered, then.

'But we're well out of season for a skrayper attack,' noted the warder.

He walked to the other side of the corridor and rotated a handle, lifting a storm shutter off a viewing porthole. Something megalithic, grotesque, was slipping through the clouds, drifting past the aerospheres of the Court's city in the firmament. Brief gaps in the cloud cover revealed a wall of dark, rust-coloured metal peppered with jagged spikes and lit by savage bursts of red light.

'What in the name of the Circle is that thing?' sputtered the warder. 'It looks like it's riding a lightning storm!'

'Not a lightning storm,' said Oliver, glancing over the guard's shoulder at the strange craft. 'It's riding the leylines.'

Oliver could feel the power of it. A spike of raw energy leeched straight from the heart of Jackals below, lifting this monstrosity up, pushing a devil's cauldron into heaven's limits. It was like a bloated flying citadel, a hideous castle riding on the energy of the leylines.

'We're opening our gun ports,' said the warder, hardly believing what he was seeing. Apart from driving off the skraypers and other gas creatures, the Court's defences had never been used in anger. From somewhere inside the city a series of small aerostats emerged like angry hornets protecting their nest, then they were past the porthole and there was a thump-thump as they ran into the attacker's fire. A backblast of burning hull fragments bounced off the

133

viewing glass, spinning ribs of hull skeleton windmilling past.

The warder noticed Harry rushing the handcart down the passage at speed. 'Hey!'

'What's the very best way to start a fight with your enemy?' asked Harry.

Running behind the cart, Oliver raised up two fingers. The two fingers he could use to push into an opponent's eyes, blinding them.

'Glad to see your time with me wasn't totally wasted.'

They nearly lost their footing as the corridor tilted, the handcart slipping across the floor with the impact of an explosion. Timlar Preston's restraining straps held him on the flatbed, but Oliver barely managed to escape having his legs crushed by the buggy. There was another explosion inside the Court of the Air. More distant this time, the impact taken by one of the spheres at the far end of the aerial city. The tenor of the klaxons changed, becoming a frantic hoot as Harry redoubled his efforts at dragging the cart forward, Oliver struggling to keep up.

'Will the lifting room to the hangar still be working?' Oliver shouted over the racket.

'Not in a minute's time,' called Harry. 'That's a separation alert.'

'Separation from what?'

'Our transaction-engine chambers have done the maths on trading blows with whatever the jigger that is out there. We're losing.' There was a rattle as a porthole next to them was covered with an iron grille sliding down the outside of the prison sphere. 'The Court of the Air is preparing to separate. Each sphere of the city becomes an independent airship and they scatter.'

Oliver gripped the handcart as the prison sphere began to list in the opposite direction. 'Scatter to where?'

'Damned if I know, this is the first time we've had to do it since I've been with the Court. There'll be a rendezvous point for anyone who makes it out alive.'

'Stop!'

Oliver looked around. It was the warder catching up with them.

'Get him back in his cell.'

'Why?' asked Oliver.

The warder stared at Oliver with contempt.

'He's just a cadet,' apologized Harry, abandoning the cart and moving back down the corridor. 'Wasn't so long ago that I slipped him out of Bonegate Jail to join us.'

The warder grabbed the handles of the handcart, pushing Oliver to the side. 'You think we're going to risk the prison sphere crashing into Jackals with fifty year's worth of captures? If this mob of rascals got out all at once, Jackals would be an anarchy within a year—' His words were interrupted by a muffled crash from down the corridor, followed by the pop of explosive compression. 'We're flushing out all of the prisoners, high category ones first, and they don't come much higher than Timlar Preston.'

Harry's hand slipped over the warder's mouth from behind, silencing him as he thrust a dagger through the man's spine. The warder arched violently and then slumped over Preston's comatose form. 'That's why I need him alive, old stick.'

'You didn't have to do that,' said Oliver.

'You're a fine one to talk. Of course I bleeding did,' said Harry. He pushed the corpse off Timlar Preston's unconscious form. 'Just like I'm going to have to drag him into an empty cell before it's flushed. Half measures won't see our people through today safely.' He snapped a chain of punch cards off the dead warder's belt. 'And he wasn't going to give us the keys to the guards' station if we'd just asked him nicely.'

An acrid burning smell reached Oliver's nose. That wasn't good. Just how badly had the prison sphere been hit? The rattle of explosions outside grew louder. Harry left Oliver to manhandle the prisoner gimbal forward while he slotted a red punchcard key into the guard station's lock. Ducking down to check inside before the armoured door had fully withdrawn into the ceiling, Harry waved his old comrade-in-arms forward. 'Nobody here. They'll all be up top in the main station, trying to work out which one of them has the most flight time on an aerosphere.'

Oliver had nearly gained the door when a series of detonations thunder-cracked in a timed sequence, then the floor veered off from under them, leaving Oliver holding the gimbal with one hand and the door with the other.

Harry staggered to the guard station's entrance and reached out to help pull Timlar Preston's unconscious form inside. 'Unfortunately, right now, I think that would be me.'

Oliver looked up. Those last explosions had been too measured to be part of the battle. Separation! Through an arc of glass in the guard station their perilous state of affairs stood revealed in its true horror. The Court of the Air had split into a hundred separate globes, many trailing smoke and flames, stabilizer rotors being reorientated into flight position, the rubber gangways and sealed corridors that had connected the aerial city drifting down now through the clouds like streamers at a country fair. Some of the spheres' gun ports were still firing, a few surviving airships looping through the carnage, razor prows thrumming uselessly with the power electric – their enemy today no pod of skraypers that could easily be repulsed with a few shocks. The vapour cloud cover generated by the city's vast array of transaction engines had cleared away sufficiently to reveal the passage of the executed prisoners; white trails like spider legs reaching out, thin lines of heated oxygen where the cells' decompression seals had been explosively blown. Every few seconds there was another pop and a new captive would be launched flailing – quickly stilled – into the airless vaults of the upper atmosphere.

Oliver could no longer see the vast hull of the enemy craft, but he could feel the weight of their evil riding the leylines like a mountain balancing on an eruption of magma. Draining Jackals of her ancient lifeforce as they flew, turning the precious power of the land against those that they would conquer. The attacker's vessel was filled with soldier slats similar to the beasts he had slain outside Tock House's walls. He brushed their minds, glimpsing memories of their war craft's construction. It had been built by stripping the mountains of Catosia, levelling them to make a honeycombed cauldron of black rock, minerals sucked out by slug-like things and excreted as a trail of panels and girders in their wake. Oliver pushed past the slats' minds, trying to locate their masters' presence. No, there were only the soldiers of the Army of Shadows inside the citadel. Strange. Oliver recoiled in disgust as he probed their essence. They were foul – it was all he could do to hold back the urge to retch. Greed. Avarice. A stripped-down core of pure selfish loathing for anything outside of the Army of Shadows. Kill. Devour. Breed. All with a fierce, demented energy about them, locking this storm of locusts to their labours with an intensity so driving it burnt Oliver's soul to behold. It had been an age since the slats had fed properly. So many centuries since they'd had a green, fresh land to strip. There was something else, too. Amusement. Amusement at the clumsy collection of locked airships that had made up the Court of the Air – that something so ephemeral and weak and subtle could count itself the guardian of an entire nation. The slats piloting the flying citadel showed their contempt by drawing up the force of the land and reflecting it towards the toy spheres they faced. Great gobs of power flaring out and lighting the floating city up the way children might burn out a hornet's nest for the fun of it. Oh, how they loved to see the hornets burn.

Shaken by a massive impact, the prison sphere's floor dipped out from under Oliver and Harry's feet, leaving them suspended in the air for a second before spilling them back down to the floor. One of the instrument panels blew behind them; a shower of sparks falling over Timlar Preston's body. Harry cursed like a navvy, getting to his feet and struggling to spin a wheel on a hatch in the floor. 'The lifeboat is a tad cramped, but there's room for two if you drop down alongside him.'

Oliver looked at Harry.

'I may be a bastard, but I'm not a coward. This is my battle and I'm not leaving it to a bunch of lousy prison guards on an aerosphere to fight.'

'The Court's finished, Harry.'

'We're never finished. We might be folding this hand of cards on the table, but the great game never ends.'

Oliver dragged Timlar Preston's comatose form towards the lifeboat hatch. How many years had the Court hunted Oliver across the face of Jackals? Fearing him. Fearing the brace of pistols that had been handed down from generation to generation of those who had worn the mantle of the Hood-o'the-marsh. The Court. His implacable enemy. More cunning than the crushers from Ham Yard. More persistent than the cavalrymen from the barracks of the New Pattern Army. The Court of the Air had always been there. The unseen eye in the sky. Always watching. Always planning. How would the kingdom see without them? What future could there be without the carefully crafted path the Court was leading them down? Oliver was missing them already. Invisible and invincible no longer – just a collection of mortals tending the civil war's legacy of democracy, blown to the four winds on a motley squadron of high-altitude aerospheres.

Oliver lowered Preston into the lifeboat, a low moan escaping the scientist's lips as he banged his spine on the iron sphere's walls. Preston fell away and Oliver dropped his feet through the hatch. 'What is the enemy going to do next?'

'After they've blinded the realm by taking us out? Well, if it was me, there'd be a right good kicking coming for any Jackelian that tries to stop them invading.'

A tinny voice broke out from a speaking trumpet mounted on the console. 'Station twelve! Station twelve, we've been boarded. All hands to repel boarders on the lower levels. They're beasts; they're—'

Harry sighed and drew out the knife he had used to kill the warder, wiping the blood off on his trousers. 'No rest for the wicked.'

'Be careful. These things are called slats and they're fast and they take a lot of killing. Their throats are their weakest point.'

Harry watched Oliver climb down the lifeboat's ladder. 'You never did say what you wanted Preston for.'

'We're going to build a cannon. One big enough to shoot us to Kaliban.'

'You're—' Harry threw back his head and laughed. 'Well, Timlar Preston's your man, all right.'

Inside the confines of the cramped lifeboat Oliver pushed Preston to one side and slipped his left foot into the sail deployment pedal. 'Stay safe, you old thief.'

'That's what I do best, old stick. Though, from the sound of it, I rather think it's you who's going to need all the luck.'

*　　*　　*

139

With a clang the escape hatch shut, Harry spinning its lever tight. He slid the dead warder's master punch card into the console and there was a clacking from the clockwork deployment mechanism as the lifeboat was lowered out of the prison sphere's hull.

'You stay safe too, boy.' Harry pulled the firing lever, the crack of two charges blowing, and the first – and possibly the last – successful prison break in the Court of the Air's history was over.

A slippery clicking noise sounded from outside the warder station and Harry turned to see the flat eyeless skull-plates of the pair of ebony monsters that had tracked his scent along the corridor. Slats, damn slats!

'That was fast work, lads.' Harry showed them his blade. 'Well done. Now, which of you two ugly slime-dripping jiggers wants some first?'

CHAPTER SIX

C ommodore Black indicated the sword rack and wiped the fat tears of sweat pouring down his forehead with the towel hanging there. Purity dropped her sabre into the wooden rail and borrowed the towel after the u-boat man had finished with it.

'You've a classic sense of blade work about you, lass. Some might say archaic.'

'Some might say unreliable,' replied Purity. 'This isn't anything to do with me. Until I came here I had never picked up a sword in my life before. If any of the children in the Royal Breeding House were caught fencing with broom handles we would be birched so hard we couldn't sit down for a week.'

'They want to raise sheep to wear parliament's tainted crown,' said the commodore. 'Not lions. Yet you fight as if you've been tutored in the arts of war all of your life.'

'Something's possessed me,' said Purity. 'My madness – whatever you want to call it. Every day it burrows a little deeper within me like a sickness, and it gets harder to tell where I begin and it ends.'

'If madness it is, it's a grand old sort. Your reflexes are getting steadier with each session. Cavalry sabre, fencing foil, debating stick, pistolry, cutlass. There are not many tricks of arms I have left to teach you. Nor, I dare say, any tricks of pugilism that mad strapping uplander Duncan Connor has remaining to pass on to you either. Just remember that the New Pattern Army fights dirty, and that you've your house's honour to carry with you.'

Purity looked around. The corpses of Kyorin's murderers might have been cleared away, but Purity could still feel the slats' lingering malevolence. 'I wish Oliver would come back. He seems to know what I am, to recognize the thing inside me.'

'Let him stay away, now,' pleaded the commodore. 'A day, a week, a month is good and a year would be better still. You've got parliament's warrant sitting on your escaped head to think about. That lad with his wicked brace of pistols draws trouble to him like wasps to a picnic. He goes off to visit the Court of the Air and the whole place comes tumbling down like a pack of cards. I could tell you tales of that lad, Purity Drake, and all the trouble he's got me into before now. Stumbling around the undercity and the sewers of Middlesteel, pursued by vicious killers. Marching across the fields of Rivermarsh while shiftie lancers tried to run my proud chest through with their steel and our own airships rained fin-bombs about my head. If it hadn't been for my quick grasp of military matters directing the armies of the Kingdom of Jackals and the Steammen Free State, why, our nation would be a conquered province of Quatérshift and we'd be nodding at each other in the street with a hello compatriot, this, and a how do you do, compatriot, that. Yes, that strange lad you're so keen to see again is fine for getting us into terrible scrapes, but it's old Blacky that everyone has to turn to to get us out of them.'

'I think whatever has been talking to me inside my head has been talking to him, too.'

'Well, I suppose it'd be a blessed release for us if he and Molly did come back early from the House of Guardians, for it'd mean Ben Carl had thrown them out, them *and* their mad plan for building a cannon to shoot Molly to the moon. I should have made an appointment an hour earlier than theirs, and used the jingle of every medal the First Guardian gave me after the battle of Rivermarsh to convince him to help keep my Molly's precious head safe on the soil of Jackals.'

'How can you say that?' asked Purity. 'You heard what Kyorin said.'

'Ah, the poor blue-skinned traveller. Torn apart and lying bleeding on the floor of Molly's bedroom. He was kind to you and no doubt a fine fellow for all the strange colour of his hide, but I've heard the dying words of a good few souls on my terrible adventures and they rarely make much sense. This wicked Army of Shadows is no doubt from one of the continents north of the polar wastes; I've seen stranger sights than your friend's eyeless monsters in the underwater cities of races such as the gill-necks, and crossed swords with far more wicked creatures in the jungles of Liongeli.'

'Either way,' sighed Purity, 'the Army of Shadows will be here soon enough. The news sheets are full of nothing but our new treaty with Quatérshift and the war.'

'The sheep are lying with the wolves now, right enough. And I can think of one shiftie we'd be well rid of to start with.' The commodore pointed towards the window of their library. 'That twitchy devil Timlar Preston, insisting that nothing else but my finest brandies and wines will to do to comfort his genius and lubricate his plans for his damn fool cannon. If there was an agent left to seize the bugger, I would place a notice in the *Illustrated*'s small ads and risk my address

143

to the Court of the Air's rascals in the hope that Timlar Preston wouldn't be sitting in my house come the new day.'

'And in doing so you would be depriving science of one of its greatest minds,' noted Coppertracks, rolling into the court-yard with a couple of his mu-bodies in tow. 'The schematics I have been helping him draft bear as much relation to our current state of gunnery as a child's catapult does to one of your redcoats' rifles.'

'Then perhaps his mad device will be good for lobbing a shell or two towards those slippery-skinned slat creatures in Catosia without me having to get close enough to unload my deck sweeper's eight barrels into their wicked hides.'

'Our cannon's range will stretch a little further than that, dear mammal,' said Coppertracks.

The commodore looked at the box the steamman's drones were bearing. 'More messages from King Steam?'

'Not this time,' said Coppertracks. 'I spent the morning visiting our old friend at Saint Vine's college.' He waved at his drones and they pulled out a series of tomes, laying the books out on a garden bench in the shadow of Tock House's courtyard. 'The college's library is always my first source for mining the depths of historic esoterica.'

Purity was quick to move over to the bench. 'You found something to help me?'

'I promised that I would,' said Coppertracks. 'Your descrip-tion of your madness, your visions, led me to a very specific period of Jackelian ancient history: the long dark ages following the fall of the Camlantean civilization. The pre-Circlean age, when the Council of Druids and the Stag Lords still ruled Jackals. The legends say that a warrior queen united the tribes and that her royal bloodline held sway until the age of ice, blood that was later to re-emerge as the lineage of the first kings. Your ancestors!'

Purity looked at the drawing inked on ancient vellum, an angular illustration of an armoured woman riding a chariot pulled by lions, her hair wild and spread by the wind. The face! The face was the same as that of the woman whose body she had shared on the ancient beach of shale.

'Elizica!'

'Elizica of the Jackeni,' said Coppertracks. 'There is not much beyond myth that we know of that period of history. What the glaciers of the coldtime didn't erase, you fastbloods did when you burned your books to keep warm, and the majority of tomes that survived the age of ice were later tossed on the fire by the Circlist church for containing too many religious references for your atheist faith's tastes. These manuscripts are copies of copies, the originals made at some personal risk by a heretic monk and buried in a cathedral meditatory.'

'The woman in my dreams really existed then,' said Purity. 'I'm not going mad!'

'Hardly,' said Coppertracks. 'The Steamo Loas are my race's ancestors and it is considered a great blessing to be ridden by the Loas, to be touched by our gods. The steammen's great pattern is not so different from the one sea of consciousness your Circleans put their faith in.'

'What do these books say about her?'

'That she was a great queen who defended Jackals from an invasion by one of the underwater races. The geographic record King Steam's scholars have compiled indicates the Fire Sea was expanding at that time, so there may well have been mass migrations by the underwater kingdoms during Elizica's age; the Kingdom of Jackals with its long coastlines would have been a tempting target for any fleeing refugees.'

Purity traced a curious finger over the raised ink of the bound volume's leather pages. It was warm to the touch, as if the monk who had illuminated the original had leaked his spirit into the illustrations. 'It's beautiful.'

'Myth always is.' Coppertracks opened one of the accompanying volumes – notes by a modern Jackelian academic. 'I dare say the reality was more prosaic. She is linked to the legends of the Bandits of the Marsh, two hundred warriors who were outlaws, fey-born and sworn enemies of the Stag Lords. This volume speculates that Elizica led the Bandits of the Marsh against the underwater invaders, and then overthrew the corrupt Stag Lords who had been making treaties with the occupiers, clearing the way for your Circlist faith to replace the druids' many gods. Monarchy and Circlism, the precursors to Jackals as we know it today – strong enough to survive even the long age of ice that was to follow.'

'A long-dead queen, now,' said Commodore Black. 'What good will she be in this fight that is coming?'

'If the Army of Shadows is composed of the slats that attacked Tock House, the help of any Loa that comes to our aid will, I suspect, be deeply welcome,' said Coppertracks. 'You were with me outside King Steam's command tent when we saw the lions running through the sky.'

'What we saw that day was a projection,' protested the commodore. 'A trick of the mind from the fey.'

'You should have more faith in the power of your land, my softbody friend,' said Coppertracks. 'Whose lions were they, running through the sky? You know the answer – when the kingdom is threatened, it is said the first kings will return from the hills where they sleep, led by a great warrior – a sword-saint. Those lions in the sky gave heart to your army when it seemed as if all was lost. The kingdom was threatened then and it is threatened now.' Coppertracks laid an iron hand on Purity's shoulder. 'And lo, our new house guest hears the whisper of an ancient queen, her life now protected by the Hood-o'-the-marsh, the *marsh*, mind, while something terrible comes upon us from the north.'

The commodore sadly met Purity's gaze. 'That is the way of it, then, lass. I would shoulder this burden of yours if I could. You already on the run from the scoundrels and dogs of parliament. Now you have to hear the whisper of some long-dead queen, too.'

'I don't mind,' said Purity. 'I really don't. All my life I've been treated like an outcast for the fits I suffered – but they helped me escape the Royal Breeding House and now I know them for what they are. Not a madness, but a gift. It's as if I've been suffocating all my life and now I can breathe again.' Tears welled in Purity's eyes. 'I think this is what happiness feels like.'

'You've a forgiving heart,' said the commodore. 'And you shame an old u-boat man with it.' He looked down at her bare feet. 'And it pains me to see you without some fine cow leather to wrap around your toes. If you will not take one of Molly's spares, will you at least let me buy you a new pair of shoes?'

Purity shook her head and picked up one of the books Coppertracks had brought back from the college. 'I need to feel the land beneath my feet. But shoes or no, I don't think I'm a sword-saint, however quickly I may have taken to your sabre practice. Can I take these books to my room and read them up there?'

'Of course you may, young softbody,' said Coppertracks, his drones collecting the remaining volumes for her as he spoke. 'But you must follow the house rules I explained when I showed you Tock House's library.'

'I remember – no food or drink, no book-marking by folding the pages, no breaking the spines . . .'

'Quite correct. Books are a little like the Loas. They allow

147

our ancestors to reach out from the past and touch our boiler-hearts with the wisdom of ages long forgotten; although with books, of course, you decide when to ride them, rather than the Loas calling upon you.'

Commodore Black looked at Purity. 'You've practised enough with sabres today, lass. But make sure you read the books in your room and not the library, now. That mad old shiftie is working in there and the further away you stay from him, the better I shall like it.'

Purity left with Coppertracks' drones carrying the tomes for her, their master thoughtfully rocking back and forth above his caterpillar tracks.

'You are wrong about Timlar Preston,' Coppertracks said to the commodore. 'He is a gentle man.'

'And the more dangerous for it. Many a smithy of pistols and blades can say the same . . . but you put the fruits of their labour in the hands of wicked men like me and the result is dead bodies on the duelling fields and fatherless children left crying after a battle.'

'Yes,' said Coppertracks, 'fatherless children. When will you tell her?'

'Tell who what?'

'Please, Jared softbody. I *am* a steamman slipthinker. I see patterns, the little patterns that make up the great pattern. While many of my less travelled brothers back in the Steammen Free State might say that all softbodies look the same to them, I have lived long enough alongside your people not to count among their number.'

Commodore Black seemed to slump and grow smaller at his friend's words. 'You're a canny one, old steamer. There's no denying that.'

'The geometry of Purity's facial patterns matched against yours was enough to pique my curiosity. It was an easy enough trick to use my vision plate to capture a magnified image of her eyes and compare the inheritance vectors against your own. I do not know how it has come to pass, but there's a ninety-four per cent level of probability that Purity Drake is your daughter.'

'It feels like another age,' sighed the commodore. 'When I was younger and still welcomed adventure. What the news sheets called the Prince Silvar affair.'

'The prince was substituted for a double,' said Coppertracks. 'Broken out of captivity from the Royal Breeding House. But I thought that was perpetrated by agents of Quatérshift?'

'So it was meant to look, that fine day,' said the commodore, wistfully. 'It was before the fall of Porto Principe, when the royalist court in exile still had a taste for mischief and I wore the face, name and title of Solomon Dark, Duke of Ferniethian. And it was no mean feat for me, even then. I had to join the redcoats, rise to the rank of sergeant and make sure I was posted to the barracks at the Royal Breeding House. I was the inside man for that blow against parliament, and Purity's mother – ah, now, there was a lady. Alicia Drake. As proud and as beautiful and as clever as any of us born free on the islands of Porto Principe. She worked out what I was about, all right, and she was the only one of those poor broken royalist songbirds they keep cooped up in the Breeding House with the gumption to help me organize the prince's escape.'

'You should tell Purity who you are.'

'How can I?' sobbed the commodore. 'I saw her mother fall during the prince's escape with a ball through her head – I thought she had died. Now I find from Purity that it was a glancing blow and that when Alicia recovered, she used her wiles to portray herself as a bystander caught in the crossfire to avoid the gallows, pleading her belly for her life. I believed my darling Alicia was dead. I didn't even know I had a daughter until Purity turned up here with her mother's name and the House of Ferniethian's eyes.'

'She will understand,' said Coppertracks.

'How can she ever do that? A father is someone you are proud of, someone to look up to. Not a fat old fool who abandons his family to a life of hell in parliament's dark, windy fortress of royalist brood mares. She would hate me for it. I would be a coward in her eyes. It would be more than I could stand and more than she could stand, too. Her life to date has already been ruined by my carelessness, and the mortal best I can hope for is to keep her safe now. I'll train her with every trick and wile that's kept me alive and out of parliament's hands, and I'll give my life to save hers if I have to, but you must promise me this, old steamer: you must never tell her who I am. Purity can never know.'

'You owe her the truth.'

'Not when the truth would hurt her more than the lie. I owe her a good life more than I owe her the wicked truth.'

'How much longer do we have left?' Coppertracks argued. 'Darkness is upon us from the north. Nothing can be guaranteed anymore. Not if the spirit of Legba of the Valves were standing guard over Tock House, or Elizica of the Jackeni for that matter. Would you let the truth die with one of you?'

'Let it be buried without either of our mortal bodies if it can,' said the commodore. 'I will keep Purity safe and that is all I can do.'

'I shall go along with your decision, dear mammal. But I fear it is neither the proper nor the correct one.'

'The people of the metal are an honest folk,' wheezed the commodore, 'you leave the lies to old Blacky. I've lived a life full of them to keep my poor skin safe from parliament's agents. And when the rest of those slippery slats turn up to make slaves of us all, you leave the killing to me. I've had a life full of that, too.'

'I will hope instead that the Army of Shadows' masters will prove amiable to reason and accommodation with the existing inhabitants of our land.'

'Is that so?' chortled the commodore. 'Well, I've got eight barrels of reason loaded upstairs and a knapsack full of shells to accommodate all-comers. And we'll see which of us is right about that point as well, before long enough.'

Coppertracks watched Commodore Black pack away Purity's practice arms, returning them to the storeroom under Tock House's grand staircase. Somewhere to the north lay the answer to the submariner's wager, getting closer by the day with the fall of every new Quatérshiftian town. Ah yes, the small patterns and the large patterns. And something unexpected coming to disrupt them all. There hadn't been many answers in the corpses of the slat creatures that had attacked Tock House, their organs rapidly dissolving in a soup of their own acidic blood, and the pistol one of them had carried defied the steamman's understanding of modern science – a solid dark thing with almost no working parts, a heat agitation matrix inside capable of releasing bolts of fire from a rotating crystal inside its barrel.

Coppertracks resolved to throw the cogs of Gear-gi-ju that evening, to call upon the Loas to shed what wisdom they could on the matter of the invaders. As if every other steamman from the Kingdom of Jackals to the Free State wouldn't be summoning their ancestors at the same time.

It was interesting, mused Ben Carl, that nobody ever took his butler for anything other than what he appeared to be. Diminutive. Bland. Someone, who, if he stood still for long enough, would begin to blend in with the wallpaper. Just another member of staff from Wolfstones, the First Guardian's official parliamentary residence on the outskirts of the capital; just another piece of furniture adorning the rooms of state. With only the two of them in Carl's office at the House of Guardians, though, it was always a temptation to refer to the man by his true title of General. Where he stood in the ever-shifting secretive hierarchy of the Jackelian political police was hard to say, but somewhere near the top, Carl suspected. Possibly poised serenely on the apex of their sharp, dangerous little organization.

'You have another find?' asked Ben Carl as the man shut the door to his office.

Carl's supposed butler placed a burnt badge on his mahogany desk – the gate of parliament confining a wolf barely recognizable, so blackened was the circle of cloth. 'This was from one of the more recoverable corpses, First Guardian. The wreckage had flattened a farmer's oast house out in Halfshire.'

'Who would have thought it possible?' said the First Guardian. 'Who would have even thought it undesirable?' Carl touched the sides of his wheelchair. The Court of the Air had mangled his legs during the troubles, the brief, failed revolution that had been raised in his name so many years ago. He should have been glad that the Court had fallen. Fallen at last like he had, escaping from one of their black aerospheres as they lifted off the ground of the kingdom, intending to toss him in a cell to rot. Now the pictures the watchers in the sky had been sending had dried up and all he was left with was the terrified reports from refugees fleeing Quatérshift and Catosia. The Army of Shadows. Everywhere. Killing and conquering and enslaving and *feeding*.

'We can preserve the peace in Jackals by ourselves,' said the general. 'Parliament's writ will not falter on our watch.'

Carl nodded. But then, who would watch the watchmen? Who would keep the political police honest now the Court of the Air had been destroyed? Dear Circle, what a turn of the wheel they had come to.

There was another knock at the door and one of Carl's aides entered on his command. 'Word from the southeastern frontier, First Guardian. The army of the Steammen Free State has been sighted assembling in the foothills near their mountains.'

'That is the best news we are likely to have all day. Thank the Circle for ancient treaties.'

The aide pulled a silver-plated watch from his waistcoat and checked the time. 'And the compatriots from our new treaty will be coming over from House Guards on the hour.'

'Three armies to face this strange new foe,' said Ben Carl. 'Jackelians fighting alongside Quatérshiftians rather than against them. We live in interesting times. There has been no word from our embassy in Kikkosico, I suppose?'

The aide shook his head.

'The god-emperor's legions will stay dug in along the pampas,' speculated the general. 'Too much dissent in his provinces to risk sending his soldiers outside their borders.'

'They'll march out quickly enough when we prove we can turn the invaders back north,' said Carl. 'He'll be into Catosia and raising the imperial standard over the city-states like a terrier charging into a fighting pit.'

'Sooner him than us, then,' said the general. 'Anyone fool enough to claim Catosia will be raising their flag over an eternity of rebellion and trouble.'

'Oh, and your other appointment is here,' said the aide. 'The appointment we weren't certain we should accommodate.'

'You should always make time for old friends and supporters,' said the First Guardian. 'Show them in.'

The aide did as he was bid and returned with Molly Templar and Oliver Brooks in tow.

'The crows that fly before the storm,' said Carl. 'And now they're flying in pairs. Why does that not surprise me?'

'I'm hoping that you're well informed,' said Oliver. 'Well informed enough not to believe all that nonsense in the news sheets about the Army of Shadows being an exceptionally aggressive horde of polar barbarians.'

'Opinions seem to be mixed on that one,' said Carl.

Oliver looked at Carl's supposed butler. 'But then, not everything is as it seems at first glance.'

Molly pointed to the First Guardian's desk. 'That badge you've just covered up with papers on your desk. If you're collecting, we've recovered something a little more substantial from the wreckage of the Court of the Air. Or should I say, *someone*.'

'You see,' said Carl towards his butler. 'I told you it's always worthwhile making time for old compatriots.'

'Let me explain just how far away we are from the old days,' said Molly. And Carl listened as she shook the foundations of his world.

When Oliver and Molly left the First Guardian's office, a sea of uniforms was being ushered into the largest of the cabinet rooms. The crimson jackets of the Jackelian New Pattern Army, the dark blue of the Sky Lords of the Admiralty, House Guards generals weighed down with braid and medals and a scattering of cyan-uniformed Quatérshiftian liaison staff – as incongruous by their presence as anything the pair had ever seen.

Molly waited for the hourly toll of Brute Julius – the bell

tower that arrowed out of the House of Guardians – to quieten before speaking. 'Do you think he will help us?'

'The Court of the Air had an inkling of what they were facing towards the end,' said Oliver. 'You could see by the way that hyena in a butler's jacket reacted, that the Court had communicated some of their suspicions to the First Guardian.'

'Maybe it was a mistake me coming with you,' said Molly. 'Everyone in that room knows that I sparked off the celestial fiction genre.'

'Just one of us would have been easy enough to write off as a case for the asylum, but both? And you could see how pale the political crusher went when I told him I was on the Court of the Air when it was attacked. There isn't a nation on this or any other continent capable of taking the wolf-takers down. The great game is changing and I can feel the fear of the unknown eating away inside them.'

Molly lifted her copy of the list Timlar Preston had composed for the First Guardian. The names of the scientists from his old cannon project team at the Institute des Luminaires, in the event that any were still alive after the purges and famines of the terror in Quatérshift. As well as the location of the abandoned mine where Timlar had hidden the parts for a weapon unlike any other during the dying days of the war. 'Now all we need is the time to build Preston's cannon.'

'The three greatest armies on the continent fighting as allies . . . you'll have your time.'

An ancient image rose unbidden within Molly – more of a feeling than anything concrete, another of Kyorin's unwanted gifts to her. The Army of Shadows' raw, rapacious savagery. Kyorin's people had built a great civilization, but the Kals' gentle instincts had made them so many cattle at the abattoir when the masters had fallen upon them.

'I'm not so sure.'

'The steammen are coming,' said Oliver, speaking the words with the reverence of a prayer. 'And Jackals has never lost a war when the Steammen Free State has been fighting by our side.'

Another of Molly's memories rose. One of her own this time, of her old steamman friend Slowcogs, who had given his life to save hers; and she had to choke back a tear. 'Have we had a good life?'

'Define good.'

'After we beat Tzlayloc and his revolutionaries, it felt as if I could do anything, achieve anything. And in my own way I suppose I have. I escaped the poorhouse. I have a living now that many would envy. Wealth. Friends who would die for me. Yet here we are a few years down the line and I'm not even sure if I know what I'm doing. Gambling everything on an escaped slave's vision. When every instinct inside me is screaming at me to run away as far and as fast as possible. What in the Circle's name are we doing here?'

'The best we can,' said Oliver. He lifted his coat and patted the two pistols that had appeared by his side. Molly shivered. The guns hadn't been there when they'd entered the First Guardian's office.

'I used to think I owned these,' said Oliver. 'But now I know that it's the other way around. And we both belong to the kingdom; the pistols' reports just an echo of the lion's roar. I know exactly what I'm doing here. I'm here to protect Purity Drake. I'm the key to keeping her alive.'

'What does that make me?' asked Molly. 'Some lonely old spinster who desperately wants to live out the plot of her last novel while the world is razed to the ground around her?'

They had reached one of the entrances to the House of Guardians, the two redcoats on duty there stamping their boots as Molly and Oliver walked past. Outside, mounted cavalry waited behind the sharp black railings of parliament. A crowd of Broken Circle cultists knelt beyond in Parliament Square, humming a meditation that sounded more like a mass moan of pain. Their numbers were swelling every day, now; more and more of the population convinced that the end of the world was nigh. That the Circle was finally breaking. Maybe the cultists were right. On Molly and Oliver's side of the railings brightly clothed hussars cantered up and down nervously. No looting yet. No riots yet, just that damn rhythmic keening.

Molly raised a hand to shield her eyes against the sunlight. There it was, just to the left of the sun. Ashby's Comet. A baleful red eye behind a thin skein of clouds. 'I hate the sight of that thing.'

'If your friend Coppertracks is right, we had better get used to it,' said Oliver. 'The comet's become another moon now.'

'A cursed ugly one,' said Molly. She looked out at the crowd. It was almost obscene. They looked as if they were praying. The Circlist faith was degrading into superstition and myths of the end-time. How much longer until they started raising false idols to save them from the Army of Shadows and the dark auguries in the sky? How much longer until the Jackelians started believing in gods again? Molly ran up to the railings. 'The new moon's just a piece of loose bloody rock! Caught revolving around us by the attraction of our world's mass. I can show you Coppertracks' formulae to explain everything you see up in the sky.'

The moaning of the cultists just grew louder.

'Get off your knees, you're Jackelians, you're—'

A hussar kicked his stallion in front of her. 'Don't go disturbing them, now, there's a good damson. They're jittery enough this afternoon.'

'They're a disgrace,' said Molly. 'What do they think they're doing? How can you allow them to do that outside parliament's gates?'

'It's hard enough to keep our lads from deserting and joining them at the moment,' said the hussar. 'If trouble breaks out in the capital now, it'll take more than the flats of our sabres to turn them aside. Go home, damson, and make sure you have a stout lock on your door, that's my advice.'

'Come on,' said Oliver, tugging Molly's sleeve. 'We'll go down to the river and hail the sixpenny boat.'

Passing under the shadow of Brute Julius the pair arrived before the low iron profile of an iron gunboat moored alongside the House of Guardians' embankment, its disc-shaped cannon turrets turned towards the opposite side of the river.

Oliver nodded towards the armed sailors on deck across from them as he waved for a riverboat to stop. 'Ready for war?'

'Yes,' said Molly. 'Ready for war. Again.'

Commodore Black touched Oliver's sleeve and pointed to the dark silhouettes emerging onto the shale of the Quatérshiftian beach, men and women clambering over large boulders as they left the silent pine forest behind them and headed for the line of dinghies. The commodore pulled a rag off his lantern to show the figures the way through the night. There were about twenty people coming out of the tree line. Burly red-coated marines from the Fleet Sea Arm were holding the craft down in the surf behind Oliver and the commodore, rifles shouldered, waiting for the advancing refugees to board the dinghies. The foreign scientists were exactly where the shifties had promised they would be gathered, with the Army of Shadows currently showing little sign of intervening in the Kingdom of Jackals' attempt to spirit away some of Quatérshift's best brains for its gunnery project.

They were a ragged gathering, these refugee scientists, led by a silver-haired man staring thankfully towards Oliver and the commodore with an odd-looking face that managed to be senatorial, proud and ugly at the same time. A lithe-legged beauty accompanied the Quatérshiftian man, at least half his years, looking stunning despite her standard revolutionary citizen's garb.

'I am Paul-Loup Keyspierre,' said the shiftie. 'Head of the Institut des Luminaires of the People's Commonshare of Quatérshift. As requested by the First Committee, I and my daughter, Jeanne, have been scouring the country for every engineer and scientist who worked on the old cannon project with Timlar Preston during the Two-Year War.'

'There's not many of you here,' said Oliver. 'I was told by Timlar Preston to expect maybe forty or fifty people.'

'You have those who are still breathing, compatriot,' retorted Jeanne, her short dark hair ruffled by the fierce wind off the sea. 'In case you have failed to notice, our country is dealing with a full-scale invasion. There may be others on the antique staff list we were given who are still alive, but if they are, they have been completely lost in the confusion of the fighting.'

Paul-Loup Keyspierre gently motioned his daughter to silence. 'Our new compatriots from the west haven't seen how bad things are here now, they cannot be expected to understand the nature of the enemy and the difficulties we have faced finding as many cannon workers as we have.'

'We'll take the time to deepen our understanding as soon as we've got your eggheads safely back to our blessed u-boat,' said Commodore Black. He waved to the Jackelian marines and they pushed the crowded dinghies out into the surf and

159

began to row back towards the low black hull of the submersible. 'There may not be much moonlight tonight, but I don't want to leave parliament's tub sitting on the surface any longer than I have to.'

Paul-Loup Keyspierre glanced around. 'This is an old smuggler's beach, yes? It is good that it is out of the way, but the lack of moonlight won't help you, compatriot u-boatman. The Army of Shadows hunt and fight at night as well as they do during the day.'

'This landing may have seen a little smuggling in and out of it,' admitted the commodore. 'The odd barrel of brandy lifted from your fine nation by plucky fellows, although admittedly somewhat in contravention of parliament's wishes and the laws of your revolution. But we'll leave the fighting to the brigades of your people's army if we can. They're trained for it and I doubt if they need the help of old Blacky when it comes to battling the Army of Shadows.'

Oliver unfurled a map while the commodore lifted his lantern over the crinkled surface, revealing a province of northern Quatérshift printed on the paper. 'We didn't just choose this beach because it's out of the way. Timlar Preston buried the components of his prototype cannon inside a worked-out mine five miles inland of here; he salted the parts away when it looked like the Two-Year War was swinging our country's way, when the RAN was raining fire-fins down around your mills and weapons factories.'

'I told you something was not right here,' said Jeanne to her father. She pointed back to the tree line and a handful of Quatérshiftian soldiers appeared leading a train of pack mules. 'The animals weren't requested at the rendezvous point because these so-called allies of ours have suddenly forsworn roast beef for mule meat.'

'So I am to trust you with the lives and fates of Quatérshift's greatest minds,' said Keyspierre to Oliver and the commodore, 'but I am only to be told of these buried components when you arrive to steal them away from my people?'

'We didn't quite know whose country it was going to be when we arrived here,' said Oliver. 'And the Army of Shadows appears to have enough force on its side that we didn't need half the parts for Timlar Preston's prototype cannon falling into its hands.'

'Old habits die hard it seems, my new friends,' said Keyspierre, a tinge of sadness in his voice.

'Your First Committee has agreed to the construction of the cannon deep in the kingdom,' said Oliver. 'Well away from the fighting.'

'Well away for *now*, compatriot,' said Jeanne. She drew a sharp-looking dagger out of her belt and made a cutting motion across her throat. 'When you are fighting the Army of Shadows, the front line has a way of quickly shifting well beyond your control; but you will see.'

Oliver rubbed his forehead as if he had a headache developing. 'I don't need to see. I can feel them here. The creatures moving about, their hunger . . .'

'Don't you pay no mind to the fey lad,' said the commodore. 'Our friends back home are already hard at work on the cannon with your countryman, Timlar Preston. You get yourselves to the u-boat and we'll all be on our way to see the blessed project soon enough.'

'No, I am coming with you to retrieve the weapon's components,' announced Keyspierre. 'I have been charged with the success of this project and if there are pre-milled parts for the old prototype still in existence, they will be key to the rapid construction of a working cannon.'

Oliver was about to protest, but Keyspierre cut him short. It seemed there was a hard edge to the middle-aged scientist

– but then, it would have been reckless indeed to underestimate anyone who had raised themselves to the top of Quatérshift's institute of science in the maelstrom of revolutionary politics. 'I have spent longer than you have avoiding the Army of Shadows' creatures, young man, searching for all the staff your parliament requested. It may feel a little less like Jackelian looting if it is I who takes away the prototype cannon's components. Quatérshift never completed the great cannon in time for the war between our two nations. I will not lose the chance to turn such a weapon against our new common enemy.'

'Take the lass to the dinghy, then,' said the commodore.

'I stay with my father,' insisted Jeanne. 'All are equal in the Commonshare, compatriot sailor. I am not some Jackelian maid who needs cosseting with silk dresses, expensive fragrances, or soft cushions for a coach ride.'

'That much I can see, lass,' said the commodore. 'But you'll be equal in death if we come across the Army of Shadows' beasts.'

Jeanne flashed her dagger angrily at the commodore. 'Who do you think has been keeping my father alive as we've been hunting down every retired scientist and engineer in the occupied provinces?'

'I take your point, now,' said the commodore, flinching back from the blade. 'And it's sharply made.'

Jeanne looked with disdain at the commodore, Oliver, and the handful of red-coated marines left on the beach to help retrieve the prototype cannon components. 'Just keep up with us, Jackelian. Everything north of that pinewood forest is slat territory. Our people are getting used to staying out of reach of the slats' talons. I hope your soldiers are fast learners.'

The commodore watched Jeanne stalk away to the train of pack mules. 'Just a quick little smuggling run, you said, lad.

4*The Rise of the Iron Moon*

I should be back in the Kingdom of Jackals, helping Coppertracks, Duncan and that rascal Timlar Preston lay down the barrelling for your blessed great gun. I'm a game fellow, but I'm getting too old for these mortal dangerous jaunts you seem so damn fond of dragging me into.'

'I bring you along because apart from me, you're one of the few who ever survives these little adventures,' said Oliver. 'You're damn unsinkable, old man.'

'Is that what I am? When my unlucky stars put me in the way of every bullet and blade our age has to offer.'

But the age wasn't finished with Commodore Black yet. There were sights of horror enough to haunt the group on their five-mile journey to the worked-out mine. Memories fit to torment the visitors to Quatérshift for decades to come. The smallest of these barbarities were the cold remains of fires where the slat companies had camped, littered with the blackened bones of the captured citizenry. The shifties might have been starved for years by the failure of the revolution to produce a decent harvest, but there had been meat enough on their bones to satisfy the foot soldiers of the Army of Shadows.

The largest of the outrages was the ruins of the city of Courau, briefly visible from the brow of a forested hill where the party rested, what was left of the place spilling across a wide valley next door to a lake. Its outskirts had been completely flattened by the sweep of war, an inner core of buildings standing intact but still smouldering from the small weapons fire of the slats. Out of the wreckage a new Courau was rising, an evil green luminosity lighting up the rubble as massive domes were raised in the heart of the old town. Made of hexagonal panels, the domes looked like the eyes of giant insects, ripped out and embedded deep in the race of man's territory. Taking the commodore's telescope, Oliver saw long

163

lines of Quatérshift's citizens being marched into the city along the outlying roads, their bodies – many of them were naked – painted viridescent by the tainted light of their conquerors' eerie constructions.

'You can't see from here,' Jeanne told Oliver, 'but the slats have branded their prisoners on their foreheads. A single triangle means they are to be kept as slave labour and used to rebuild the city to the Army of Shadows' template, a double triangle means they are to be farmed. See to the right of the domes, the low glass structures that resemble greenhouses? They are pens where our people are fed slops and fattened. If you were watching during the day, compatriot Jackelian, you would see the slats pulling out the ones they intend to consume. If you were close enough, you could hear the screams of our compatriots begging for the slats to select someone else, anyone else, someone fatter or younger or older or healthier. Fighting each other to be at the back of the pens. The food pens are where the Army of Shadows keeps the children it captures. If you waited for morning you could watch adults throwing children forward when the slats come to select the day's cull, infants whose parents have already died and have no one left to protect them.'

'You see now why I came with you,' said Keyspierre, his voice like steel as he stared grimly towards the conquered city. 'There is no price I would not pay to lift the hand of this terror from our land. If the cannon the Hero of the People Timlar Preston tried to build during the Two-Year War will turn back this invasion, then I will construct it with my own hands if I have to, one rivet at a time.'

'Sweet Circle,' whispered Oliver. 'This is where their hunger leads ... I felt it like a sickness in the north, but I had no idea.'

There was a tear running down Commodore Black's fat

cheek, soon lost in the scrub of his black beard. 'Ah lad, I don't need to be fey like you to feel their evil. This is the future we are looking at, for everyone on the continent, unless we find a way to turn them back.'

'We must unseat them quickly, before their beachhead is established further,' explained Keyspierre. 'The Army of Shadows has captured six of our cities in the north, but they have only begun building like this in two of them. The conclusion we have drawn at the Institute des Luminaires is that even using our captured compatriots as slave labour, the slats do not yet possess the numbers to construct more widely. We believe that the Army of Shadows' rate of advance isn't currently being dictated by the obvious military superiority of their weaponry over our own, but by the paucity of their forces on the ground.'

Commodore Black laid a hand on Jeanne's shoulder. 'You're not alone in this fight, lass. I never thought I'd be glad of the sight, but as we left to sail for you, Jackals' roads were packed with regiments of redcoats marching east towards the border, our skies dark with the high fleet's airships preparing to fly out here.'

'And King Steam's knights are coming down out of the mountains to reinforce our regiments,' reassured Oliver. 'The forces of three nations to turn back the Army of Shadows, with Molly's damn great cannon to carry the fight back to the devils' homeland. To pay them back for what they've done to you here.'

Keyspierre seemed briefly encouraged by their words. His nation had often been on the wrong end of the cannons and bomb bays of the RAN's indomitable airships, and the shifties had taken enough beatings from King Steam's knights, both before and after the revolution in Quatérshift, that it seemed possible that their three combined armies could stand up to any invasion. Even against beasts like the slats. Even here, hiding in the hilly woods with a view out onto the ghastly scorched remains of one of the Commonshare's great cities.

But any courage they might have taken from the pair's words faded as their train of mules came in sight of the worked-out mine where the components for the original cannon had been buried. As they gazed across at the latest horror being wrought by the Army of Shadows from the protection of the tree line, a dark shape the size of a house smashed out of the pine trees to their rear, a split second away from crushing the life out of them.

Hardarms allowed himself a moment's pride as he crested the top of the hill, one of the last before the undulating hinterland of the Steammen Free State gave way to the windswept moors of eastern Jackals.

Below lay the steammen army, without doubt the greatest the people of the metal had ever assembled. Every order of knight steamman was represented in those ranks, the order of the Steel Rose and the order of the Vanadium Lance, Hardarms' own order of the Pathfinder Fist, banners snapping in the wind from the poles attached to their bodies. They sounded like an earthquake on the move, the orchestrated stamp of their feet almost drowned by the fighting hymns that lifted up to the sky. Close to seventy thousand voiceboxes singing in perfect unison. Every now and then, when the clouds parted, the steel and iron of the vast moving mass became a surf of glinting limbs and weapons, pressure repeaters coiled to boilers, drums rattling with balls. It was not just the orders militant on the move down below, there were a hundred legions of common steammen, militia who had answered King Steam's call from the high mountain villages, towns and cities of the Mechancian Spine. King Steam was taking a risk, stripping the Free State of so many of their people; trusting the paper of the freshly inked tripartite pact. How things had changed. Now, it seemed they would stand or fall together, the three mightiest civilizations of the continent. The Kingdom of Jackals. Quatérshift. The Steammen Free State.

Hardarms rested the iron palms of his two manipulator arms on his hip and swung his two war arms – sharp, razor-flowered spears – to clear the kinks in his joint seals. His reverie at the sight of their host below was quickly broken by the sound of bickering slowly following him up the slope.

'Can you not move any faster? It is not dignified for a personage of my status to be seen trailing the main body of the force in this way,' came one of the voices.

'Now don't you be getting your steam up. How many damn tonnes do you think you weigh? You can thank the blessings of Steelbhalah-Waldo that the paths down the mountain actually took your damn weight without us both taking a tumble down a gorge.'

Hardarms looked around, clearing a burst of smoke from his single steel stack. Lord Starhome, a long silver shell some two hundred feet long, was being borne slowly up the slope by the articulated tractor cradles of Mandelbrot Longtreads, the hoary hauler not the slightest bit impressed by the noble graces emanating from one of the largest of the steammen army's holy artefacts, only recently removed from the Chamber of Swords.

'It does not matter,' Hardarms called towards the hauler and his quarrelsome load. 'Within a day's march the army will turn north to rendezvous with our Jackelian allies and we three will have left them and turned south towards Halfshire.'

'And up until that point I should be borne alongside the

royal standard and the command staff,' insisted Lord Starhome.

'Oh, should you?' grumbled Mandelbrot Longtreads, his skull unit rotating around on his cab to stare at the long silver shell. 'Well then, why don't you just fly? Why don't you hover like a great big fat Jackelian airship above the royal standard and give my tracks a rest from hauling your noble carcass the length and breadth of the continent?'

'I shall fly soon enough,' retorted Lord Starhome.

'Now!'

'Oh, you lowly ignoramus.' Lord Starhome's silvery mirror-like surface flashed crimson for a second as the artefact allowed fury to overcome his usual haughty attitude. 'You dirty ore-hauling miner, you think to question *me*?'

'Lord Starhome may not safely fly here,' said Hardarms, detailing the shortcomings that the powerful relic would never admit to a lowly miner. 'He moves by distortion of the weak-strong force of mass. The radioactive poisons generated by doing that within the gravity field of a celestial sphere would, I have been told, be immensely dangerous.'

'But you are expected to pilot him?' said Longtreads.

'After we are safely free of the gravity-well of our home, I shall do just that.'

'I assure you, you will not,' said Lord Starhome. 'I am quite capable of setting my own trajectory without your hands on my controls.'

'I rather think that is what worries King Steam,' said Hardarms. 'You know what cargo you carry inside you. The looking-glass device is almost as valuable as your own shell, and I shall not allow it to fall into the hands of the Army of Shadows intact.'

The long silver capsule seemed mollified by the knight's grudging flattery and ceased arguing with the steamman carrying him up the hill. 'Whoever sets my course, I shall be free of this tugsome ball of dirt soon enough. I was never meant to be captured by the tiresome pull of a world's mass.'

'My understanding is that the people of the metal dug you out of our tiresome dirt, rebuilt you and gave you one of our own soul-boards to reactivate you,' said Hardarms. 'Some gratitude for repairing you after your crash would be in order. You are at least part-steamman now.'

'Pah,' said Lord Starhome, 'my place is soaring free in the great darks. Once I was a ship-to-ship packet, a launch for creatures so mighty you cannot even begin to imagine their power. I have crossed between galaxies, borne on craft larger than your pathetic world, relativity sails billowing in front of a furnace of screaming matter that would make your sun seem like a glint of light on my hull.'

'Shoot him now,' begged the steamman transporting Lord Starhome.

'Ah, but he is our shell,' said Hardarms. 'Now we must take him to his cannon.'

'It's hard to believe a steamman soul lives in this quarrelsome piece of quicksilver.'

'Only to patch up the damage in his original fragmented intellect, broken by a too-hard landing,' said Hardarms. 'His escape from our home will be both his and our own salvation.'

Longtreads rotated his vision plate upwards to stare at their baleful new moon, a pale crimson shadow in the daylight, just visible between the fingers of cloud. 'By the beard of Zaka of the Cylinders, while he's about it, I wish he would burn that red abomination out of the sky.'

Hardarms' iron hand reached down to touch the satchel that bore the package from Mechancia's observatory. Papers and real-box images sealed with the wax emblem of King

Steam himself. To be passed to Coppertracks and his soft-body friends. 'You don't know the half of it,' he muttered.

As if the gods had answered Longtreads' request, the pale circle of the new moon began to disappear under the rolling scuds of an advancing storm front. Shadows began to lengthen across the moorland below, a creeping crimson twilight trailing across the vast assembled orders of the steammen knights.

'The Army of Shadows,' growled Longtreads.

'Stop where you are,' ordered Hardarms. He drew a magnifying assembly out of his satchel and clipped it over his vision plate. 'Now I can see why the survivors fleeing the fall of Catosia chose such a fitting name for the enemy.'

'But can you see their army?' asked Longtreads, his tractor treads stalled on the slope.

'There's something at the other end of the moors, but the smoke from our people's stacks is obscuring my view of it. Ah, that's better, the wind is clearing the smoke, it's—'

'What? What?'

'This is a joke, surely,' Hardarms' voicebox called back down the slope. 'There are just two creatures out there. Ugly, eyeless things like the offspring of a bony black slug that has mated with a mantis; and they are manning a cannon, or perhaps it is a mortar, so stubby is the mechanism. Is this all they have to field against our forces?'

'They insult us,' said Longtreads. 'A deliberate slight. May the Loas appear and curse their spawn down to the fiftieth generation.'

'Our gun boxes are walking forward through the army's ranks. Our bombardment will speak our answer well enough—' Hardarms was cut short as a wail of anguish sounded from Lord Starhome's silver shell.

'What?'

170

'I feel it,' called Lord Starhome. 'Oh my giddy sensors, I have not felt such a thing for a millennium.'

Longtreads' skull rotated to directly face his heavy load. 'I'm a simple miner, you length of noble rust, speak plainly now.'

'A neutron-level force,' replied Lord Starhome. 'Like the parsec-tossed light of the neutron stars that once glinted off my belly inside the Nebula of Dreams.'

'Is it dangerous?' asked Hardarms.

'It—' the shell-shaped ship stopped for a moment. 'Step into my shadow, steamman knight. NOW!'

Hardarms leapt back down the slope towards Longtreads and his cargo, a crackling dome of green energy forming instantly behind him and enclosing Hardarms, Longtreads and Lord Starhome under a suffocating blanket of raw power.

Hardarms tried to speak to Lord Starhome, but the half-steamman craft's hull was humming loudly like a tuning fork, his voice faint under the effort of casting a magic he had long forgotten; low as it was, Hardarms still heard the craft's ancient mantra. 'My shields can deflect particles at point one-C under lightspeed, my shields can deflect particles at point one-C under lightspeed.'

Then the mantra was drowned out by a terrible burst of light and an explosion, the green energy of their shield fizzing beneath the onslaught. The field umbrella covering them flickered and died and for a moment Hardarms thought that their protection had been vaporized, but the craft had only let it fall after the neutronic field front had punched past.

Hardarms mounted the crest of the rise again to take in the scene. Every tree on the moor had been uprooted, every bush and blade of grass flattened, and radiating out from a blackened core, the valley below was filled with the corpses of steammen. Nothing was left at the epicentre of the blast.

Hardarms could even see where some of his comrades' shadows had been left etched into the soil, while beyond this lay a felled forest of the people of the metal – bodies intact enough, but their soul boards, crystals and circuits scrubbed of every last iota of sentience by the neutron-level force front. Little more life left down there than in the metal ores that Longtreads trundled down from his mountain mine. A handful of bodies at the periphery jerked and shook as their secondary systems tried to come back online, limbs vainly twitching now they had been burnt clear of all intelligence, of all pattern. Near the flattened standard of King Steam a few warriors stood activate but deeply shocked, the energy shields of their own ancient artefacts from the Chamber of Swords falling away now that the enemy's vicious field front had passed.

Of the Army of Shadows' cannon and its two gunners there was no sign, but those that they had sacrificed themselves for were visible now – a distant black horde advancing under the cover of the unnatural clouds to mop up the few survivors that still stood, startled, shaking, before them.

Hardarms turned to stare down at Longtreads. 'How fast are you without your load?'

'How fast?' The cantankerous steamman miner was insulted by the very question. 'I can carry over a hundred tonnes of ore and not think it too much. Free me from my load and my treads can move with the speed of a gun-box shell, as if the shadow of the Dark Lord Two-Tar himself were chasing me.'

'I fear that something just as bad soon will be,' said Hardarms, climbing up onto one of the trailers and thumping on Lord Starhome's skin to open a door in his silver shell. 'Go back to the Free State and report what you have seen, miner. Tell King Steam to look to the defences of our capital. Only the rocky depths of the mountains can protect us against such weapons.'

'And where do you expect *me* to go, to lighten this dirt-hauler's trailers?' asked Lord Starhome. 'I cannot reach the void with my impellers. I have told you, gravity is too distortive down here.'

'Crane Lord Starhome off your trailer,' Hardarms ordered the miner. 'Then clear our vicinity at your top steam.'

Lord Starhome watched as his silver shell-like body was lifted away from the miner's tractor cradles and lowered down onto the grass. 'You are not thinking of what I—'

Hardarms pointed in the direction of the black horde pouring across the moors. 'Fire your engines anyway.'

'I cannot reach escape velocity.'

'I'm not asking you to. Flop across the land like a dying fish, bounce us like a frog escaping boiling water, but move us out of here!'

'Flop!' shouted Lord Starhome. 'I don't flop! If I open a warp inside a gravity-well this deep, you'll have an explosion that makes the neutron weapon we just saw detonating look like a wax candle being lit.'

Hardarms gazed in the direction of the low, fleeing form of Longtreads, the dust from his wake kicking up into the air behind him. Longtreads was every bit as fast as he had boasted. To ensure he was obeyed, Hardarms brandished the golden ring that King Steam had given him before he departed the Free State, etched with control circuits so fine even a steamman's vision plate had trouble resolving them. 'You are sworn to obey me. You have your orders and we will move.'

'Oh, we'll move all right. We'll move, the whole bloody land will move, and you'll die of gravity particle poisoning. My reactors are *inside* my shields. The only use I can put my shields to is to cushion our eventual crash landing. I can't save you if you board me. It'll be a slow, lingering, painful death for you. You might be better off staying here for an instant end at the hands of those things.'

'But they,' Hardarms pointed towards the darkening clouds of the Army of Shadows, 'will die also.'

'Oh, give me the stars again,' wailed Lord Starhome. 'Free me of the petty land disputes and foolery of ground huggers and give me instead the infinite sky.'

'And you can give me my engine ignition,' ordered Hardarms, swinging through the portal that Lord Starhome had created in his hull.

'A minute, to override every safety protocol my great creators wisely placed in my systems,' spat the craft.

A screen formed in Lord Starhome's nose, giving Hardarms a near-perfect view of the moors as seen from the front of the holy artefact. 'The Army of Shadows is closing in.'

'Sit in one of my pilot seats at the front,' urged Lord Starhome. 'You'll fry a margin slower inside the protection of my internal acceleration dampeners.'

Hardarms had to retract his two spear arms to fit, but he positioned himself onto one of the transparent chairs, his manipulator arms grasping the controls that extruded out from the hull. More to make him feel better about his predicament, he suspected, than to give him any real control. He looked nervously at the rapidly advancing clouds. 'Are you ready to fly?'

'Ha!' laughed Lord Starhome. 'Fly? We're going to scud across this dirt ball like a flaming angel of hell and my every impact is going to leave a burning crater a mile wide.'

'Is Longtreads outside your launch radius?'

'Don't you worry about that common little miner, his troubles are over.'

A roar sounded from the back of the long, sleek shell, louder and louder, until Lord Starhome had to scream over his protesting impellers to be heard. 'It was an eon ago, but the system jumper that gave birth to me gave me two pieces of very emphatic advice. The first was this: never, never, never *ever* attempt to warp gravity within the mass signature of a celestial body with an active magnetic core.'

Hardarms flipped the iron blast hood down over his vision plate. 'And the second . . . ?'

Lord Starhome's reply was lost to posterity in an explosion so ear-shatteringly loud that its echoes were heard back in the mountain passes of the Steammen Free State.

Jeanne pushed the commodore and Oliver out of the way of the great dark beast rearing up behind them, a shower of oily liquid spraying them from a whale-large mouth, giving the two men a hasty glance at multiple sets of rotating teeth. The apparently limbless creature, as tall as a two-storey house, crashed through the remaining trees and slid across the clearing. Oliver and the commodore picked themselves up, astonished, as Jeanne ducked into the woods behind them to see if there was anything else about to come ploughing through.

The monster was a giant elephantine slug undulating silently across the grassland, powerful enough to push down trees as if they were mere blades of grass. Dozens more of the creatures were busy consuming the landscape under the light of the new comet moon, burrowing into the hills of Quatérshift and occasionally emerging maggot-like from the slopes. Hot clouds of foul-smelling mist were rising from the giant slugs' bodies, trails of it spearing up into the dark sky. It made for a hellish sight. They were mining the earth, consuming everything they came across, loudly grinding up rock and ores with their circular maws. Wherever the beasts surged they left trails, not of slime, but lines of objects discarded in the grass, hexagonal plates and piping, machine-parts and boards, objects that

175

obviously had a utility other than fertilizer for these slopes after their feeding.

Jeanne re-emerged from the woods and shook her head at her father. 'Just the slugs, this time. No sign of any slats or slaves coming to pick up their shit.'

'I didn't sense it,' said Oliver. 'It was as if—'

'They lack even the wit of cattle,' said Keyspierre, 'but they are creatures of the Army of Shadows, nevertheless. If you stand in one's way it will attempt to consume you, but they are so insentient that you can walk up behind one and freely put a torch to it – then their greasy skin burns like lamp oil. Usually, we'd set fire to the whole filthy pack of them, but the slats are aware when we kill them and come calling to see who has been making mischief. The beasts are living mills, organic factories churning out the building blocks of the Army of Shadows' machines and cities. Teams at the Institute des Luminaires have been studying the creatures' excretions when we have managed to steal them, but we have so far divined little of the parts' purpose or secrets. We are like monkeys cracking open a fine watch and marvelling blindly at the cogs and gears as we shake them out onto the dirt.'

'It's not the parts that are squeezed from their arses that I'd be mortal worried about,' wheezed the commodore, pointing to the entrance of the old abandoned mine in the hills. 'If they're inside the hills making a feast of them, they might be inside the mine. It could be the parts to Timlar Preston's great beast of a cannon they're putting on their supper menu.'

Oliver seemed hypnotized by the sight. Any campaigning force lived off the land while it fought, but Quatérshift wasn't being looted, it was being infested, the landscape remade as a hell by the Army of Shadows. The words of the ancient warrior woman who had appeared like a ghost before him drifted back to mind. *Even together, the two of you are not enough to defeat that which you will face.* Molly should have been here with them, not back in Jackals; she could have put this in one of her books.

Jeanne motioned forward the shiftie troops holding the train of mules. 'Let's scoop the cannon parts up. Keep your eyes open for slats, compatriot Jackelians, and try not to get killed inside the mine. I won't be able to watch your backs so well when I'm digging.'

CHAPTER SEVEN

Molly stepped out of the mail coach, the only passenger to alight, and looked around. Halfshire was one of the kingdom's last ancient border counties before the uplands began in earnest and there wasn't much to its acres except for pine forests and isolated farms nestled in the shadows of crags like Mount Highhorn. She absently raised a hand to stroke the flank of one of the four midnight-black mares tethered to her coach; the horse she was touching was looking suspiciously down at the steamman trailing up the path towards them.

'I thought you might arrive via the canal,' Coppertracks called out.

'It's hard to get a berth on any narrowboat, now,' said Molly. 'Even carrying full parliamentary papers. With the merchant marine grounded, every mill owner and shopkeeper from Hundred Locks to Calgness is shipping their goods by the waterways. Prices have gone through the roof.'

'Are things that bad?' asked Coppertracks.

Molly nodded her head back to the mail coach's escort. A troop of Benzari Lancers, stocky mountain people from the hinterland south of the Kingdom of Jackals. Hardy little warriors who competed fiercely for the few vacant places in the Royal Benzari Regiment each year. Ferociously loyal to their regiment's oath and deadly with the curved blades hanging from their black breeches.

'That's who parliament are trusting to keep open the Great Middlesteel Road. There hasn't been a desertion from the Benzari Regiment since they were formed.'

'Have you heard any news of Oliver and the commodore?' asked Coppertracks.

'No, but things are turning to the worse in Quatérshift. The news sheets are full of how the shifties sent their Third and Seventh Brigade to the north and both forces just vanished without a trace. Sixty thousand men gone, the country's been split in two by the Army of Shadows.'

Coppertracks raised an iron hand towards the sprawl of makeshift barracks; manufactories and buildings that had been raised inside the forest clearings, hidden from the sight of whatever eyes the Army of Shadows might have high in the sky by green netting hung between the trees. 'We only have a handful of the experts on Preston's list, and without those parts buried in his mine we'll have to attempt to mill the cannon components ourselves. We can do that, but it's time we don't have—'

Molly waved her hands to quieten down the nervous steamman. If she knew Coppertracks, he had been working day and night without a rest. He was pushing himself to the point of exhaustion to complete the massive cannon. 'Let's trust the commodore knows the old smuggling routes out of Quatérshift as well as he boasted he did.' Molly glanced up at Mount Highhorn, its grassy slopes bare except for crimson fingers of light from their strange new red moon. 'I can't see supports for the cannon being installed?'

179

'This isn't one of your celestial fiction novels, Molly soft-body. The cannon will not tower up the side of that mountain. It's flat.'

'Flat?'

Coppertracks pointed to the heart of the forest below. It was hard to tell where the ancient forest began and the new canopy of camouflage netting ended. 'It resembles a seashell, a spiral winding around itself. There has never been a cannon like it before. Timlar Preston is one of your people's greatest minds. During the Two-Year War he was designing his wave-front cannon to be hidden inside a mountain, far from the reach of airship bombs. We, unfortunately, don't have the time to excavate the mountain here, so instead we're lying the spiral gun's barrelling down across the forest floor. Yes, the fellow is truly a genius.'

'I think Timlar had a little help,' said Molly.

Poor, dead Kyorin. He should have been alive to see his desperate scheme bear fruit. They began walking down the path to the forest camp, Molly's coach and escort turning back along the trail. Up above the slope's melting snow stood the honeyed stone of a squat round Martello fort, a rusting airship tower rising behind its walls. The fort was manned with redcoats now, but the airship dock hadn't seen any traffic for a long while. The fort had no doubt been abandoned long before the camp was established, a relic of the ancient Jackelian civil war reoccupied by rough circumstance.

The camp might be hiding from view, but as Molly walked closer to the trees she could hear the hammering of steel and the hiss of gas torches. 'Has Duncan got over his disappointment?'

'He works as hard as any other welder or smelter in the camp. He may not admit it to himself, but he's clearly more usefully deployed here than fighting with the regiments,' said

Coppertracks. 'He and Timlar Preston share their passion for rockets together; that is a small consolation. I think it is Purity we must worry about.'

'People here don't suspect . . . ?'

'No, the false citizen code we acquired for her is solid. And as a seamstress for the cannon's rubber lining she is as accomplished as any of the factory children that have been drafted in here. But Purity is changing. She is so possessed by the Loa that it is now impossible to see where she begins and that which rides her ends. The other softbodies here can sense the difference. They don't know what it is, but they feel it all the same.'

Molly sighed, looking up at the evil new moon of the comet in the sky, before entering the cool, shadowed cathedral of the forest. 'Everything's changing, old steamer. And not for the better. We just have to hold it all together long enough for this cannon to be completed.'

'I tossed the cogs last night,' said Coppertracks, 'to read the auguries of our project in the trail of Gear-gi-ju.'

'And what did you see revealed?'

'The single skein,' said Coppertracks. 'The non-duplicated circuit. This project is both our peoples' last hope of survival. Without its success the race of man and the people of the metal will be exterminated by this Army of Shadows.'

'No pressure on us, then,' said Molly. Damn Kyorin. The murdered slave was right and the final vision the Hexmachina had sent to Molly had been right – and she would so much rather they'd both been mistaken about everything.

'I fear for the timely completion of the project,' said Coppertracks. 'If Oliver and the commodore fail to bring back those components from Quatérshift; if my people fail to deliver what we need to see you safely to Kaliban . . . so many chances to fail, and there are other problems here, problems of our own making.'

Molly raised an eyebrow.

'The evening's project review meeting is about to begin. Come. See for yourself . . .'

Coppertracks led Molly under the canopy of trees, dappled shadows falling across an entire town that been raised in miniature here, hidden in the lee of Mount Highhorn. Raised on her word and that of the escaped slave still haunting her memories. Molly suddenly felt very small, a vessel for something so large that it overwhelmed her humanity. All that scale, pitted against a tiny voice of doubt that was wholly her own: what if I'm wrong? What if Kyorin was mistaken, or just a dupe of the Army of Shadows, released to sow confusion and distract the kingdom from the fight for life in the defence of its homeland? Just who – or what – were they building this peculiar cannon for?

The building Coppertracks led Molly to had been constructed so recently she could smell the freshly logged pine. When the steamman opened the door and she saw who was arguing around the table inside, she gasped with shock. 'What is *he* doing here?'

Coppertracks indicated a vacant chair and the empty space next to it for him to tractor up to the table. Opposite, a group of scientists sat with Lord Rooksby at their head. Rooksby looked angrily at Molly – her assistance to Coppertracks at the Royal Society presentation obviously not forgotten.

Coppertracks tuned his voicebox to a whisper. 'You know how parliament likes to work. Every opinion on a project as important as this one has to be balanced by an intellectual counterweight so all views can be considered.'

'We're not a bloody parliamentary committee,' hissed Molly, taking her seat. 'We have a job of work to do here.'

A tall man with long black sideburns nodded at her from the head of the table. The camp commander, by the look of the worry lines creasing his forehead. 'I see that we have our mission's progenitor with us now. I am Colonel Buller, of the First Corps of Engineers, the lucky soul the House of Guardians have charged with ensuring the success of this undertaking. I don't suppose you bring with you the parts we have been promised, damson?'

'I have a crate or two that might come in useful,' said Molly. And she did. There was hardly a theatrical supplier in Middlesteel that she hadn't visited in her efforts to craft the disguise she was planning to use on Kaliban. Blue skin dye and white robes to match the natives' clothing – identical to garments glimpsed in the dreams that assailed her now. Kyorin's dreams. 'But not the components for the cannon. They're in the process of being secured from our new allies out in Quatérshift,' said Molly.'

'But secured to what end, Damson Templar?' asked Lord Rooksby. 'This entire project is misconceived. It is clear the Army of Shadows hails from one of the unexplored continents of our opposite hemisphere. The very idea that they have travelled here from one of the neighbouring celestial spheres is an arrant nonsense. We should mount this long-range artillery piece we are constructing on a turntable so that we can direct its fire towards the occupied provinces of Catosia and Quatérshift. At least then we shall derive some utility from it beyond fanning the flames of your ridiculous new fashion in novels.'

'I assure you, my Lord Commercial, the Army of Shadows is far from fictional.' Molly looked down the length of the table. 'Where is Timlar Preston?'

'He seems to be of a rather nervous disposition,' said Colonel Buller. 'I have excused him his attendance at our meetings to benefit his health.'

The colonel and Molly exchanged glances. And the excusal,

no doubt, did wonders for the productivity of the real work they were doing here.

'I have been thinking,' piped up a small narrow-faced man. Where had Molly seen him before? Then it came to her. The literary talk her agent had organized for her to attend last year at one of the theatres in Douglas Lane – he had been one of the other writers in attendance, riding her coattails on the fad for celestial fiction. No wonder Rooksby was chafing. Along with the Royal Society, parliament had drafted in the other obvious advisors to the threat posed by the Army of Shadows . . . celestial fiction authors. 'We know that the Army of Shadows originates from the polar wastes. Perhaps they don't come from the outer darks, but the inner ones! They might have travelled up a tunnel from the centre of the Earth. There are many ancient legends that suggest there is the entrance to a cavern system at the pole that leads to the centre of our world. In which case it is not a cannon we should be constructing here, but a vast drilling machine. One capable of burrowing into the heart of the invader's empire of the inner core!'

Molly rolled her eyes in frustration, noting the wave of blue energy circling lazily around inside Coppertracks' crystal skull at a uniform rate. He was bored, but at least he was diverting his intelligence to his mu-bodies scattered around the camp and continuing some meaningful work through his drones. She, meanwhile, was trapped here in this debating society of idiots and loons.

Duncan watched Purity peer down the tree-shaded length of the canal. The Halfshire Navigation's passage through Highhorn Forest was one of the main reasons why parliament had chosen to site the camp so close to the isolated lumber mill they had built their facilities around.

'Will they be with the canal boats?' asked Purity.

Duncan Connor scratched his stubble. 'I've been told that both Oliver and the commodore are safe.'

Duncan didn't say that they wouldn't be receiving the long-awaited parts from Quatérshift now if their two friends hadn't made it back safely from the voyage. Large shire horses pulling flatbed carts were arriving to receive the cargo, Timlar Preston himself anxiously waiting with the project's engineers to see if all of his components had been recovered and transported back without damage.

'I can show Jared the new sabre strikes you've taught me. Do you think he'll be pleased?'

'Aye, that he will.' Duncan raised a smile.

Purity glanced over to the wagon Duncan had driven up to the edge of the canal, the familiar oblong of his battered travel case stowed under a pinewood seat. 'You're not planning to leave us to try taking the recruiting party's coin again?'

'I've spent too long here, now,' said Duncan. 'Helping build this bonnie-looking cannon for parliament. At the very least I want to see if it actually works.'

'It'll work,' said Purity. 'Kyorin wouldn't have asked Timlar to help us build it if it wasn't going to work.'

'Yes, there is that.'

'Soon I'll see Kyorin's home, probably meet the friends of his he told me about when we were on the run in Middlesteel. He said he'd left a wife up there.'

Duncan nodded. There was about as much chance that he, Molly, or any of them would allow Purity Drake inside the cannon as they were likely to load up the First Guardian himself and blast him off towards Kaliban.

A murmur of anticipation passed around the crowd at the canal docks as the first narrowboat rounded the corner into view, her small steam engine driving a single rear-mounted paddle as she pushed a spear of smoke up through the pine forest's canopy. The lead craft was followed by another long narrowboat, then another, a low foldable wooden roof in front of each cabin concealing the cargo that had been procured from Jackals' neighbour to the east. More and more narrowboats turned the curve and hove into view, a veritable armada, and in the lead boat waiting on the cabin step stood the familiar figures of Commodore Black and Oliver Brooks.

Pulling into the lumberyard's mooring channel the lead craft slowed to a drift and the commodore jumped onto the ground to tie up the narrowboat. Oliver stepped out behind him and headed over to Timlar Preston.

'We were getting worried you wouldn't turn up,' called Duncan to the commodore, leading his horse and cart backwards towards the channel.

'And you would have been a lot more worried if you had but known what we were facing out in Quatérshift,' said the commodore, his breath momentarily departing as Purity walloped into him. 'But I shouldn't speak of such things in front of you, Purity. Your nights' dreams are troubled enough without me adding to your imaginings.'

'I want to hear the truth as well,' said Purity. 'Those slats that killed Kyorin, there's more of them in Quatérshift?'

'A mortal terrible host of them,' said the commodore. 'Crawling all over the north. We were lucky we had that wicked lad Oliver Brooks riding with us, for it was only his dark senses that helped us navigate across the shiftie provinces without attracting the Army of Shadows' attention.'

Duncan patted his cart's flatbed. 'You found the components the shifties had buried?'

'Greased up inside crates at the bottom of Timlar's abandoned mine, just where he said they'd be. And that was as near as we came to failing in our task. There were still ores in that mine and the Army of Shadows has a terrible plague of monstrous black slugs the size of houses sliding over the conquered provinces of Quatérshift, eating anything and everything in their path and shitting out a trail of machinery in their wake for their slaves to collect. They were burrowing into the side of the hills where our mine stood like a Circlist vicar making merry with a teacake. If we had arrived a day later with our train of mules, I dare say we would have found the hills and the mine consumed, and Timlar's cannon parts a tasty dessert to round it out for them.'

'Living factories . . .' said Duncan in astonishment.

'Not so strange to someone who used to guard the southern frontier, I should say, eh, soldier? Some of the same black arts that devil of a caliph practises down in Cassarabia,' said the commodore. 'Although the cleverness of the caliph's womb mages only stretches to teasing living creatures out of his slaves' wombs. I dare say if he could teach his creations to eat rocks and sand, then shit out swords and pistols after the meal, he would be about it quick enough.'

The commodore watched Purity run over towards Oliver, now that the young man had finished explaining to Timlar what had been retrieved. Work crews moved in to draw back the narrowboats' wooden roofs and expose the cargo.

'How bad was it?' asked Duncan.

'As bad as it can be, lad.'

'How can it have come to this?' said Duncan. 'These creatures have travelled all the way from another celestial sphere, such an unimaginable distance, and for what?'

'For a supper long denied,' said the commodore. 'Aye, and we are to be their main course. Before I left, before I saw the ruins of the shifties' country, I was still in half a mind as to the truth of the matter of this Army of Shadows. I thought perhaps that Molly's imagination had laid her a little too open

187

to the ravings of a slave's broken mind, poor Kyorin escaped from the polar barbarians of the north or the satraps of Cassarabia. But you only have to see the fate of the poor shifties to know that the perpetrators of such crimes are free of any ties to this green and pleasant place we call home.'

Duncan watched one of the last narrowboats tie up at the lumberyard docks and a party of dishevelled-looking travellers climb out; more shifties by the looks of them. There was a man at their head, silver-haired, accompanied by a beautiful young woman. Timlar Preston seemed surprised to see the senatorial newcomer and the two were soon closeted away for a private conversation.

'The fruit of our u-boat's voyage, Paul-Loup Keyspierre – some grand nabob from the shifties' Institute des Luminaires,' said the commodore, seeing the direction of Duncan's gaze. 'And the girl is his daughter, Jeanne.'

'A political, then,' said Duncan.

'No doubt a good compatriot to survive as head of their hall of science without tripping and falling in the great terror,' said the commodore. 'And at least clever enough to see which way the wind was blowing in his homeland. Rats always swim out of a burning u-boat, a long stream of them kicking away from the torpedo bays.'

'If it comes to it,' said Duncan, 'and we need to get Purity away from the hubbub, what's the port out of Spumehead looking like?'

The commodore shook his head. 'There's not a steamer ticket to the Concorzian colonies to be had for neither love nor money. The west coast is as thick with shopkeepers on the run from the storm front as there are flies circling the turd pile fallen out of your fine mare's rear. If you still remember the way to Cassarabia from your regimental days, you might be better lighting off down south.'

188

'If the caliph has any welcome for me, it's in his torture gardens or on the slave block,' said Duncan.

'Is that the way of it, then, the usual fondness of foreigners for our redcoats? Well, if there's three arms of the compass denied to you now, there's still east. Quatérshift is as good as rolled up, but you could reach the Holy Kikkosico Empire on the other side of the slopes of the Mechancian Spine, take a caravan across the pampas. But—' he reached out to touch Duncan's sleeve, '—there's one blessed thing you must know. Running changes a man. After too many years of it, you wake up not knowing whether you're home, or just bunking down in an impostor of a place you're pretending will do for the same.'

'The Kingdom of Jackals is your home,' said Duncan.

'So it is, or should I say so it might have been, six hundred years ago, before Isambard Kirkhill's gang of shopkeepers seized the land.'

'You're not going to run, are you?'

'No,' grinned the commodore. 'I'm a sight too tired to run and a sight too old to remember a new alias. So let the slats come for old Blacky and prize my sharpened sabre out of my cold fingers if they dare.'

Duncan watched as the commodore lumbered over to the scientists he had rescued from Quatérshift, before turning to haul the crates out of the narrowboat, the long boxes still dark from the dust of the mine where they had been secreted.

<*It wasn't Purity you were worried about, was it?*> said the voice from inside Duncan's travel case as he dropped the first crate next to it on the back of his cart. <*You were thinking of running with me before we're attacked by the Army of Shadows.*>

'Was I?' Duncan went back for a second crate, balancing the load across his muscled shoulders.

<It won't make any difference. Not to me.>

'Don't talk like that,' spat Duncan. 'I'd run if I thought it would keep you safe. But it won't. Those ugly kelpies from the Army of Shadows will arrive wherever we flee to soon enough, and the stronger for having consumed all the nations between us and wherever we end up. We might as well make a fight of it, here, on our home soil.'

<Do you have a battery of rockets to kill them with?>

'No, I'm not in the Corps of Rocketeers any more,' said Duncan. 'You know that. But I might just have a bonnie cannon to do the job.'

As the cashiered soldier dropped his crate into the cart there was a massive explosion and for a second Duncan thought that one of the canal boats' cargoes had detonated – some explosive cache fused early – but the shower of leaves and loose pieces of timber was rattling off the forest canopy from above. Whatever had struck Highhorn Forest had fallen well wide of their canal path.

Duncan pushed the precious travel case under his cart in case they were being mortared, dipping his head out as Coppertracks came steaming past. 'I thought the first gunnery test was scheduled for next week, old steamer?'

'A message,' said Coppertracks. 'I received a message from one of my people seconds before the explosion. It said: "Coming in hard. Landing on my shields."'

'Hard!' Duncan blinked as a piece of blackened bark fleeted off his forehead. 'Even the dafties of Dennehy's Circus don't make landings any harder than that.'

'I believe the cannon's vital component promised to me by King Steam has arrived,' said Coppertracks. 'Though not in quite the manner that I had been led to expect.'

The steamman was the master of understatement. The task of unloading the components from the canalside forgotten,

190

the project workers began to run towards an unexpectedly felled section of forest.

At its centre, the smoking, silver form of a shell-like capsule lay embedded in the super-heated mud. An imperious steammen voice roared out at Duncan and the others, as they stood clustered around the broken trees and boiling mud, looking at the crash site in amazement.

'Precisely which part of me being stuck in this foul gloop do you witless ground huggers think I'm enjoying? I am sure some of you possess the sentience to clutch a shovel and begin digging me out.'

Coppertracks rolled forward. 'Lord Starhome, I presume.'

Skyman First Class Hanning polished the glass face of his heliograph as he waited for fresh signals from the lamps of the lead aerostat in the *Revenge*'s squadron. Mounted beneath the airship's chequerboard hull, lower than the gun ports, lower even than the fin-bomb bays, the h-station was a tiny domed nodule, manned by an adept in the code that allowed the Royal Aerostatical Navy fleets to move in synchronized flights.

It was a solitary calling, manning the h-lamps, but the job did have its consolations. Lamp men were always privy to the captain's orders from Admiralty House – at least when they were communicated in the field, rather than via the wax-sealed written orders handed to skippers before a stat pushed off. The quick wits needed for coding the messages – as well as their confidential nature – meant that h-operators were treated with the courtesies of a petty officer's rank, even when they hadn't passed the board exams for such: extra grog, PO's rations, and spared deck-scrubbing duties. And they got a better view of the scenery and the skies bar all but the wheelman on the bridge, or maybe the spotters in the crow's nest.

Right now, the skyman looked out on as respectable an assemblage of both soldiery and the fleet's sleek ships as anyone sitting on his wooden seat in the *RAN Revenge's* h-station had ever seen. Hanning let his eyes wander to the nearest of the *Revenge's* sister craft. There was the *RAN Diligence,* his first berth as a greenhorn, running proud next to the *RAN Flying Fox* – the *Canny Fox,* or *Old Canny* to her crew – said to be one of the luckiest hawks in the Fleet of the South; never brought down by squall, ground fire, or any of the foes she had ever been dispatched against by the Kingdom of Jackals. Just a couple of the hundreds of airships gathered here today, their shadows a reassuring sight for the earthworms of the New Pattern Army below. And the Circle knows, they were marching in numbers that hadn't been seen since the Battle of Clawfoot Moor, when parliament's forces had smashed the rump of the royalist army so many centuries earlier. There was the Heavy Brigade, their exomounts' green scales glittering in the sunlight; the Twelfth Glenness Foot and the Sixth Sheergate Rangers, redcoat columns two abreast in full marching order; the iron land trains of the Royal Corps of Rocketeers, steam from their black stacks obscuring the racks of Congreve rockets primed and ready for battery fire; the green uniforms of the Middlesteel Rifles, walking in ragged skirmish order at the head of the infantry columns. The tactics of the New Pattern Army hadn't altered substantially since they had been perfected by First Guardian Isambard Kirkhill centuries earlier, but then why improve on perfection? Besides, the earthworms in the regiments always relied on fighting in close coordination with the Royal Aerostatical Navy, and the Jackelians' monopoly on airship gas had served their nation well when it came to defence.

Occasionally, one of the clockwork-driven horseless carriages mounted with an oversized version of Hanning's h-lamp would flicker into life below, requesting an update from the flagship or reporting the findings of the army's mounted scouts. If the musings of the command staff from House Guards were found to be mildly pertinent they would be circulated lazily among the high fleet's airships a while later. They did worry and fuss so, the braided and medal-breasted generals of the army – but then, they weren't drifting hundreds of feet out of range of the effective fire of the foreign brigades which the kingdom's armed forces were called to suppress. Where the high fleet sailed safely and omnipotently above the fog of war – often adding to it by dropping fire-fins and gas shells onto the battlefield – the poor benighted scrapings of the regiments had to face every hail of shrapnel, hot shell and ball that the enemy tossed at them.

No wonder jack cloudies were hailed as the heroes of the nation and welcomed into every jinn house and drinking establishment with offers of a song and a round freely stood, while the earthworms had to be press-ganged into the regiments, or recruited from the ranks of those facing transportation to the colonies to an alternative service under the sharp tongues – and sharper floggings – of the army's sergeants.

Hanning's musings about the good luck of his employment were interrupted by a clatter of bony feet coming down the ladder to his little glass bubble of solitude. It was Ti'ive, the young craynarbian midshipman bearing a note scribbled in the captain's hand for him to translate into lamp flicker.

'Another one for the *Thunderbolt*, if you please, Mister Hanning.'

Hanning checked to make sure he still had line of sight to one of their flagship's h-stations (as a flagship, the *Thunderbolt* had the unusual honour of possessing four h stations – fore, aft, port and starboard), then the skyman flicked into action the flint igniter on the side of his lamp's gas assembly. Hanning

193

looked at the note he had been handed by the officer and harrumphed. The skipper was asking permission for the *Revenge* to break east to make contact with the missing steammen army. The steamers were a day late for the planned rendezvous, and it seemed the skipper considered it unlikely that the Free State's usually punctual army would allow themselves to fall so behind schedule.

'I doubt if we'll cut any orders independent of the fleet, sir,' opined the lamp operator. 'None of our hawks have been taken since we've started sailing convoy fashion.'

'The captain's worked with King Steam's fellows before, and he's a sight more concerned by their non-appearance at the border than our flag officers seem to be at the moment,' said the young middie.

'And has he said anything on the bridge about the six missing brigades of Quatérshift's finest that were meant to be waiting on their side of the border to join up with our earthworms?'

'Jon Shiftie?' Ti'ive said, fiddling with his starched officer's uniform. 'Only that they're not fit for much beyond the fine art of retreat anyway, and that it might be better all round if the shifties took to their boot leather now, rather than folding a flank under fire and leaving good Jackelians exposed to the Army of Shadows when things start getting thick down below.'

Hanning started to blink the message out to the *Thunderbolt*. 'I saw Jon Shiftie fight in the Two-Year War, and I'd sooner have a few regiments of their bluecoats to add to our number than not. Even if their backbone does owe a debt to political officers with pistols ready to cut down anyone who tries to run, I reckon their boys held their lines well enough under our hawks' shells last time around.'

Skyman First Class Hanning was trying to talk over his

nerves. Everyone on board the *Revenge* had been nervous since they had crossed the border into Quatérshift. It wasn't just the sight of the dead Cursewall that had once been raised to separate the two nations, now drained of the very power of the land that once fed it. Not just the missing brigades the shiftie attachés had promised and failed to deliver to the House Guards staff. Not even the uneasy alliance with their most ancient of foes. It was the fact that they were sailing into a war of aggression for the first time, breaching a covenant that was timeless for the people of Jackals. Jackelians kept to their borders and, as stalwart as they were in their nation's defence, they had no taste for empire. The very idea of crossing into another nation and taking the fight to an enemy they hadn't even caught sight of yet felt unseemly. And it was a wrongness that had seeped through the airships and unsettled every jack cloudie serving in the four fleets.

Hanning was still clacking out the message to the flagship when Ti'ive's sharp eyes spotted the *Thunderbolt* making a more basic communication, the craynarbian crying out at the sight of the all-ships command – a bright red pennant running up the flagship's spine ropes, flapping in the wind. *Enemy sighted.*

The flagship's h-stations flashed new orders for all to see, not bothering to single out any one ship of the line, and all the other airships picked up the message for general relay until the fleet fast became a sea of winking stars. *Form line. Engage.*

Hanning dashed out the orders on his pad, ripped off the top sheet and passed it up to Ti'ive. He might not have been sitting in the crow's nest up top, but the skyman could see the ruby-red storm front rolling in from the north. One minute it was sweeping in above the distant hills and the next minute they were swimming in it, thick, red, as if the blood of everyone in Quatérshift below had been turned into steam and blown over the high fleet.

'Have you ever seen such a thing?' asked Ti'ive.

Hanning was trying to think what to say when a lance of light and fire jetted past the *Revenge*'s aft, so hot that he could feel the glass of the h-station's dome burn with it, a sudden wave of thermals buffeting their airship and briefly clearing away the crimson fog. And beyond the *Revenge*, the *Flying Fox*, the lucky *Fox* – was revealed cut in two down her middle – the whole mid-section of the stat's hull vaporized in a cloud of superheated celgas. As broken now as her luck. Both the surviving sections of the airship tumbled away, spilling burning sailors and ballonets into the mantle of tumbling debris: the melted keel catwalk, exploding engine housings, celgas netting and flailing bracing wires, all steaming white hot from the enemy's strange heat ray.

Both sailors were struck dumb, but a voice sounded from the corridor above the tunnel that led down into the h-dome. 'They're above. They're above us!'

'What is it?' Hanning shouted up. 'Has the crow's nest sighted something? All I can see down here is—'

Seven or eight streams of energy similar to the last one jetted past, rocking the *Revenge* like a pigeon tossed by a tornado. Hanning fell off the operator's bench, Ti'ive sprawling about somewhere above him – his hard craynarbian shell cracking into the dome's glass.

Having lifted himself back up, dazed and bruised, Hanning blinked away the images torched on his retina to see a garden of bright red flowers – blooms of fire and smoke and blazing jack cloudies. 'Sweet Circle. How can they do this to us?'

Ti'ive tried to steady himself, as the airship and its h-dome

196

rocked from side to side like a fairground ride. 'What's the matter with our damn airships today?'

Something caught Hanning's attention on the ground and he pulled his gaze away from the field of mushrooming destruction in the sky to look down upon the smashed ranks of the New Pattern Army in full ignoble retreat: the redcoats of the Light Infantry; the green uniforms of the Rifles; the cherry-trousered Hussars on their steeds, all retreating. Adding to the terror below was a rain of airship girders and the boiling ballast water falling from the *Flying Fox*. A few regiments of the infantry were trying to pull back in a disciplined line, but they were collapsing ragged against the sea of black – an undulating dark mass of the beast-soldiers of the Army of Shadows. Jackelian artillery units were attempting to set up their guns under the cover of the House Guards, each large cavalryman protected by an armoured gutta-percha cuirass, riding high and heavy on their exomounts; but the riders were encircled by a scattering of slats that had already broken through the collapsing squares of the West Pentshire Regiment. There were a few puffs from the heavy rifles carried by the House Guards before they were knocked off their mounts by streams of springing black creatures and torn apart.

The last glimpse of the ground Hanning had was the desperate uncoupling of artillery pieces from the trains of horses by their gunners before they too were swarmed over, then the unnatural cloud enveloped the *Revenge* and Hanning's dome was sealed once more inside a sea of dense crimson mist.

Hanning and Ti'ive looked at each other in shock. So used to flying above the carnage. So used to drifting high above the fog of war, dispassionate angels of destruction, directing the New Pattern Army and smashing any force foolish enough to break the Jackelians' peace. Now the two sailors suddenly found themselves as much subject to the vagaries of war as any confused redcoat, stumbling through the thick clouds of rifle and cannon smoke that settled over every battlefield.

Ti'ive yelled in shock as the eyeless face pushed itself up again the outside of the dome, tapping a curious, clawed finger against the glass.

'It's got a sail-rider's rig on its back,' shouted Hanning, not so panicked he didn't forget to draw his pistol from where it lay tucked into his belt.

Homing in on the sound of the two sailors, the beast drew its talons teasingly across the glass, leaving scratch marks on the crystal surface, then it threw itself back and disappeared into the crimson mist.

'It was whispering,' said Ti'ive.

'What?'

The craynarbian looked at his comrade. 'Didn't you hear it, Mister Hanning? It was whispering something in a language I didn't recognize and it was clicking, clicking like a blood bat. By jingo, they see by the sound of their throats – no wonder they prefer to fight inside this deadly red pea-souper of theirs. They must hunt by the screams and whimpers of their victims.'

Hanning shook his head – no, he hadn't heard the monster's whispers. The craynarbians were long diverged from the race of man through millennia of jungle survival, the hairs on the back of their skulls giving them a sixth sense lacking in their soft-skinned cousins. But Hanning heard the yells and shots from somewhere on the other side of the *Revenge* clearly enough, the distant echo of pistol fire reverberating through their wooden corridors. Hanning pulled a crystal charge out of his belt and broke open his bell-barrelled gun, pushing the shell into the breech.

He had solved the mystery of what had happened to the missing airships of the merchant marine. But after today – bar a few clerks of supply manning the inkwells of Admiralty House – there wasn't going to be anyone left in the Royal Aerostatical Navy to warn.

CHAPTER EIGHT

C oppertracks exited the long, low building of the camp's infirmary and indicated the door he had left open for Molly, Oliver and Purity to enter. 'The poisoning my patient is suffering has declined to residual levels. There is no danger of infection now if you talk to him.'

Hardarms had been dragged out of the smoking silver shell he had crashed in, and while the steamman warrior had accomplished his main charge – bringing Lord Starhome safely to the cannon project in Halfshire – the price of his success was the gradual failure of his proud metal body. For most of the time he had been unconscious – only Coppertracks' efforts had kept him alive even this long.

'And the steamman knight asked for me by name?' said Purity.

'He did,' admitted Coppertracks.

'But how did he—?'

'King Steam will have told him,' said Oliver. 'And that canny old steamer is so close to the Steamo Loas, he might as well be a spirit himself.'

'I thought King Steam was young,' said Purity. 'Barely out of his childhood.'

Oliver shrugged. 'The body, perhaps. His mind is the latest incarnation of a monarch older than the mountain behind us.'

'Soul,' corrected Coppertracks. 'King Steam's mind is unique to his latest body; it is his soul that is passed down through the generations.'

They entered the infirmary and were guided by Coppertracks to the room where Hardarms had been isolated. There was a smell of rubber in the room; wet, rotting and foul. One of Coppertracks' drones lay deactivate in the corner – sacrificed by Coppertracks to care for the dying pilot. The dead mu-body was speckled with flaking brown where the rust of the radiation sickness had eaten away at its shiny shell. Hardarms was – if it were possible – in an even worse state, his entire body a quilt of raw brown-and-red metal, the hardened armour of the steamman knight eroded by the final advances of the gravity warp poisoning.

A faint light pulsed behind the knight's vision plate as he noticed the three newcomers ushered in by Coppertracks. 'The male softbody I recognize from my sharing of cables with King Steam. Oliver Brooks of the race of man, halfling child of an Observer. The older female must be Molly Templar, which makes the younger . . . Purity Drake.'

'You know me, then?' said Purity.

'My sovereign knows well the part of you that is awakening with the land,' said Hardarms. 'As he knows your two companions here, from our last time of troubles.'

'Well, this latest time of troubles we're suffering seems to be going from bad to worse,' said Oliver. 'Has Coppertracks told you of our news sheets' reports of the rout of the RAN and the New Pattern Army inside Quatérshift?'

Perhaps it was a side effect of his radiation poisoning, but Hardarms seemed hardly disturbed by Oliver's information. 'Of course, Oliver softbody. When I saw the destruction of

201

the steammen army it was obvious that no force of the race of man could match our adversary. Not if every nation in the world poured its resources into a single regiment and marched against the Army of Shadows as one.'

'Did the king speak of me?' said Molly. 'Did he speak of the fate of the Hexmachina?'

'The god-machine is a cousin of the people of the metal,' said Hardarms. 'King Steam knows the Hexmachina has been locked in stasis, sealed away in the deep bowels of the world by our foe.'

'And he's not worried by that?' Molly had to restrain herself from shouting. 'I threw the Wildcaotyl back beyond the walls of the world with the Hexmachina's power. You can't count on me to save you all this time . . .'

'You are a knight without a steed,' said Hardarms. 'A duellist without a sabre. His majesty asked me to tell you he understands how frustrating that must be for you.' Hardarms stretched out and took Molly's hand, pressing something into her palm out of sight of the others. Molly looked down. It was a gold ring, etched with lines so thin she could barely see the complex patterns that had been engraved on it.

'For Lord Starhome,' whispered Hardarms as Molly bent down to catch the whisper from the knight's voicebox. 'You will know how to use it when the time comes.'

'Your sympathy is all very well,' said Molly, hiding the ring away in her pocket, 'but your army has been exterminated too, and Jackals now lies defended only by militia with pitchforks, fencibles who fire two training shots a year and a couple of RAN cadets in training ships.'

'And I wish that were not so,' said Hardarms. 'Just as I wish that a tool for slaying gods had proved more effective against a mortal foe. But wishing will not make it so. Wishing will not bring either of our nations victory in this fight.'

Hardarms leant over to retrieve his satchel from a table next to his bed, removing a sheaf of papers. 'And I also wish I had better news to bring to you than this...'

Molly took the papers being proffered. She winced as she felt the steamman's pain swelling up inside him. How could he bear it? Every sensor along the length of his body was flaring in agony. Molly forced her gaze down onto the papers and saw images of a large sphere that seemed to be made of rust-coloured iron, accompanied by commentary pencilled in by the hands of the king's councillors.

'The images are from the new observatory in Mechancia,' said Hardarms. 'Real-box pictures enlarged from our largest telescope.'

Coppertracks trundled over to handle the pictures, scanning them with his vision plate in fascination. 'I have never seen the like of this before.'

'Oh, but you have,' said Hardarms. 'Every time you glance up at the sky and curse our baleful new moon swinging in orbit around the Earth.'

'This—' Coppertracks looked again at the images '—this cannot be Ashby's Comet? Where is its ice, the rubble, the—'

Hardarms extended a weak manipulator arm towards the ceiling. 'Burnt off, fallen away. And that which remains beneath is what we once mistakenly thought was a comet. As you can see, our foul new satellite is an iron moon.'

'Then, dear fellow, Ashby's Comet was never a natural phenomenon?'

'And its path around Kaliban and back to Earth no random accident of celestial mechanics,' said Hardarms, his voicebox losing volume as he spoke. 'King Steam's scholars have re-visited all our theories of astronomy and can come to no conclusion save that this iron moon is some monstrously sized tool of the Army of Shadows.'

'But the Army of Shadows appeared well before the iron moon was captured by our world,' said Molly. 'I saw the enemy in my vision from Kyorin. The slats were crossing the celestial darks in shells that ride beams of light all the way across to our home.'

'I have no answers for the iron moon's presence or intent,' said Hardarms. 'But I don't need to see its corroded red alloy to know that fell, evil moon was created above Kaliban by our enemy. See here the last image taken at the observatory before we left for the Kingdom of Jackals and mark it well.'

Coppertracks held up the final image, a snapshot of a long silver thread extruding from underneath the iron moon down towards the bottom of the picture. 'Like the thread from a spider.'

'And growing longer each day,' said Hardarms. 'Extending down towards our world's surface! King Steam's scholars believe the enemy means to use the cable to anchor the iron moon to our world, somewhere towards the Army of Shadows' stronghold in the polar wastes. The iron moon is slowing, now. Soon, the moon will orbit no longer, but will be joined to us in a stationary position.'

'Anchored to what end?' asked Purity.

'None that is good,' said Hardarms.

'A lifting room!' exclaimed Molly. 'I cleaned enough vents in the capital's pneumatic towers to know what you can use a cable like that for. You run supplies and material up and down its length.'

'A lifting room that can travel high into the heavens and beyond,' said Purity in disbelief. 'Now there's a thing for one of your novels, Molly.'

'Such a colossal undertaking,' said Coppertracks, allowing a tone of wonder to sound from his voicebox. 'The minds that are capable of such a feat of engineering. . . we must appear as savages to them.'

'They may have arts that are not yet known to us, brother slipthinker,' said Hardarms, 'but it is *they* that are the savages. I have seen these slats. Bestial things with no sense of living within the harmony of the great pattern. They have no code, they have no honour. They are naught but a dark flame that will burn all of creation to stay afire.' The knight extended a trembling manipulator hand out to Coppertracks and the steamman bent close to hear the warrior's whispered words.

'How can we fight them?' said Molly, the desperation of their pathetic little cannon put into perspective against the incredible might of such an enemy. 'How can we fight creatures that can construct moons out of iron and craft bridges between the celestial spheres themselves?'

'With what makes us alive,' said Hardarms. 'With passion and imagination and the compassion we feel for our fellow living creatures in the great pattern. With what makes us different from them; and with *her*.' The dying steamman warrior pointed at Purity. 'That was the message King Steam asked me to relay to you three softbodies. That you will save us, Purity Drake, and that you, Oliver softbody, are the key.'

'But I'm a nobody,' said Purity. 'I've a price on my head. I could barely survive an attack by a couple of slats.'

'You *are* Jackals!' Hardarms' vision plate briefly flared with his old light. The steamman seemed to shrink back in his bed. 'Pray – the Loas grant that be – enough.' At last he fell silent, that great steamman warrior, Hardarms, captain of the Pathfinder Fist; the visor above his darkening vision plate slid down to seal his skull in the final reflex of a creature of the metal.

Purity looked at Coppertracks. 'What did he whisper to you?'

'He gave me his true name for his funeral rites,' said Coppertracks. He looked at Molly. Had his keen vision seen her receive the ring from Hardarms? 'And he said that we should not trust Lord Starhome. He is only partially a steamman and his systems will revert to feral ways with each week he spends outside the Chamber of Swords beyond the civilizing influence of the people of the metal.'

'You have to let me come with you now,' demanded Purity. 'You heard what King Steam told us. If there's a way of beating the Army of Shadows on Kaliban, I can help us find it.'

'We'll see,' said Molly, trying not to sound dispirited. Oliver was the key, Purity was their last hope. And Molly? She was a riderless knight who merited only King Steam's sympathy now. 'We have to get our damn cannon working first.'

Before Lord Starhome went wild. Before the Army of Shadows came across the country's borders and found them defended only by private fencibles old enough to be Molly's grandparents.

Before the *end*.

Duncan Connor took the heavy riveting gun from Commodore Black, the submariner looking perfectly at home among the other burly navvies and hulking engineers putting the finishing touches to Timlar Preston's cannon. The strange gargantuan snail-shell, cast from iron, wound its way around the forest floor amid the flash of welding torches and the hammer of machines. There was no rifling inside the iron tubes welded together to form the cannon's massive spiral. Instead, its barrel had been lined with rubber panelling to form a vacuum, steam engines drawing out all air from inside.

Timlar Preston's plan was for Lord Starhome to be loaded onto an ammunition cradle above the heart of the spiral and then slid down into a breech to be injected inside the airless cannon. Once inside, the steamman craft would be fired out with a great detonation – the cannon's power augmented by an additional series of blasts from firing rings, chasing the craft all the way around the spiral. Pressure from the blast would build up in the barrelling behind Lord Starhome at an exponentially increasing rate, riding the vacuum in ever wider slingshot circles around the cannon, until, finally, the shell would pierce the membrane at the muzzle of the barrel with a velocity so fearsome that Lord Starhome would be flung free of the pull of the Earth – into the dark void in which the steammen swore their strange artefact could fly. All the way to Kaliban and the homeland of the Army of Shadows.

It was a mad, daring dream. Yet Duncan had faith in Timlar Preston's plans. Decades before, during the Two-Year War, Preston had hit upon the same innovation that was to cost Duncan his position in the Corps of Rocketeers. No more explosions through the crude mixing of explosive fuel, but a *controlled* detonation, spraying the highly corrosive and combustible blow-barrel sap into a mixing chamber using hardened glass nozzles. Where Duncan had envisaged a new generation of long-range rockets being developed by the state armoury of the kingdom, Preston had refined the notion of a wave-front cannon, a simple iron tube that could accelerate a shell so fast it could escape the very grasp of the world itself. Preston had originally dreamed of using his creation to send a party to the moon, with explorers wearing diving costumes and brass tanks of air inside water-filled shells to survive the detonation of the cannon. But the Two-Year War had put an end to Preston's peaceful ambitions as surely as Duncan's radical ideas of warfare had derailed the career of the once lauded Connor of Cassarabia.

Duncan Connor pushed the head of the heavy riveting gun against the iron face of the barrel and squeezed the trigger, the coiled pipe back to the pressure drum jumping off the dirt like a snake that had been stepped on.

Commodore Black inspected the cleanly sunk rivet with satisfaction, pulling a fresh bolt from the sack slung over his shoulder. 'As neatly done as any navvy back in the submarine pens of Spumehead could manage.'

Duncan held onto a strut and looked down the scaffold. To the right, one of the engineers from Quatérshift had stopped fiddling with the components of an injector ring as Paul-Loup Keyspierre talked at him.

'There's something not quite right about yon one,' said Duncan.

'His foreign accent, is it?'

'No, it's the way people react to him, all the staff who arrived at the project from Quatérshift. Just look at that scientist, Jared. How still and pale he is. I've seen simple farm laddies and lasses being given their first lumps by a drill sergeant with less fear than that on their faces.'

'Ah well, he's the skipper of their boat, right enough. Back across the border Keyspierre would have the power to strip a man of his position and send work-dodgers off to organized communities. That's the power to starve you and your family, or imprison you in a living death – until you'd come to welcome the real article when it moved you along the Circle.'

'It's more than that,' said Duncan. 'It's a different sort of fear. And then there's his daughter. She stalks about like a panther.'

'She's sleek lines, that Jeanne, I'll give you that,' said the commodore. 'But the terrors of the revolution have been raising ladies mortal resilient across the border, that's all there is to the girl's manner. Compatriot Keyspierre and his daughter are decent enough salts at heart. Jeanne was quick enough to save me back in Quatérshift, when one of the Army of

208

Shadows' giant slugs was about to transform the iron in my blood into another wicked brick for their city.'

Duncan said nothing, but he seemed to cling onto his doubts.

Having finished with the scientist working on the firing ring, Keyspierre walked down along the curve of the cannon to stop underneath the scaffold where Duncan and the commodore were working.

'Commodore Black, I see that your contribution to the effort here stretches beyond your rather curious specialist knowledge of the channels off my nation's coastline.'

Duncan noticed the man's voice was deep and smooth, his Jackelian accent very nearly flawless.

'Just doing my bit, Compatriot Keyspierre,' said the commodore. 'A bit of Jackelian elbow grease to help chivvy this mortal fine piece of engineering along to completion.'

'Grease being applied to a scheme generated by the inspired minds of the glorious revolution,' said Keyspierre.

'But cast,' Duncan called down, 'from Jackelian iron. Aye, much the same as the barrel on a redcoat's Brown Jane. Your people are not strangers to our rifles, I believe.'

'So it once was,' snorted Keyspierre, the nostrils of his large nose flaring. 'I can see how well our cannon is polishing up. A pity we did not have a few of these formidable devices completed during the Two-Year War. Who knows which way the winds of fate would have blown if we had been able to shell the House of Guardians when they were debating the continuance of their war against us.'

'An interesting question, for sure,' said the commodore.

Keyspierre nodded, before starting to walk away. 'Quite. But we speak of the past, when it is the future both our countries needs to look to now. Please do pass my compliments on to the noble workers helping complete this most ingenious feat of gunnery.'

'They must have a different set of history books across the border,' bridled Duncan as the man left their earshot. 'I was sure it was the laddies in Quatérshift who invaded us during the Two-Year War.'

'As I recall, most of their books were fed into the fires on the boilers of the shifties' steam-driven execution machines during the purges.' Commodore Black looked at the figure of the departing institute official. 'Ah, well. All friends together now, eh?'

Radford and Sykes lengthened the run of the nets alongside their shallow-draught fishing keel. It was usually such easy work this far from the estuary, where their competition was few and far between. The Gambleflowers splintered into a dozen channels around the marshland of Monymusk before reforming into a single course that snaked all the way out to the coast. The marsh was usually thick with insects and the river crabs, and the fish and birds that fed on them. But something was scaring the fish off today, with the result that the pair's nets had been empty each time they hauled them back on board.

Sykes cast an eye at the lonely fish still flopping about the catching crate on their foredeck. 'It'd be nice to have some friends for Mister Trout here. Some companions, so that we'll have something more to show for the day's labours than an ear-wigging from Damson Sykes when I get back home.'

'Never seen anything like it,' said Radford, pulling his leather hat down tight against the chill marsh air. 'Empty, today.' He nodded to the east where the river cut through Middlesteel. 'You expect bad waters down by Old Reeky; but then when the capital's mills have got a stink on, the fish all head up to us. Look at the bugs flitting over the water. Got to be something wants to bite on them today.'

The lines holding their net seemed to judder at his complaints and both men began to haul the net in. 'That's more like it.'

Sykes winced. 'Is we stuck? This is heavy, Circle it is.'

The pair of fishermen heaved at the lines until the pulley began to run again and the net lifted up. They swung the catch over and down onto their foredeck.

It landed with a heavy slap and Sykes advanced on it, scaling knife in hand. 'What's this, then?'

Radford sucked his breath in as the wash of water dragged blackened cloth away from the sodden mass under the net and revealed the pale white stretch of a human hand against their boat's boards. 'It's a floater!'

Sykes bent down to loosen the net from around the body. 'Poor unlucky bugger. Ain't seen one of these for years, not since I worked the six-penny boat in Old Reeky.'

Radford watched his friend uncover the corpse. 'Must have come down with the morning tide from the sea. Wonder if this is the fellow that's been putting off our fish?'

Sykes tapped the flat of his knife thoughtfully against his bushy beard. 'Now then, I think we knows him. Last week. Don't you remember? He came down to the docks, wanting to know if there were any inns with spare rooms left in Sheergate. One of the carriage folk wanting to travel on to Spumehead for passage out to the colonies.'

'I think you may be right,' said Radford. 'He was a flush jack with his pocket book. Bit too full of himself for my taste.'

'Have to be a dreadful severe sinking right off the coast for him to roll in this far with the tide, mind.'

'Could be so,' said Radford. 'Steamers have been running full to Concorzia for weeks, putting out dangerously low on their waterlines from what I been told.'

Radford was bending over to help Sykes clear the corpse entangled in their net when their little boat jolted to port, a pitter-patter rain of thuds pushing their hull back into the marshy reeds of the bank. Trying to keep their balance, both men dropped the tangled netting and swayed to the other side of the boat.

Down the river, thousands of bodies drifted face down with the tidal waters, as if a forest of humanity had been felled and loggers were moving the harvest downstream. Blackened, burnt clothing; men, women, children, all dead. Sykes reached down into the water and pulled out a sodden blue sailor's cap floating by to inspect its name badge. The Jackelian Navy Ship *Excellent*, one of the huge ironclads that had been guarding the harbour entrance at Spumehead. It appeared there would be no sudden influx of new colonists arriving in Concorzia after all.

Both men were so intent on watching the horrific migration of death following the tide towards the capital, that they failed to notice that the swelling mist rising behind their backs was tinged with veins of crimson, an ominous reflection of the blood-filled waters of the Gambleflowers. In fact, it took Radford and Sykes minutes to hear the hollow bony clicking deadened by the fog. And by the time they saw the hulking black silhouettes of a legion of slats cutting through the cover, it was too late for either of them.

Two new burnt, torn-up bodies joined the black tide and bloody waters heading down towards Middlesteel.

Molly could see that the camp commander, Colonel Buller, was getting irritated – possibly due to the pressure he was under to deliver a successful test firing this afternoon – especially considering almost everyone involved in the project was thronging around the spiral-shaped cannon as if a festival day had been declared – whether their schedules of work said they should be labouring right now, and whether they were invited or not.

Everyone was desperate to see whether the great contraption – this bastard fusion of Jackelian engineering and Timlar Preston's Quatérshiftian genius – was going to live up to their hopes or blow apart in an explosion that might put a volcano to shame.

The colonel leant over the wall of the firing station, a platform built on stilts like a tree house with a panoramic view of the organized chaos below. 'Sergeant, clear those work-shy layabouts away from the firing rings – filling the reservoirs is dangerous enough work as it is, without being jostled by malingerers.'

Soldiers from the Jackelian Corps of Engineers pushed back the navvies that were getting in the way of the careful work of filling the glass-lined fuel reservoirs. Molly approved of the commander's caution. When it came to dealing with the volatile explosive liquids needed to drive their engine of gunnery, human error would be enough to scupper the whole project.

'He's in a snappy mood, today,' said Purity.

'I'm afraid we won't get too many chances to do this,' said Molly. 'Timlar Preston has calculated that the force of any more than four firings will wreck the cannon's barrel beyond use. Two test firings to calibrate, one live, and one left in reserve: that's all the chances we'll have.'

Molly should have resented Purity, but try as she might, she couldn't. The young escaped royalist had been filled with the power of the land, just as Molly's own connection with the power she had taken for granted had been snapped. She had been as young and eager as Purity, once. But this was the way of all things. Youth faded. Cynicism deepened. When Molly looked in her mirror to brush out her red coils of hair she saw lines on her forehead that she found hard to recognize sometimes.

'Well, manners don't cost anything,' said Purity.

213

Yes, she saw more than a little of who she had once been in the young Purity Drake. 'I hope you've been busy building up a stock of rubber lining for the cannon, young damson. Because after today's test firing it'll all need to be re-laid for the next attempt.'

Purity wrinkled her nose in disgust. 'I go to sleep in my bunk and all I can smell is blessed rubberized sheeting.'

Molly smiled. 'You've been spending too much time with the commodore.'

A uniformed engineer came into the firing station and saluted Colonel Buller. 'We have the blank shells on the loading turntable, sir. I've finished testing them, and I can report they match Lord Starhome's dimensions and weight exactly: we are now ready to fill the first shell with sand to approximate the flight crew.'

'Fill it with sand equal to ten people's weight, captain,' said the colonel, pointing to a turntable mounted above the spiral-shaped cannon where Lord Starhome and a series of blank shells rested in metal cradles.

'Ten!' Molly started. 'I wasn't planning to take passengers—'

'Apart from me,' interrupted Purity.

Colonel Buller looked surprised then vexed. 'I thought Lord Rooksby had told you . . .'

'Told me what?' Molly demanded.

'You are not to be allowed into the craft on the day of the launch. The party to Kaliban is to be headed by Rooksby. Parliament felt that you were too close to this project and your motives may have been tainted by your association with one of the foe's natives.'

'Tainted! Molly shouted. 'This is *my* cannon, and the native you're so concerned about gave his life to make sure it was constructed.'

'That is as may be, damson, but the guardians on the

214

committee overseeing this project are firmly of the opinion that the expedition to Kaliban will have far more chance of success if it is appropriately composed of a selection of scientists, ambassadors and soldiers. I think upon reflection you will agree that professionals are better suited to survive the hardships of the journey, as well as scouting the weaknesses of the enemy while finding and negotiating with potential allies. Certainly better suited than writers of penny dreadfuls and—' he indicated Purity, '—shoeless seamstress friends of the author.'

Molly's face was turning crimson with anger. 'This is *outrageous*.'

'No, Damson Templar, it is *expediency*. If the tales from our army's survivors are to be given credence, we are currently facing complete military disaster. Your vision contributed to the marshalling of resources necessary to complete the cannon, and parliament now judges your contribution honourably discharged. We cannot possibly stake our nation's survival on the fate of a single celestial fiction author.'

'Parliament now judges,' spat Molly. 'I know who's been pouring poison in the right ears. Oh yes, Lord Rooksby has changed his tune since the RAN was defeated, that dirty snake of a scheming jigger. When I arrived here, he was swearing blind that the Army of Shadows had marched over the polar ice from the other side of the world, not come from Kaliban. He said this cannon was a joke and now he wants to bloody *command* it?'

'This is madness,' protested Purity. 'You can't do this to us. Molly was touched by Kyorin, she knows things that are vital to—'

'Young lady, half my comrades have been touched – touched by the Army of Shadows and lying dead in the killing fields across the border in Quatérshift. I rather think that the House of Guardians is very well-decided in this matter.'

'We shall see!' Molly stalked off. 'We shall see how well they've bloody decided.'

Molly ran down the ramp from the firing station, ignoring the sound of Purity still attempting to argue the colonel around, brushing past a gaggle of scientists coming up the ramp. Oliver was in the crowds below, pushing through the spectators from the forest's mills and manufactories and smelting works. He could see how angry she looked.

'What is it?'

'You're the Circle-damned key, why don't you ask your friend Purity up there.'

'Molly – what?'

But she was through the crowd of navvies and heading towards the turntable where Lord Starhome and the test shells waited, the half-steamman craft's bright hull in stark contrast to the grey iron of the testing shells modelled on his pattern. The turntable was designed so that each shell could be rotated to face the injection-run down to the breech of the spiral-shaped weapon. An operator in the cab of a crane was exchanging shouts with the muzzle loaders as Molly shoved past the soldiers, climbing up the ladder to the turntable.

Lord Starhome was still in the breech-facing position, while a gang of engineers focused their attention on one of the blank shells next to him, preparing to drop heavy sandbags inside a hatch in the shell's side. Weight enough to match the gang of pirates who had stolen the voyage to Kaliban away from under her nose.

There was a door-sized hole in Lord Starhome's hull, the living metal flowing around the edges while Commodore Black passed equipment through to Duncan Connor. 'Have you come to help us, lass?'

Molly climbed across the turntable, ducking under the nose of one of the reserve shells. 'Help you . . . ?'

'Coppertracks is inside, he is going to use the keen eyes of his shiny celestial boat to track how high we shall shoot today.'

'I am not *his* boat,' said Lord Starhome, tetchily. 'I have agreed to cooperate in this endeavour out of my steadily stretched good graces, that and the increasingly slim hope that this primitive explosive slingshot you have constructed will be able to restore me to my natural environment.'

'Let's not keep you waiting any longer, then, my lord,' snapped Molly, slipping the control ring Hardarms had given her over her finger and pressing it against Lord Starhome's cold, slippery hull. 'Recognize operator function.'

'If I must,' sighed Lord Starhome.

'Lass,' said Commodore Black as Molly swung through the opening. 'What are you about?'

Molly glanced back outside the ship for a second, alerted by shouting. Redcoats were moving through the crowds below, burly-looking provosts; she knew exactly who they were coming to arrest.

'I'm going to save the kingdom, Jared. Every thick-witted guardian in parliament, every useless civil servant working in Greenhall, and every treacherous thinker in the Royal Society.' Molly turned to Duncan Connor and Coppertracks. 'Get off.'

'Molly softbody, my monitoring apparatus has been fitted into Lord Starhome, I cannot simply—'

But Molly manoeuvred around the supplies stacked in the back of the ship, slipping into the cockpit at the front. 'Seal the bridge off.'

At her command the walls of the ship flowed like quicksilver, separating her from Coppertracks, Commodore Black and Duncan Connor.

'Please lass,' the commodore's voice sounded from behind the wall. 'You're not ready to cast off now . . .'

'They've left me with no choice. They're planning to snatch the expedition from under me and give it to that blackheart Rooksby.'

'Let him have it then,' cried the commodore. 'Let it be his wicked bones that are left strewn across the angry sands of blessed Kaliban.'

'If we don't stop the Army of Shadows, it'll be the Kingdom of Jackals that ends up as a desert. Get off, now, all of you.'

'Please . . .'

'Can you load yourself into the cannon?' Molly asked Lord Starhome.

'I'm held by the turntable's clamps,' said Lord Starhome. 'But I have a magnificent communications array that includes a light transmission mechanism that would serve to burn them off.'

'Do it!'

'An official order to launch? Your whim is my command.'

Molly could hear banging on the other side of the wall and Coppertracks' voice pleading to no avail with the half-steamman craft, when a hiss of melting metal sounded from outside.

'I'm the only one that understands,' said Molly. 'Kyorin showed me, not them. I have to do this.'

'I really don't care,' announced Lord Starhome in a detached manner. 'If it means I am free again, oh by the light of my creators, yes. To be free of this place and able to chart my own course again. Nearly there. I've melted the port clamp away, time for my starboard chains to go.'

'Jump out,' Molly yelled back towards the wall. 'Unless you're planning to come to Kaliban with me, you all need to abandon ship now.'

'You foolish woman,' a muffled voice shouted back at her, in an arrogant tone that she recognized from far too many tedious meetings at the camp. Lord Rooksby.

'We are days from being ready for anything but a practice firing,' called another voice in a Quatérshiftian accent – Keyspierre. They were arguing loudly with Molly's friends in the back of the craft. She could hear the shifties' daughter shouting for cutting tools to be brought on board.

'You're the fool, Rooksby, to think you could steal this cannon from right under my nose with parliament's blessing.'

'You may be inside there, compatriot,' called Keyspierre through the wall, 'but the cannon firing mechanism is outside on the cannon and controlled by us. You can stay loaded in the breech until thirst and hunger bring you to your senses.'

'Show me what is happening outside,' Molly ordered. 'Is he right?'

Lord Starhome turned the front of his nose transparent, revealing dozens of engineers and soldiers abandoning their posts, even a couple of Coppertracks' mu-bodies, all of them running towards the turntable. 'Correct enough in the literal sense of his words. Are you ordering me to assist you in firing the cannon?'

'You know the answer to that, ship.'

'I shall take your answer in the affirmative, little ground hugger, and allow you to correct me if I have grasped the wrong end of the stick.'

There was a keening protest on the other side of the bulkhead from Coppertracks' voicebox. It sounded as though the steamman had fainted.

'He's not the only one who can spread his consciousness among drones,' said Lord Starhome, pleased with himself. 'Quite acceptable. And the drones are not even mine.'

Outside, the mu-bodies the ship had possessed were running

for the fuse station at the centre of the iron spiral. On the other side of Molly's impromptu bulkhead the banging had grown ferocious.

'Last chance to get off,' yelled Molly, 'or—'

She stopped as the sky above the camouflage netting grew dark, rolling scuds of an unnatural crimson storm front advancing at an accelerated pace.

The Army of Shadows had arrived at Mount Highhorn.

Purity sensed the wrongness in the sky even before the soldiers' shouts sounded the alarm; an instinct gifted to her by that ancient queen from Jackals' past. She was outside the firing station and heading for Lord Starhome when she looked up; a cloud of darting sail riders riding the ruby storm front in, hundreds of black triangles beginning to peel off and fill the air above – slats whistling over the tree line. Her hand fled to her belt, but she was weaponless. All the sabres and guns she had practised with were in a chest under the commodore's cot. She made to run back towards the barracks, but the sudden jostle of soldiers and navvies – either running to their stations or running out of harm's way – pushed her back.

Then, suddenly, Oliver was by her side, moving effortlessly through the crowd.

'The Army of Shadows is here,' shouted Purity.

'Yes,' said Oliver. 'There's one of their flying citadels behind the red clouds, riding the leylines and coming around Highhorn Mountain. When they get above us they're going to burn the entire camp to the ground and our cannon with it.'

'How did they know we're here?'

Oliver pulled her to one side as a great beam of heat struck out from one of the sail riders' weapons, shredding the camouflage netting above them. 'Perhaps they followed Lord

220

Starhome's trail of destruction across the county. Maybe they've just reached Halfshire anyway.'

'If they're here, then they must have already fought their way through Middlesteel.'

Purity made to run for the barracks again, but Oliver stopped her and pointed to the forest's edge. 'Yes, and that's why we must head into the wilds. No towns. No roads.'

'I haven't even got a pistol.'

'I've got two,' said Oliver.

With the burning netting falling around the clearing the first slats were starting to swoop down, sail rigs passing through the crackle of rifle fire from the soldiers. Purity watched transfixed as Lord Starhome's long silver length slid down into the breech of the cannon and the firing hatch at the centre of the spiral sealed shut behind the craft.

'Molly,' shouted Purity. 'She's inside the cannon.'

'She has to launch before the slats' flying castle reaches us.'

'I need to get on board,' begged Purity. 'They need me on Kaliban, you have to help me get on board that ship.'

Pushing out of the crimson clouds, the outline of the Army of Shadows' ugly citadel emerged above them. It was riding the leylines on a dozen blasts of energy, scouring the land below, swarms of eyeless soldiers arrowing out on sail-rider rigs from cavernous maws cut into its rock-like sides. The fortress had a terrible organic quality to it, like a wasps' nest carved out of granite and metallic ore. There was no refinement to the Army of Shadows' art. Just raw energy and matter stripped out of the land and turned against any living thing dwelling below. Dozens of leathery black globes hovered around the citadel in the air, held aloft on whining circles of blades that rotated so fast they were a blur to the eye and a buzz upon the ears. Evil red light glowed from hundreds of weapon loops dotting the citadel, while in its shadow, the

221

slopes of Mount Highhorn had turned dark from a plague of Kaliban's advancing legions. The slats made a horrendous cricketing noise as they drew nearer, the chattering sonar throats combined with the clicking of a thousand fangs rubbing together at the thought of fresh flesh to feed on.

From behind the cannon a solitary figure ran into Purity's view, the gun's creator, Timlar Preston, waving his hands wildly to attract the attention of the slats circling above. 'I recognize you. I recognize you as creatures of learning. There must be no more bloodshed between us. There must be peace!'

Peace. What was the fool doing?

'You are a sentient race,' yelled Timlar. 'We can work together, there is no need for this.'

His calls towards the sky finally invoked a response: a bolt of heat enveloped him before dissipating in a blast of steam to reveal a blackened carcass collapsing to the ground. In the end, the Quatérshiftian genius had achieved peace only for himself.

Purity tried to pull away from Oliver's grip and make towards the cannon. 'They're getting ready to go, I *have* to travel to Kaliban.'

'Molly's already inside the gun,' said Oliver. 'It'll be a miracle if she launches before the cannon's destroyed. They don't have time to take on board extra passengers.'

'I can sense the commodore inside the cannon, Coppertracks and Duncan too. They didn't even know Kyorin. He came to *me*, he rescued *me*.'

'Maybe he did,' said Oliver. 'But the land came to you too, and she came first. You're part of Jackals and the kingdom is going to need you to resist the invaders.'

'It needs me here to run away again? That's what you want us to do, isn't it.'

<*You can fight,*> said the voice inside her head. <*You will lead and others will follow.*>

222

'I'm just a girl.'

<So was I, when the invaders came from the sea, but our land is ancient enough to protect both of us.>

Gloom deepened about them in the shadow cast by the crude flying citadel of the invaders. Mount Highhorn was now hidden by billows of crimson clouds boiling out from the ground underneath the unholy war machine. Oliver and Purity began running in earnest now, towards the fringes of the camp where it met a sweep of dense pine. At last it became clear why the sail riders hadn't landed in force on the cannon. With an enormous roar, a pillar of flame left the citadel and ploughed through the forest like an earthquake, drawing down onto the cannon.

Purity stumbled as the blast of heat from the terrible beam hit her. Behind her, fire burst one of the cannon supports and the metal spiral started to collapse to one side as an ear-splitting explosion from the ground answered the flying citadel's heat weapon. The first eruption was followed by an incredibly quick sequence of follow-on cracks, and it felt to Purity as if the teeth were shaking in her head as each firing ring added its voice to the immaculately timed crescendo. Then the citadel's heat ray sliced across the huge metal sculpture below igniting the unexpended fuel in the cannon's reservoirs and the entire cannon lifted off the ground. Pieces of the wave-front weapon blew across the clearing, wedges of shrapnel embedding themselves in the tree trunk Purity and Oliver had taken shelter behind. As if enraged by the successful firing of the cannon, the Army of Shadows' flying citadel began to rotate, its killing beam of energy twisting across the rest of the project, the hidden timber buildings that had been their home riding into the air in splinters and a firestorm of burning trees.

Purity couldn't sense the life force of Commodore Black,

Molly or the others. Was that because they were dead? Or – she risked a glance from behind the shrapnel-shot tree. There was a thin trail of vapour climbing out from the clearing as if the sky had been scratched up towards the heavens. Had Lord Starhome been intact as he was blown out of the muzzle of the cannon?

'I think they were given the gun before the cannon was hit,' said Oliver. 'But I'm not sure. It was a damn close thing.'

'Molly,' said Purity, tasting the acrid smoke in the air. 'Commodore Black, Coppertracks. Oh, Circle, please let them be alive.'

They had gone, left her behind, just like her mother and brother had slipped away from her to die, leaving her to go on alone.

The storm of beasts circling on their sail-rider chutes was gliding lower, ready to mop up any survivors of their flying citadel's bombardment.

'Let's go.'

'Where?' asked Purity. She followed Oliver deeper into the forest; not running, but fast enough so they might put the camp quickly behind them and keep up a steady pace for hours.

'Right now, anywhere but here.'

<*You know where you must go,*> said the voice in Purity's mind, accompanied by images of the trident-carrying queen. <*The call is strong within you now.*>

Oliver nodded. 'Curse your eyes, but I do.'

'You can hear Elizica speaking inside my head?'

'That's funny, I thought she was inside mine,' said Oliver.

The light grew fainter all about them – somewhere above the canopy of pine, the sun was setting unseen. Setting on the destroyed cannon project, setting on the Kingdom of Jackals.

'The slats like to hunt in the dark,' said Purity.

'They may see at night,' said Oliver, drawing his two strange pistols. 'But they've never fought the night.'

Something in his voice struck a chill sliver of fear into Purity's heart. Those two guns of his seemed to glow like death in the gloom, yet this young man who could overhear her madness appeared possessed by one far deeper than her own. He wasn't the master of the brace of evil pistols anymore, they were the masters of him.

'Where does Elizica want you to go?'

'To die,' said Oliver. 'She wants me to go to die.'

CHAPTER NINE

Purity stumbled through the trees, her legs numb from walking, her discomfort anaesthetized by the complete aching tiredness she was swimming through. Oliver was a constant by her side. It was almost like having her brother back alive with her: the shared madness – the voice inside their heads – a kinship nearly as thick as blood. And they could both sense the presence of the Army of Shadows, the slats' leathery black globe-like craft suspended under buzzing blades whisking through the cloudy starless night, dropping off scouts to hunt down the survivors from the Highhorn camp.

The two of them might have already cleared the forest if it wasn't for the necessity of continually doubling back on their tracks. Blind though the slave soldiers of the Army of Shadows were, they were possessed of a keen enough sense of smell to keep their hunting packs hard on Purity and Oliver's trail. Purity doubted if they had any inkling of what she and Oliver really were – but the foe had obviously been stung by the existence of the hidden cannon, a level of engineering far beyond what they had expected from their prey in the kingdom.

Survivors might possess knowledge of that engineering, knowledge that the slats didn't want reaching any of the other nations of the continent before they, too, were conquered in turn.

Oliver hadn't said any more about where they were going, the dire fate he had mentioned; but right now, Purity hardly cared – she would settle for half an hour of sleep and the guarantee she wouldn't be ripped to shreds by the talons of one of their pursuers before she awoke.

'Are we going to die?' she asked Oliver.

'If we do, we'll have a lot of company. The entire land's dying. They're making a corpse of Jackals.' Oliver took Purity's arm and pushed the sleeve up, allowing the drizzle to touch her skin. Her arm itched as the rain fell upon the white flesh. 'That flying citadel has infected the rain here. This is just the start. We must go on.'

'I'm tired.' Purity tried to shut out the sight of the red haze of moonlight smudging the rain clouds above the canopy of pine. Corruption in the heavens, corruption in the rain. Just the two of them to stand against it all, two kestrels, flying against the full fury of a storm. What difference could the two of them make?

'Why me?' Purity yelled her rage up at the iron moon. 'Why did this have to happen? What have I ever done to deserve this?'

'It had to be someone,' said Oliver, quietly. The look of resignation on his face shocked Purity to silence. What did she look like to him? She almost felt ashamed.

'I'm sorry.'

'Don't be,' said Oliver. 'I was given these two pistols by a Circlist reverend. He had been the Hood-o'the-marsh before me. He and I were connected, just like the Circlists believe all of us to be connected. Connected by the guns, or the land,

227

or by our humanity. That's why we're going on. Because we have to. Because if we don't, nothing else will.'

She followed him. Purity and Oliver left the forest behind and trekked across the heath.

Hours became days.

It was strange, Purity mused, it was like the end of the world – as if the kingdom had been emptied. They hadn't met any other survivors from the camp since they had thrown off their pursuers.

Highhorn had been an isolated stretch of the country even before the war, and when they came across villages and roads they found them abandoned. Once the two of them had seen a valley filled with a dozen house-sized slugs, slowly devouring the trees of a pear orchard, a trail of hexagonal plating excreted in their wake. The slugs emitted a diffuse crimson steam that rose in vapours, trailing languidly towards the sky. No wonder the days had become an intermittent twilight, a crimson-toned gloom as the enemy's creatures set about their work – converting the land into useful resources. Even the enemy's soldiers seemed to have vacated the countryside. There was the occasional wasp-like humming in the distance to mark the passage of one of their leathery flying globes, but no more sightings of their flying citadels, no more pursuit by the eyeless monstrosities that marched under the enemy's banner.

Oliver and Purity might have been the only ones left alive in this strange, empty landscape.

Purity came to a stop. 'I wish we could find some food, a cottage, anything.'

Oliver pointed to the north. 'The nearest small town is that way, about a day's walk. But it's empty, the Army of Shadows must have reached it.'

'How can you tell?'

'Because if it was otherwise there would be people there,'

said Oliver. 'And I would feel their evil. We'll stop and rest a while. I can make a poacher's fire. If I build it right it won't give off much smoke.'

An hour after Purity and Oliver left, a scout for the Army of Shadows was bent over the remains of their fire, its eyeless black head pushed up against the stones, sniffing at the ashes through a cluster of breathing folds. Its fangs clicked together in anticipation. Not old at all. And from the scents heading off, there were a couple of fine meals waiting for its pack.

Not for the first time, Molly wished that the ugly mood inside Lord Starhome would prove as mutable as the hull of their half-steamman craft. Once the crushing ferocity of the launch had been replaced by the strange waterless floating of their voyage, the shell-shaped ship had started to metamorphose, his living metal flowing into a new shape that was half-manta-ray, half bat. Lord Starhome was rapidly growing larger around his passengers. Sucking up the dust and grit of the celestial darks and incorporating it into his fabric. When they reached Kaliban, the expedition might be travelling in a craft a hundred times as large as the shell shape Lord Starhome had assumed to survive his ancient impact with the mountains of Mechancia – if the members of the expedition managed not to kill each other before they arrived.

Molly was coming to regret having opened her cockpit to the others she had inadvertently kidnapped for the voyage.

'I, sir, am invested with the authority of the House of Guardians,' insisted Lord Rooksby. 'I have full command of this expedition by order of parliament.'

'You carry no authority over any compatriot of the sovereign people of the Commonshare of Quatérshift,' retorted Keyspierre.

His daughter Jeanne nodded vehemently by his side. 'The launch of this vessel was made possible only by the sweat and genius of the Institute des Luminaires and the ruling committees of our people.'

Commodore Black pointed towards the back of the craft where Coppertracks had vanished into the storage hold with Duncan Connor. 'You might as well decide on Coppertracks as the skipper of our expedition, for this craft belongs to King Steam and we're on steammen soil by the nautical laws, while your parliament of shopkeepers and congress of the mortal committees of Quatérshift falls further away with each hour we travel.'

'A ridiculous suggestion,' said Rooksby.

Lord Starhome's disembodied voice sounded around them. 'Am I merely a chattel, then?' He showed his displeasure by allowing the field of artificial gravity he had recently created for them to fluctuate, the expedition members briefly subjected to a twinge of nauseous flotation.

'That's enough,' said Molly to Lord Starhome, who was showing worrying tendencies towards independence. As the craft grew larger, the percentage that was steamman – that owed any loyalty to the Free State – was being diluted. Molly fingered the control ring Hardarms had given her. How much longer until they were left riding a wild, masterless stallion through the endless night?

'We do not need to be lectured by you, Jackelian,' said Keyspierre's daughter, pointing an accusing finger at Molly. 'If it was not for your reckless interference we would be on a properly equipped and outfitted vessel of exploration, with trained soldiers to protect us instead of your gang of misfits and sightseers.'

'This is *my* expedition,' snapped Molly. 'I received foreknowledge of the invasion by the Army of Shadows. My gang of misfits got Timlar Preston back alive and saw my cannon completed, and without us amateurs, you—' she waved at the two shifties '—would be meat for those monsters' larder in your corrupt little compatriots' paradise, while you—' she pointed at Lord Rooksby '—would be on a clipper on the other side of the world blundering about looking for the Army of Shadows' non-existent homeland.'

'Aye, Molly has the size of it,' said the commodore. 'And more to the point, if it wasn't for her small blessed act of piracy back in the kingdom, the Highhorn cannon would have had a test shell loaded when the Army of Shadows came calling to destroy it, and we would all be sitting around its ashes toasting our bread in its fires, if we had the mortal life left to do so.'

'You, sir, are a fool,' shouted Rooksby at the commodore, stalking away to one of the other cabins. 'You are all fools. Lesser minds that don't possess the wit to realize the consequences of what you have done.'

'Your rebellious act of petulance may well have cost both our nations their future,' said Keyspierre, withdrawing with his daughter down one of the corridors that Lord Starhome had formed in his starboard wing. The shiftie's voice echoed back as he walked away. 'I fear the imagination of a novelist will serve very little purpose against the strength of the foe's might when we reach their home.'

Molly slumped back in one of the craft's acceleration chairs. 'Have I done the right thing?'

'You were true to yourself,' said the commodore. 'And it's the knowledge inside your head from that poor unlucky fellow Kyorin that we must look to, to guide us to the blue lad's friends.'

Molly bit her lip. If they still lived. If they could find them. If Kyorin's people had a way of beating the Army of Shadows.

If they could even understand the weapon and discover some way of using it against the enemy. Molly tried not to despair. It sounded so desperate when she thought about it, but the dead slave's words had proven true so far. He had given Timlar Preston the knowledge the great inventor needed to finish the design of his wave-front cannon. Kyorin's pessimistic predictions about the Army of Shadows had proven true at every vicious turn of the kingdom's futile attempts at defending itself.

'You didn't even want me to go on this voyage,' said Molly. 'And now I've lumbered you and the others with the expedition too.'

Commodore Black looked at the image of their home receding on one of Lord Starhome's screens, a small blue sphere against a field of velvet night. Blue save for the northern pole, where a red infection seemed to be spreading out, smoky coils of crimson clouds obscuring the cancer eating away at their world. And above it all the ugly red coin of the iron moon. 'Ah, poor Purity. I should have stayed to protect her. Coppertracks was right, and I am an old fool for not having settled matters honestly.'

Molly was puzzled. 'What did Coppertracks say?'

'It doesn't matter now,' said the commodore. 'My mortal wicked stars have given me the fate that I deserve, and that's to be cast off on this perilous journey, into the heart of the enemy's dark territory. As if facing their monstrous slat soldiers on the good soil of my home wasn't burden enough. Now I must be thrust deep into a nest thick with their kind, where the Army of Shadows' writ has run as law for an age. Even my bones will know no rest when they are lying bleached on their red deserts, so far from the Kingdom of Jackals and all that I hold dear. But I'll accept the fate of a fool, if only the fickle lady of chance goes kind on our friends back home.'

'We'll save them, Jared,' said Molly, 'we'll save them all. Oliver will look after Purity until we get back, and we'll find a way of smashing the Army of Shadows. Kyorin said the answer lies on his home and that is where we must go.'

'So it seems,' said the commodore. 'I shall stay here then and watch our home as it gets smaller, dwindles to a glint of light in the sky, and put my trust in a strange blue man fleeing the storm that now rages in Jackals. And put my faith in you, lass, who once saw us survive the undercity and the dark legions of Tzlayloc and his demon revolutionaries.'

Molly left the commodore to his brooding. She was just a woman now, without the might of the Hexmachina to call upon. Lord Rooksby was right. A mere author of celestial fiction. How in the name of the Circle was she going to bring them back alive from this one? She felt as if she was spitting against a tornado. Picking her way down one of the ship's new corridors, Molly went aft to find where Coppertracks had disappeared to with Duncan Connor. The canny steamman was up to something, but her instincts told her she would be better off not drawing attention to that fact in front of Lord Rooksby and the two shifties.

Lord Starhome's voice followed her as she walked down the craft's passage. 'How you softbodies achieve anything is beyond me. So fractious. Always arguing.'

'We'll work it out between us,' said Molly.

'While you are about your painfully slow cognitive processes, do you have any idea where you wish to be deposited on Kaliban?'

'The face,' said Molly. There was nowhere else. 'Take us to the carving of a face. There will be a city nearby – the last city on Kaliban.'

'Oh, my sensors can resolve plenty of cities on the surface,' said Lord Starhome. 'Mausoleums, mainly, they have the appearance of having been dead and empty for centuries. You organics certainly don't know how to clean up your mess after you, do you?'

'But there is a city near the face, with living people? Kyorin's race and their masters.'

'Yes, yes,' said the half-steamman craft. 'Locating it is quite easy. I just have to follow the glow of dirty isotopes and the filthy concentration of pollutants.'

'Take us there,' said Molly. 'That's where this fight will be settled.'

'Fight?' The sneer was audible in Lord Starhome's voice. 'Like two drunkards brawling over a half-empty bottle of jinn. You should stay on board me, little ground hugger. I could show you such sights: rainbows glistening off the water particles of the Wormwood Nebula, the seventy sun system of Leo A, all the wonders of the cosmos.'

Molly twisted the control ring on her finger. At times, the tracery of circuits on its golden surface burned fit to scald her skin. It was taking more and more of the ring's failing power just to keep the ship in check. 'Stay on course for Kaliban.'

'Of course,' muttered the craft. 'Of course. So futile. The races of your home will be murdering each other long after you and I have died, and that's an immensely long and full life for me. It's just a good thing you people breed like bacteria in a bog down there. Always more bodies to throw into the fray if you wait a generation or two.'

'Kaliban,' ordered Molly. 'Just take us there.'

She could hear Duncan Connor talking to Coppertracks up ahead, and rounding the corridor, she found the two of them in among the boxes of supplies that had been half-packed when Molly had stolen the craft. Along with something else stowed at the aft of the hold. It appeared to be a looking-glass, circular and as tall as she was, but there was something strange about its surface – a quicksilver movement, flexing like water, distorting what it mirrored. And the circular looking-glass was mounted on top of a sphere held up by six iron legs that might have been borrowed from a metal spider. Coppertracks was fiddling with the sphere, adjusting something, but the whole thing looked wrong, out of place. The senses that once allowed Molly to pilot the Hexmachina, the weirdness in her blood, called out to her that here was something that should not exist in their world.

'What are you doing with that? It's a machine, isn't it? So dense, so many parts packed in at such a small level. . .'

'The others aren't behind you, lassie?' asked Duncan.

'They're off sulking,' said Molly. 'Or in Rooksby's case, probably busy detailing written charges against me seeing as he's parliament's chosen head of our little excursion.'

'That insidious mammal,' said Coppertracks. 'A life in politics would at least have spared the Royal Society his divisive presence, even if it would have done little to advance the principles of Kirkhillian democracy.' The steamman closed the panel on the sphere, passing a small set of tools to the single mu-body that had been on board at launch. 'Your affinity for matters mechanical serves you well, Molly softbody. What you see here is our second gift from King Steam, almost as precious to my people as Lord Starhome himself.'

'It's like this, isn't it?' said Molly, indicating the hull of the void-faring craft. 'It's not truly of the people of the metal.'

Coppertracks' crystal skull dome flared in concurrence. 'One of the advantages of cycling his soul through the great pattern on the path towards eternity is that King Steam has picked up many a strange curio down the ages. Do your symbiote senses tell you what this is?'

Molly held her hand out in front of the circular looking-glass. 'It – it is a door. But how can that be, and where does it lead?'

'Imagine you held the very stuff of existence and sliced it in two,' said Coppertracks. 'Two halves of a membrane that stays connected no matter how far apart you then separate the two parts.'

Molly reached out and touched the surface of the looking-glass. It felt cold, wet, like water and oil mixed. But when she pushed on the surface, nothing happened, it was a solid. 'A doorway. Then this machine has a twin, two looking-glasses connected.'

'Its twin resides in the deep halls of Mechancia,' said Coppertracks. 'Within King Steam's palace. The sphere sitting beneath the mirror contains a grain of contra-matter that can open the doorway, though not for more than a minute – so great is the tension between the two membranes. The energy needed to equalize each brane-field quickly destabilizes the mirror and destroys it beyond use. We may travel through it only once.'

'This is how King Steam intended for us to get home,' said Molly.

'Rooksby and those two shifties mustn't ken about this until we're ready to tell them,' said Duncan. 'They would want to use the doorway immediately, go back to King Steam's land for a properly resourced expedition. I don't trust any of those three dafties not to abandon the voyage and leave the rest of us to hang.'

'Not that they could, now,' said Coppertracks. 'I have just finished encrypting the ignition mechanism of the sphere. Only Duncan softbody and myself can activate the looking-glass gate.'

Molly pointed to herself. 'And me, I need to know the key.'

'That may not be prudent,' said Coppertracks.

Molly was shocked. 'What do you mean?'

'You have received an uninvited infusion of knowledge into your mind from a native of Kaliban,' said Coppertracks. 'There are some among the Free State who would consider that a transgression, a virus.'

'Dear Circle,' swore Molly, 'you sound like Rooksby now. That virus you're so glib about has seen us well on our way to Kaliban.'

'Kyorin may have been a pawn of his masters, dear mammal. Have you not considered the possibility this whole voyage to Kaliban might have been a test? To see whether we possess the abilities to directly threaten their home – a test that if passed, may decide whether we are all to be exterminated rather than merely enslaved and farmed.'

'You really think that's the case?' asked Molly.

'King Steam's council considers it a possibility, however remote, along with a hundred other options that do not match Kyorin's story and explanation for seeking our help. We know so little about our attackers, beyond the ease with which the Army of Shadows has vanquished all our attempts to resist their advances. It is possible they may even have used your bond with the Hexmachina as the mechanism to trace and imprison it within our world. We carry with us a gate that leads straight to the heart of my people's kingdom. I hope you understand King Steam's caution in how we exercise its activation.'

'You know me better than that,' said Molly.

'You I do know,' agreed Coppertracks. 'Kyorin and his race, however, are a different breed of softbody. We have yet to see the Army of Shadows' true masters with our own eyes. How can we be so sure that Kyorin and his blue men are not the masters of Kaliban's vicious soldier race?'

Their argument about Kyorin's intentions was cut short by

Lord Starhome's intervention. 'There is something coming towards us.'

Molly looked at the hull of the craft. 'Surely we are not at Kaliban yet?'

'No, that we are not. But there's something forward of my sensors, coming up fast and it's like nothing I have ever seen before.'

Molly frowned. Now what were they facing? 'Could it be a fleet of the shells that the Army of Shadows used to travel across to our world . . . ?'

'It's nothing physical,' said Lord Starhome. 'More like a wall of energy, a wall that resembles nothing which I am familiar with.'

'Aye, it may be a Kaliban weapon,' said Duncan.

'I am conversant with the screens and shielding of countless void-faring entities,' said Lord Starhome. 'And I can assure you that this is no such primitive deflection mechanism. I'm trying to resolve its nature, but it is actually defying my sensors: there are fundamental fluctuations moving along the stuff of existence; I can detect positrons moving backward in a storm above the field's surface. It appears immensely strong, yet I can hardly get a lock on it; even now we're this close. You're lucky I didn't just fly straight through the field unawares.'

'I trust your own shielding is fully activated now,' said Coppertracks, nervously.

'Naturally,' boomed Lord Starhome's disembodied voice. 'At my current most impressive velocity you would be dead from micro-dust impacts and radiation poisoning many times over if my shields were not functioning. I can shelter next to the skin of a sun if I have to. Still . . . a haze of positrons moving backwards, I have never seen such an outlandish sight, not once while traversing two galaxies.'

Molly dug deep in the confused jumble of memories and recollections that Kyorin had left to her, but there was nothing forthcoming from the residue of the slave's soul to suggest he had any inkling of a wall of exotic energy protecting Kaliban. But her gut spoke volumes. 'Pull away! Pull away, Starhome, I have a bad feeling about this.'

'Pull away?' said Lord Starhome in derision. 'Do you think that I am one of your clockwork-driven horseless carriages that can be swerved into a side road at the tug of a lever? I have been accelerating up towards light speed – it will take me the rest of the journey to brake. This field is too wide to avoid, you may only make a slight modification to the speed at which you wish my bow to cross it.'

Duncan Connor ran over to his precious battered travel case, as if he could use its weight to smash through the unknown obstacle. Coppertracks stopped fiddling with the looking-glass gate they had stowed away. Was the steamman now suffering from the temptation to activate it and leap through to safety in Mechancia before their ship struck the barrier?

'It's coming up fast,' said Lord Starhome. 'Brace yourselves for a collision.'

Molly's hand struck out for one the girders supporting the store room, gripping hold of the cold silver surface a second before the ship's lanterns went dark, gravity lost in a storm of crates, overwhelmed by a roaring explosion and a scream of agony from Lord Starhome. Then they were lost in a spinning, careening mass of metal that had been their craft.

It was time. The Hexmachina had finished modifying the workings of her internal components as best as she could. It was hard to tell whether her plan would work. Trapped inside the centre of the world in a cage that could modify and adapt

239

itself in response to all of her attempts to escape. A cunning cage built for only one purpose. To contain the Hexmachina while the power that fed the god-machine was bled away, slowly starving her to death. But would the cage be clever enough to detect what the Hexmachina had done to herself? The cage was cunning, but not self-aware; the Army of Shadows had stopped short of giving it a soul or real intelligence. But that did not mean it was stupid. A mousetrap was a dumb machine, but no mouse in its right mind wished to be caught by one.

She could not escape, the Hexmachina, not in any form that would be recognizable as her. But her lover the Earth knew the god-machine well, and the Hexmachina could feel the throb of the world's pain outside her prison: the planet's soul, its very lifeforce, leeched away by the invaders from Kaliban. And the Kingdom of Jackals. Jackals was part of the Earth. Its soil and stone both ancient and true. Jackals, so ran the whispers of the lava outside, now lay ready. With a moment's fierce concentration, the Hexmachina forced open a pinprick-sized tunnel in the unnatural lattice imprisoning her form, flipping the cage's molecules to a liquid state before firing a stream of her essence out through that pin-sized channel.

The lattice that imprisoned her instantly detected the change of state in part of its structure and moved to contain the Hexmachina, modelling the altered laws of physical stasis used by the god-machine and overwriting the infected mathematics to close the tiny tunnel that had been hacked into the cage's fabric. The minuscule channel was closed, cutting off the stream, leaving the depleted, shrunken form of the Hexmachina inside. Depleted, but elated – for outside, a wave-front of energy was passing through the magma at the speed of sound, ready to be caught by the kingdom and stored in the old way.

Stored in stone, just as the druids had once done. After all, the Hexmachina was at heart a device for opening and closing doors. For keeping dark gods out of the world. And there was an ancient door that badly needed opening, while yet another had to be shut on the Army of Shadows.

The Hexmachina's prison was complete again. The tiny breach had only lasted a second and the cage had learnt that trick and put in place a series of running equations to prevent another such hack against the fabric of matter. Yes, the enemy knew her well. But then, that cut both ways. She knew them, and their filthy kind should have burnt themselves out like a spent plague long ago.

Now it was up to the land above. And the last queen of Jackals.

CHAPTER TEN

A dream of flying, and when Molly opened her eyes – ignoring the throbbing pain at the back of her head – it had come true. Molly was drifting above a storm of crates and shock-loosened supplies. The ship's lantern flickered, adding to her headache, but showing Duncan Connor swimming across to her. She looked down. A belt had been stretched across her stomach and looped around one of the room's silver girders to stop her floating away in the ocean of cargo.

Molly rubbed her neck. 'I think I'm going to be sick.' Then she saw that Coppertracks' little drone was helping Connor move around, one iron hand on his ankle while another gripped one of a series of handles formed onto the wall.

'It's not so bad,' said Duncan. 'Aye, like falling with a sail-rider chute, but none of the wind. You had better get used to it. We've been without gravity for a couple of hours and I don't think we're getting it back.'

'Is Lord Starhome all right?'

Coppertracks' voice sounded remotely from the drone's voicebox. 'I am attempting to restore some of the steamman components that burnt out. He cannot even remember

242

Jackelian. I am communicating in hexadecimal code, but our ship only seems to remember his creators' tongue.'

Lord Starhome's disembodied voice sounded in response, half a song and half an alien screech. A shudder ran down Molly's spine. It was nothing anyone on her world had ever heard the like of before, and Starhome sounded very annoyed.

'Our craft's surface has been badly ablated,' continued Coppertracks. 'Many of Lord Starhome's sensors and the external components he had grown on his surface were ripped off as we passed through Kaliban's defences. His shields held, though, or we would be dust upon the void.'

Another alien howl followed, the singsong static hectoring and strident. Molly let Duncan undo the strap he had secured her with. 'How dangerous is Lord Starhome right now?'

'Well, we're still floating about,' said Duncan. 'And I don't think that's entirely because of the damage. I'm not sure if he remembers who we are, or if he thinks he's got a wee infestation of rats aboard.'

Sweet Circle. Molly winced as she followed Duncan and the drone out of the cargo hold and back up towards the bridge, hand over hand on the holds in the wall. What was to stop Lord Starhome opening a door in his hull to suck them all out into oblivion? The cold gold band of her control ring was still on her finger, but it felt as useless as a broken pair of stirrups on an untamed stallion.

'You realize,' barked Lord Rooksby as Molly entered the command deck, 'that treacherous native Kal must have known that his home was defended by a killing shield, and you—' he pointed at Molly '—by your own admission carry around his knowledge inside your dim-witted little skull.'

They were all drifting around the open space, tethered by belts to various girders, handholds and seats – only Keyspierre's daughter looked comfortable. She moved across the air like a ballet dancer, gracefully arching her back and using a wall to kick off before gripping a seat on the other side of the bridge.

'I certainly didn't know about the shield,' said Molly, 'and I don't think Kyorin knew about it, either. Why trick a handful of us up here just to kill us?'

The commodore bunched his hand into a fist. 'You're a mortal nasty piece of work, Rooksby, and I've a mind to teach you a few manners.'

'You, sir, are not even meant to be here,' said Rooksby. 'If parliament's writ had been followed, you and your menagerie of freaks would be sitting back in the kingdom and letting a professional expedition venture forth to Kaliban.'

'Ah, my lord commercial,' spat Commodore Black. 'Parliament's writ runs a long ways distant from the strange shores we've set a course for, and if you keep on with your poisonous jabbering, I'll be minded to float over there and toss you and your rotten House of Guardians-given title out of this ship of ours.'

'Please,' said Coppertracks, his iron hand inside an instrument panel at the front of the craft. 'A little peace for me to work. I'm nearly done. I have stripped two of the three steamman logic drums used to rebuild Lord Starhome, replacing the components in the least damaged of the trio. Paul-Loup softbody, if you would pass me my magnetizer, I shall attempt to close the new circuit I have built inside here.'

Keyspierre took one of the instruments floating in the air and passed it across to Coppertracks, the steamman examining it and tutting. 'No, the circuit magnetizer, please, *that* one.'

Exchanging instruments, Keyspierre passed Coppertracks the magnetizer and Coppertracks gave a nervous squirt of steam from his stacks before closing the broken circuit. The ship's lanterns dimmed for a second, then returned to full illumination, followed a moment later by the weight of gravity – gradual enough that they all landed lightly on their feet – or in Coppertracks' case, treads – from wherever they had been anchored.

'That's better, now,' said the commodore, winking at Jeanne. 'A fine figure of my girth needs to feel the weight on his boots and know which way is up and which way is down.'

A disembodied sigh sounded around them, hopefully Lord Starhome finding his full cognitive abilities coming back to him.

'Are you recovered from the effects of the weapon?' asked Molly.

'Weapon?' said Lord Starhome, impatiently. 'An ineffective sort of weapon I would say.'

Molly rubbed the back of her bruised head. 'Not from where I'm standing. How far to Kaliban now?'

'I'm having to regrow most of my sensors,' said Lord Starhome. 'But let me see, I can still feel the unpleasant tug of gravity and – yes, we're almost upon the ugly red-looking place. Even more disagreeable than that water-soaked rock of yours where my magnificent form was trapped for millennia.'

'Then we shall land outside the face of Kaliban,' said Molly, 'and hope that we didn't set off any alarms by breaching the Army of Shadows' shield.'

'Land?' said Lord Starhome. 'I don't think I care to.'

'You don't care to . . .' Keyspierre's daughter drew a knife from her boot and threatened the ship's exposed console. 'You have your duty, compatriot, by alliance with the Commonshare.'

Lord Starhome's laugh echoed around them. 'Please, little ground hugger, please don't scratch me with your eight inches of sharpened steel. You might take some of the burnish off my hull.'

Molly brandished the control ring on her hand – and noticed that it was glowing a sickly yellow. 'By the loyalty you owe to King Steam, I command you.'

'My apologies,' the eerie, disembodied voice took on a dark tone. 'I don't really *do* landings. I spent far too many aeons interred under the surface of your disgusting dirtball to want to exchange my freedom for a similarly tedious experience beneath the sands of that sucked-out husk whose orbit we're coming into.'

'My people rebuilt you,' pleaded Coppertracks.

'Oh, but I have been rebuilding myself since we launched,' said Lord Starhome. 'Particle by particle, and doing a far superior job of it. There's very little of your people's art left within me now.'

Molly's control ring was giving up the ghost, smoking hot, too little left that was steamman for it to re-establish its hold. 'You shall land where I order you!'

'Oh, I think we can both get what we desire,' said Lord Starhome.

Coppertracks vanished in front of Molly as a hole opened up in the deck beneath his treads; Commodore Black, Keyspierre and the others yelled in alarm as similar apertures swallowed them up.

'Well, mainly me, actually. Out with the old . . .'

Molly tried to lunge towards the exposed control panel, but she was too slow, an opening taking her feet away from her. She found herself flying along a tunnel, squeezed by the living metal of the craft like a throat about to gob out a fruit pip. Out into the infinite night.

It was cold on the heath. Oliver watched Purity shiver as she was exposed to the chill autumn winds, the grass and bracken crunching underfoot as the evening formed a frost.

He was used to the cold, though. There was always a chill at night. Where there were trees around them, they were losing their leaves, tinged as red as the baleful moon squatting unnaturally in their sky. Purity had fallen silent. Was she thinking about where he was leading her? And then Oliver saw it – the heath dipping in front of them before rising into a slope. A slope crested by a stone circle.

There were similar artefacts scattered all across the Kingdom of Jackals: burial circles, circles of astronomy, circles of power where the leylines crossed and intersected. Many were treated with reverence by the order of worldsingers, those that called themselves sorcerers, but surely not this one – so far away from the industry and homes of the race of man. This isolated, wind-blighted heathland that had grown out of the forest's borders and never seemed to end.

'There's nothing here, just a circle of standing stones,' said Purity.

'Nothing but the land,' Oliver told her.

Purity flashed him a look of concern – something in his voice seemed to be worrying her. Dejection? Acceptance? Relief? A dissonant blend of all of these? But then, she didn't know what he was going to have to do here. Even if he succeeded, things were unlikely to turn out well. Not for him, at any rate. And he probably wouldn't be doing Purity many favours either. Oliver led her across the grass, his riding cloak billowing in the breeze that whipped across the bleak open space. There was a mist rising out of the grass around his boots. A marsh mist. They slipped into the centre of the circle of stones, granite menhirs at least three times their height. There was a sense of stepping into another world up here, of isolation. Separation. One of the stone sentinels stood twice as tall as all the others, its shadow like the hand of a clock across the grass, descending over a menhir fallen in front of it – there to serve as an altar?

Oliver moved in front of the circle's tallest stone, letting the wind blow across his face. The night carried a scent that was not altogether pleasant: rich and boggy.

'What's that smell?' asked Purity.

Oliver pointed to the horizon. 'There's a marsh a mile ahead.'

'You sound pleased about that.'

'The marsh and a darkness over it. What more can a man ask for?' Oliver lifted the brace of pistols out from his belt and gave them a theatrical twirl. Showing off. Anything to distract him from the twinge of fear freezing his heart, the shadow of a dark foreboding.

'You look after yourself, Purity Drake,' said Oliver.

Purity took a step towards him, but the wind picked up suddenly and pushed her back. Oliver slammed the barrels of his pistols into the altar stone, a finger's width apart, planting them like saplings that might grow into oaks. He was kneeling down, head bowed before the rough-hewn rock.

'What—?'

<*He is the key*,> whispered the ancient voice.

Beneath Oliver's boots the ground was trembling, the two pistols glowing brighter and brighter, cruel stars set upon the land. Oliver yelled and shut his eyes. This was it, then. Circle, he hadn't expected it to hurt quite as much as this. Changing and burning and changing and . . .

There was a rumbling under Purity's feet, then the pain of the intense light started to dwindle and she blinked tears out of her eyes, trying to focus on the spot where Oliver had been standing. He had vanished, completely disappeared, but the two pistols had been transformed into a sword: tall, silver and sheathed in marsh mist. A sword. Bleeding steam into the evening air, its blade sunk halfway into the fallen menhir.

'Oliver,' shouted Purity. 'Where are you?'

<*He is the key,*> repeated the ancient voice.

'Please don't leave me, Oliver. Don't leave me here all alone, not like everyone else.'

<*He has been freed. The part of him that is fey has passed to the land of the fast folk, far beyond the feymist curtain.*>

'Oliver . . .'

<*The part of him that was of this land stands before you still. He abides within the blade.*>

'He's not a sword,' said Purity. 'He's a man. And he's more than those two cursed pistols he carries. What kind of queen are you, what kind of creature, to do this to him?'

<*The kind that has passed into the land. My blood has become the streams that run down from the mountains. My flesh is the soil that lifts up each summer's harvest to your people. Pick up the sword, Purity Drake, see if my blade speaks to you.*>

Purity stood before the blade, the true edge of the sword captured by the rock, its hilt protected by a basket – a guard shaped as the face of a lion. The blade sang through her, wind blowing over its edge and splitting along the basket, whistling out of the lion's sculpted metal teeth along the buckler. 'The sword's caught inside the rock.'

<*A queen with my blood was destined to carry this weapon.*>

'I am all that's left of my line. The last of my house.'

<*Then you must believe in yourself. This is an old test, as ancient as the bones of my land. Take the grip of the sword and set it free of the rock.*>

Purity's hand reached out, feeling the wind funnelled through the guard, as if the lion of Jackals was blowing onto her fingers. She hesitated, her hand wavering above the sword's

249

pommel. 'It's not just Oliver inside the sword, I can feel something else. More than the land, more than you . . .'

<*The blade contains a little of the essence of the god-machine. It is the power to split worlds.*>

Purity shivered. A *little* of its essence. Now it had been revealed to her, she could feel a similar energy humming in each of the stones circling her. The rest of the power was stored, but stored for what purpose? 'The Hexmachina. Oh, Molly. Why did you have to go to Kaliban without me? This is your legacy, not mine.'

<*No. Molly Templar serves as a symbiote for the god-machine. Like Oliver, she could join with the blade, but she could never carry it. That is your heritage, Purity. Do not hesitate, do not show fear. This is your blade and your destiny alone.*>

Purity bit her lip and reached out to wrap her fingers around the grip, a spark of fire leaping out between its crosspiece and her skin, burning, but burning with a fiery cold. The sword slipped out of the fallen menhir with a rasping song of stone, as if its granite had been shaped to be the blade's sheath, the long silver length of the blade so thin and light the metal might have been folded with air.

She had it! Purity gazed at the blade in wonder. 'The sword hardly weighs a thing.'

<*So, a queen after all. Like so many things, the weight of the blade is felt in other ways. By the deeds you will be called towards. Now, strike the tallest stone and strike it well.*>

Purity clutched the grip harder, strange symbols flowing down the metal like light on the waters' edge as she did so. 'The sword will shatter against the stone. I broke one of Jared's practice blades on much less than that.'

<*The one who carries it may shatter, but never the blade. It is no mortal sword. It is the last hope of Jackals wielded*

by the last true queen of this land. Its power is as limitless as your belief in yourself. Now, bow to the stone in front of you and strike it with all of your will.>

Purity spun the blade twice in slow windmill turns, then lashed out at the menhir. At first, just for a second, Purity thought she had missed it, though the Circle knows how she could have done so at such a short distance. No impact, or clatter of steel on rock. Then Purity realized she had *not* missed her target. The top half of the menhir was sliding down the slope she had carved through it, tumbling to the side with a heavy rumble. As the stone fell away, a volcano fire lifted out of the section still resting on the grass, leaping from rock to rock until the circle of stones was a carousel of flames and light. It was being discharged, all the power of the god-machine. The space between each menhir had become a gate of energy, crackling and shimmering in the cold air and filling the hilltop with a fire-grate warmth. Figures began to step from out of the gates, silhouetted against the burning energy behind them for a moment before it winked out of existence.

<Hail,> said the voice inside Purity's head. *<Hail, the Bandits of the Marsh.>*

Bandits? Purity glanced around the darkening circle. A handful of figures. Four of them. Three men and one woman. The legends of Elizica of the Jackeni from Coppetracks' books came back to her. Two hundred warriors who had fought to free the land from the invaders from the sea. A sword-saint to lead them. 'Aren't you about one hundred and ninety-six bandits shy?'

<The sword is only as powerful as your belief, Purity Drake. You should have believed more.>

One of the figures was wearing an archaic metal breast-plate with a high steel collar, his hair shorn brutally short like

251

that of a Circlist monk. 'This is the queen? She is but a girl, a shoeless child.'

'We have slept an age,' said the oldest of the bandits, scratching at a scruffy silver beard. 'Under the hills and far away. Would you know her better if she carried a trident, Samuel? Only those with the true blood of Elizica running through their veins may summon us.'

'How much royal blood flows through her flesh, old man? There are only four of us here. Where are all the others?'

'Show some manners,' commanded old Silver-beard.

'Have the gill-necks returned from the ocean?' the monk-like bandit asked of Purity, obviously trying not to snarl out the words.

'No. We face a different invader,' said Purity. 'We've been at peace with the underwater kingdoms for as long as I can remember.'

And she was meant to save Jackals with these four strange-looking anachronisms? Wearing dark marshmen's leathers studded with iron pins. Even two hundred bandits couldn't be considered an army – what could she do with this motley group? Offer to field a damn game of four-poles? Purity sighed. 'The ones attacking us are called the Army of Shadows and they have legions of slave soldiers called slats fighting for them.'

'The enemy always has legions, that is what makes them worth fighting. I am Ganby Meridian,' said the old fellow with the silver beard. 'My three companions here are Jenny Blow, Samuel Lancemaster—' he pointed to the tall, monk-like figure, then indicated the rangy black-faced bandit standing by their side '—and this taciturn fellow is Jackaby Mention. You speak very strange Jackelian, lady. We must have slept longer than we expected. How are you known among your people?'

'Just Purity, Purity Drake. You are truly the Bandits of the Marsh?'

'These three are bandits,' said Ganby Meridian. 'I myself am not fey, although I found myself attached to their outlaw ranks by curious happenstance, being of the noble order of druids before circumstances drove me into the margins of the marsh waters.'

The sole woman in the group sniffed the air. 'It wasn't circumstances; it was a baying mob of your own people, old man. This Army of Shadows, young shoeless queen, do they smell like damp rodent fur, no, like bats . . . ?'

'They don't smell of anything,' said Purity.

'Jenny Blow is never wrong,' noted the bandit Samuel Lancemaster. He pointed outside the stone circle down towards the bottom of the slope. 'Her nose knows.'

Purity saw them. Black shapes, a hunting pack of slats, clicking with their rattlesnake throats and surrounding the base of the hill below. There were dozens of the horrors down there and it had taken all of her friends to slay a small handful of slats back in Tock House. The memory of Kyorin dying in her arms leapt back at her. She and the Bandits of the Marsh were about to discover the difference between the Army of Shadows and the invaders from the sea they had once fought, to experience it very directly indeed.

The old man who claimed to have been a druid appeared frozen in terror at the sight of the slats. 'Always are we outnumbered!'

The tall one, Samuel Lancemaster, removed a knuckle-duster-like device from his armour and it extended into a full-sized spear at his touch. The other two bandits seemed content to move by his side, unarmed, while the druid overcame his terror enough to cower behind the hastily formed line.

253

'But rarely are we outclassed,' Samuel shouted down to the enemy.

<*Your sword,*> the voice whispered to Purity. <*Raise the blade in front of you.*>

Death came up the hill at them.

CHAPTER ELEVEN

M olly had expected to tumble into the airless certainty of
an icy death out in the celestial darks, but instead she
found herself colliding with Commodore Black inside the
storage chamber at the aft of Lord Starhome.

'This is disgraceful behaviour,' called Coppertracks, his sole
drone hanging onto his master's tracks as the treads rotated
uselessly in zero gravity. 'You owe your existence on the great
pattern to King Steam.'

'You're wasting your breath, now, with him,' said
Commodore Black. 'The wicked ship's not in any mood to
listen to reason.'

'Him!' said Lord Starhome in haughty revulsion. 'You damn
ground huggers couldn't even get my gender right. Can a male
give birth?'

Molly halted her drift by kicking off the frame of the
looking-glass gate, which was anchored by some unknown
force to the deck. Their craft had closed off the holes that it
had used to suck them into the hold. Also vanished was the
sole door exiting the storage chamber. 'You're saying that
you're *pregnant*?'

'I am cleansing myself. All the components that were forced upon my body by your steammen surgeons, all the abuse you've heaped upon my noble frame, all squeezed out.'

Coppertracks sounded astonished. 'You can self-replicate?'

A porthole formed in the side of the hull, to reveal that the hold where they were trapped was curling out from the main body of the craft like clay being pulled off a potter's wheel, fat globs of living metal falling away into the star-studded darks. 'And you're the cleverest of your kind, steamman? The creators help you!'

'You promised me Kaliban!' Molly shouted at the ship.

'All yours,' said the craft, dipping in a graceful turn and bringing the ugly red eye of Kaliban up to fill the window. 'You're even lined up to hit the upper atmosphere above that hideous stone face you're so keen to visit.'

Rooksby banged angrily on the hold's hull. 'Hit? How are you expecting to land?'

'Oh, but that's rather the thing: I'm not,' came the disembodied voice. 'Look after my soul board. My soul is your burden now.'

Around them the hull started to reform, becoming a sphere, and the porthole showed the bat-like form of Lord Starhome disappearing, a faint nimbus of distorted gravity squeezing the craft away through the aether. Their storeroom had become a lifeboat squeezed off the body of the main ship. Starhome was marooning them!

'You traitorous steamman mongrel,' yelled Rooksby.

'Mamma,' a young female voice echoed around the sphere. 'Please don't leave me. Come back.'

'Oh sweet Circle,' swore Molly.

'There's something big out there, a red sphere, getting larger,' squealed the newly born craft's voice. 'I'm falling into it.'

Gravity was gradually being restored by their proximity to

Kaliban, the supplies and members of the expedition attracted to the hull. The very *hot* hull, getting hotter with each second.

'You need to assume a shape that will shed heat, young knight of the steammen,' announced Coppertracks. 'And a shape that will brake our descent. Otherwise the friction of entering Kaliban's atmosphere will incinerate us all.'

'Are you my papa?' asked the craft. 'Some of my organs appear to match the pattern of your frame.'

'A brother, perhaps,' said Coppertracks. 'Of the race of the metal. Your older, wiser brother.' He seemed pleased with that idea.

'What is my name, brother? My designation?'

'For the love of the Circle, steamman,' shouted Lord Rooksby. 'Forget about your cursed name. My boots' soles are steaming. You must grow wings, fly!'

'Nonsense,' argued Keyspierre, being steadied by his daughter as the craft bounced under their feet. 'A shell, compatriot craft, form yourself into a cannon shell. That is the best shape to assume.'

'Use your shields,' ordered Molly. 'That was how your mother survived her crash in the mountains of Mechancia.' *Shelter next to the skin of a sun*, indeed. Time to put the craft's boasts to the test.

'Yes,' said the young voice. 'That's an idea. I can grow those, I know how.'

Molly nodded in desperation. 'Good girl. Grow your shields now.'

'No, not grow shields, shields need to be projected out,' replied the voice. 'I mean grow a shield generator inside my body. I can start to gestate the seed of one within a week.'

Commodore Black groaned. 'Ah well, lass, it was a mortal fine try.' He spat on the porthole and watched his spittle crackle into steam. 'It's blessed unlucky to be falling to our deaths on any ship without a name, so I'll give you a name, you silver-skinned beauty, if you could but see us safe to Kaliban's hateful sands below. I baptize you the *Sprite*, the *Sprite of the Stars*.'

'Really now, that is no name for one of the people of the metal,' protested Coppertracks, holding onto his drone body as the newly born ship jounced in the turbulence. 'You shall be called Lady Starsprite. For this craft is still a daughter of the Free State and a champion of the Chamber of Swords.'

Around them the hull started contracting, assuming a pear shape, concentrating mass under their feet at the base of the teardrop. Was this a better shape than a sphere for diving down onto Kaliban? Molly felt a nudge from Duncan Connor.

'Even if we can save ourselves from a cooking in this oven, we're going to be killed by the impact of landing,' whispered the ex-soldier. He was clutching his travel case like a talisman. 'But we can use yon steammen portal to escape. A minute open would be long enough for us all to jump through.'

Molly tried to ignore the climbing heat and think clearly. Abandon the mission? Come so far, risk so much, only to flee back home at the last moment. But what use staying if they all died?

'Aye, I know, it sits bad with me too,' added Duncan. 'But this young foal has no shielding. So high up, we are going to be murdered in our breeks trying to get down to the ground.'

With a tremendous slam, a pocket of atmospheric turbulence spilled Molly onto the floor. She looked out of the window. All she could see was a line of fire fleeting up towards the black edge of space. It would be so easy. Step through the steammen's strange looking-glass gate. Save their lives. Keep them all alive: alive for as long as it took the Kingdom of Jackals and all the nations of the continent to fall to the Army of Shadows.

*   *   *

A hundred thousand miles away, the craft that had once been known as Lord Starhome folded space around her hull, squeezing the universe harder and harder and building up an impressive head of speed. Free, so gloriously free at last. Her sensors were almost fully regrown, a little dive through an asteroid belt having added enough matter to more than make up for the damage she had suffered helping those ingrate little ground huggers on their foolish mission.

She rotated her newly formed sensor array to capture an image of the starfields hanging densely around her, little twinkling motes of gravity from the nuclear furnaces that burned so distantly. Where to go, what to do? So many choices. So many wonders of creation to explore, far from this dreary little solar system where the fickle hand of fate had chosen to maroon her for an interminable age. Time to feed the surrounding constellations' patterns into her systems, compare them to the master maps she held deep within her, take a bearing, and get on with the rest of her sublime existence.

It took an hour of frantic diagnostic checks for her regrown sensor systems to realize that something was very wrong. But not with her sensors.

With the universe around her.

How strange it was to be attacked by these invaders, the slats loping up the hill like killer apes, terrible eyeless faces marking Purity and the Bandits of the Marsh's positions with their chattering throats. The slat horde hurled themselves up the slope towards the circle of standing stones with an animal-like tempo, but some of them were carrying rifles, flinging burning bolts of energy towards them rather than bullets. It was as if they were being attacked by a pack of ravening wolves who had only discovered sentience a couple of minutes earlier: which was no less odd than the style in which they were received at the crest of the slope.

Purity brushed the bolts of fire aside with her blade, turning them on its mirrored surface, as light as air in her hands, using it as instinctively as breathing. There was something reassuring about its unearthly heft. Only when the slats had closed with them outside the stone circle did Purity realize what it was – holding the blade was like holding Oliver's hand. He had become the blade itself and if he had once been a shade of death stalking across the land, in her hands the sword felt as if it was capable of so much more.

Samuel Lancemaster leapt forward by her side with a roar and headbutted one of the attacking slats, twisting his spear as if his weapon was the sail of a windmill. It was then she saw why Jenny Blow and Jackaby Mention hadn't bothered to produce weapons when the slats had surrounded them. Jenny Blow opened her mouth and started projecting a banshee scream, the force of it cracking into the slimy black chitin-like chests of the attacking slats, hammering them off their clawed feet. In amongst their ranks Jackaby Mention ran at a speed so fast he had turned to a blur, only briefly visible in the seconds between slowing down to kick and strike at the slavering slave soldiers.

Whatever the slats had been expecting to face on top of the hill, it wasn't this! Also lost to sight was the long-in-the-tooth druid – but then Purity located him, the old fox trying to hide behind the stones in the centre of the circle – stumbling and cursing as the slats came at him, his fighting style a curious mix of retreating and simultaneously turning to fling the sorceries of the worldsong at his pursuers. His silver hair tossed flaring under the night sky as wild sparks of wizardry hissed and recoiled around the inside of the stone circle. It was like watching a drunken pugilist weaving among a gang of toughs, landing blows and avoiding their flashing fists by his chance, clumsy stumbles. Except these fists had talons attached to the fingers, one of the clawed hands lashing past Purity's face as she weaved back herself. <*Poison,*> the sword seemed to whisper to her, the organic compound of the corrosive secretion flashing through her mind. She could understand it, see how to render the posion benign inside her blood if she was clawed. What in the name of the Circle was this blade of hers, how much was it capable of?

Jenny Blow arched her head around, the gale from her throat sweeping the slats trying to circle her into the side of one of the stones. Samuel Lancemaster strode into the space that had been created, casually lashing out with the butt of his spear and nearly breaking a slat in half. He was big, but his strength went far beyond his size; the fey bandit seemed able to strike with almost superhuman strength, the blunt trauma of his spear strikes killing with a single blow every assailant that came at him. At least, Purity never saw any of the slats get back up to have a second attempt at him.

As quickly as they had come at them the storm ended and they were standing alone under the shadow of the stone circle, Purity's blade twitching in her hand like a diviner's rod seeking water. Corpses littered the slope around their feet while the blur that was Jackaby Mention slowed to a standstill in front of them. His marsh leathers were crisped with a sheen of ice.

'Where is Ganby?'

'I am here,' a voice sounded behind one of the stones and the old druid appeared, brushing mud off his breeches. 'I have seen off the last of them.'

'Did you enjoy your rest, old man?' snorted Jenny Blow.

Purity hoped so. When the Army of Shadows realized how many slats had vanished, this part of the country was going

261

to get very dangerous indeed. They would have to leave here as quickly as they could.

Purity ran her hands along the shelves of the abandoned village's sole shop, emptying the contents stored there into a sack. Each tumble and crack of can upon jar brought back the memories. The attack upon the hill, slats leaping up towards the ancient stone circle. Her sword humming in her hand, sucking up the bolts of fire from the heat-agitation weapons of the beasts. Drinking fire from the air. And then there were the four Bandits of the Marsh. Awoken from the dark corridors between the worlds and full of surprises. Like Jenny Blow, who could tell the sex of a hare a mile away with her thin nose, Jenny who had remarked offhandedly that it had been she who had taught King Steam to fight with the modulations of his voicebox. The ancient fighting art of the steammen knights. Did they really owe all their martial skills to this short, barrel-chested female bandit?

Just four. Four out of two hundred Bandits of the Marsh. If only she had been stronger, could have struck the stone with more of her might. Kept the portals between the stones open for longer, awakened more of the sleepers.

Samuel Lancemaster poked his head around the door to make sure Purity was all right. She could hear the fire crackling in the back room's hearth, dry broken furniture feeding the flames.

Purity held up one of her finds. 'Ham.'

Samuel grunted. 'More canned victuals.'

'Back in the Royal Breeding House this was currency.'

Samuel shook his head, perplexed. 'Your land is a strange one, lady. The nobility held as prisoners by their own council. King and queen kept only as symbols.'

Purity took the bag through to the back room, tossing it

next to the supplies they had found in the cottages of the abandoned village. It was a good haul. The people must have moved out very fast. Evacuated by the county constabulary or – well, the alternative did not bear contemplation. 'Only the old nobility, the royalist cause. You won't find any of the Lords Commercial inside the Royal Breeding House.'

'And these Lords Commercial,' said Ganby Meridian, his silver beard tinged yellow by the firelight. 'They are given their titles by your parliament of shopkeepers, or by your hostage-queen?'

'Neither,' said Purity. The conversation was making her uncomfortable, calling forth too many memories of the patriotic songs and lessons she had been forced to learn by rote in the cold school chambers of the fortress where she had grown up. 'They are decided by the tables and logs of Greenhall, the treasury office of the Guardian Chancellor. You are automatically granted a title after you have paid a certain amount in taxes to the state; the rate varies and is voted on each year by parliament. The more money you pay, the higher your precedent in the lists.'

'Hmm,' groaned Ganby, the disapproving noise rumbling at the back of his throat.

'Is it so different, Ganby Meridian, from the queen we placed on the throne of the Jackeni, or the council of druids deciding who would rule among the stag lords?' asked Jenny Blow.

'To become a druid took years of hard study and mastery of the worldsong. You had to prove yourself worthy of tasks as weighty as selecting a new ruler. My ostler I would trust to care for my horse, my smithy to shoe her. But to look inside the heart of the person I would call Sovereign? I am not sure I would trust such a matter to my ostler or smithy.'

Samuel smiled and tossed the leg of a table into the fire

grate, sparks spitting against his silver breastplate. 'Has Ganby mentioned he was a druid long before he joined our ranks?'

'Yes,' added Jenny Blow. 'Before his crimes and knavery saw him thrown out and drawn towards the margins of the marsh's waters as an outlaw.'

'Pah,' said Ganby. 'If I ever stopped lying, I would disappoint you. These are strange new days indeed. Queens who are mutilated and kept in chains, councils of standing chosen by those who have none, and a faceless legion of monsters walking the world. Fighting those gill-necks from the kingdom below the waves seems as a blessing in comparison to this new war.'

A knot of anger tightened inside Purity. 'My friend Oliver gave his life to free you for this war.'

'Not just us *four*,' said Jenny Blow, pointedly.

'That's enough,' said Samuel. 'We four answered the call and you speak to the true queen of the Jackeni, that much you must know.' He knelt down in front of Purity. 'My spear is your spear, as it was for Queen Elizica.'

And what a spear it was. By activating a hidden control, Samuel could collapse the weapon into a nasty weapon shaped like a knuckle-duster that could smack bricks out of a wall. When he was thinking, he would sometimes snick the spear out to its full length and then swing it back to its fist-sized shape, rattling the air with the noise of the spear's reorientation.

'A queen without boots,' pointed out Jackaby Mention from his chair, wiping his lips with relish as he set about the contents of one of the tins.

Purity looked across at the brooding black bandit. 'You wear no shoes either.'

Jackaby raised his bare toes and wiggled them. 'I meant it as no insult. I run faster when I have none and I like to feel close to the bones of the world, the earthflow.'

Ganby drew Purity to one side. 'They mean no harm by their words. They are touchy around normal people.'

Purity wasn't sure if she should feel flattered or frightened that they considered her normal. 'You mean those who aren't fey?'

'Quite. In our age the druids made sacrifices to keep the killing, changing clouds of the feymist at bay – children were bound and cast into the feymist curtain. Most died, but some did not.' Ganby indicated his three companions. 'Those that survived the changes of the warping mist were considered cursed and hunted without mercy by the land's tribes. Where else could they hide but the great marsh? They have little love for the affairs of mortals and as loyal as they became in the end to Elizica and her lion throne, I fear they see only a little of her in you.'

'I wish there was none of her in me,' said Purity. She picked up the sword from the stone circle. 'And I wish that I hadn't been given this.'

Ganby rubbed his beard thoughtfully. 'I remember another young woman standing before me, saying the same thing about a trident she had retrieved from a lake.' He sighed. 'We slept for an age to reach this strange new time, when she said she would need us again. That was not easy for us, nor for you to be the one to receive us. Let us see if we can make it worth the while for both of us . . .' He took Purity's sword from her, carefully weighing it two hands. 'Do you know what this blade is?'

'Sharp,' said Purity. 'And the sword contains a little of the essence of my friend Oliver . . . and of the Hexmachina.'

'They are facets of it,' said Ganby. 'You have described it a little, but they are not what the sword *is*. It is a maths-blade, a tool to manipulate the worldsong.'

'Maths?' said Purity. 'You mean sums and adding up? What does that have to do with sorcery and the worldsong?'

'Everything,' said Ganby, his hand sweeping out to encompass the room. 'All that you have seen, all that you will see, everything that you are, these are all mathematical constructs. The song of the world is composed of notes, the notes are composed of waves and strings, and they can be modelled and manipulated by an adroit mind. When you change the factors of an equation, you change its outcome. The worldsingers' training allows them to tap into the flow of power within the earth and change the equations that underlie the world, by hand, spell and mind.' He indicated the other bandits sitting around the fire and handed the blade back to her. 'The fey carry some of that ability innately. Your sword is a tool that allows you to manipulate reality. It cuts through stone so easily because it can change the equations of existence that define how matter should interact with its surface.'

'More than a sword,' whispered Purity.

'An essential truth,' said Ganby. 'I would never have shaped it as a sword myself. When you give someone a hammer, every problem tends to look like a nail. I would have made it a book, or perhaps a slide rule.'

'What can I do with it?'

'What can you not?' Ganby indicated she should hold the sword out. 'A start would be to tear a hole in the veil of the world and free our fellow Bandits of the Marsh from their sleep of ages. You managed to do it for the four of us.'

'But there was power in the circle of standing stones,' said Purity. 'Helping me. I could feel it flowing through me. The power of the god machine, the Hexmachina.'

Ganby waved his hand impatiently as if this were a mere trifle. 'Pah, there is more power in the human heart and the imagination of a child than there is in any stone circle or blade. You can use the sword. Just feel the lingering aura of

266

our sleep and then reach to the place where the energy is connected. Tear a rent towards it using your blade.'

Purity clutched the pommel of the sword and symbols started to flow down the flat of the blade. She could feel the connection the old wizard had spoken of. Thin tentacles of else-when connecting the four bandits to the place where they had slept away the centuries. Spinning the blade, she tried to cut a portal in the air, reach the sleeping place. Instead of a rent forming, the arcs of her blade left scratches of golden light hanging in the air, shrinking and diminishing before the threads blew away like candle smoke.

'I can't do it,' said Purity, frustrated, proffering the blade back to Ganby. 'You're the great druid, you open the gateway for your friends to come through.'

He took the sword out of her hand, gripping it properly in a fighting stance, the symbols creeping along its surface disappearing, the blade's silver brightness darkening. It had died in his hand. 'You see, just a cold length of metal. Something to bash away at an enemy's helm with. I could never get Elizica's trident to work for me either. This is not my sword.' He passed it back to Purity. 'It is yours.'

Purity took a few more swings to the same negligible effect. The maths-blade was becoming heavier where once it had seemed so light. 'I can feel it, the place you came from. But I don't have the power of the stones to channel through the blade to break across to it.'

'Power is not channelled through the blade,' said Ganby, sadly. 'It is channelled through the one that wields it. And you have everything that you need to wield it, save the belief that you can. That you deserve it.'

'But that's the thing. I'm not sure I do. I certainly never asked for this.'

'Yes, your ancestor was tutored as a princess of battle from the age she could first walk,' said Ganby. 'I am sorry to ask so much of you so quickly, Purity Drake. Time will bring you what you need.'

Purity looked out of the back room's window, the iron moon gazing back down, a rusty squinting eye. 'How much of that do we have left?'

'There will be enough time and enough battle, both.'

Purity nodded. Yes. There was an entire continent full of monsters to practise her new maths-blade against.

CHAPTER TWELVE

Molly picked herself up from the jolting deck and shouted to be heard above the roar of the re-entry flames outside. She might just have a way to stop them burning up above Kaliban! 'Coppertracks, can you join cables with the ship?'

'The craft is steamman enough for us to share our minds.'

'Starsprite,' Molly called, 'make yourself ready.'

A silver cable extended like a tentacle from the wall. 'My skin is hardening outside, a shield of ablative polymers forming. It feels better now. We're finally clearing the mesosphere for the stratospheric envelope. I can see it. Do you think my mother knew this would happen? Do you think she loved me just a little?'

'Coppertracks has a trick for you that you can't call upon by instinct,' said Molly, watching the ship's cable snake towards a port opening in her steamman friend's chest. 'Your turn, old steamer. The sail-rider rig we cut Duncan out of at Tock House; show your young relative here the schematics for it. Starsprite, when you have the plans, peel off part of your hull to form the rig's sail triangle.'

The fire inside the crystal dome of Coppertracks'

transparent skull began wheeling in eccentric patterns while the transfer was in progress, the steamman giving a little whistle of alarm from his stacks at just how fast the newly born craft was absorbing his wisdom. Fast then faster, then it was over. Above them, the roof of their pear-shaped capsule started to flow downwards, stopping just short of their heads, their porthole elongating and moving in front of the craft's nose – quicksilver sails lashed by the wind-shear growing into existence outside; one sail above them, two smaller stabilizer canopies to either side. As soon as her new wings had fully formed, the young craft began to roll, arrowing down in a spin.

'How do I control myself?' screamed the craft.

'Form the sail rider's control bars and pulley system inside here, down by your nose,' ordered Molly. She glanced at Duncan Connor. 'This calf of a craft might not have a clue about how to make a landing, but how about one of the wild boys of Dennehy's Circus?'

Duncan looked pensively at the control bars, guide lines and deflexor handles forming in the front of the young ship. Outside the porthole, the brilliant red arc of Kaliban's continents and waterless seabeds curved out before them. 'This is a wee bit higher than any sail rider ever attempted a touchdown from.'

Molly tried to ignore the rattling of the newly formed struts as Duncan climbed over the scattered supply bales to slide into the control rig. She screened out the nervous mutters of Lord Rooksby – was that a Circlist meditation he was repeating? – disregarded the cold, angry eyes of Keyspierre and his daughter. Duncan Connor had possessed skill enough to land his burning rig in Tock House's garden, the only survivor of the Army of Shadows' annexation of the Jackelian skies. And here they were now, tumbling down over the enemy's old home. It was a calculated risk, but she wasn't going to give up now. Not after coming this far.

Molly turned as a crack sounded behind her. Commodore Black was rummaging through the supplies, emptying the contents of each crate onto the floor. Then he found what he was looking for and with a grunt of satisfaction pulled out a bottle of medicinal whisky. 'Let us say a thanks to the board of supply's clerks back in Highhorn, for they saw fit to outfit us with the very thing to calm our nerves. Along with—' his hand swept the debris of his scavenging '—this other junk.'

'Jared, those are supplies we need,' said Molly. 'Compasses, pistols, tinned food, blue skin paint so that we can pass for native Kals.'

'No, lass,' said the commodore, unstoppering the bottle. 'This is what we need. A toast to Duncan and his skill, swooping here and there like a blessed hunting hawk. I've had my fill of being treated like a wave-tossed cork by fate. Fired out of uncommonly sized cannons, living in the belly of steammen vessels crossing the celestial darks, cast away like a plummeting stone over the enemy's stronghold.' He took a swig from the bottle and offered it to Keyspierre but the shiftie scientist looked disgusted. 'No? Suit yourself. Ah, it's good. This'll put hairs on your chest. No, it's the solid land for me from now on. My boots firmly on the ground, even if the land is that of wicked Kaliban.'

Rooksby yelped as they started to roll again, Duncan grunting and pulling the craft back on course. His face was beaded with sweat and his lips pulled so tight he was drawing blood with the force of his concentration.

'Your piloting is magnificent,' announced the young Starsprite. 'It is like having an organ for atmospheric flight inside me. I can feel what you are doing. How you're using the side sails to brake and turn us. But we're going to pass through a wall of turbulence at the borders of the tropo-sphere, I can feel it flowing ahead of us.'

Molly had to stop herself from yelling as the battering outside renewed itself with fresh vigour. As if sensing the fear inside her passengers, Starsprite formed a series of pews topped with railings to hold onto across her deck. Molly clutched at one until her knuckles stood out on the back of her hands like white stones on a Spumehead beach. Then they were slip-ping towards smoother currents, the shaking abating.

'Can you not increase the size of the main sail triangle?' called Duncan from his position in the nose.

'I do not have enough material,' replied the craft. 'I know the proportions of the sail are wrong but my hull is already as thin as I dare squeeze it.'

'We're gliding too heavy for a brake and tug landing,' said Duncan, banking the craft. 'I'm going to try and spiral us down, long wide figures of eight all the way to the ground. Keep your eyes open for a straight stretch of sand for our final glide in.'

Molly moved to the front and stared out of the elongated porthole. She could see the face of Kaliban, the carving no bigger than her thumbnail. Lord Starhome had been as good as his – her? – word, after all; dropping the expedition down on top of the monumental carving like a sycamore seed sinking to the ground. Shadows of canyons and mountains crisscrossed the land below – if summits were visible at this height, they must be on a scale that dwarfed the craggy ranges of the Jackelian uplands. Molly closed her eyes and waited for the jumbled headache of Kyorin's memories to cast adrift a suit-able landing zone. *There.* To the south of the carving, long undulating dunes of dust-thin sand. She could see them in her mind's eye, blowing and shifting in front of a sierra eroded by the fierce sands into a forest of toadstool-like capstones.

Molly pointed out the stretch to Duncan. 'Place the tail of your last loop in the shadows of the carving's chin, there's sand enough to skim down for a long, low landing.'

Duncan grunted in affirmation, not taking his concentration away from the porthole for a second. 'Aye, I see it, I see it.'

Molly's head was throbbing now. It was painful, accessing the jumble of memories that Kyorin had dumped into her. Increasingly so, each time she tried it. What, she wondered, did the pain mean?

Someone was behind her. Jeanne and her father. The young shiftie seemed fascinated by the crimson vista circling in front of the transparent material of the porthole. 'Those lines out there. They are the same canals the steamman presented at the Royal Society.'

Who had told her? Coppertracks was humble about his achievements and Lord Rooksby had no reason to talk about his rival's findings.

Molly nodded, warily.

'A remarkable achievement,' said Keyspierre, his mood improving now they had hope of a landing. 'The Kals surely must have organized themselves as a commonshare and laboured mightily to achieve such a network.'

When it came, the final meeting with the ground was blisteringly fast. The craft tore through the barrage of rolling dunes with whip-cracking explosions of red sand as each impact slowed Starsprite a little more. Then there was a long tearing sound as her belly caught the sand, sliding for what seemed hours before they stopped. Molly was shaking as she got to her feet. She hadn't realized how terrified she had been during the long fall towards Kaliban and now the shock of their arrival was catching up with her. For a moment she wondered if the impact had affected her eyes – everything seemed to be turning red. But it was Starsprite. Their craft was changing the colour of her hull, the texture becoming grainy red rather than silvery smooth – camouflaging her lines – blending in with the sand in which she had settled.

'Open the door,' said Molly. 'Let's see where we are.'

'I haven't ordered that,' Rooksby practically shrieked, his nerves in shreds.

Molly pointedly ignored him and jumped out of the hole rippling open in young Starsprite's stern, landing ankle deep in the ruby sands. She felt light on her feet, springy. The pull of this world was only two thirds what she was used to back home. Then the intense wall of heat struck her. It was like walking into an oven, thick, cloying. Circle's teeth! Molly noticed how near they had come to a canyon drop starting only ten feet away from the Starsprite's nose. No hint of this in Kyorin's memory of the landscape. Ten feet from a plunge to – she looked over the edge – the walls narrowed down to an impossibly deep death, as if Kaliban was an apple and someone had run a knife around its circumference in an attempt to cut it open. The floor of the ravine was filled with a stream of dark thrashing flesh. No accident of geography, then – she was looking at more of the Army of Shadows' slave machines. Mining worms.

Molly turned away from the foul sight, allowing herself a brief snatch of exhilaration. They had actually done it. All the times Molly Templar had written of explorers landing by airship on one of the moons, finding bizarre alien lands, and now she was actually following in her literary creations' footsteps. Molly looked around, drinking in the strange sights. No greens, no blues, everything tinted by the colour of blood, a wasteland of endless deserts. Her euphoria dwindled. How she wished one of her novels' clever, fast-thinking heroes or heroines were here instead of her. Jack Riot or Emma

Cochrane. Either of them would have been able to make a much better bid of their desperate last attempt to save the Jackelian people than her.

There was a thump behind Molly as Coppertracks and the commodore exited the craft. The steamman slipthinker's two wide caterpillar tracks made for an effortless passage across the fine sands.

Commodore Black peered over the edge of the ravine and shook his head in repugnance. 'Look on the canyon floor down there. Those are the black slug machines of the Army of Shadows, the same wicked things I saw infesting Quatérshift. Thousands of the foul creatures wriggling around down below like a river of terrible worms.'

'There's nothing left,' said Molly, sadly. 'They must be cutting new ravines like this all across the world, but they've sucked the place dry. No more minerals, no more gases and oils, no more deep-water aquifers. Kaliban really is dying.'

'We see before us how our world will look in a couple of thousand years,' said Coppertracks, 'if we fail to turn back the Army of Shadows.'

'Then we won't fail, Aliquot,' said the commodore. 'For even a Cassarabian tribesman would turn their nose up at this wicked empty heat-blasted land. It's certainly no place for any honest Jackelian.'

Duncan Connor swung out of the craft followed by the two shifties and Lord Rooksby, the latter strangely reluctant to examine the landscape for all of his protestations of the right to command their expedition.

'How does this compare to the deserts of Cassarabia?' Molly asked Duncan.

'The scale of things was a wee bit more humble in the caliphate,' noted the uplander. He was standing with his back to the canyon and staring towards the carving. The great face

275

of Kaliban rose out of the dunes, as high as a mountain that had been levelled straight by the hand of gods.

Interesting, thought Molly. You could only see the features of the face from above, but the angular rise of a thousand flat terraces, some as tall as Middlesteel's pneumatic towers, demonstrated that the carving was no freak of geology.

'An idol, sir, of the natives' gods,' said Lord Rooksby, dismissively.

Molly shook her head. 'Those terraces used to be hanging gardens, I think, and this desert a great forest. There hasn't been water to run through its sluices and waterfalls for many hundreds of years.'

So strange. Seeing all this for the first time, but not for the first time. Everything carried with it the strangest sense of déjà vu and it wasn't even hers.

'Pah, it shows very little sophistication,' said Lord Rooksby. 'Compared to the noble proportions of Jackelian architecture such a barbarous carbuncle only demonstrates the superiority of the race of man.'

'I disagree with your conclusions,' said Keyspierre. The Quatérshiftian handed his daughter a folding telescope that he had secured from the supply crates. 'It was clearly a high civilization, and that we stand here in the ruins of their world certainly does not bode well for our mission to uncover our invaders' supposed weaknesses.'

'The people must persevere,' said Jeanne, clasping her fist to her chest. No doubt one of the many sayings parroted by the children of the revolution.

'There is no other course,' agreed Keyspierre.

Molly indicated the carving's lee side, to the west. 'That's where the last great city of Kaliban lies. Half a day's walk from here.'

'Does it have a name?' asked Duncan.

Molly's head was throbbing more than ever with the weight of memories. 'Iskalajinn. Not that the locals speak it with their lips, only up here.' She tapped the side of her head. 'It is the Kal word for the end of all dreams.'

'Ah, lass,' said the commodore. ' I have no trouble speaking my mind, but I've never talked *with* my mind before. I'll happily paint my face blue, but the first time I talk with my thirsty lips I'll give the game away.'

'Blue face or no, you'd only ever pass for a Kal in the dark of night,' said Molly. 'You're far too tall and broad. You too, Duncan. There are no Kals with muscles like yours. You'll have to keep watch on the city from outside.'

'And I presume I would be correct in thinking there are no steammen on Kaliban, Molly softbody?' asked Coppertracks.

Molly shook her head, sadly. 'I don't think the Army of Shadows' masters trust the life metal. They prefer their slaves organic and pliable. You should stay here with the ship.'

Duncan shook his head. 'I'm the only one who knows how to survive in a desert, lassie, and there's a good reason why Cassarabians travel in caravans across the sands. It's how you stay alive. We go together. Me, the old steamer and the commodore will hole up outside the city. Close enough to come and get you if you're discovered.'

And that left the three people she least wanted to infiltrate the last stronghold of the Army of Shadows on Kaliban with. Rooksby and the two shifties, none of whom showed any inclination to trust the instincts she had inherited from Kyorin. She barely trusted them herself, thanks to the unforeseen canyon they had nearly tumbled into. But right now, the runaway slave's decaying ghost was all they had to keep the expedition alive in the heart of the enemy's fastness.

*　　*　　*

Of all of the expedition members, Molly quickly realized that Duncan Connor demonstrated the most proficiency at moving through the fine soft sands in the white robes that Molly had dredged from Kyorin's memories and had made up in Middlesteel. There seemed to be a knack to travelling across the sands in a steady way without letting your boots be sucked down – without making each step a struggle to withdraw the sole. But then, Connor of Cassarabia had surely gained enough practice during the years when he had earnt that moniker. He had told them the Cassarabian name for the fine, sapping dunes they were wading over; melah. One of at least fifty names the warring, fractious tribes he had held the southern frontier against possessed for sand. And Duncan's knowledge stretched to more practical purposes, too. Tying up the belts and laces of the undulating white robes was second nature to him, leaving mere strips of blue-dyed skin visible under their headscarves.

Only Coppertracks moved without the protection of the Kal sand-traveller's garb. But then there was no disguising his iron body, and his two wide caterpillar tracks seemed far better suited to skimming across the sands than the long legs of the race of man. Each hour of travelling brought the colossal carving closer, rising higher and higher above them until the sun rotating through the purple sky dropped the face's shadow across them. The last inhabited city of Kaliban had been positioned so that its streets would be sheltered in the carving's shade at the full height of the midday sun. Now they were given the same protection from the rays of the furnace heat.

'Perhaps I should have stayed with the ship,' said Coppertracks. 'My hull is too burnished. I glint in the daylight for any scout of the Army of Shadows to see.'

And Starsprite's pleas had been so intense and plaintive, begging for company – so soon after her abandonment by her

278

mother. But the young craft was as hidden as she could be and a great deal safer than any of the rest of them. They would be back, if they survived. Unless they convinced the Army of Shadows to build another cannon for them, the looking-glass gate stored inside Starsprite's hull was their sole way home.

As the expedition members moved towards the last city of the Kals, from time to time they would stumble over something partially hidden by the sands. An ancient reminder that Kaliban had been a very different place before its occupation by the Army of Shadows. It was in such a find that Molly left Coppertracks, Duncan and the commodore: a cracked-open dome, empty and half swamped by sand. But it would serve as shelter from the dust devils that whipped across the surface of the land, as well as the hunts of the slat patrols.

'Molly,' called Commodore Black. 'How long are we to leave you before we come looking for you?'

'We'll be back in two or three days at most,' said Molly. 'Stay here and mount a sentry. The slats prefer to patrol at night and Kyorin has memories of other things in the desert, experiments of the Army of Shadows' womb mages that have been released to exterminate the free Kal.'

Both Rooksby and the two shifties bridled at leaving behind their pistols from the supply crates, but Molly insisted. Kals did not own such things, nor would they have used them if they did. Nothing would give them away more quickly than if they were found carrying weapons.

The remaining four members of the expedition approached Iskalajinn at twilight, the sun setting behind the carving, revealing a glass-slag sprawl nestling against the rise of the face of Kaliban, low buildings spilling across the sea of dunes and then rising high on terraces set against the carving. The light of the furnace sky was slowly replaced by a green shimmer from the emerald geodesic domes of the Army of Shadows that rose on the far side of their slave city of tenements, thousands of hexagonal panels shining like insect eyes ripped from the skull of a mantis. Molly had a sense that the Kals were almost never allowed inside the comfort of the domes – and if they were, they were even more rarely ever seen again. But the thoughts bubbling out of Kyorin's memories suggested that he believed that there were gardens inside, running waters and a climate far more agreeable than the dire oven that their slaves laboured in. The Kals' whitewashed habitations were built of a quartz-like material, extracted by chemically processing the sand and moulded in blocks of narrow streets to protect against the sun, each dwelling topped by a long curved wind tower designed to funnel the slightest of winds down to the rooms inside and cool them.

'This is the great bastion of the Army of Shadows?' said Rooksby, his voice disbelieving, looking at the glitter of the overlapping domes. 'The slums of Whineside seen from the top of Tavistead Hill are a more imposing sight.'

'Oh, there were many more of them, once,' said Molly. 'But as the land's bounty has been exhausted, the Army of Shadows' numbers have been controlled down to what you see here.'

'There are enough of their spawn in Quatérshift,' said Jeanne, 'and they seemed plentiful enough to me as they overran our territory.'

Keyspierre glared at his daughter. 'You are coming close to voicing defeatist sentiments, compatriot daughter.'

'I saw the gnawed bones of our people outside Courau, compatriot father,' said Jeanne.

Keyspierre's face went red at the tone of insolence in her voice and for a moment Molly thought that he was going to strike her, but he obviously thought better of disciplining his daughter in front of them. 'Try remembering that when you see the faces of the monsters responsible for their deaths.'

'These Kals, sir, are cowards,' said Rooksby. 'With so few of the enemy's number left here, why have the natives not risen in revolt? If only we had the marines along that were meant to be here. Just a handful of them and we could have seized this pathetic hovel. Damn these Kals' eyes.'

'You'll be able to measure their bravery soon enough,' said Molly. 'If we can meet up with Kyorin's comrades.'

There was a location that burnt particularly bright in the jumbled buzz of memories that was Kyorin's legacy to her. Outside the walled city, a place where the slat soldiers rarely came. She found it easily by the presence of the seventy-foot high cacti, their leaf sails – vast moisture traps – slowly rotating. Taps had been drilled into them, but the queues of Kals had thinned out now that the previous day's collected water had slowed to a mere trickle through the plants' veins.

Molly led the four of them into the shadow of one of the emptied cacti and bade them wait cross-legged. It was ten minutes before one of the water-keepers left his plant to come over to them.

'Are you sand-born?' he asked using mind-speech. 'If the slats hear that nomads are travelling close to here and begging for water they will—'

'We are travellers,' said Molly. 'From afar.'

The water-keeper stepped back, gasping as he saw Molly's lips opening and closing to form the words.

'What did you say to him?' Rooksby demanded, watching the shocked water-keeper hustle back to his cactus and beckon his apprentices closer.

'You'll know soon enough.'

'What have you done, now, you foolish woman?' hissed

Rooksby. 'Is it not enough you had to drag us here without the soldiery to finish off the Army of Shadows . . .'

'We'll find out soon enough if Kyorin still has friends here among the oasis regulators,' said Molly.

'This is not how such things are done,' said Keyspierre.

'I bow to a Quatérshiftian's greater knowledge of how informers and the secret police work,' said Molly. 'But as I'm the only one here who can communicate in their language, we'll do this my way.'

Molly's way proved adequate, for when one of the water-keeper's assistants returned, it was with a female Kal, her face uncovered by the enveloping white headscarves the rest of them were wearing. She knelt before Molly and pressed the skin of Molly's forehead with her thumb. Molly felt a gentle tickle inside her skull, then the headache of Kyorin's memories rising. Molly winced in agony as the female Kal withdrew her thumb and rubbed it with her forefinger. There was a smudge of blue dye where the sweat of Molly's forehead had made the theatrical face paint moist.

'Clever,' said the woman. 'But do not bring your blue faces too close to any slats. They have very good nasal receptors and your scent is, I suspect, different enough from ours.'

'We are friends of the slave engineer Kyorin,' said Molly. Her head throbbed with pain. There was something about this female that was causing Kyorin's memories to thunder inside Molly.

'That much is clear. Why else would the residue of his soul burn hard inside you?' said the woman. 'And you use old speech. Keep your lips closed when we get inside the city. I shall do such communicating as may be required.' She looked at Rooksby and the two shifties and repeated her words in Jackelian.

'You understand us!' said Keyspierre.

The woman sighed, leading them away from the oasis and towards the city. 'It's quite unnerving seeing someone with blue skin speaking like a slat, all fangs and tongue and teeth. Yes, I understand Jackelian, Quatérshiftian and about a dozen more of your languages. One of my family received training for a position on the expeditionary force.'

'You are our compatriots, then,' said Jeanne. 'You are fighting the Army of Shadows.'

'We resist their aims,' said the Kal, bitterly. 'While also serving duty as their slaves and food source. I am not sure if the former outbalances the latter. It would have been better if one of the plagues that followed the loss of our medical technology had wiped us out entirely, then the masters would have starved to death before they ever reached your home.'

'Does your cell's revolutionary tradecraft allow us to know your name, compatriot?' asked Keyspierre.

'Why not? If I am caught with you we are all dead anyway,' said the Kal. 'My name is Laylaydin.'

'Are you taking us to meet the great sage?' said Molly. 'Kyorin said the sage has a way of defeating the Army of Shadows.'

Laylaydin shrugged. 'So it is said. But he does not live in the city. The nomads in the deeps of the desert wastes hide him. He would not survive for long here in Iskalajinn with the slats' nose for uncovering saboteurs and detecting resistance to their occupation. You shall be taken to a place of safety until we can send for one of the sand-born to take you to the great sage.'

Molly stopped as she noticed that the palm-like trees that had so far lined their path had given way to glass-slag crucifixes, the emaciated dead bodies of Kals hanging upside down from each cross.

'They were part of the resistance?' whispered Molly.

283

Laylaydin shook her head. 'No, look, their bodies do not bear the torture marks of interrogation. These are petty criminals. The ones on the left were caught teaching the young to read, while the ones hanging opposite were exposed indulging in a ritual sharing of ancestral memories using mind-to-mind contact. Technically neither crime carries the death sentence – that would be too wasteful of the Army of Shadows' dwindling food stocks – but you have to survive more than five days on the cross to be cut down. It is so hot now that it is very hard to survive five days.'

Rooksby looked as if he was about to gag at the sight. 'Damn you for sheep. How can you let the Army of Shadows treat you like this? You Kals might almost be part of the race of man, save for your cyan-coloured skin. Why do you not fight them?'

Laylaydin looked pityingly at the Lord Commercial, exposing her wrists from underneath her robes. There were two great ugly weals of flesh where the nails had been driven through them. 'I lasted the five days up there for birth crimes.'

Birth crimes. Molly rubbed her temple at the pain of the memory rising inside her. 'Your children . . .'

'They were fed to the slats as sweetmeats after they were found to have passed the threshold for powers of the mind. The masters require their cattle to breed true. My blood code carries a recessive pattern of how our race once existed, which is why they sterilized me when they cut me off the cross – so I could not have any more children quick of mind with the potential to be raised as sages. Our streets are ahead, please, you must walk in silence now.'

Molly and the others needed little encouragement to do so.

Travelling north along the cobbled country road with the woods on either side for cover, Purity was unnerved by how empty the landscape seemed to be. Where they passed through a village, the houses were abandoned, possessions tossed about in the yards, gates unlatched and banging in the breeze. It couldn't have been more than a week or two since the Army of Shadows invaded, but already nature was reclaiming the gardens. Weeds rising from in between paving stones, once manicured lawns overgrown, brown leaves lying curled and uncollected.

Occasionally they came across the corpse of a horse by the side of the road, the saddle removed and its rider fled. Ridden to death in an attempt to escape the advancing slats? The gates by the toll cottage were unmanned, the little wooden boxes where pennies were dropped for the upkeep of the roads rattling full and uncollected. The road that Purity and the four Bandits of the Marsh were currently following rose up a hill before twisting down into a long valley, its floor covered in a yellow-green mist.

Purity made to go down the valley path, but Jenny Blow laid a hand on her shoulder. 'No, that is no mist, it smells unnatural – a false odour to it.'

'What does your nose suggest?' asked Samuel Lancemaster, resting against his spear as if it were a lamppost.

'War gas,' replied Jenny Blow. 'A barbarian's weapon. Does the Army of Shadows possess such filth?'

Purity shook her head. 'I don't know – I didn't see the slats use gas when they attacked us at the Highhorn camp. But our redcoats do and the Royal Aerostatical Navy have gas shells in their fin-bomb racks.'

'There may have been a battle below,' said Ganby.

'I could run through the valley,' suggested Jackaby Mention. 'Fast enough that I wouldn't have to breathe it. Find out what lies below.'

'No,' said Purity. 'If that's dirt-gas it will burn your skin

285

off – and the Circle knows what the Army of Shadows is capable of producing.'

'Then I shall clear it away,' said Jenny Blow, taking a deep breath, her chest expanding to an unnaturally large size.

'Allow me,' said Purity, drawing out her maths-blade. 'You'll be gusting that back onto the Jackelian highway.' And she needed the practice.

Ganby nodded in approval and Purity held out the sword, pointing it towards the valley. She could feel the composition of the gas through the sword, heavy and complex, a name rising into her mind from the blade that meant nothing to her – *dichlorodiethyl sulphide*. But she could see the chain of bonds stretching out inside the cloud, ladders and ladders of particles, all connected. She felt the throb in her hand and visualized the bonds realigning, millions upon millions of them, reforming and changing their shape, becoming harm-less celgas – the rare substance that floated the hulls of the RAN's airships. Within seconds the newly transformed lighter-than-air cloud was rising, clearing the valley below and revealing a terrible sight.

'I am glad to see that our practice sessions are bearing fruit,' said Ganby.

Purity wasn't. She would have been better off leaving the valley shrouded. Bodies littered the road snaking through the valley, grey dots scattered across the way. Horses. People. Overturned carriages.

'A gas assault,' said Samuel Lancemaster in disgust. 'There is no honour in war fought by such methods.'

It was no better at close quarters, the figures below twisted into hideous shapes, white foam hanging out of their bloated lips. Everywhere there was a terrible garlic reek. These people were refugees by the look of them, carts and wheelbarrows piled with precious possessions. Not much to look at really

– mantelpiece clocks, a few prize gardening tools, bundles of clothes and – then Purity saw *her*. She stopped in shock. It was Emily from the Royal Breeding House, lying on the flatbed of an overturned cart, her eyes crying tears of dried blood and staring up sightlessly towards the cold autumnal sky. Purity bent over to look across at the other bodies. There were Flora and Edith from Dorm Five, the two young duchesses stretched out across the grass. More familiar faces sprawled along the side of the road.

'There are bodies in uniform up here!' called Jackaby Mention. 'Are these your soldiers?'

'Second Mounted Rifles,' said Purity, looking at the corpses. 'They were often assigned duty at the fortress.' She had nearly said home, but the Royal Breeding House hadn't been that, even when she had still been a prisoner of its halls. How many times had she wished a terrible death down on Emily's head for all of her torments? Egging the other royalist prisoners on to single Purity out for her madness and fits. But this . . . Parliament must have been evacuating the house's stock south, not wanting a repeat of the invasion by Quatérshift, when the shifties and their revolutionary allies in the kingdom had run half the old order through their steam-driven killing machines. Her mother. Her brother. It looked like the premium on the old royalist bloodlines was about to rise even higher. If the House of Guardians were left a land to reconvene over.

'There is something wrong here,' said Ganby.

'You always say that, old man,' said Jenny. 'Any excuse to run away.'

Ganby pointed to two bodies locked together. One was a redcoat of the Second Mounted Rifles, his face covered by a neckerchief to protect against the fumes before he had been overcome. His bayonet had been stuck through the chest of another soldier wearing a Jackelian uniform, but not from a regiment whose insignia Purity recognized. Save for the bayonet thrust, this soldier would have lived: his face was covered by a gas mask with brass goggles concealing his features.

'These travellers were attacked by their own soldiers,' said Ganby.

'There's no food,' noted Samuel Lancemaster. 'Any supplies these people carried have been looted. They were ambushed down here.'

Sweet Circle, had it really become so bad in the world outside Highhorn while Purity and her friends were constructing parliament's secret cannon? Soldiers fighting each other for supplies? Raiding refugees for their few paltry belongings. Where were the raiders' officers, had there been a mutiny in the ranks?

'Yes,' said Purity, 'it was our own troops. The slats would never have left good food on the bone like this.'

Jenny Blow tapped her nose and pointed to the left. Jackaby Mention became a blur, running up the side of the valley and disappearing into the woods. After a minute he returned, the smear of his form coalescing in front of them, wiping a frosting of ice from his dark aquiline nose. 'There was a camp up there, the remains of a fire pit still smouldering and a great many empty shell casings in the tree line.'

'They've gone,' said Samuel Lancemaster, thumping his spear angrily in the mud.

'We must focus on the Army of Shadows,' said Ganby. 'We have no time to track these killers. There will always be people easily driven to brigandage by brutal circumstances and a poor harvest. We did not wake to follow a queen again for the likes of them.'

'I would have a harvest of their skulls if I ever come across such cowards,' said Samuel. A shaft of sunlight glinted off his silver cuirass, becoming a sunburst.

Ganby saw how Purity was staring at the bodies of the dead breeding house inmates. 'Did you know them?'

'No. I thought I might know them, but in the end I never did,' said Purity. 'They were Jackelians, just Jackelians. Like me.'

The plan to capture a slat alive for interrogation sounded a lot more achievable when it was being discussed around a campfire with the Bandits of the Marsh. Now Purity was actually facing the prospect of having to entice one into chasing her, the sense of the plan was melting away in the harsh light of day.

Perhaps it was the shock of seeing Jackelians collaborating with the slats, whip-wielding overseers from the race of man lording it over the slaves. Broken Circle cultists who had finally achieved their exalted position at the feasting tables of the end times. That they had transferred their worship of the iron moon to veneration of the invaders who had come down from it was bad enough; but that the collaborators felt so little sympathy for the lines of slaves labouring under their whips – slaves who had been their neighbours and friends a little while ago – that was unforgivable. The Broken Circle cultists had the smug, self-satisfied look of gamblers who had backed the right bird in a cockfight, and the fact that the loser was left bleeding in the pit mattered not a jot to them. It was the same look she remembered from the staff at the Royal Breeding House, a look that Purity knew well enough to loathe.

The Kingdom of Jackals was being transformed into a nation-wide version of the Royal Breeding House – its occupants not raised as royalist songbirds, but kept as fattening farm animals and beasts of burden. A little piece of Purity had, ever so briefly, felt a touch of gladness that the Jackelian citizenry was finally getting a taste of the existence she and her ancestors had been sentenced to; but that unworthy feeling had been squashed when she'd seen the look of misery on the slaves' faces.

The Army of Shadows' vassals were chained to each other at the ankle with slippery grey cables that resembled snakes; the poor devils branded and struggling under the weight of hexagonal panels. Bringing the components back from the swathes of destruction being worked by the invaders' living factories to the ruins of Crosshampton where the slaves were erecting a new emerald-domed city.

Purity moved the leaves on a bush to get a better look at the slaves.

'How is it that I am to play the part of the bait?' Purity whispered to Jackaby Mention, 'when it is you who can run so fast?'

'I only have two speeds. I can walk or I can run,' said Jackaby. 'And when I run, the wind itself envies my heels.'

Purity stared out towards the slat they had singled out for capture, the beast standing guard over the line of Jackelians struggling past it. 'Precisely.'

'They would be made wary by both my age and my speed if it was I who had to give the hound a taste of the hare. Chasing a young female is something that should come naturally to them.'

'The overseers, perhaps,' said Purity. 'I'm not so sure about the slats.'

'We shall see,' said Jackaby.

Purity glanced back into the woods. She couldn't see Ganby, Samuel Lancemaster or Jenny Blow, but she hoped they were still hiding back there, waiting to incapacitate the slat. Purity rested her blade against a tree and turned round to say something to Jackaby, but he had already disappeared to warn the others that it was time.

Slipping past a thicket, Purity wandered out into the trail of flattened trees, took a couple of purposefully blundering steps into the open, and pretended to see the slat soldier guarding the chain gang for the first time. She followed her discovery up with what she hoped was a convincing scream. The slat's flat oblong head spun around with a hiss, the sound of her scream all it needed to home in on her presence.

Purity turned and pushed back through the thicket, ignoring the yells of the collaborators and warning shouts from the line of slaves. Grabbing at her sword, Purity ran as fast as she could. She could hear the crashing of the undergrowth behind her as the slat followed. She could feel the hunger inside its mind, such a craving to tear and feast on her flesh. More yells came from the human overseers further behind. They had decided to join the pursuit too, but they weren't a quarter as nimble as the slat, its claws ripping apart the undergrowth like a living machete.

At last, as agreed, there was a peculiar roaring sound: Jenny Blow's deadly voice stripping the bark off the trees like the rattle of a hundred woodpeckers at once. On the explosion of sound, Purity opened her bag of ground-down pepper grains and scattered them behind her, thwarting the slat's only other tracking sense. It hardly mattered, the deafening reports were blinding the beast and it crashed through the undergrowth to one side of Purity, its talons slashing angrily at the bush as if it was trying to silence the noise by slicing at the forest. It was concentrating on the source of this deafening irritation and Purity slid underneath a fallen trunk, gripping her sword securely in case the slat changed its mind. How long to wait before heading after the slat? She was about to step out when she heard someone else moving through the undergrowth. Peering out from behind the tree trunk she caught a glimpse of blue skin slipping through the trees. It was one of Kyorin's people, following the slat's trail. A male Kal. Had he used the diversion to slip his chains of bondage and come to try to save her? He was wearing a white robe wrapped around his body, his belt empty of tools.

'Over here,' whispered Purity.

The Kal looked around, his slim body slipping through the trees and raising a hand in greeting.

'Can you understand me?' asked Purity.

'Yes,' said the Kal, his mind-speech reaching across to her and his lips broadening into a smile.

'I was a friend of Kyorin, when he was alive,' said Purity. 'Did you know him?'

'I did,' said the Kal, advancing through the trees. 'We trained together. You say *when* he was alive. You saw him die?'

'A pack of slats killed him,' said Purity. 'They hunted him down. I tried to save him from the monsters but I couldn't.'

'Of course you couldn't,' said the Kal, moving in front of Purity. 'A slat warrior is bred only to slay and you are just a girl.' The Kal's smile opened wider and two massive fangs sprouted down from his upper jaw. 'A very juicy young girl, bloated with salty fresh blood.'

He leapt at her neck, trying to sink his fangs into Purity's flesh. She reacted on instinct – hers or Elizica's – and punched the Kal's stomach deep with her sword's buckler, winding the blue man and sending him stumbling back.

'You'll taste all the better, for that insolence, my sweet,' laughed the Kal, taken aback by Purity's attack but quickly recovering his composure. 'I'm going to drain every bit of your blood and leave your body a husk before I toss your marrow to my slats to feed on.'

'Taste this instead!' Purity waved the tip of the maths-blade threateningly in front of the Kal's chest.

He was looking for an opening and swaying like a cobra for another attack when there was a blur and a buffeting, the Kal carried back almost too fast to follow and slammed into a tree. There was a sickening thump as the Kal's body joined with the tree trunk and the blur materialized to a stop in front of her. Jackaby Mention crackling with frost. The Kal was dead. Nothing could have survived being slammed into an oak tree at that velocity.

Jackaby kicked the corpse, making sure the creature was slain. 'I thought you said that the blue skins were slaves taken by the Army of Shadows? That they were our allies?'

Purity stared at the corpse, horrified. So she had. How could she have been so wrong about Kyorin and his people?

CHAPTER THIRTEEN

I skalajinn before sunrise was a city made dark by the shadow of the colossal face, slag-glass houses dimly lit by green globes that hung off joists drilled into their rough crystalline walls. These ancient lanterns drank in the sun's rays during the furnace-like days and trickled it back out as a faint glow for as long as their energy stores lasted. Molly and her companions had waited a day already in one of the Kal safe houses, and this was the second they were spending in Iskalajinn.

Molly, Lord Rooksby and the two shifties were being led through the narrow streets in silence by their guide Laylaydin, along winding passages that ascended between the terraced houses as they climbed higher and higher, up the side of the great face of Kaliban. Had it been the Army of Shadows' idea to concentrate the last of the dying world's resources here, in the shadow of the wreck of the Kals' once great civilization? A reminder that the Kals' age had come, gone and been eclipsed by their all-powerful conquerors.

Molly was desperately aware that they would have to send word to her three friends hiding outside the city before too long. Before one of them attempted something rash and came looking for her. Molly didn't have another day to spend in this city, waiting for a guide to the great sage to be procured, ignoring the tedious complaints of Rooksby and the pair of Quatérshiftians. Molly's head throbbed harder and harder, it seemed, each hour. So many things that seemed familiar, firing off tiny flashes of agony as she tried to avoid recalling why they'd meant something to the runaway slave.

It hadn't helped that there had been nothing to do in their last safe house but watch the Kals who shared their slag-glass hideaway tending the bean-like things growing on terraces in the central courtyard, fed by a trickle of the water collected from the well each day. The Kals would take almost religious care in trimming the vines and bearing away their visitors' stool pots to empty as manure on the rock basins. A complex array of shutters allowed just the right amount of sun to slant through and warm the beans.

Molly was about to press Laylaydin as to why they were being moved between safe houses when the Kal woman stopped them and pointed down to a street on a lower terrace. A company of slats was moving along in two lines, the beasts at the head riding high in saddles on something that looked like a cross between an eagle and a giraffe, an impossibly long neck surmounted by a wickedly sharp beak. There weren't many Kals out in the bitterly cold hours of the early morning yet, but those that were threw themselves to their knees, not daring to look up at the convoy. Not daring to gaze upon the windowless silver-blue metallic capsule being borne through the streets by seventy naked Kals, keeping the capsule aloft at shoulder height on long ceramic poles.

'It is one of the masters,' whispered Laylaydin, indicating the glow of the hulking domes at the end of the city. 'They hardly ever venture out of their city, now.'

Molly thought of the tentacled, octopus-like monstrosities

she had seen in Kyorin's vision, plotting the invasion of her home. She shuddered. Was the master bobbing around in the comfort of the last of the world's water inside that capsule?

'You don't think the masters suspect we're inside Iskalajinn?'

'No,' said Laylaydin. 'That procession is heading out on the road to the travel fields. There are still a few deep-cast mines and facilities scattered across our land with resources not yet stripped.'

Travel fields. Molly looked at the sky, but there was no sign of the leathery globes that the Army of Shadows used instead of airships, ugly windowless spheres suspended under rapidly spinning metal blades.

'If they knew we were here, compatriot Templar,' said Keyspierre, 'we would be dead.'

'Or worse,' said Laylaydin. 'Yet you almost sound approving of their efficiency.'

Keyspierre shrugged. 'Efficiency is always to be admired, wherever it is found.'

Laylaydin snorted. 'Between them, the masters and their slat pets have gnawed the last of the meat from our land's bones. That is efficiency of a kind. But I pity it and I shall save my admiration for more worthy endeavours.'

'Well said, damson,' Lord Rooksby agreed. 'They are our enemy, Keyspierre, and it is the bones of our people back home they're busy devouring.'

'Quite,' said Keyspierre, looking knowingly at his daughter as they kept to the shadows of the empty street. 'And I have seen nothing since we arrived in this heat-blasted land fit to help us shake their seeming supremacy.'

'Kyorin thought otherwise,' said Molly.

'An escaped slave,' laughed Keyspierre. 'Who lacked even the means to return home save for the ingenuity of the Commonshare and our cannon.'

'Be quiet!' snapped Laylaydin. 'You don't know what you speak of.' Seeing that those she was leading were taken aback by the shattering of her usual serenity, she added, 'Kyorin was my life mate, an illegal union made outside of the masters' breeding laws. The slats took our children, and now he is gone from me too.'

Molly was nearly lost for words. 'I'm sorry.'

'In the normal course of things his last memories would have been shared with me,' said Laylaydin. 'For all of the masters' breeding strictures, they still have not managed to entirely eliminate our higher powers from the blood line.'

Molly bit her lip. No wonder she had detected a resentful edge to the way Laylaydin dealt with her. 'Kyorin died well in my land.'

'There are no good deaths,' said Laylaydin, 'only bad ones, only the release of our pain. My people's time here is nearly done.'

Laylaydin ushered them into the igloo-like entrance of one of the highest houses nestling against the great carving. Rooms had been blown like bubbles inside the slag-glass building, floors softened by the brightly patterned carpets Molly had seen female Kals weaving using threads stripped off their bean plants. At the end of the house one of the carpets hanging tapestry fashion across the wall was pulled back to reveal a tunnel. A passage burrowing into the great face of Kaliban. The rough-hewn excavation ran only a short way through the structure before joining a series of conduits that had perhaps, once, channelled water to the hanging gardens outside. A trail of fluorescent arrows was marked on the walls of the sluice system and the group followed the long-dry passages to the edge of a precipice. Steps led down to a vast chamber lit by hanging lamps, ancient pumping machines and water filtering equipment lying derelict around its edges.

Circular drain holes marked the walls of the chamber at head height, hundreds of dark pipes staring back at them. The floor of this cavern hidden inside the Face of Kaliban was dotted with Kals, some eating fruit at long tables formed by stone slabs, others reading, or sitting cross-legged in circles, humming and meditating.

'This is the heart of the resistance,' announced Laylaydin. 'Many of those here are criminals with slat destruction orders hanging over them. Some are deserters who refused to assist the slats with the invasion of your land. Others are merely sympathizers drawn to our aims.'

'This?' said Keyspierre, looking around the nearly silent empty space in derision. 'This is your revolution? Surely this is a joke – where are your sabres, your weapon smiths, your bomb makers? Where is the training in arms being conducted? The lessons in assassination?'

'We resist in our own way, not in yours.'

Keyspierre looked indignant. 'Please do not lecture me on the ways of revolution, compatriot. Before the tyranny of the Sun King was swept away by the forces of our glorious commonshare, I survived two years on the run from the king's secret police as a Carlist subversive. This, compatriot, is not how you cut off the oppressor's hand.'

'Nor do you defeat your masters by becoming them,' retorted Laylaydin. 'Our land was very different from yours before the occupation and the coming of the masters. We had few meat eaters in the geographic record of our world. The pattern of our ecos was based on a vast network of elaborate cooperating systems that straddled the land. We had no word for violence, none for murder or crime.'

'The perfect commonshare,' said Jeanne in reverence.

'And its end the perfect tragedy,' said Keyspierre. 'But you have since been taught the concept of cruelty well enough from the Army of Shadows. We travelled here to find allies, not sheep willing to step meekly up to the farmer's knife.'

'You came because of the rumours that the great sage has a way of defeating the masters,' said Laylaydin. 'But first we would know that you are fit to receive it.' Laylaydin indicated the largest of the circles of sitting natives to Molly. 'Your friends' weak minds could not survive our sharing, but your mind is different, Molly Templar.'

'I have machines in my blood,' said Molly, sitting down in a place that had been made for her. 'I was an operator of the Hexmachina, the last of my land's god-machines.'

'It is said that our own veins once bubbled with such machine-life,' said Laylaydin. 'But the masters feared our longevity, quick minds and the other abilities our machines gave us, and burnt all traces of the life metal from our bodies. We are mere shadows of our ancestors now, cripples bred into cattle to sate the appetites of the masters' slat armies.'

'But you can still share memories with each other.'

'Yes, but we end up nailed to the cross when we are caught doing this,' said Laylaydin.

'Or worse,' added Molly.

The skin of the Kal next to her had been darkened to near indigo by the sun and he still wore his dusty desert robes bound tight. 'You speak lightly of such things.'

'As lightly as a nomad walks across the dunes.'

'Perceptive, too,' said the Kal. 'Well met. Yes, I am your guide. My name is Sandwalker. I have come out of the salt flats and would suffer the fate of all free Kals if I was discovered inside the last city.'

'Your accent is different from Laylaydin's.'

The Kal wiped his hand on his white pantaloon-like trousers before taking Molly's. 'I only shared the learning of your

299

tongue this morning. Your words still come hard for me. I will grow fluent as I practise more.'

Molly started. Since this morning! She had already received an inkling of what it was like to be part of a network of living minds from Kyorin, but here was the example made flesh. What miracles had the Kal civilization accomplished during its heyday? How far had they fallen to end up here, mere farm animals and slaves?

Laylaydin sat down in the group, and with the circle of hands complete, Molly felt the pain she associated with Kyorin's memories abating, subsiding to such an extent that it was only now that she realized the dead slave's gift to her had become a constant dull throb within her. Memories began flashing past. Drawn out of her like grubs pulled from an apple with a set of tweezers. Kyorin on a dock in Middlesteel, leaping into a river with slat hunters firing darts at him, running sodden through the cold streets, communicating with Timlar Preston inside the cells of the Court of the Air, being helped by Purity Drake. On the run together with the young royalist. Then the images accelerated faster still, Molly's own recollections this time. Flashes of the Hexmachina, the war she had once fought against the demon revolutionaries so many years ago, the cannon construction at Highhorn and her three friends waiting for her in the ruins outside Iskalajinn.

Molly caught only brief glimpses of the minds of the others sitting in the circle as they probed her memories. Why were the Kals being so careful not to show her their own histories and pasts?

'Enough,' said Laylaydin, releasing the hands of the two Kals sitting to either side of her. 'Oh, my Kyorin, all that way for this.'

'What is it?' said Molly. 'There's something you're not telling me. Why weren't you sharing your thoughts with me? What have you got to hide?'

'To put it simply, your mind is already full,' said Laylaydin. 'Kyorin gambled that your symbiote machinery would be able to handle the weight of all his memories driven into you so fast, but I fear your mind is not as sophisticated or evolved as ours. Have you been experiencing headaches?'

'I—' Molly considered lying, but what would be the point? 'I have.'

'The machines inside your body are concentrating around your brain, trying to cope with the weight of his knowledge. But they are burning up under the strain. Your mind is cooking inside your skull, Molly Templar, caught in a vicious circle. The more machines die in your blood the fewer there are to carry the load and the faster those remaining burn up. I am so sorry, but my life-mate filled you with his soul and the vessel of your body is too weak to be able to carry it.'

'Take the memories out of me,' Molly struggled to keep her voice calm. 'Your damn husband put them in, you can take them out of me.'

'We eased your pain as much as were able when we were joined, but such cleansing is merely a balm on your wounds. We are unable to clear you of the remains of Kyorin's soul.'

'*We* are unable,' said Sandwalker. 'But there is one who can help you. The great sage is not like us; he is what our people once were before the occupation. He could unentangle the pathways of the mind of even someone as strange as you who have travelled so far to stand by our cause.'

Rooksby and the two shifties were staring at Molly with horror, as if her condition might be contagious. She had to bite back an insult. 'We were going to see the great sage anyway. Now we have two reasons to go.'

'You must stay here, compatriot,' insisted Keyspierre. 'Let

301

our Kal compatriots care for you while we travel to seek the weapon and your cure. Are we to travel through the desert bearing you on a stretcher? Your presence will only hinder the prospects of the expedition succeeding.'

'Not a chance,' snapped Molly. 'I'm going with you.'

There was a rise of excited voices at the far side of the chamber.

'Tallyle! You're alive,' said Laylaydin, spotting the Kal who was walking down the steps to the chamber. 'We heard that all of the engineers working at Processing Ten were fed to the slats when the station was decommissioned.'

'Not all of us,' said the Kal, shaking hands with the other natives eagerly pressing in around him.

'This is our leader,' said Laylaydin, proudly. 'The infiltration of the Jackelian scouting force was his plan.'

'And the allies we hoped for have arrived just in time,' said the Kal.

'In time for what?' asked Molly.

'Why, to feed my hunger,' replied the Kal, a pair of deadly pearl-white fangs sprouting from his jaw, his tongue whipping out obscenely to lick at his lips.

Purity came to the clearing where the Bandits of the Marsh were holding the captured slat just in time. Hanging in the air like a conjuring trick while Ganby stood by muttering a spell, the captured slat was watching Samuel Lancemaster heat the edge of his spear inside a fire. A blaze that Jenny Blow was encouraging to iron-foundry heat with her breath.

'What are you doing?' demanded Purity.

'We have our prisoner,' said Samuel. 'Now we are going to begin our interrogation.'

Purity looked at the spear tip glowing orange in the fire. 'You can't do that.'

Ganby reached out to tap the hard black chest of the slat. 'This bone armour doesn't stretch all the way around its body. These slat creatures are like craynarbians, the joints of the legs, arms and neck have soft areas to allow their limbs to bend.'

'We might have grabbed the wrong creature,' said Jackaby, appearing behind Purity in the clearing. 'The blue men aren't the slaves we believed. One of them attacked the young queen, sporting a set of fangs that makes a lie of their fruit-grazing diet, unless they have apples in their land that fight back like bears.'

'Now that is interesting,' said Ganby. 'From chattel to soldier with one small lie uncovered. Clever, like the gill-necks when they invaded. How many stories did we hear about them which turned out to be lies they had spread to sow confusion among the tribes? But it makes getting the truth out of this one all the more imperative.'

'You can't torture the slat,' said Purity. 'It's our prisoner, you can't treat it like—'

'Like it would treat us if our positions were reversed?' said Ganby. 'Nobody has a taste for this, but it is necessary. You should go if you find it unpleasant.' He turned to the prisoner. 'Now, my friend, Jenny Blow heard you giving orders to our people in our tongue, so I know you can understand what I am saying to you.'

All the Bandit of the Marsh got for his trouble was a stream of guttural chattering from the slat's fang-encrusted mouth, the same language Purity had heard in Molly's bedroom from Kyorin's killer.

Samuel withdrew his burning-hot spear from the fire. 'Let me help you remember our language, beast.'

'No!' Purity stepped forward, drawing her sword and holding it above the hovering slat like a divining rod.

'You do not yet possess the skill to use your maths-blade for such a subtle task,' said Ganby.

'Less subtle than a burning spear?' Purity ignored the druid's words and felt her blade flutter above the slat, drawing in the essence of the creature, revealing it for what it was. 'So young,' gasped Purity.

The blade drew in information from the creature's cells, memories imprinted at a primeval level in the thing's brain. The slat was barely two years old – so short a life. Their kind only lived up to five years old. Everything was instinct: its drive, its hunger, its anger, its loyalty, its knowledge – weapons, fighting, obeying – all burnt into it as reflex, the slat fashioned as artfully and intentionally as the edge of a bayonet. Cast not in steel, but in flesh. A living weapon gestated inside a tank alongside thousands of its brethren. The sword probed down the slat's body. No gender, no reproductive organs, just pea-sized hollows where the seed of such things lay suppressed and wizened. This was hardly a creature at all, just a mutilated piece of artificial flesh given a spark of life and set loose to be thrown upon the sabres and rifle fire of the Army of Shadows' enemies.

Purity felt a terrible pity for it, mixed with contempt for the creators of such a thing – that its masters could warp the sanctity of life to such an aim.

'Good,' said Ganby, watching waves of light twisting out from Purity's sword. 'Now the mind. Where are the slats concentrated, what are their armies' weaknesses?'

Purity ran the blade up to the slat's eyeless skull. Had the old goat arranged the slat's torture to goad her into using the sword like this? Just another lesson from the sly druid. Purity's sword began to pulse, shifting its power to match the complex patterns stamped across the slat's mind, picking at the memories that went beyond mere instinct. A dark chamber, the slat using its throat to bounce noise off thousands of its brothers, practising claw strikes against granite posts, seeing the world in reflections of sound. Darkness and light the same. Barely two days old. Feeding, fighting. But weakness? Where were their armies' weaknesses here in Jackals? Finally she saw what she was searching for, the blade blazing with the information it had extracted, turning the possibilities and modelling them, showing Purity a potential way to victory. Could it be possible?

But just the *chance* of it.

There was still the matter of Kyorin and the nature of his people. Purity began to probe for answers but the slat had realized what she was doing, felt its mind being opened, and began to howl in terror. Purity felt the impulse in its skull before she realized what it was. Another reflex, buried deep, and made as fundamental as the instinct to breathe. The twin poison sacs that fed its fangs with a viper-deadly bite exploded inside its throat, poison coursing back through its veins towards the twin heart chambers thumping within its chest.

The slat's body, still suspended in the air, flexed briefly then fell still: with its last breath it hissed *slat, slat,* and started reeling off a line of numbers before it fell to silence. Purity's sword dug out the numbers' meaning from the creature's dying mind. The numbers were its name, allocated at birth as its wet, dripping flesh slid out of an open tube. The slats believed that repeating them at death would admit them to the warriors' afterlife. So simple, so brutally short-lived, but they had still developed a culture passed on in secret throat-clicks – a piece of existence discrete from the all-encompassing control of their masters.

Ganby sensed the expiration of life in the beast and let its body drop to the grass of the clearing. 'Suicide. It killed itself rather than tell us anything.'

'No, it wanted to live,' said Purity, sadly. 'Its own body turned against it.'

Samuel Lancemaster brandished his spear angrily. 'My way would have—'

'Ended the same way,' said Ganby. 'Probably a lot faster too. The slat only realized what Purity was doing to it when she touched its mind. It would have suicided as soon as you tortured its flesh.'

'By the tail of Old Mother Corn,' swore Jenny Blow. 'What is that foul stench?'

Purity pointed down to the slat. 'The same thing happened to the ones that attacked us at Tock House. Coppertracks told me their blood becomes acidic after death, melting their organs and making a post mortem impossible.'

Ganby rolled the decomposing corpse out of the clearing. 'The Army of Shadows doesn't want anyone to gain the knowledge of how their pets are created.'

Purity wrinkled her nose in disgust at the idea as much as the smell. Surely there wasn't a womb mage or worldsinger on the continent who would want to create such a monstrosity as a slat, not even in Cassarabia? 'I don't care how the slats are created, because now I know where the Army of Shadows' weak spot is, where the slats are massed. Where they fear attack!'

The Bandits of the Marsh looked at her, and only the crackle of the fire Jenny Blow had raised sounded inside the clearing.

'There,' said Purity, pointing to the iron moon, a pale red disc in the afternoon sky. 'That's where the Army of Shadows' masters are. Waiting for their new cities to be built and their slat armies to crush the fight out of the last of us before they take permanent residence down here.'

'You want us to destroy an entire moon?' said Jackaby Mention in disbelief. 'Had this beast been up there?'

'I don't think so,' said Purity. 'I only got a brief flash of its memories of the north before it died, but I think it was a guard on their lifting room. The slats have many legions protecting their cable up to the iron moon.'

'My feet have carried me far,' said Jackaby. 'But never as far as a moon. Jenny Blow's breath cannot reach it, nor Samuel's spear, nor even the spells of a cowardly old druid.'

'But I have this sword, and I think it's sharp enough to cut the stake lines that anchor the iron moon to our world,' said Purity. 'You wanted to know how to hurt them: breaking their cable will do that. Now the iron moon is joined to our land, their cable is incredibly taut. Cut the cable and it will whiplash back with all the force of the turning of our world, slice the masters' fortress into pieces and spill the Army of Shadows into the night.'

'A beanstalk,' laughed Ganby. 'Take an axe to the beanstalk and the giant comes tumbling down.'

CHAPTER FOURTEEN

Molly watched in horror as the leader of the Kal's revolution pulled Laylaydin to him and sank his newly appeared fangs into her neck, holding the woman tight as she collapsed, the skin around Laylaydin's neck throbbing as he sucked the blood out of her body at a staggeringly fast rate. Molly's spell of paralysis was punctured by the screams of the other natives in the chamber, scattering as a line of slats burst in through the main tunnel entrance, cutting apart the running Kals with bolts from their rifles. The blue-faced Kals nearest the door were dragged to the floor by leaping soldiers and torn apart. Molly was desperately trying to find the other members of her expedition amidst the confusion; she thought she saw the fleeing form of Lord Rooksby hitting the floor as a slat rifle-butt clubbed him from behind. But where were the two shifties? Then a passing bolt of fire skimmed past her eyes and she lost her vision to an explosion of fierce light and a blaze of dots. Molly stumbled, trying to rub the explosion of tears out of her eyes, flinching as a hand grabbed hers.

'This way!' It was the voice of Sandwalker, the nomad Kal,

dragging her through the screams and the crackling sound of the slats' discharging rifles.

'I can't see!' Molly shouted, nearly tripping over something soft and fleshy on the floor.

'Duck your head,' warned Sandwalker, the weight of his fingers forcing her head down. 'Keep going, the floor is flat.' His voice was echoing – it sounded as if they had entered one of the water pipes in the cavern's walls.

'What was—?'

'No talking,' snapped Sandwalker in his mind-voice. 'Slats hunt by sound and these tunnels carry noise far. Hold my hand, stop when I stop, go when I go.'

Molly ran with the nomad as fast as she could, trying to keep the sound of her panting low and controlled. Sometimes they climbed up what felt like small slanting passages. There was no sound of pursuit behind them that Molly could hear, but she flinched at a hissing noise. A peppery scent filled the corridor.

'Something to destroy their sense of smell if they track us this far,' said the nomad's mind-voice.

After running for what seemed like hours Molly found her sight coming slowly back to her, although it was hard to tell in the dark of the sluice system; she could just see a lantern in Sandwalker's hand, something that looked like a round flat black stone throwing out a strong beam of yellow light straight ahead. The face of Kaliban was large enough to contain thousands of miles of these tunnel systems. How did the nomad know which way to turn? She tried to search her inherited memories but the stab of pain that came back was like a knife slicing across her skull. Damn Kyorin's memories overheating her brain, it seemed they were going to kill her slowly even if the slats and their fang-mouthed friends among the Kal didn't finish her off sooner.

As her vision returned properly Molly started to panic, the weight of the walls crushing in on her. Her hands were trembling, her heart thumping with the feeling of being buried underneath hundreds of miles of stone.

Sandwalker stopped. 'We can talk now. Any slats who came after us will be lost miles behind. Are you sick?'

'I don't like enclosed spaces,' said Molly. She had been a stack cleaner in her poorhouse days, forced into the tight spaces of Middlesteel's pneumatic towers; and the tunnels of this carving were far too similar to the conditions she had endured then.

The nomad laid a hand on Molly's forehead and shut his own eyes. She could feel the weight lifting, clearing – the shuddering of claustrophobia along her body abating as the Kal pushed into her mind.

'You will last until we get outside. This fear lives very deep within you and it would be dangerous to remove it entirely. Let me see your face.'

'That hurts.' Molly winced as the Kal gazed into her left eye, staring at her iris from different angles. Then the right eye.

'Blast blindness, mild. You are lucky. If the rifle shot had been nearer it would have boiled both your eyes inside their sockets.'

'Are you a doctor, too?'

'No, I am a stupid, ignorant sand-born primitive with the dust of the desert still fresh on my trousers.'

Molly ignored the caustic remark. 'With fangs or without? I was under the impression your people were plant eaters.'

'You mean Tallyle back there? As you saw, he is not one of us anymore. Search your Kal memories for being made a gift of *the hunger*.'

Molly tried, but the pain was too great and she had to

stop. Nothing was returned by the part of her mind that was Kyorin.

Sandwalker saw the pain she was in and shook his head as if she had failed a test. 'Poor fool; Tallyle must have let the slats take him alive. The masters have turned him into a carnivore. He survives on blood now. The masters corrupted his body inside their machines, as a warning and a punishment and a source of ironic amusement. He now follows only his endless appetites in their service.'

Molly didn't need to hear the disgust in his voice to know that there could be nothing worse to the gentle herbivores.

'The Army of Shadows sees it as an improvement, no doubt,' said Sandwalker. 'And for the masters it is the easiest way to turn a select few of our people into eager collaborators. Nothing wasted, you see. The masters drink our souls – our very life essence. Then those of us they have given the hunger drain our blood. Finally the slats feast on the meat and bones that are left. A little something for everyone in the cruel pyramid of life they have shaped, with us crushed at the bottom as their cattle.'

Molly listened to his words in horror. And now the Army of Shadows' masters had new acres to farm, herds that had yet to be depleted. Her entire nation, and the rest of the continent.

The Kal indicated a ladder inside a pipe positioned above their heads.

'We're still going upwards?' asked Molly. 'We've been travelling through these garden sluices for hours.'

'Garden sluices?' Sandwalker snorted. 'The gardens on the walls outside needed only a fraction of the water that would have come through here. Don't you know what the face of Kaliban was?'

Molly shook her head.

311

'A power mill, once. The greatest on Kaliban, fed with water for fuel and harnessing the very power of the sun itself.'

'A giant steam engine.'

'Of a sort,' said the nomad. 'Our people have forgotten so much. A whole population murdered and farmed and controlled down to the few that live in the last city now.'

'But you remember in the desert?'

'A little more than is safe for us,' said the Kal. 'Which is why it suits us to be looked down on as ignorant root-grubbers by the city-born. We free Kal are usually as stingy in our sharing with our kind in the last city as they were with you. The city-born are infiltrated too easily by those who have been twisted against us by the masters' hunger.'

'And you really have a weapon to defeat the Army of Shadows?'

Sandwalker nodded. 'So it is said.'

'One that you haven't used yourself.'

'It is how I became a servant of the great sage. I travelled to seek him out as a boy, to beg him to give the weapon to me, so that I might use it.'

'He didn't give it to you?'

'He only told me it would not help us,' said Sandwalker.

'You do not defeat your enemy by becoming him,' Molly repeated the words of Kyorin's wife. 'But if your people are pacifists, would you have been able to use the weapon if the great sage had given it to you?'

'I once slit the belly of one of the masters' twisted abominations crawling through the desert towards me at night to feed on my body,' said Sandwalker. 'I do not think it so different. A matter of scale, perhaps.'

'Maybe there's hope for your people yet,' said Molly.

'I fear otherwise,' said Sandwalker. 'Else the masters' blood would be on my hands, and your help would not be needed.'

312

Her hands. Molly focused her blurred vision on her fingers. She had been the guardian of Jackals, once, the last symbiote operator of the Hexmachina; had wielded the power to cast down gods. But the Army of Shadows had entombed the Hexmachina inside the heart of the world as easily as a butterfly collector pushing a prize specimen into an empty matchbox. What weapon could the Kals possibly possess to stand against such a force? How terrible would it have to be that they had never used it? And how monstrous did they think the race of man was to actually unleash such a horror against the Army of Shadows?

After a further hour of travelling, Sandwalker stopped by a wall. The surface looked featureless enough to Molly, but Sandwalker placed his fingers on it and there was a click, followed by a section of the wall sliding into the ceiling. A dark shaft lay on the other side of the opening, squares of light activating as Molly stuck her head through, a long line of luminescence, smaller and smaller down towards a vanishing point. Craning her neck around, she saw the lights stretched away into the darkness above her, too. The shaft must extend from the very foot of the carving to its top. Molly took some convincing to step out into the air at Sandwalker's urging, but she finally acquiesced after he used his torch to demonstrate how the flow of gravity's polarity had been reversed inside the vent, the shaft serving as a lifting room. It was the oddest sensation, floating upwards, every sense in her body crying out that she shouldn't be falling heavenwards, quite unlike the weightlessness she had briefly experienced inside Lord Starhome – and that had been bad enough.

Odder still was the sight that greeted her when she stepped out of the door at the top of the shaft. Not the fact that they were standing under the beating sun on the rim of the face of Kaliban's mouth – a dark chasm, which Sandwalker told

313

her, had once expelled water vapours as the giant power source's sole pollution – but the shape of the creature that was waiting for them. Taller than Molly by a couple of heads, green scales shining in the light, two massive wings wrapped around it like a cloak to shade it from the heat. It was a *lash-lite*, or something as near identical to the people of the wind that made their nests in the Kingdom of Jackals' mountains as to make no difference.

'This is Baxcyteen,' introduced Sandwalker. 'His people work with us against the masters.'

'The few of us who are left,' said the creature, its eagle-like beak opening, the feathery scales of its muscled neck quivering in the heat. 'The slats still visit the mountains to burn our villages where we have not concealed our caves well enough.'

Even the whistling accent in his speech put Molly in mind of the lashlites. Her novels often featured races similar to the race of man being discovered on one of their moons, so perhaps she shouldn't have been so surprised to discover that the pattern of her world's other species might also be repeated on other celestial spheres.

'I shall not keep you from your home for much longer, brother of the wind,' said Sandwalker. 'Can you bear the two of us down to the dunes outside the city?'

'I flew you up here,' said Baxcyteen, 'and two will not be so bad for the glide back down. But we must be quick, for if gravity is on our side for the journey down to the sands, it is our only ally. The slats have been passing overheard in their flight balls. I think they suspect free Kal are abroad in the salt wastes.'

'They have good reason to, my friend. We were betrayed in the city. Another of our people has been given the hunger and many of the resistance lie dead behind us.'

Baxcyteen hissed in frustration. 'They seek you, Sandwalker, and they would burn my wings from me for helping you. Come.'

Taking each of them under one of his arms, the lashlite waited for his passengers to grip on tight, then unfurled his massive wings and ran forward until he found a strong enough thermal, beating up into it and rising above the face of Kaliban. They were riding heavy with their combined weight, even Molly could tell that. She kept her eyes shut for most of the flight down, only the churning inside her gut indicating the means of their escape. They were still in the shadow of the carving's chin when the three of them put down on the gloriously soft and safe sands. Molly steadied her beating heart while Sandwalker unfurled two pieces of diaphanous white silk-like material from a pouch around his waist and helped the lashlite fix the cloth to his wings. 'A present from the free tribes of the south, traded through our friends in the city, Baxcyteen. I would have accepted a little more if I knew they were going to be betrayed and the exchange shut down.'

'A good present,' said the lashslite. 'A fair trade for your life this day. Your people in the south are canny.'

As the sun struck the material it began to turn orange, the same colour as the sands, matching the ground perfectly. Even standing a foot away, Molly could barely see the creature.

'My tent is also made from memory silk,' said Sandwalker, seeing how she was staring at the lashlite. 'It is a meta-material. The silk also bends sound around itself, so the slats cannot see it, and matches the heat of its surroundings so the twisted creatures in the desert cannot hunt us through our body warmth.'

Sandwalker waved to the lashlite as the lizard-man took a

run down the dunes, and threw himself up into the air. A brief shimmer of his memory silks then Molly's rescuer vanished out of sight.

'I was rather hoping your friend might be able to whistle up some of his flight and fly us all out of here,' said Molly.

'We do not know where his villages are, just as he does not know where the great sage hides. Our two people meet at barter points scattered throughout Kaliban, and hope our rendezvous are not betrayed while we wait.'

'The slats want the great sage so badly?'

'You have no idea,' said Sandwalker, wrapping a turban above his blue-skinned forehead. 'My tribe's sage is called Fayris Fastmind and he is as our people once were. The masters fear him as if he were a plague that would make an end of them. There were many sages once, but over the centuries our secret holds in the wastelands have been betrayed and uncovered. We have so few of them left now. Fayris Fastmind may be the last of his kind, and he is certainly the most powerful. I think the masters suspect that he has the power to destroy them and if the Army of Shadows has one defining trait, it is that they cannot bear to suffer that which they cannot control. Even the wastes left by their uncontrolled appetites have been infected by their twisted spawn to exterminate the few Kal that live free and evade the slat hunts.'

One of Kyorin's memories of the creatures haunting the outskirts of Iskalajinn surfaced unbidden and Molly stumbled, nearly fainting with the pain of it.

'I fear for you, Molly of the Jackelians,' said Sandwalker, helping her to her feet. 'Your second soul is growing too heavy for you. We should find the others in your party and leave here at once.'

*   *   *

'Ah, lass,' cried the commodore, seeing Molly peering over the broken fabric of his half-buried dome. 'I was about to go out searching for you, so long have you been gone.'

The commodore and the others were not alone in the dome. Coppertracks and Duncan Connor stood behind the corpse of a vast blue snake-like thing – its circumference wider than an oak tree. The creature was lifeless, a sabre driven through the middle of its three eyes, multiple whip-like tongues lolling across the dome's floor.

'Lucky you did not come back last night, though, when this terrible beast came slithering out of the dark with a taste for my mortal legs in its wicked sharp mouth. But it met its match when it tried to add brave old Blacky to its diet.'

Duncan coughed.

'Well, with a little help from our ex-officer of the rocket corps, here. I see you've brought our guide at last, but where is that rascal Lord Rooksby?'

'I'm afraid things didn't go well in the city,' said Molly. 'He's as likely dead, along with Keyspierre and his daughter.'

'Surely not, Molly softbody,' said Coppertracks, the steamman's iron hand gesturing behind Molly and Sandwalker. 'Unless *they* are a mirage.'

Molly whirled around. It was the two shifties, Jeanne and Paul-Loup Keyspierre following the trail out of Iskalajinn together.

'Stop them!' Sandwalker pushed Molly to safety behind the commodore. 'They may have been twisted by the masters and turned against us. They may walk with the hunger inside them.'

Commodore Black drew his pistol, breaking the gun and feeding a charge into its breech. 'That does not sound too good, my blue-skinned friend.'

'How can we be sure?' Molly whispered.

'One of us must risk their life by getting close enough to check.'

Molly was about to say that she would do it, but the nomad was already off. Sandwalker ran up the dunes towards the two shifties. The expedition desperately needed the nomad alive, or all of them would be doomed to wander the desert aimlessly until the slats finally hunted them down. Sandwalker stopped in front of the pair and after a brief heated conversation, Jeanne and Keyspierre opened their mouths and allowed the nomad to inspect inside their jaws for newly grown fangs.

'What is going on, lassie?' asked Duncan. He had drawn his pistol, moving to stand beside Commodore Black and the steamman.

'The Army of Shadows has a little trick to commission you inside its ranks,' said Molly. 'It involves turning you into a monster with a taste for drinking blood.'

Keyspierre and his daughter obviously passed Sandwalker's inspection as he waved to Molly and her friends and then led them down the dune towards the ruined dome. Predictably, the two shifties were not happy.

'Are we also to be given a turn to test you for the mark of the enemy?' Keyspierre spat.

Molly opened her mouth and stuck her tongue out at the scientist. 'Test to your heart's content. How did you two get away from the Kals' hideaway?'

'In much the same way as you, compatriot, I would imagine,' said Jeanne. 'We ran for our lives when the Army of Shadows broke into the resistance base. We ducked down a tunnel that eventually led to another of the Kals' safe houses. The so-called revolutionary that lived there couldn't understand a word of what we had to say, but he knew we were trouble with more following us. He packed us off with these bags of supplies and led us to the edge of the city.'

'He gave us this, too.' Keyspierre produced a red hexagon

made of what looked like gutta-percha with interlocking triangles moulded on its surface.

'It is the harvest mark,' said Sandwalker. 'The Kal you met has been chosen in the lottery to feed the slats and the masters at the next cull, and – I am ashamed to say – to feed our own people who have been given the hunger. It is the city-born's tradition to pass the token to a friend the day before they are taken, to remind us why we resist the occupation.'

'Did you see what happened to Rooksby?' Molly asked.

'Your aristocrat friend was captured,' said Keyspierre. 'I saw him clubbed down and dragged off struggling by slat soldiers before we escaped down the tunnel.'

Sandwalker was not happy with that news. 'He is alive and he knows you are waiting here? Your friend's blue skin-dye won't fool the interrogators for a minute. They will give him all their attention when they realize he is not a Kal. Every slat on Kaliban will be combing the land around here soon, looking for interlopers from the race of man. Pack your supplies now.'

'You will still help us?' asked Molly, trying not to sound as if she was pleading.

'It is very dangerous,' said the Kal. 'But the stakes are high. I will take you to where I think the great sage is hiding, but if the slats look to be following us . . . you understand I cannot risk the great sage's capture. I will flee and you will have to make your own way through the wastes as best you can.'

'Where you *think* he is hiding?' said Molly. 'I thought you were the great sage's servant. In the name of the Circle, when did you last see him?'

'Three years ago,' said Sandwalker. 'Even that much contact with him is dangerous. The great sage normally changes his lair every few years, but if another member of my tribe tells him of Laylaydin's death and the hunger being given to Tallyle

319

before we arrive, he will move immediately as a matter of precaution. You were present at the fall of the largest resistance cell in Iskalajinn.'

'Then we must go now,' insisted Keyspierre. 'The survival of everyone in the Commonshare and the Kingdom of Jackals rests with your leader.'

Sandwalker drew a diagram in the sand with his finger. 'This is where we are.' He scratched a circle around their position. 'This will be the circumference of the slats' initial search and sweep. We must move beyond this area and push into the deep desert far faster than they anticipate. After that, my sand craft will protect us from whatever slat patrols are scattered more widely. But there is only one way to travel so rapidly and it is particularly dangerous.'

Molly's skull began throbbing, the meaning of the nomad's suggestion filtering up through Kyorin's memories.

'We must ride the canals,' said Sandwalker.

The canals of Kaliban. How many of them would survive the canals?

There was a brief flurry of sand as the leathery globe touched down, bone-like legs extending from holes and lending the craft an insectoid look as the blur of blades above the sphere slowed to a halt. A hatch opened in its side and Lord Rooksby was roughly pushed face down into the dune by a pair of slats. A moment later the corrupted Kal, Tallyle, appeared in the hatch, jumping down to land beside the prisoner.

'On the face of it,' noted Tallyle, 'I would have to say things aren't looking good for you.'

'It was here,' pleaded Lord Rooksby, cowering behind his captor. 'It was. I have a perfect memory for geography. Here, sir, is the ravine, there is the carving of the face, the mountains over—'

'Yet, I find no ship,' said the Kal. He knelt down to face the quaking Rooksby, licking his tongue across his massive extended fangs. 'Just as there was no one back at the ruined dome, and I know you didn't grow wings to fly here across the celestial void from the Kingdom of Jackals.'

'But there was the snake,' begged Rooksby, spittle flying wildly out of his mouth and puddling in the sand. 'The dead snake inside the dome. You could see the remains of their camp. And the ship we arrived on was here, I swear it. Your terrible machine knows I am telling the truth.'

'There is that,' said Tallyle. 'But our slats haven't had much practice on your breed inside the interrogator before. You are either a lot more clever than you look or a lot more stupid.' He looked at the pair of slat soldiers. 'You do have some needles and blades you haven't tried in the interrogator yet?'

One of the slats bowed. 'Yes, Carnivore Tallyle.'

'There we are, problem solved. And the interrogator isn't the only machine we can put to work on your body. The masters will be very pleased to be given a novelty such as you to play with.'

The two slats picked up Lord Rooksby and carried him shrieking back into the globe. Tallyle had a last glance around then tutted in frustration and climbed up into his craft.

After the globe had lifted off and was disappearing towards Iskalajinn, a tiny orange-furred creature resembling a beaver pushed its head out of the sand and started chirruping, more of its family doing the same around the dunes. It instinctively understood that the slats would feast on any members of the warren caught moving around in the open.

The creature chattered in alarm as a sudden massive eruption of sand startled it, a metal whale rising out of the dunes opposite.

321

'That was exciting,' said Starsprite. 'I found some of those sand roots you like to feed to your litter while I was hiding.'

The little creature warbled in disgust at the unnatural interloper – torn between its ancient instinct to cooperate with other species and the flight instinct that had more recently been imprinted in its blood memories – then it ducked back down to check on its warren.

'Oh well,' said Starsprite. 'Thank you, it was a good warning call, anyway.'

Unnoticed by either Starsprite or the half-steamman ship's new mammal friends, the slat scout that had dropped out of the transport's other side pushed aside its rifle and started clicking in satisfaction under the shadow of its sand-coloured camouflage cover.

Carnivore Tallyle would surely let it have its selection of the next cull's meat for finding the missing ship.

Commodore Black looked at the wide width of the canal alongside Molly, dabbing at his nose in disgust with a handkerchief. The smell of the brown sludge flowing down its length was overwhelming, worse than any slurry pit or Middlesteel tannery works.

'You cannot be asking us to swim across that foul mess, Sandwalker?'

'I am not,' said the nomad. 'What you see flowing down there are pollutants expelled from the masters' processing centres. The acids in the canal would burn your skin off and blind you before you could make six strokes. There used to be seas of this filth when we still had seas. Now even the pollution from the masters' machines and mills is put to use in their automated transport system.' He indicated a series of dark ceramic barges piled with metal plating being swept along by the flow of filth. 'The very last of Kaliban's bounty pulled from her deep heart to be assembled into ships that will carry the masters across to their new home on your world.'

'This is it?' said Molly. '*This* is your plan for getting a head start on the slats?'

'This particular canal runs all of the way out to the last of the polar mines,' said Sandwalker. 'It passes deep through the desert. And there are the empty barges travelling back towards the mines.'

Molly looked at the automated barges, small black oblongs chained together in convoys by rusted cables, running unloaded deep into the desert. The barges rode high in the sludge on catamaran-style hulls, tube-shaped engines on each hull powering them forward and leaving a wake of bubbling muck behind. Every barge had a dome the circumference of a barrel rising at the front of its prow.

Jeanne said what Molly was thinking. 'The barges don't look that big, compatriot. Will they take our weight?'

'They are powerful enough to float a load of many tonnes down from the mines,' said Sandwalker. 'The real problem we face is that black dome mounted at the front of each barge. It is a thinking machine, similar to one of your transaction engines. The masters grew tired of our sabotage attempts and thefts from the canal system many centuries ago – those domes will detect us if we board a barge, then detonate a cache of explosives moulded into its keel. We will have three or four seconds at most until the barge qualifies our presence as an active threat rather than just a sand vulture landing on its hull, then there will be a quite spectacular explosion.'

'Now I'm a game fellow for a lark,' said the commodore. 'But I think I shall take my chances with the wicked Army of Shadows and its minions nipping at my heels rather than jump down onto one of those terrible things.'

'Stealing a barge and its cargo is a rite of passage among the free Kal of the salt wastes,' said Sandwalker. He produced a handful of coin-like objects from underneath his robe. 'You hit the top of the dome hard with this disk, like so, to activate it. The disk also contains a thinking machine – a powerful model designed to subvert the barge's controls. Keep it pressed down on the dome and when the train of barges is under our command, I will re-instruct the lead unit to increase speed and stop when we are far enough into the desert to avoid all but a long-range slat patrol.'

Duncan unslung the supply packs the commodore was carrying and tied them around his own back, dangling them across his battered travel case. 'If a wee Kal bairn can make the jump . . .'

'I will jump first,' said Sandwalker.

'I'll go behind you,' said Molly. She fingered the coin-like device the nomad had given her. 'I'll take the second barge.'

The others called out their numbers and Commodore Black came in second to last, his barge in front of Jeanne's. 'What a cruel life this is. I'll match a sabre with any enemy, but now my mettle is to be tested by leaping like a poor frog into the foul burning excretions of the Army of Shadows. What a shameful end for my rare genius.'

They waited five minutes for the combination they needed. Then it happened, barges were passing on both sides of the canal, the convoy on their side moving closer to the wall of the canal to avoid the barges passing in the other direction. Sandwalker ran towards the edge of the sand-blown embankment, hurling himself off the side. Molly took a deep breath and followed, one step, two, then she flung herself away and out, keeping her eyes locked on the flat oblong of the second barge, as if just looking at its hull would be enough to draw her down safely onto its surface. It tipped to port as she hit with a painful jolt to her ankles, the catamaran blades taking a second to stabilize against her weight, and Molly had to fight not to roll over the side into the burning effluent below. But something else had detected her weight, too, the mound at the front of the barge lighting up with an evil red light and emitting a caterwaul siren. Molly practically flung herself across the dome, slapping her coin on its top. It was as if she had plunged a dagger into a skull, the light inside the dome flaring up and then dying, the siren running down to silence.

Sirens were rising and falling behind her as the others landed on their barges and struck the sentry machines with Sandwalker's miniature transaction engines. Despite the heat of the sun in the purple sky, Molly was cold with sweat. All the sirens had fallen silent expect one. Something was terribly wrong at the end of the barge train.

'Your coin, lass,' Commodore Black was shouting. 'Use your coin.'

Jeanne was standing up behind her barge's dome and she raised an empty hand aloft. 'I slipped on the sand up there, it's gone.'

'Leap across to my barge, lass. Come on, it's your only chance.'

Jeanne drew her knife and lashed at the cable holding her barge to the end of the train. 'My barge will kill us all. The people must prevail.'

'No, Jeanne!'

But it was too late; the current of the canal carried Jeanne's screeching barge away from them and she opened her fingers in a final farewell. Then there was a flash of light and fire and the walls of the canal rattled with debris, splashes of filthy liquid spattering Molly's barge. Jeanne was gone. Blown to the uncaring winds.

On the next barge down, Keyspierre picked himself up and

325

looked coldly at Molly, turning his back on her as if she was responsible for his daughter's death. If only Molly hadn't launched them early from the kingdom, if and if, all of the infinite *if onlys*. Molly collapsed onto her own barge, watching the particles of metal in the sludge catch the afternoon light. Borne with the stench towards the heart of the wastes.

CHAPTER FIFTEEN

'We need to find a sailboat,' said Jenny Blow, watching Samuel Lancemaster's broad muscles bulge with each dip of his oars into the water. Purity didn't consider it likely that they would. They were following the River Ald west, and it appeared as if the desperate refugees who had preceded them had stolen every available boat.

'We were lucky enough to find this old thing hidden in the reeds,' said Purity.

'When we get to the coast we may have more fortune in the harbour towns,' speculated Ganby. 'Something to carry us north towards the Army of Shadows' terrible great beanstalk.'

Purity didn't voice her worries, but she doubted that too. All the large craft would have been used to flee to the colonies in Concorzia; anything small enough for the five of them to manage would have been seized to flee south or out to one of the isles. While she had been busy at Highhorn, it looked as if the entire kingdom had fallen into madness. Purity had even seen boats burnt in the river, not by the Army of Shadows, but by Jackelian turning against Jackelian. At least the current was pushing them in the right direction.

'I'll fill some sails fast enough,' said Jenny.

'My rowing is not quick enough for you?' asked Samuel. 'Or would you prefer to give Jackaby a turn?'

'I have my pride,' said the black bandit. 'I am not a living paddle to be dropped behind the transom.'

The conversation stopped, for as they rounded a corner, they discovered the course of the river blocked by a sixpenny steam ferry, its cabin covered in faded advertising hoardings that had seen better days – *Smith-Evans' Balsamic Cough Elixir*; *WW Mackinder's of Middlesteel and her Gold Medal Pianos* – and under the passenger bench awnings a group of men waited, rifles and pistols clutched and pointing towards Purity's rowboat. An order to heave to was shouted out from the sixpenny steamer. Were they brigands? Whoever they were, their boat looked sound enough and the twin stacks behind the cabin were emitting wisps of steam.

'Why do you block our way?' Samuel shouted from the front of their boat.

'We guard the approach to Wainsmouth,' a man wearing a brown flat cap called back.

Purity stood up so her voice would carry across. 'Wainsmouth still has people?'

'More and more every day,' shouted the man on the steamer. 'It is the last free town, unless any of the upland cities are still left standing.' He gazed down, obviously bemused by Samuel's archaic cuirass and tall spear. 'Is that all there is of you? All right, pass on, friend.'

Samuel rowed them past the passenger boat with three swift, strong strokes while Purity gazed back up at the men.

A free town, still. Perhaps with an equally free sailboat to carry them north? Their luck was turning at last.

* * *

The guard on the sixpenny ferry had been correct about more people turning up at the last free town every day. Outside Wainsmouth, the old town walls were packed with crowds queuing up in front of a line of tables for the chance to be admitted to safety inside.

Names, ages and occupations of those being admitted were recorded in ledgers, along with many other details. Few people seemed to fail whatever criteria were being applied to entry. The family in front of Purity and the Bandits of the Marsh was gushingly grateful that they were to be given sanctuary, the woman full of spite and bile over some village they had tried to enter on their way to the town whose desperate inhabitants had chased them away as thieves, waving pitchforks and birding rifles.

At one point, a couple of redcoats came trundling towards the town gate in an empty cart pulled by two grey shire horses. There was a short, disappointed exchange of shouts, then the cart was admitted back inside Wainsmouth proper. It sounded to Purity as if the cart had been out scavenging for something, but had found no luck on its search. She hoped it wasn't for food from the farms dotted along the South Downs. The mob of refugees might turn into a besieging army if they were turned away for a lack of supplies now.

They were a motley collection keeping order among the mob outside Wainsmouth. The country constabulary in their black frockcoats, redcoats from the regiments, even some shifty-looking fleet naval arm tars. But the desperation for food and shelter meant that the crowds were kept naturally pliable by their desire to be given sanctuary. No one protested too much when they were relieved of their packs of food and whatever other provisions they had with them. The rough-shaven men taking down the bandits' details accepted Purity's trade as seamstress without query or question, and although

329

she had to surrender her sack of tinned goods, Purity got her strange sword through wrapped in cloth, and Samuel Lancemaster his spear – collapsed to its knuckleduster configuration and slotted into a carry space in his chest-piece.

The people on the desk showed a little more interest in Samuel's breastplate, asking him if he had been with the heavy cavalry to carry such a cuirass, but when the bandit demurred, the guards lost interest and waved them all through towards the town gates. Lucky that they did. A couple of nights before, Samuel had told Purity that the armour was part of his body, fused to him. Trying to take it off would be like trying to remove his ribs.

'Here are your tokens for your first day's meal,' the deskman said. 'Duties get assigned the day after. Go down to the largest warehouse on the quay. There's benches and food inside, servings are on a rota.'

Once inside the walls Purity had a fine view of the town sloping down towards the port. The large harbour was protected by a sea fort, built down the hillside and into the water, strong round towers connected by iron walkways and pocked by concrete cannon domes. Wainsmouth's waters looked bare of boats, only a couple of fishermen's stubby two-mast trawlers tied up where there were moorings for hundreds. But there was one vessel in the water to fill the majority of the empty berths. It was a u-boat of the fleet sea arm, lying as long in the water as a dreadnought with a conning tower as substantial as a fortress. Her bow had been cast as a regal lion, teeth and muzzle caught in a steel snarl – each of her eyes a cluster of torpedo tubes. Purity gawped. How the commodore would have loved to be here to see this titan of the deep. Triple gun mounts on her forecastle, double water-sealed cannon turrets on the stern. Her name was embossed in cursive script on the black hull, each raised letter painted

330

bright red. The *JNS Spartiate*. Parliament's ensign, the cross and gate, fluttered on her flagstaff, a red field bisected with a white cross, the portcullis of the House of Guardians on the upper right-hand corner, the lion rampant in the lower left. A vessel that defied all of the kingdom's enemies to take her.

'A beauty, ain't she?' said a constable standing behind Purity. 'They'll never overrun Wainsmouth while we have her guns protecting the town. Now move along, get yourself fed down at the quay before you block up the way here.'

'These are the Jackeni of our age,' said Ganby, approvingly. 'People who know how to honour the tradition of hospitality.'

'I wonder if their hospitality might stretch to giving us a berth on that vessel down there?' Jackaby Mention pondered.

'These people need her here,' said Jenny. 'How many women and children in this town now shelter under her guns? I can fill the topsail of one of those fishing boats down there just as well.'

'A pity,' said Jackaby. 'The watchman was right; she is a beauty as fine as any. But you are correct, they need it here. You are ever our conscience, Jenny Blow.'

'And your bloodhound,' said Jenny. She pointed towards the quay. 'I can smell a stew bubbling in the pot down in the warehouse.'

'A stew, not a roast?' said Samuel Lancemaster, sounding almost disappointed. 'Well, anything will be better than the jellied chunks of bully I've been picking out of cans since we arrived here.'

It had been raining earlier that morning and the steep cobbled streets down to the quay were slippery – Purity nearly lost her footing several times. *Bare feet are conscious of the land. They feel the bones of Jackals, connect with the blood of the world. You will know when the time is right for shoes.*

331

Indeed, and how her friend Kyorin had approved of those words from Elizica. Was that good guidance, now? When the Kals were cooperating with the Army of Shadows, trying to sink their fangs in her throat. She had the blood of queens running through her veins. She had the maths-blade concealed on her back and she had the Bandits of the Marsh fighting by her side. It was time she stopped being the nation's breeding house ragamuffin and began acting like its one true queen.

Purity thought she detected a pulse of disapproval from the spirit of Elizica of the Jackeni at her pride as she walked towards a cobbler's halfway down the road to the bay; but then, Elizica of the Jackeni hadn't needed shoes, or anything else in the way of clothes, for a very long time. What did she know?

Purity asked the Bandits of the Marsh to save her a seat at the warehouse. Behind the hexagonal panes of the shop's curved bay windows were all sorts of shoes, boots and sandals ranging from the fine to the workaday. But it looked dark inside the shop, and there was a sign reading 'closed' behind the door's sidelight pane. Oh well. She was about to follow the bandits down the rest of the hill when a rustling came from inside the shop and the sign twisted around to read 'open'.

'There we are,' Purity announced to the air and Elizica. 'Fate after all.'

There were oil lamps inside, but their wicks stood dry behind glass – saving fuel, but making the room dark and unwelcoming. In the gloom a boy shuffled forward with a stool for her, an apprentice with a wooden stump below the knee of his left leg. His voice had an annoying grating quality, as if he was trying to ingratiate himself.

'The master bids you sit, damson,' said the boy. 'Be out soon.'

He hobbled over to the door, locked it and twisted the sign to read 'closed' again. Strange. Why had he done that?

'Aren't you going to light the shop, lad?'

'Short of oil, that's so, damson.'

It was then that Purity heard a knocking outside the cobbler's shop front, someone tapping on the window panes. Had Ganby or one of the others come back to fetch her? She was about to rise to see just who it was when a wet, sickly-sweet rag was pushed down on her face, her head yanked back.

Purity struggled against the foul stench to reach her sword for a couple of seconds before blackness overtook her.

In one of the Wainsmouth warehouses, two thugs wearing the ill-fitting uniforms of county constables stepped over slumped bodies. Some were spilled across the long pine tables, others fallen off the benches onto the stone floor. The collapsed refugees were being pulled unceremoniously through a door at the back like sacks of grain and dumped on the flatbed of the first of the carts waiting outside.

'I thought this one was going to start creating for a moment,' said the thug, pointing to Jenny Blow's body sprawled across the chest of Samuel Lancemaster. 'Look at her brown marsh leathers. Bloody bogtrotter, acting as if she's some grand lady. Sniffing at her plate like the meat has gone off.'

'What's been added to the food doesn't have an odour,' said his friend. 'Ain't the chief cleverer than that? I think she was sniffing at the meat in the pot.'

One of their workers was bending over to get a grip on a body and the thug lashed out with his boot, catching the worker in his stomach and sending him rolling winded into a bench. 'Get about it, you dogs. Faster, less you want to join these 'uns in the butcher's store. There's plenty more fresh fodder waiting outside the walls to come in.'

Purity's eyes blinked open. They felt swollen and itchy but she couldn't reach them with her hands, couldn't even see her limbs. She was lying horizontal in total darkness inside a crate so narrow her arms lay pinned down alongside her ribs, unable to twist an inch. Claustrophobia swept in. She didn't even have the purchase to kick at the walls with her bare feet, or thump at the roof pressed tight down on her forehead.

Something snapped inside her and Purity gave herself to wild panic, thrashing and screaming in the darkness.

CHAPTER SIXTEEN

S andwalker had taken something like a brick out of his pack, and placed it on the floor of the tent. Glowing orange, the heating block pushed back the chill of the freezing desert night with a circulating warmth that belied the frosty atmosphere under the silk-like canvas. Along with the silence from Keyspierre, the reek of the canal haunted Molly. Had the pollutants infused Molly's clothes or was it merely the memory of the canal persisting in her nostrils, along with the vision of Jeanne disappearing in the sudden fire-flash, the siren on her barge silenced as pieces of it ricocheted off Kaliban's mighty canal works?

Molly broke the quiet. 'You've not spoken of Jeanne since we climbed out of the canal.'

'What is there to say?' remarked Keyspierre, rubbing tiredly at his stubble. 'She died to save us, so that we might reach this great sage of the Kal. She put the preservation of the Commonshare of Quatérshift before her own life – as I would expect any good compatriot from my nation to do, as I would do myself.'

'You're a cold one, Keyspierre,' said the commodore. 'She

335

was your daughter, man, your blood. Would you not have done anything for her?'

'Do not presume to tell me how to grieve for one of my own,' said Keyspierre.

'One of your own, perhaps,' said Coppertracks, the steamman – sitting furthest from the heat of the brick while he generated his own warmth from his furnace. 'But not your blood, I believe. Her iris shared about as many inheritance vectors with your eyes as it did with the scratches on my vision plate. She was not your daughter, dear mammal. Now that she is dead I think you owe her – and us – the truth.'

Duncan Connor sat bolt upright at the news. 'I kenned it. There was something not quite right about the pair of you numpties from the start.'

'You know nothing of me,' snapped Keyspierre.

'I know that you are no scientist,' said Coppertracks, the steamman's voicebox becoming uncharacteristically firm. 'Your understanding of the gunnery project at Highhorn was the superficial sort I would expect to come from a potted briefing on wave mechanics. And aboard Lord Starhome you didn't know one end of a fully functioning circuit magnetizer from another.'

'You're just an informer, aren't you?' accused Molly. 'A shiftie stooge sent to keep an eye on your scientists at the Highhorn project?'

'Is that how highly you think the Commonshare values the survival of its citizenry?' said Keyspierre, sadly. 'That it would dispatch a menial merely to spy on its scientists' fraternization with your Jackelian friends? You are wrong! I am a colonel attached to Committee Eight of the People's Commonshare of Quatérshift, charged with ensuring the success of our mission to Kaliban at any cost. At *any* cost.'

'So then, the wolves have been let out to run free.' The

commodore sucked in his breath. 'Your kind I've heard tell of before. Seven central committees operating under the rule of the first, and the eighth that doesn't officially exist at all. You're a wheatman is what you are, as bad as any of the dirty agents from the Court of the Air.'

'A typical Jackelian mangling of our tongue,' said Keyspierre. 'It's huit, you dolt.'

'A secret policeman by any name,' said the commodore. 'Ah, poor young Jeanne. I did not know you for what you were.'

'She was a loyal servant of the Commonshare. Her real name was Jeanne de la Motte-Valois, a compatriot lieutenant attached to Committee Eight.'

Commodore Black suddenly leapt at Keyspierre, landing a punch on the shiftie's chin and sending them both sprawling, the intelligent fabric of the tent trying to reflect their forms back at them as they flailed and rolled under one of the brace poles. Only Duncan Connor was strong enough to haul the u-boat man off Keyspierre, pulling the commodore away as he tried to land a boot in the Quatérshiftian's face.

'Jared!' Molly shouted, shocked by her friend's sudden explosion of violence. 'What in the name of the Circle do you think you're doing?'

'Why don't you ask this wicked wheatman,' spat the commodore. 'Ask him about the Quatérshiftian aristocrats who escaped with their lives to Jackals but without their children. Tell us about your secret police's schools, Keyspierre, where wheatmen stole the young from the revolution's death camps, training and honing the ones who were strong enough to survive to become fanatics to serve your cause.'

'The job of the people is to serve the people,' said Keyspierre. 'Would you rather I had left Jeanne to die in a camp? She was young enough to be re-educated. She didn't deserve to

337

be condemned for the accident of her noble birth any more than our gutter children deserved to be left to starve outside the gates of the Sun King's palace. And I'll take no lessons on how to treat aristocrats from a Jackelian. Jeanne lived as a productive sentinel of the Commonshare; my people never kept her as a living archery target to be trotted out for a stoning every time parliament needed a distraction.'

'I can see there's aristocratic blood in your veins,' said Commodore Black, 'because you're a royal bastard right enough. She was never *your* daughter to take.'

'You insult me! She was a daughter of the revolution,' said Keyspierre. 'One who gave her life to keep your useless carcass walking through the desert. And after this is over—' Keyspierre patted the knife tucked under his belt '—I shall demonstrate to you how very foolish it is to strike a ranking colonel of the people's brigades. What is it you call it in the kingdom, grass before breakfast?'

'That's a mortal fancy name for a duel,' said Commodore Black. 'But if you've a plain taste for a little simple murder, I'll give you satisfaction and we'll see which of us is planted in the soil after the dark deed is done.'

'That's enough,' ordered Molly. 'You two can lock horns after we've saved Jackals and—' she looked meaningfully at Keyspierre '—Quatérshift.'

Sandwalker shook his head in dismay. 'Your friends bicker like slats fighting over the finest cuts torn off one of the city-born.'

'Our people do that when our nerves fray, when we lose people we were fond of,' said Molly. 'Apologies. It is unnecessary.'

'Well,' said Sandwalker, 'then you have all come to the right land. Kaliban is the realm of the unnecessary. Lie down and I shall attempt to ease the pain in your skull.'

Molly did as she was bid and Sandwalker laid his blue-skinned fingers on her forehead, the throb inside rising then easing and pulsing back to something more bearable.

'The very desert we trek through is unnecessary,' continued Sandwalker, his fingers browsing her scalp. 'Every grain of sand, every electrical storm, every dry riverbed: all the products of our masters, a mentality that gorges itself until the cycle of life is broken with no hope of repair. The light that burns the soil, the storms that now ravage the world, the waves that lap no longer in our seabeds, they once gave my people the energy they needed to live peacefully within the cycle of life. But the more sophisticated your civilization, the more fragile its structure, the more you rely on the cooperation and specialization of the Kal who stands beside you. Millions upon countless millions died on Kaliban when the masters and their slat legions arrived. Almost everything we knew was lost, much of the rest looted and wrecked by the Army of Shadows. No more living machines to be raised as crops. No more learning permitted to our children. Now, thousands of years later, all we are left with are paltry splinters of knowledge. An imperfect remembrance of the fact that the objectionable existence we find ourselves trapped in is a cruel, needless perdition compared with the paradise we had created for ourselves. A paradise we would have willingly shared with the masters and their slat armies if they had but asked.'

'You sound like a professor friend of mine,' said Molly. 'Back in Jackals, she's an expert on a classical fallen civilization called Camlantis. I think the Camlanteans had a little of the life you remember. At about the same time as your civilization, too, I think. They fell to our own barbarians, though, the Black-Oil Horde. We didn't need the slats to destroy our land's paradise.'

339

'How very sad,' said Sandwalker. 'How much better if our two peoples had met in those ancient days, rather than like this, in the ruins of the Kal civilization. What marvels might we have achieved together as friends?'

'Kyorin showed me how the Army of Shadows flies like locusts from sphere to sphere, reducing the land to a husk before moving on.'

'I once heard the great sage theorize that they are getting better at controlling the convulsions of our world as they consume it. Who knows, with enough millennia to practise, perhaps they will have learnt how to live within the cycle of life by the time they reach the very last unharvested celestial sphere that spins around the sun. They will have all our ghosts to teach them.'

'It won't come to that,' insisted Molly. 'We'll stop them, Sandwalker. Trust me. It's what my people do best, killing and fighting.'

'Carnivores,' sighed Sandwalker. 'Well, we have tried everything else over the centuries. Now it seems we shall have to trust your people to do what they do best.'

After the nomad had eased away the worst of the pain inside Molly's head, she went to sit next to Coppertracks, who – if the swirling patterns of energy inside his skull were anything to go by – had something occupying his own mind.

'A penny for your thoughts, old steamer. Are you worried about Quatérshift's involvement with the expedition now that you know the truth about Keyspierre and Jeanne?'

'No I am not, Molly softbody. That Quatérshift would involve someone like Keyspierre in the expedition is wholly predictable of that paranoid nation. I have a deeper concern, one concerning the rituals of Gear-gi-ju.'

'I saw you calling your ancestors' spirits earlier today,' said

Molly. 'You need to be careful how much oil you shed at your age.'

'Calling, indeed, but calling without any answer at all, dear mammal. I have never experienced the like of this before – ignored for one calling, yes, but like this? Night after night, day after day of complete emptiness as I toss my cogs. It is as if the Steamo Loas have, to speak plainly, completely forsaken me here.'

'There is the distance to consider,' said Molly. 'How many million miles are we from the Steammen Free State here on Kaliban?'

'Physical distance means nothing to my ancestors,' explained Coppertracks. 'They exist outside distance in the realm of the spirits. No, there is something else to account for this void, something that I am missing. I cannot believe the people of the metal's ancestors have abandoned me in this land. So much is strange about this wasteland the Army of Shadows have created. There is something terribly wrong here, and it is staring me directly in my vision plate, yet I cannot see it.'

Molly had no answer for her friend.

If even the gods of the steammen had forsaken Molly and her friends in the dark wastelands of the Army of Shadows, what did that say about the expedition's chances of success on Kaliban, now?

Sandwalker was leading the expedition along the dunes in the welcome shade of fluted columns of basalt – giant anthills towering as high as any Middlesteel tower – when Coppertracks stopped, his tracks entangled in something. As he pulled at what was caught up in his caterpillar treads, a series of cables was revealed and a black box fell out of the side of the crumbling rock of the basalt, yanked free by the steamman's efforts.

Seeing what had happened, Sandwalker came running back. 'Don't touch the box!'

Coppertracks gingerly placed it on the sand.

'Is it a snare or the like?' Duncan asked, helping the steamman untangle the cable from his treads.

The Kal nomad shook his head. He picked up the box and examined it, then pushed it back into the face of the basalt rise. 'An old fibre communication line. Our tribes had them hidden around the desert, but the Army of Shadows discovered the cables and adjusted their machines to detect the mechanism of light transmission we had believed was secure. It was centuries ago, but we lost half the free Kal before we realized how the slats were suddenly finding our caravans and hidden bases.'

'I wonder if they were doing the same back in Jackals?' said Molly. 'Reading our crystalgrid messages before they attacked, learning about us?'

'Undoubtedly,' said Sandwalker. 'The masters do not like to leave such things to chance when they lay their plans.'

'Fate has been blessed unkind to your people for you to live like this,' said the commodore. 'Scuttling across the sands, always an eye open for the enemy, fearful even of sending a message, where every stranger of your race you meet might be hiding a fearful set of fangs to sink into your flesh.'

'It is certainly not any way of life we would wish for our young,' smiled Sandwalker. 'Stop here for a rest. Eat your food but conserve the water, we have little left.'

In the lee of a rise now, the expedition members did not need further urging. Even sitting in the shade they found the arid heat draining. They were travelling day and night, trying to keep ahead of the slats. Molly brushed the sand off her billowing white trousers and made her seat on the gravel of the rise.

Keyspierre passed the sack of food he had been given back in Iskalajinn to the nomad. Sandwalker rummaged around gratefully in the bag and removed one of the long bean-like vegetables, squeezing a green pod out of its end to chew on. 'You are very generous in your sharing. You should eat more of these yourself, Keyspierre. They contain a juice which helps your body retain water.'

'Alas, compatriot, I am an unashamed carnivore,' said Keyspierre. 'I shall stick to my tinned fare, even though Jackelian canned beef is far removed from fine steak that has been shown the flames of a fire for the requisite two minutes.'

Molly could see that the nomad found the idea of what was inside their supply cans quite disgusting, almost as strange as the idea that something as precious as tin would be used just to preserve rations.

Watching Keyspierre spoon out lumps of jellied meat, the commodore began to sing one of the oldest Jackelian drinking songs, each verse hummed out between swigs from his canteen. '*Should the shifties dare invade us; thus armed with our poles; we'll bang their bare ribs; make their lantern jaws ring. For you beef-eating, beer-eating Jackelians are sorts; who will shed their last blood for their country and king.*'

Molly met his eyes and the commodore fell to silence. Keyspierre hadn't risen to the bait, but at this rate, one of them was going to run the other through before they reached the lair of the great sage.

Sandwalker led them across the shifting sands of the dunes for two more days and nights. Then they climbed an escarpment to a sandstone plateau where they were presented with dramatic views of whirling, tornado-like storms scouring the desert floor below. One of the ravines they passed contained a thin scrub of vegetation and a pool of water, but the nomad refused to allow them to go down, saying only that the tarn was a false oasis, containing creatures twisted by the Army of Shadows. Traps, always traps. Climbing through the maze of gorges and gullies was time-consuming, but the alternative – risking the low floor of the desert with its dust devils – was too dangerous to contemplate. Those storms could rip apart even the nomad's tough tent fabric and would scour the flesh off the Jackelians' bones within minutes if they were caught in the open.

Luckily for the expedition, the height of the plateau also allowed Sandwalker to use another of the devices from his pack, a flimsy kettle-sized pyramid of transparent panels that he would religiously assemble and leave outside their tent each night. By morning a thin trickle of water had formed inside a plate in the pyramid's centre, capturing the dew of the sunrise, and he would refill their dwindling canteens as best he could.

On their fourth day crossing the plateau they spied a pair of silver machines walking across the desert floor on a nest of whipping, cantilevered metal tentacles, bodies like teardrops pockmarked by round smoking holes. The tentacles looked like magnified versions of the organic ones Molly had seen on the masters' bodies in Kyorin's memories. Molly couldn't tell exactly how large the machines were, but to be able to see them stumbling through the desert at this distance, they had to be truly massive. For once, Sandwalker didn't require that the expedition members scurry off and conceal them-selves in a ravine. These were blind, stupid machines, part of the masters' network of devices to tame the atmosphere and stop Kaliban's weather from turning more vicious than it already appeared.

Every extra day burning under the Kaliban sky only stiff-ened Molly's resolve. If they couldn't find a way of defeating the Army of Shadows here, then this life would become the fate of the Jackelians' descendants. Living feral like rodents, crawling in-between the Army of Shadows' cities and surviving on whatever crumbs they could scavenge from their soiled world. It didn't matter that Molly was a mere shadow compared to the power she had possessed when she had piloted the Hexmachina. Nor were the petty rivalries of her world's nationalities of consequence – they had no home under this boiling Kaliban sky. Here, Molly and her friends could be only prey or predator.

A day after they had left the plateau behind, Molly began to suffer additional physical side effects from carrying the weight of Kyorin's memories. As well as the headaches, she was struck by bouts of muscle cramps, nausea and drowsiness. She was slowing them down, now, and in a territory they needed to pass through fast. They were traversing an area of sand mists, grains that had been beaten as light as flour by the sun and the storms, and which now blew as a fine silicate across the *Aard Ailkalmer Issah*. Even the name of the territory being pronounced by Sandwalker was painful to Molly, the alien Kal syllables echoing like a battering ram inside her skull.

By the third day Molly started to suffer waking hallucinations, seeing faces briefly in the shadows and dust hazes, hideous leering goblin-like devils that might have belonged to the dark gods from before the Circlist enlightenment. She would flinch in alarm and swear at them before they snapped back to being mere shadows of rocks.

Sandwalker insisted Molly suck on strips of blue salt and chew the bitter pods from the vegetables in his supplies to help alleviate the symptoms – her heated brain made increasingly susceptible to sunstroke. But Molly could tell from the way the nomad looked at her now that he was seriously worried about her condition. It seemed as if Keyspierre's prediction that her affliction would become a burden to the expedition was proving correct after all. The pain inside Molly's mind swelled and ebbed. Increasingly when the pain was on the rise, she would become confused, her mind experiencing things that had once happened to Kyorin as if they were happening to her now, or seeing things that made no sense at all. Once, she even thought she had come across Duncan hiding behind a basalt column and talking to his precious battered travel case as if he was expecting an answer. She was going mad, slowly. Then not so slowly at all.

Molly caught Keyspierre looking at her as they trudged along the dunes, his eyes deceitful and narrow under the turban that protected his face from the blowing dust.

'Stop looking at me!' Molly shouted.

'Compatriot?'

'I know what you are planning to do.'

Duncan Connor was ahead of Molly, holding a guide rope to stop them becoming separated in the endless floating sand haze. 'Are you all right, lassie?'

'He's planning to kill me!'

Duncan looked back at Keyspierre. 'What are you about, man?'

Molly threw herself towards the uplander. 'Keyspierre's planning to slip a cushion over my face and smother me in the tent tonight so I don't slow us down, or he'll cut my rope and leave me to wander alone out here. Anything, Duncan, anything to ensure we get to reach the great sage. All for the people, they must prevail. The people.'

'Molly,' said the ex-soldier, feeling her forehead. 'You're burning up, lassie.'

'Don't let him kill me! Duncan, please, I saved your life

from a blazing sail-rider rig back in Middlesteel, now's your chance to repay me by saving mine.'

'There are a good few in this blasted land that deserve to die, compatriot,' said Keyspierre, coming towards her, 'but I do not count you among their number.'

Molly took a step back and fell over something buried in the sand. 'Liar, you dirty shiftie liar. You'll kill us all to make sure you reach the great sage!'

Sandwalker appeared out of the haze. Unslinging his canteen and helping Molly to her feet, he was about to offer her a sip from his water, but then he spotted what she had tripped over and stopped, his eyes widening in shock. Jutting out was a long fused tube of sand that had been petrified into glass. 'This is fresh.'

Duncan Connor knelt down and examined the glass. 'It's not the spoor of one of the kelpies that live out here, is it?'

'A beast,' said Sandwalker. 'But not a living creature. This is the sand flash left from a lightning strike on the dunes. There is a permanent pizo-electrical storm we call the Beast, but it normally rotates eight hundred miles north of here. The masters' systems are truly failing if the storm has moved so far south.'

Molly tried to break out of line and flee into the haze, but Commodore Black caught her and pulled her back. 'No, lass, that's not our way.'

'Keyspierre wants us to die,' insisted Molly. 'He knew the storm was here. You have seen what his people are capable of, Jared. He wants the great sage's weapon just for Quatérshift, not for us. We all have to die.'

'I'll not lighten that secret policeman's reputation,' said Commodore Black, 'but this is your fever speaking, lass. Your imagination is swinging wild on the yardarm with your sickness.'

Why couldn't the commodore see what Keyspierre was doing, was planning to do to them all? He was so dangerous.

'We don't have time for Molly to rest,' said Sandwalker. 'We must be skirting the fringes of the stormfront or we would already be dead. We have to clear the basin and the storm area before we are—'

His words were cut off by a tremendous burst of light in the sand haze, an ozone stench and a sound like a cannon being given the fuse right next to their ears. Coppertracks' sole remaining mu-body was blown apart by the lightning strike, cut in two, sent spinning into the dunes.

A wave of aftershock from the discharge rippled through the sand haze, making the skin along Molly's hand twitch as if someone were pinching it.

They had met the Beast and they were balancing inside its maw.

CHAPTER SEVENTEEN

With a scraping sound, the lid of Purity's crate was wrenched off, blinding her with the sudden flood of light. Pulling her aching body out of the crate, Purity saw she was in a room lit by a solitary gaslight on a circular table. And there! There was the one-legged jigger who had attacked her, accompanied by a steamman, an old four-armed affair wearing a leather apron over his iron chest, hung with hammers, pins, scissors and other tools of the cobbler's trade.

'What—?'

'Quieten down,' said the apprentice boy. 'We had to hide you. There were men looking for you who thought they had seen you come into the shop.'

Purity rubbed at her swollen eyes, the skin of her face red and peeling where the apprentice had drugged her with his rag.

'Leather cleaner,' noted the apprentice. 'As good as a teeth-puller's gas if you're not wearing a cobbler's mask.'

'Or don't have a boiler heart not much subject to the vagaries of atmospheric composition,' said the steamman. 'My name is Cam Quarterplate and this young softbody is my apprentice, Watt.'

'What in the name of the Circle are you doing?' Purity shouted. 'Those men at the front of the shop were my friends.'

'The men who came looking for you weren't the ones you went walking down the hill with, that's so,' said Watt. 'They were the chief's men, damson.'

'Chief?' said Purity. 'What chief? Are you two foot-shodders completely mad?'

'That's what the softbody who now runs the town calls himself,' said Quarterplate, his twin stacks nervously quivering out a trail of smoke, his voicebox set low to a whisper. 'They came out of Middlesteel, a horde of them. Convicts, we think. From Bonegate or one of the other large prisons. Wainsmouth belongs to them now.'

Watt nodded sadly. 'And everyone inside the walls is as good as their slave. Rumours I heard in town say their chief used to be a leech-monger, a doctor who was waiting the rope in Bonegate for poisoning rich patients after the carriage folk had changed their wills to favour him.'

'But there are soldiers outside the gates,' said Purity, shocked, 'and that vast u-boat sitting in your harbour . . .'

'There are men *dressed in uniform* outside the gate. Our garrison cleared out months ago with the rest of the army to march east to the war in Quatérshift,' said Watt. 'And the chief's brutes took the *Spartiate*'s crew just like they've taken all you refugees. The *Spartiate* sailed into harbour looking for fuel. Except we haven't got any, of course. If we did, the chief and his men would have seized the u-boat and sailed off to Concorzia like all the bloody guardians did when the capital and parliament fell to the Army of Shadows.'

'This is no free town,' said Cam Quarterplate, the outrage seeping through his voicebox. 'The only freedom we have here is to be made deactivate if we go against the chief. That duplicitous fastblood has made a deal with the slat creatures.'

'Don't you see, damson?' protested Watt. 'We don't have the victuals to feed a tenth of the people who have come to camp outside Wainsmouth's gates. You refugees come here with supplies, the chief's men steal them off you, and then you leave as food. Food and slave labour for the slats. There are not enough of the bloody monsters in Jackals for the Army of Shadows to hunt down everyone yet, but when people on the road hear of our free town and the free feeds down in Wainsmouth's warehouses, they all make their way here readily enough. The slats are licking the bugs off the flypaper in Wainsmouth.'

'Will one of you two please tell me what happened to my friends?'

Watt cast his eyes ashamedly to the floor. 'They've been drugged, damson. Not everyone survives the dose of what they slip in the warehouse food, but them that does is paralysed for about a week. Your friends will be chained up in the sea fort's dungeons. No RAN airships come calling here now, but the Army of Shadows does. Every week, in those ugly hovering aerostats they rattle through the sky in, with nets underneath to carry away all their slaves and meat.'

'It is true,' agreed the steamman.

'But they don't know you're here, damson,' continued Watt. 'They've already searched our shop for you, when you were nailed inside the crate. You're not on the worker count, you won't be missed here. If we can get you out of Wainsmouth . . . you have to find the people coming here, tell them what will happen to them – spread the truth about the last free town!'

'They'll know I'm here, all right,' said Purity. 'When I free my friends.'

'Don't be stupid, damson,' begged Watt. 'The chief's men are animals. When they stormed the town they made our

351

defenders strip, then they covered our fencibles and the county police in oil and burnt them down in the square like it was bloody Smoking Prester Charles Night, made everyone in the town watch it, too, so we'd know what we'd get if we went against them again. If they catch you, you'll end up just like the people we find floating in the harbour after they've been tossed from the sea fort.'

'Oh, those poor fastbloods,' said Quarterplate, the iron fingers on his four hands flickering in dismay. 'The sounds that drift across from the sea fort at night. It's enough to make one deactivate one's sound baffles. Those poor, poor people.'

'My people,' said Purity.

Watt and Quarterplate ducked as Purity extended her arm and her sword burst out of its sheepskin wrap and flew across the room to wallop into her hand. The cobbler's backroom suddenly did not seem so dark, the light of the maths-blade scouring away the shadows.

'*My* people!' she yelled.

The man sitting on the old mayoral chair of Wainsmouth had more of the manner of a king than a mayor, even if he had completely failed to dress for the part. He reclined against the cushioned chair-back sporting a tattered officer's uniform looted from the regiments, covered by a sheepskin waistcoat, while a dark stovepipe hat warmed his bald white scalp. At his feet a woman was chained to the floor.

Two thugs dressed as redcoats dragged Purity Drake's bruised and bleeding body closer so he could get a better look at the prisoner.

'I'm flattered,' said the chief, sizing up Purity. 'Most of the occupants of this miserable little town are trying to scale the walls to get out every night. But you, my fancy, you actually have the temerity to try to scale my fort's walls to face me.'

'What do you want done with her?' asked one of his thugs.

'I don't suppose you can converse on any learned subject with distinction – music, contemporary theatre, any literature other than penny dreadfuls? No? Circle forbid I should actually find any source of diversion here.'

Purity spat a gob of blood onto the floor from her swollen mouth. 'Did that amuse you? Let's talk about you dying, you hairless slug.'

'Not on my rug, you filthy young ruffian,' sighed the chief, averting his eyes in disgust. Two of the bruisers in his court of convicts ran forward, vying to be the one to clean away the mess. 'You know, your voice puts me in mind of a singer at the capital's pleasure gardens, Fanny Thornhill – I never cared much for her arias. A little too strident for my taste.'

One of the chief's men came into the chamber ill-dressed as a county constable, pushing Cam Quarterplate and his apprentice Watt in front of him.

'You should not have done this wicked thing, Watt,' quivered the steamman.

'I assure you,' said the chief, 'he should have done.' He pointed down at Watt. 'May I presume, my fancy, that this is the part of our sad play's script where you beg me for money or a position in my little fighting force of felons?'

'I just want my ma back,' said Watt. 'You've got her here in your cells.'

'Good grief,' said the chief, lifting his stovepipe hat to rub at a rash on his bald pate. 'The tastes of some of my brutes. I do hope she's fairer in complexion than you.'

Purity struggled in the grip of the guards, trying to lunge at Watt. But they were too strong, and Purity had taken quite a beating when they captured her scaling the sea fort's walls. 'You jigging little foot-shodder, you said you would help me!'

'You, you're as mad as a bag full of weasels,' laughed Watt. 'Waving some rusty old sabre about and raving on about how you're the true ruler of the kingdom. You were going to get yourself killed anyway, now at least I can use you to help get my family back.'

'I believe I'm currently occupying the position of the last ruler of Jackals,' said the chief. 'Monarch of the ruins and rubble and rats and all else that is crude and base. That is all that is true *here*, now the veil has at long last dropped away from civilization's unsightly face. But I'm afraid there's only room for one chief. Bring that foolish little thing towards me.'

The thugs forced Purity forwards and down to her knees while the chief rummaged in a black surgeon's bag by the side of his makeshift throne. 'Kill or cure, it's an old quandary. Now, here I have the very thing I gave my third wife. A connoisseur's choice.' He grabbed Purity by the cheek and stuffed something inside her mouth, then closed her nostrils until she choked and swallowed it.

He held his hands out regally, one of the thugs running over to clean them with a hot towel. 'That's a very rare fungus called Shadowjack's Kiss. When it is dried and crumbled, a few grains of it mixed with mercury can cure the sweating sickness.' He waved Purity away from his presence. 'Bed her down in the cells. She'll begin to suffocate in an hour when her throat is too distended to admit air into her lungs. Make sure one of you dogs calls me to the cells to observe the girl's symptoms well before she goes purple. She'll only have five minutes of really first-rate choking for me to see before her end.'

Purity tried to say something, but she was still coughing

and gagging from the slimy, foul-tasting toadstool. Her tongue was heating up as if someone had rested a hot poker on it.

The chief indicated Watt. 'I also have a prescription for our little one-legged cobbler. Take him down to the cells with the girl, find the little snitch's mother and make him watch while you cut her throat, then you may cut the young rascal's for his troubles.'

The chief's thugs dragged Purity away with the two cobblers, the young apprentice struggling and screaming in anger at his betrayal while the court of convicts laughed, jeered and poked at them on the way out.

'Well,' said the chief, as his three prisoners vanished. 'You can't do right by doing wrong, can you?'

'And the old steamer . . . ?' asked a guard.

'He's saved us the trouble of rounding him up with the others,' said the chief. 'The blue-skin who arrived with the slats brought fresh instructions. All steammen inside the walls to be held ready in chains for transport by the time the next quota is due.'

His lieutenant looked surprised. 'They can't bloody eat *them* too, can they?'

'I rather think they are displaying the instincts of a mechomancer in this matter,' said the chief, drawing an imaginary scalpel blade through the air. 'I'm sure they'll tease a few of King Steam's secrets out of the people of the metal before the last of them has been dissected.'

The chief nudged the woman chained by his feet and she brushed back her elaborate coiffure and picked up the book she had been reading aloud, *Purges, Physics, Clysters and other Allied Sciences*.

'Read on from page two twenty, my fancy, cutting for stones.'

One of the henchmen coughed nervously.

'Speak,' commanded the chief.

'We're a little shy on our quota this week. We could always pass the cobbler's lad to the slats . . .'

'Oh really, is that all?' The chief waved his underling's concern away and indicated to the woman that she should continue reading. 'I have faith that there will be more people banging at the town's gates by tomorrow. The fecundity of the filthy poor, breeding, always breeding. If there is one thing there is always an abundance of in this doleful life, it's the sight of the great unwashed masses befouling your doorstep. Trust me on that.'

Trust him. After all, he had once been one of Middlesteel's most distinguished doctors.

CHAPTER EIGHTEEN

A bolt of electricity flashed down the dunes and erupted behind the expedition, showering Molly in sand, making the red haze they were running through sputter with dispersing energy like crackling popping on a roasting pig.

The sand had never seemed so untraversable as Molly desperately tried to keep up with Commodore Black and Coppertracks over the slow, sucking dunes. Anything but fall back alongside Keyspierre. If Molly slipped out of sight of the others for a moment the shiftie would try to murder her, she could see just how he would arrange it. So easy. Trip her and push her face into the sand, strangle her and leave her corpse to be claimed by the shifting sands or fried to ashes by the lightning storm. Just another victim of the Beast, like Coppertracks' decapitated drone.

Poor Molly Templar, so unfortunate, dying on the expedition she had been the catalyst for. An adventure too far for the foolish author and her friends, overreaching her talents, overestimating her resources and fortitude. Just a sad little workhouse girl made good whose luck had finally run out. But would there be anyone left in Jackals to mourn her? No! Keep hold of the line; don't lose sight of the others.

Around Molly the dust haze was thickening, coalescing under the fury of the Beast's pizo-electric whipping, almost a sandstorm now. *Shelter*, her burning mind's Kal instincts screamed at her. No, don't dig down. To camp inside the maw of the Beast would be to invite disaster, death from the wild scourging energy. Molly flinched as there was a triple crack, a wave of bright light flaring ahead of her, geysers of sand blowing back from the Beast's assault. Then she was walking over cracking glass, the sand-flash so fresh it was still hot. Steam from the slagged sand assaulted her nostrils and a wave of nausea lurched inside her. It smelt like hog's pudding – barley and pig's offal baked inside pastry. But that was just a trick of her nose, surely, her senses distorting everything?

Molly bent over and began to vomit. This was no good. How much water was she expelling out of her gut along with her last meal? The expedition was almost out of water now, and food too.

A figure emerged out of the sand haze, like a sketch from the *Middlesteel Illustrated News*. A pieman opening his barrow to expose the hot charcoals at the bottom of his iron box.

'I don't want hog's pudding,' heaved Molly as the seller indicated his fare.

Molly screamed. It was Purity Drake's head lying inside the pie-seller's barrow, human limbs piled alongside. The slats, the slats were devouring Purity, consuming everything Molly cared about in the kingdom.

The lines of the pieman's sketch danced and reformed into Keyspierre's face. He was shaking her. 'Compatriot!'

'The pieman's fare,' said Molly. 'It was human meat.'

'Your line, compatriot.'

Molly looked down. The guide cable she was holding was smoking at the end, unconnected to the rest of the expedition. That last lightning strike must have sheared it. Sweet Circle, she was alone with Keyspierre, the others blundering ahead somewhere in the sand haze, still following on behind Sandwalker.

Molly slipped out her knife. 'Purity was trying to warn me.'

Keyspierre stepped out of the way as Molly lunged at him, the blade passing through the space his chest had been occupying a second ago. 'Not going to cook me, not going to chew on my ribs, you jigging shiftie scum!'

'You've lost your mind, woman!' Keyspierre caught Molly's wrist and moved to one side, twisting her around and making the knife fall out of her hand; but she had seen what he was doing and had slipped the treacherous Quatérshiftian agent's own blade out of his belt with her other hand. She slashed at him with it, cutting his arm, then tossed the knife into her right hand and went for his gut before he could register the switch. He wanted to cook her flesh, but it was going to be his organs lying spilled on the sands. Then she was tumbling through the air. The damn secret policeman had second-guessed her move, converting her movement into a – she thumped down hard on the sand, Keyspierre's weight smashing onto her back before she could get up.

Keyspierre pushed Molly's face down into the blanket of sand, his left hand reaching around to encompass her neck, strangling her. Choking sand spilled into her mouth and she tasted salty grit as she lost consciousness. Salt. Salt to season Molly for the fire the Quatérshiftian agent was going to cook her flesh over.

*   *   *

Purity was dragged along the damp dripping length of the sea fort's dungeon level, the old supply cellars fastened with iron chains around the doors, faces of human produce pressed up against the bars or sprawled inside, paralysed by the criminally insane doctor's drugs. That was one thing you could say about an army of convicts, they knew how to lock down tight the unfortunates who were to be the slats' fodder.

Purity could feel her throat swelling, the muscles burning around her neck, growing increasingly numb as the poison the chief had stuffed into her worked its bile inside her.

'Shall we toss her in with the sailors from the *Spartiate*?' one of Purity's escorts asked the turnkey.

'No, chief wants the crew kept to themselves, in case we turn up some fuel later. Chuck her in with the rest of the meat.'

'She won't be shipping out with the Army of Shadows,' explained the guard, twisting Purity's arm further behind her back to stop her from thrashing. 'She's only got until the end of the hour. She's been "cured" right enough by him upstairs.'

'Best we keep her fresh, then.' The turnkey beat a rifle butt against the door's bars, making the few prisoners that were on their feet retreat in fear. 'Back, you vermin. You might be dinner, but we've got dessert here, and we'll be wanting her out again in a bit.'

Watt and Cam Quarterplate were being shoved along the corridor a few steps behind Purity.

'When my friend opens the dungeon door, you point out your ma, just as quick as you like,' threatened the apprentice's guard, waving a knife in front of the two cobblers. 'Otherwise you'll find out what else this is good for cutting off before you croak.'

'But my ma's your wife, that's so,' spat Watt, who had taken some lumps on the way down the sea fort's steps himself.

360

'My dad gave her a little of the hey-jiggerty while you were locked inside Bonegate Gaol.'

Watt was slammed against the wall and the guard was about to make good on his threat, but Purity was close enough to Cam Quarterplate now. She gestured in the air and her maths-blade leapt out of the steamman's vertical stack, her sword glowing white-hot from the superheated exhaust of Quarterplate's boiler heart. There was a brief burning agony as Purity seized the grip before she used its power to transmute the heat into a flash of blinding light. Watt had his eyes closed, and, as agreed, his master had flipped the cover of his vision plate down – but for the guards, that flash was the last thing they were going to see.

Purity hardly needed the part of her that was Elizica of the Jackeni to show her the thrusts and steps of the dance – the feathery burden of the maths-blade curving and twisting and carving. When she was finished, six men lay dead at her feet. It took a second more to direct the sword's force along her own body and isolate the swelling tide of the poison making her throat muscles bloat and turn purple. Her blade passed the chemical signature of the ascomycete toxin through her mind and she twisted at its bonds, snapping the chains of the chemical as easily as if she was breaking a necklace of daises.

Then silence apart from the cries of the seagulls flying on the other side of the fort's thick walls. Outside the dungeon door the two cobblers were staring at Purity in shock. The way she must once have looked at Oliver Brooks, the Hood-o'-the-marsh, before the strange young man's existence had been joined with the land and her terrible blade.

'That was vengeance,' said Purity, shaking.

'That much was clear, Purity softbody,' said the steamman.

'How did you know?' asked Watt, looking at the dead

361

guards at his feet in horror. 'How did you know this scum wouldn't send me and old Cam back to the town for turning you in?'

'I had a life of people like the chief telling me what to do,' said Purity, sadly, 'back in the Royal Breeding House. That's just how his kind use power, when they have it.'

'You *are* the queen,' said Watt, looking at Purity's strange glowing sword. 'Sweet bloody Circle, I don't know whether I should hug you or throw a brick at you.'

'I have the land's blade and the lion's heart,' said Purity. She slashed at the chain securing the dungeon door, sending the thick iron links splashing out in a cloud of liquid metal. 'And my Jackelians are not a people to die quietly as they are dragged to the butcher's block.'

The few prisoners who had recovered from their paralysis fled to the damp walls inside the chamber Purity had forced open. Purity banished the darkness with her sword's fire. And there in the light were the Bandits of the Marsh. She burnt the toxin within their bodies, burnt it inside all the prisoners until they had recovered the use of their limbs, standing up sweating and groggy; or, in the case of the four Bandits of the Marsh, as furious as a swarm of wasps trapped under a cider glass and then released.

Purity looked at her fuming bandits. 'You said back in the valley of the war gas that we didn't have time to sort out the lesser evils on the way to fight the greater one. Do you still feel the same way?'

'You are learning, I think,' coughed Ganby, rubbing life back into his numb legs. 'And not just about the mastery of conversion a maths-blade gives you.'

'You no longer have to ask me,' said Jenny Blow, bending her knee in front of Purity. 'You can now command me.'

'I have had my bellyful of this place,' spat Samuel

Lancemaster, pressing on his cuirass and ejecting his knuckle-duster, sending the waking prisoners stumbling back crying in alarm as he extended it out to a spear twice his height. 'I have been conscious for hours, listening paralysed to the cries of sobbing children in the dark and the threats from those honourless cowards outside that dare style themselves brigands.'

Jackaby Mention looked down at Purity's bare feet. 'Yet you still have no shoes, my queen.'

Bare feet are conscious of the land. They feel the bones of Jackals, connect with the blood of the world. You will know when the time is right for shoes.

'No,' said Purity. 'But I have an army here and a navy in the dungeon down the corridor waiting to be cut out of their chains.'

And it was time to use them.

Ganby inspected the spear. It had been a most impressive throw, straight through the chief's chest and two of his toadies, to land embedded in the metre-thick casement of the sea fort; the part of the fort's wall that hadn't been reduced to rubble by the *JNS Spartiate's* cannons when the u-boat's crew had been reunited with their gun mounts. It was no wonder Samuel Lancemaster had to wedge his boots against the wall to retrieve the spear. Extricating themselves from the now truly free town of Wainsmouth might be a little trickier, however.

Ganby shook his head at the sight of the gathering crowds coming out along the harbour slope onto the walkways and surviving Martello towers of the sea fort. Even the townspeople who hadn't fought to chase the chief's men back into the surrounding hills when they realized the u-boat was on their side. Perhaps especially them, as well as all the fools who had taken the Army of Shadows' appearance as a sign of the breaking of the Circle and the end times.

How they begged and pleaded with Purity Drake to stay and make their town her capital. Soon they would be bringing sick children to Purity and asking for the queen's touch to cure them. The gullibility of the desperate. But did Ganby have the right to look down on their superstitions? He had traded on many of the same deep needs when he had been wearing a druid's robes. Pah, so much for the Circlist heresy and their half-witted humanist religion without gods. When the kingdom's people had stopped believing in the druids' many deities they had not begun believing in nothing, they had started believing in *anything*.

Purity stood on the ruined floor of what had been the chief's throne room to make her address to the mob.

'Your town's walls may feel safe.' Purity's voice carried out beyond the cry of the seagulls. 'But they are an illusion, the illusion of safety and comfort and the familiar. The slats will come tomorrow and if we kill them still more will turn up when they realize this town is no longer a nest of collaborators.'

'Where then?' someone called. 'Where can we go?'

'Back to the land!' Purity called. 'You are the sons and daughters of Jackals and your land will shelter you. The regiments have failed you, the slats hold sway over our sky, and so this must be a guerrilla war from now on. The forests and mountains will shield you and you will prey on the slats before they prey on you.'

'Stay!' the crowd begged. 'Lead us into the land.'

Purity held her sword out. 'I *am* the land and the land is *me*. My path lies north, into the heartland of the Army of Shadows. I intend to take our u-boat and drive this blade into the chest of every slat that stands between me and the destruction of that red abomination squatting in our heavens. Those of you that have any fight left in you, those of you that have the taste for vengeance, you'll find your fill of it if you follow me into the foe's heartland.'

A u-boatman in the crowds pointed down to the *Spartiate*'s black hull bobbing in the harbour. 'Our old girl only has enough expansion engine gas left in her tanks to run the screws for half an hour, maybe an hour at most. You'd be lucky to reach Hundred Locks in her.'

Purity bent down and picked up a drinking glass from the floor, placing it on a collapsed column. The oversized flagon only had a lick of red wine left in its bottom. She held her maths-blade over it and the dribble of wine began to bubble and froth, rising higher and higher until a stream of it was spilling over the edge and flooding out across the debris-strewn concrete. Ganby had to stop himself tutting aloud as people jostled in the crowd to try to get a taste of the wine, crying that this torrent was their queen of legend's own blood.

'Her tanks can be made full,' said Purity. 'As can her cannons, and her torpedo tubes – but that means nothing unless I can fill her decks with stout Jackelians with the heart to teach the Army of Shadows what it means to invade our country. To teach them why they will never count themselves masters of this land as long as one free Jackelian remains alive to stand against them. Can I fill her?'

The crowd yelled their approval.

'Can I fill her?' Purity held her sword aloft and the sun turned it to fire as a shaft of light broke through the clouds to strike the roaring crowds out on the ruined sea fort.

Ganby nodded in approval. They would need all the help they could get. The chief's force of convicts might have spared many of the u-boat's ratings from the Army of Shadows' hunger, but they certainly hadn't been planning on taking along the *Spartiate*'s marines. Replacements for the troops that had been fed to the slats would have to come from the town's volunteers. Yes, Purity was doing well. She had asked Ganby on the journey here why Elizica of the Jackeni was no longer coming to her in waking dreams and visions. Purity only had to stare in a mirror to see the answer to that question.

The disgraced druid walked over towards Purity as the surviving senior officer they had freed from the *Spartiate* – a first lieutenant of the fleet sea arm, his uniform caked in dust from the assault – emerged to talk with the queen.

He was indicating some of the men in striped sailor's shirts in the crowd. 'They've got families in the fishing villages down the coast – wives, children. They've asked to be excused to see how they fare before they join our venture.'

Purity looked at the collection of sailors, respectfully clutching the round hats decorated with the crest of the *Spartiate* in their hands. 'You want to go back for your children?'

'What man wouldn't, damson?' said a boatswain.

'What man wouldn't?' echoed Purity, sadly. 'Let them go. But we will sail when we sail.'

'You know what many of them will find out there,' said Ganby as he came up to the queen.

'They are leaving as fathers,' said Purity. 'But they will come back as avenging angels. When you have no family to worry your conscience, you have no fear.'

'Please don't hold onto that hardness,' said Ganby. 'It is a bitter seed to plant within yourself.'

'It was never planted by me,' said Purity. 'Those that sowed it are about to reap their harvest.'

A cold autumn breeze came off the waters and chilled Ganby Meridian's bones. It would be colder still in the north. This girl had become their queen and now some small part of him wished that she had not. The u-boat officer and the surviving sailors were starting to make a way for Purity down to their vessel, but they needn't have bothered – Ganby watched the queen walking through the crowds, the people of Wainsmouth parting like a sea for her.

Samuel Lancemaster came up to Ganby and planted the foot of his newly retrieved spear alongside the druid's boots. 'We're out of our time, druid, so much unfamiliar but so much the same.'

'What did you expect?' said Ganby. 'A peaceful old man's death thousands of years ago would never have suited you or the other bandits; on a bed of straw, surrounded by grandchildren and pushed out under the stars to see the sky overhead one last time.'

'You sound like such an end would have suited you just fine, druid. These people treat us like heroes now,' said Samuel. 'But if we save them, it won't take long for their fear of us to return and their gratitude to fade to a memory. Then we'll just be bandits hiding on the margins of the marsh waters again.'

'There are worst things to be,' said Ganby, 'than fey.'

'I know why you followed Elizica to sleep under the hills with us,' said Samuel. 'The druids you betrayed by fighting alongside us were not forgiving types, were they? They would have made a festival of your end, old man, for helping end their sway over the Jackeni.'

'There are no druids in this land any longer; they are as lost to these people as the legends of the Bandits of the Marsh. But the Army of Shadows, now, they truly scare me. They are like wrathful gods in the heavens. When we fought the gill-necks they only wanted to usurp our rule over Jackals for their calflings' sakes, to make our territory their own. I understood their motives, even when I was digging spike pits on our beaches to kill them. But these dark ones, they would gnaw on the Kingdom of Jackals' bones until it is less than dust. I can feel the lifeforce of our land being drained, my sorceries fading along with it.'

'You always did jump at your own shadow,' laughed Samuel. 'Now you have an army of them to worry about.'

'Mock, then,' said Ganby, irritated. 'Your spear arm will be tested soon enough when we arrive at the bottom of their beanstalk.'

'I have a bad feeling about this,' said Samuel in a fair imitation of the druid's voice before he walked off.

Ganby held out his left hand flat in front of his face. It was trembling. He reached out with his right hand to hold it steady. There were worst things to be than a coward, too. Like dead.

Purity saw Watt and Cam Quarterplate waiting for her on the other side of the sloping road outside their shop's bay windows. There were plenty of people in the street between them now; people loading up their possessions on carts and abandoning the town, others coming down to the harbour and the *Spartiate* with hunting rifles or the weapons the fleeing convicts had thrown aside. Purity crossed over to them and saw that Watt had a package under his arm.

'Are you coming to the north with me?'

'Not I, damson,' said Watt, slapping his wooden leg with a hand. 'How do you think I lost this? Mangled by a shell-loading cable when I was thirteen on a seadrinker not much different from that old girl down there. My days as a u-boat boy are over, that's so.'

'And you fastbloods will still need sturdy boots,' said the steamman, 'out in the forests and the hills.'

'More than ever,' said Purity. 'To stay ahead of the slats.'

Watt held out the parcel he was holding. 'It ain't right for a queen to go around without covering up her toes.'

Purity put her hand on the wax paper then smiled. 'Lay them aside for me. It'll give me something to look forward to when I come back.'

Clutching the parcel with mixed feelings, Watt watched Purity walk away. She had been lucky that she had left a good footprint or two back in the dust of the shoe shop's floor. The shoes he had made for her would have fitted perfectly if she had tried them on. Perhaps they would have reminded her of him, too, when she glanced down at them every so often. Oh well. Purity Drake looked like a queen and talked like a queen, but Watt was a parliamentarian at heart, and he was voting with the one good foot that his service in the fleet sea arm had left him with.

'Good luck,' the apprentice whispered.

'I rather think,' observed Cam Quarterplate, 'that you were growing quite fond of her.'

Watt looked down briefly, embarrassed, and clomped his wooden leg down on the cobbles. 'You know what I like about working for you, Cam? You never made fun of me for this, not even when all the customers were having their little jokes about young Master One-Boot working down at the cobbler's. Not even then.'

Cam Quarterplate's skull unit rotated towards the sky. 'The great pattern needs many different threads in its weave. Look up there. The birds are heading south, young softbody.'

'Too bloody right, old steamer.'

369

Watt hurried back into the shop to pack the rest of his tools up.

The slats were coming back to Wainsmouth. You didn't need to travel all the way to the icy north to find the Army of Shadows.

CHAPTER NINETEEN

ommodore Black rubbed the grit out of his face. 'There! Is that what my poor mortal eyes think it is?'

It was. Coming out of the sand haze was a figure with a body slumped over its shoulders, briefly silhouetted against the last pizo-electric crackle of the raging beast of a storm.

'My ancestors' cogs be blessed,' said Coppertracks, his vision plate magnifying the distant image. 'They made it out of the storm! It is Molly and Keyspierre softbody.'

Even Sandwalker's normally stony face momentarily cracked into a smile. The group stopped and turned to look behind them in amazement, as if the pair might be a mirage cast by the heat of the day pounding down on them from above. They unslung their backpacks into a pile on the sand as they gawped at the miraculous sight.

'But I fear she doesn't look well,' added the steamman.

'The storm has slowed us down,' said Sandwalker. He pointed to a distant peak piercing the empty sky. 'We must make better time towards the mountains or Molly will surely die on the way.'

'What have you done to her?' shouted the commodore as

Keyspierre stumbled to a stop in front of the expedition. 'She's as bruised as a barrel of lemons hauled through a storm tossing.'

The secret policeman unshouldered Molly and lay her body down on the dunes. Sandwalker was immediately at her side with a canteen; trying to give her the derisory dribble of water that remained to them.

Keyspierre squared up to the commodore, throwing the strip of severed guide rope at the u-boat man's feet. 'Thank you, compatriot, for rescuing the little author.'

Commodore Black lunged at the shiftie, but Duncan caught him.

'He's brought her back out of the storm, man, all the way through the lightning. The bampot didn't have to do that.'

'He was as likely using her blessed body as a shield to take any bolts that were coming his way.'

'I was obliged to render Compatriot Templar unconscious,' said Keyspierre. 'Her sickness has left her unhinged. She woke up screaming that I had eaten her hands, then tried to throttle me with the very fingers that were supposed to be inside my stomach.'

'Why did you do it?' asked Duncan. 'You could have just left the lassie to the storm, claimed that she was separated from you.'

'If you ask me that then you have no code,' said Keyspierre, 'and even less idea of what the Commonshare stands for. We are all equal and all equally worthy of saving. No officer of Committee Eight would leave a compatriot behind.'

'I will carry her,' said Coppertracks as Sandwalker finished administering the last of their water. 'This heat has less influence on my organs and my treads can roll as well over the dunes with Molly softbody's weight across me as with my own.'

Commodore Black laid his hand on Molly's forehead. Her only response was a small moan. 'Ah, poor lass and poor us. We've fought so hard and come so far and this is the end of us, out here. Molly burning up under the weight of Kyorin's soul. Your blessed paradise made a hell, Sandwalker, a small taste of the fate of our beautiful green Jackals. My genius has been tested before, but never by a land so fearfully arid and an enemy so cruel as the Army of Shadows.' The commodore slipped his bottle of medicinal whisky from his pack. 'But I still have this, even if our water canteens are as dry as a sea-drinker hull sailing too close to the magma of the Fire Sea. A rare taste of home so we can remember the kingdom's lochs and hills before we all leave our parched corpses stretched out here.'

Duncan lunged for the bottle, but the commodore was too quick, moving it to the side and pushing away the ex-rocketman's hand. Duncan was furious. 'Are you mad, Jared, wanting a dram of that stuff? With no water you can't drink whisky out here in the heat of the day.'

'I may not be an old hand of the southern frontier like you, but I know what drinking whisky in the desert does to a man,' said the commodore. 'But here it is, I'm dry, and as great an adventurer as I am, even my brave frame can't be murdered twice. I'll keel over from this wicked sun long before I keel over from the stomach cramps.'

Taking a greedy swig from the canteen, the commodore wiped the drips from the side of his mouth and offered the bottle to Duncan and Keyspierre.

'I'm still going to kill you when this is over,' said the secret policeman, taking the whisky, drawing a quick measure and then passing it across to Duncan Connor.

'What sort of filthy wheatman would you be if you did not?' said the commodore.

Duncan took a nip, made a face and spat the foul-tasting stuff out onto the sand. 'Sweet Circle, man, I've drunk raw jinn distilled by tribesmen that tasted better than that. How much alcohol is in this wee bottle?'

'Alcohol!' Sandwalker snatched the bottle, sniffing at it in horror before corking it shut. 'Fools! You've actually brought a solution of alcohol out onto the plains?' The nomad drew his arm back to hurl the bottle as far as he could, the commodore about to leap on him to save it, when they saw it. 'You'll attract . . .'

The thin branches of what looked like a tree were rising up over the dune in front of them, quivering in the air. A horrendous buzzing filled the empty wasteland and the thin branches became the spread of twin antennae on a giant ant, its chitin a mottled orange, the same shade as the sand, hovering under twin buzz-saw wings, two leathery globes swelling out on either side of its thorax.

Sandwalker tossed the bottle as far and as hard he could, and like a gun hound fetching a falling pheasant, the flying ant curved through the air and snatched the tumbling green glass with one of its six jointed legs. Then the monstrosity flipped around and came straight for the members of the expedition. Everyone scattered, Coppertracks ducking as he reversed backwards at full speed clutching Molly's prone form, the huge insect's rotating forewings nearly clipping the steamman's transparent dome skull in passing.

It went right through the space where the expedition had been standing, scooping up all their piled packs – the potpourri of food scents too strong for the insect to ignore.

'Our blessed supplies!' Commodore Black shouted, running up to the crest of the dune after the creature. 'My bully beef!'

On the opposite side of the dune was a rough circle of ground a lighter colour than the surrounding sands. Fat orange larvae were coming out to feed as the giant ant opened the expedition's belongings with its scimitar-sharp mouthparts, its antennae flickering in a dance as it scented and sorted the chemical traces coming from each pack. Commodore Black didn't need to notice the similarity between the flying ant and the slats' hovering globe ships to know that here was another of the mutations scattered across Kaliban by the terrible Army of Shadows. Where was his blessed gun?

'Leave our food there,' ordered Sandwalker as he sprinted up the dune, pushing the commodore's pistol down towards the sand. 'That flying ant is only a male drone left to tend the nest's young. The female soldiers and workers will be out foraging with their queen – there will be dozens of them, more than enough to hunt us down as prey.'

A grand course of action. One ruined by Duncan Connor sprinting up the slope behind them, roaring as if he had just lost his mind, a pistol in one hand and a straight Jackelian cavalry sabre in the other. 'It's got her, it's got her!'

For a moment Commodore Black thought that his friend was talking about Molly, but a quick glance back down the dune showed that she was still resting in Coppertracks' iron arms. 'She's safe, lad!'

Connor of Cassarabia was over the crest of the hill and dashing down in frenzied kicks of sand towards the ant. It was then that Commodore Black saw it. The flying insect had ripped open Duncan's travel case, scattering bleached white bones across the bronze sand, one of them a skull so small it had to be that of a human child.

The head of the insect darted up as it saw Duncan racing towards the nest and the larvae in its charge. Raising its abdomen and dipping its antennae in warning like a charging bull, the insect took off towards Duncan, but the ex-rocketman triggered the charge in his pistol, blowing out the ant's right compound eye in a shower of ichor. Off balance now, the ant continued to fly towards Duncan, the Jackelian launching himself into the air and landing on top of the creature's thorax underneath the twin rotating wings. Now the flying ant was furious. This was prey – prey fighting back! It clumped down onto the dune and angled its wings to blow a sandstorm back across its body, always enough to dislodge any parasite foolish enough to try to pierce its chitin.

In the midst of the gale Duncan yelled an upland battle cry and slammed his sabre down through the join between the head and thorax of his furious mount, decapitating the ant in one swing. As the massive insect's wings stopped rotating, Duncan was off, smoothly rolling away from the beast's back and running towards his broken case and the bones lying across the sands, slashing at the fat orange larvae as they reared up and tried to lunge at his legs.

Commodore Black and Sandwalker were quickly at Duncan's side, leaving the others on the crest to gaze down bewildered at the carnage and the giant slain ant, watching Duncan stuffing the bones into his travel case and trying to lock the lid back on it.

Duncan was mumbling at the sand, barely registering their presence. 'I'm sorry, lassie, I'm sorry they did that to you.'

'Are you suffering from heat exhaustion, Duncan Connor?' asked Sandwalker. 'You could have died. Do you know how dangerous these colonies are?'

'Don't look at her, man,' begged Duncan. 'She hates people glowering at her now.'

'Who, lad?' asked Commodore Black.

'My wee daughter, Hannah.'

'These are just blessed bones.'

'She's different now, that's all. Hannah hates people having

376

a shufty at her. Nobody else understands, only her father does, only me, always me.'

'We have to go,' urged the nomad, bending down to gather what supplies had survived the larvae's feeding frenzy. 'The drone's mates will return and we must be far away when they do.'

'It wasn't my regiment's fault,' said Duncan, standing up and clutching the broken case to his chest, 'when we fired on the raiders with our gas rockets. We didn't realize the raiding party had already stolen people from the upland villages for slaves. Everyone was wearing sand robes. We thought they were coming out of the desert, not going back towards Cassarabia, not going *back*.'

Commodore Black gently laid a hand on the ex-soldier's shoulder. 'She's just bones, lad, she's dead.'

Duncan shook his head. 'No, it was my wife who died, not Hannah. No one understands that Hannah's just a little different. My wee girl, my bonnie wee girl.'

But Commodore Black understood now. Why the New Pattern Army hadn't taken Connor of Cassarabia back into the fold even when the enlisting parties were desperately sweeping every lane in the kingdom's towns for fresh recruits to face the Army of Shadows. How many years had Duncan been travelling with his daughter's corpse rotting in a suitcase? Part of him must know, deep down. The part that had been taking coin for suicide callings like the circus of the extreme.

'We have to protect Hannah,' insisted Duncan. 'Protect her from the Army of Shadows. Those black-hearted kelpies will take her for a slave, make her suffer the same as Sandwalker's people.'

Commodore Black looked at the ex-soldier. 'We'll save her, Duncan, we'll save all our darling girls back in the Kingdom

377

of Jackals and stick our boot hard up the Army of Shadows' arse while we're about it.'

Sandwalker retrieved a thin black tube from his torn pack. He rotated its head to reveal a tiny spray hole. 'We must pass through the territory of the ant colonies to reach the mountains. This will help us survive.'

'What is it, lad?' asked the commodore.

'A synthesized version of the pheromone a queen ant uses to attract her workers and soldiers to her. If we are pursued, one of us must sacrifice themselves for the group. Once the pheromone is applied to a robe, the colony will chase only the one who has been sprayed. If this was my tribe's caravan, it would be traditional for the oldest and the sickest to be appointed as the lure.'

Commodore Black glanced nervously at the massive blade-like pincers of the dead ant's mouthparts. If it came to it, who would be selected in such a mortal awful lottery?

Which one of them would have die to save them all?

Molly woke up to burning pain slicing through her head, haunted by the shadows of things she wasn't quite sure were phantoms, or Kyorin's memories, or events that were actually happening to her now. She was being carried. Yes, the expedition to reach the great sage. To find the weapon. And to cure her, before her mind fried under the endless heat of the Kaliban sun and the weight of the strange memories.

She was being borne in someone's arms; her head so weak she couldn't even turn to catch sight of who it was. But she could see the great rise of a mountain in front of them. So tall, as were the ants. Two giant ants! Coming towards her, as big as shire horses, pincers snicking together hungrily. Molly tried to yell but her throat was too dry. She was placed on the ground and left there. The monstrous pair of ants were still coming forward, six legs apiece, sharp orange legs like lances jabbing at the ground. The head of the nearest ant dipped down, its antennae brushing against Molly's forehead, marking her scent. This treachery was Keyspierre's work, it had to be! The dirty shiftie secret policeman was sacrificing her as an offering to these monsters. Abandoning her as food to save his skin.

Now Molly's paper-dry throat summoned enough saliva to scream.

CHAPTER TWENTY

Even miles distant, Purity could hear the thunder of the *Spartiate*'s guns as the first shells began to drop on the domed city that the Army of Shadows had built on the coast. Or rather, the dome that had been raised by their slaves' labours. Purity, the Bandits of the Marsh and their small volunteer army had come across a few of the pits where the slats had tossed the bones of dead polar barbarians after consuming those who had been worked to death. Nothing wasted.

Purity hoped that there were some of the ugly tentacled masters the slats bowed their eyeless heads to inside that dome . . . and not just because it would make it easier to entice the slat legions away from the hideous white beanstalk anchored in the frozen soil of the north. She wanted the masters to be there because, for just a moment, it would mean that the invaders might feel a fraction of the fear that the Jackelians had while the slats were rampaging across their home.

'It is working,' observed Samuel Lancemaster, brushing the falling snow out of his face. 'The slats are being recalled back towards their city.'

'They fear an assault from the sea,' replied Purity. 'Rightly so – for all the slats know, we might have dozens of u-boats waiting under the ice pack to surface.'

Columns of slats were forming up, emerging like beetles from snow-submerged buildings blasted into the hard ground of what had once been the polar barbarians' territory. Soldiers appeared in the shadow of their beanstalk, the hideous white appendage disappearing into the snowstorm and the night. No sign of the iron moon here, the baleful rusting eye of the Army of Shadows hidden like the home of the gods on its heavenly mountaintop. Only the occasional flicker of red light as capsules rode up the beanstalk. These were the same capsules Molly Templar had described crossing the celestial darks, now turned into lifting rooms. Purity arched her neck up towards where the giant cable disappeared into the whited heavens. It was at least the circumference of one of the capital's lofty pneumatic towers.

Yes, Purity had a good view of the beanstalk from the brow of the hill. But by her side the druid Ganby was paying little attention to their target. The closer they got to the drained leylines of the distant north, the more nervous the old man had become. Now he was lying alongside Purity shaking like a jinn-house lush without the coins for his next glass.

'Would that we did have such an underwater armada,' said Ganby. He rubbed his face into the snow, moaning as a circle of leathery globes squatting around the beanstalk started to hum into life, rising under their buzzing blade-wings before angling away across the hills.

'Eating snow won't make a man of you,' laughed Jenny Blow. 'We'll throw the hearts of a couple of slats on the fire for you later. That'll fatten you up.'

'The soil is so barren. They've drained the energy from the land. I'm too weak to fight them.'

'And you thought you had the sweating sickness the day before I met the gill-neck's prince in single combat,' said Samuel. 'Do be quiet, old man.'

'Is he always like this before a battle?' asked Purity.

'Every one I've seen,' confirmed Jackaby Mention. 'Except this time I believe he may have just cause for his humours.'

'This is my first battle.'

'I know. Your job is to sever the ring of cables anchoring the beanstalk to the ground,' said Jackaby. 'The rest you may leave to us.'

The rest. It sounded so easy. The element of surprise might carry them through the defences to the foot of the towering beanstalk, but how long could they last – how long would *she* last – hacking the anchor cables off it, before the Army of Shadows responded with force enough to overwhelm the small band of attackers?

It was then that Purity saw him, trying to hide down in the crowd of volunteers. Watt! Despite all his protestations, the young cobbler had returned to his old calling in the fleet after all.

She walked towards him, and seeing that he had been rumbled, he gave up trying to conceal himself amongst the crouching line of volunteers.

'I thought you were going to head into the forests with the other refugees from the port?'

He looked embarrassed. 'The old steamer can keep them in shoe leather well enough without me.'

'Your talents might be better off employed back on the u-boat. You'd be safer there.'

'You're a fine one to talk.' He held up a small rifle. 'I'm not out here to protect you, you know. After I was invalided out of the fleet, I promised myself I'd never die on one of those tin cans. I needed the air, that's why I'm here.'

The air. It was about to get a lot more bracing. 'Well, you look after yourself, Watt.'

He reached out and put a hand on her arm as she was about to go back to where the Bandits of the Marsh were . waiting. 'I've got your shoes tied up in my pack. I made them myself. I sized them using one of your footprints from the dust back on the shop's floor.'

Purity laughed. 'Really? Thank you. I'll try them on when we've cut down the beanstalk. It'll be something to look forward to.'

Purity walked to the head of the hill and turned about to address her volunteers crouching down on the side of the slope like a hundred and fifty white ghosts, her voice competing against the storming winds and the distant thundering guns of their u-boat. 'I know many of you are scared, many of you are wondering if you will see your homes again right now. So I'm not going to ask you to fight your way through the slats down there . . .'

Shouts of mortification sounded back through the whipping snow.

'No, I'm not going to ask you to fight your way through slat legions and hold that ground down there. But here's the rub. I have decided that ugly bone-white beanstalk rising out of our ground offends my eye. It's unsightly. So I'm going to take a stroll down there and chop it to pieces. Perhaps you'd like to come and see me do that?'

Her volunteers shook their rifles in the falling snow.

'Then you're invited for a stroll!' shouted Purity. 'And if we bump into any slats down there, just remember that one stout Jackelian soul is worth fifty of their slave soldiers.'

'You have heard your queen. Not one of you is to die,' commanded Samuel, 'until you have sent at least fifty of those flat-faced bastards back to whatever foul underworld they worship. I shall kill twice that many myself and count them merely practice for my spear.'

Purity rose and pointed her maths-blade down towards the beanstalk. An explosion erupted from the base of the hill, the first of the Army of Shadows' mines detecting the gravity wave sent from her blade, then there were hundreds of sprouting flowers of fury setting each other off around the perimeter, arcs of shrapnel shredding the slats that had been standing behind the safety line with their rifles shouldered. At the first sign of attack, anthill-like structures next to the underground entrances of the slats' barracks started to spew out clouds of red gas, the cloaking mist the creatures used to blind their enemies and tip the balance in favour of their sound-sight.

Purity shook her head. Not this time – the sword blazed in her fist and the gas clouds became fierce jets venting from a hoop of red volcanoes around the beanstalk before returning to gaseous form far above the encampment.

'I think the Army of Shadows deserves to see us come calling,' called Purity, waving her sword. 'For your families. For your freedom. For Jackals!'

As one they rose behind Purity, charging down the slope. Purity was not thinking about the slippery iced rocks under their feet, not thinking about the driving wind or the black chattering forms spilling out from the Army of Shadows' underground barracks. Not thinking about how she would have to lead anyone who survived back to the *Spartiate* if the raid succeeded, harried every step of the way by the enemy's legions.

Jackaby had dragged Ganby Meridian to his feet and was pushing the druid along with the rest of the kingdom's last ragged army. Behind them the wind multiplied twenty-fold, a gale picking up broken rock from the rubble of the minefield and making a storm of flint chips over the base of the beanstalk, slats howling as their armoured skeletons were torn to pieces by the gale. The wind subsided as Jenny Blow halted for breath. Purity and her raiders were on the flat now, following fast after Jenny's storm as though they were redcoats charging behind a rolling artillery barrage.

That was when the first of the rods started to rise from buried hatches surrounding the minefield, shining black poles each topped with a rotating globe studded with sharp crystal tips. Samuel Lancemaster shoved Purity to the snow as bolts of fire began to streak out of the spheres, leaping red sparks that cut through the ranks of the Jackelians. Rifles went spinning though the air as their owners fell clutching blackened chests and burnt off stubs of limbs. A second volley of sparks lashed out of the rising fence, splitting the falling weapons into fragments.

'Movement!' shouted Samuel. 'The fence detects movement. Get to the ground and lie still!'

Purity looked around. Her force were throwing themselves down to the snow and trying not to shiver on the freezing ground. But there was Jenny Blow, still on her feet and trying to shatter the poles' spheres with her voice. Jenny Blow had once taught the knights of the Steammen Free State how to modulate their voiceboxes and shatter organs inside a ribcage, but she would teach no more. Homing in on her from all sides, the fence whipped Jenny in a crosscut wave of spitting sparks, slicing her to pieces. The last dying notes of her throat emptied into the wind as she fell back and lay sprawled across the ground, little veins of crimson spreading across the plain's snow. Purity had detected the minefield, but not this lurking fence of burning fire . . . Jenny's death was on her hands. Fool, fool of a girl. She was a breeding-house ragamuffin, not a queen, not a leader. What use was her bravado out here?

Ganby lay across from Purity, muttering, his frantic eyes darting between the crackling poles in front of them, a forest of death raised to protect the beanstalk. 'We're dead, we're dead. Death awaits us in the north.'

And Purity had led them to it.

Molly came out of unconsciousness yelling, the thunder roaring in her head as she tried to make sense of the vague shapes she could see in the dim light. She was being carried by one of the giant ants, her body lying across the foremost pair of its legs. As Molly was borne bobbing through a dark rocky tunnel, flashes of light hit her like bayonet thrusts from somewhere to her side. The nest, she was in the ants' nest, being dragged deep into their colony. Nausea and fear swelled around her in a sea of agony, the insect's antennae stroking her hair as she screamed and flailed in its grip.

Wakefulness came and went, the spear-clacking noise of the monstrous insect's legs on rock drumming across her. Then she was being taken through a chamber, pale light from a distant source in the roof glinting wickedly against the ant's compound eyes. Its legs lifted Molly forward; painfully twisting her neck she saw that it was carrying her towards a wall dotted with dark circular holes and lifting her into a tube. Oh, sweet Circle! A memory of the spider web that often seemed to be woven outside her bedroom in Tock House on cold autumn mornings came back to Molly. The spider happily spinning little white packages and sealing the flies against a leaf for its young to consume.

Molly tried to lever herself out of the tunnel, but the ant had sealed the tomb down by her feet. Shut in. Trapped. Just like when she had been a stack cleaner crawling through the tunnels of Middlesteel's towers, the enclosed spaces pushing down on her, crushing the life out of her. She had survived that, though. Survived the short career of a poorhouse stack-cleaning girl.

Molly was feverishly kicking at the obstruction under her feet when something came crawling out of the other end of the tunnel and snapped tight onto her head.

Surrounded by the cries of the wounded and dying raiders, Purity was desperately trying to work out a way to disable the fence of murderous poles that had risen to protect the Army of Shadows' facility. She could deflect a couple of the killing sparks with her sword, absorb a few more, but the enemy's defence barrier encircled the beanstalk. Every time one of the Jackelians moved they were detected and cut to pieces. Just like poor Jenny Blow.

More slats were spilling out of the barracks; it wouldn't take long for the beasts to form up behind the killing fence and pick the Jackelians off like farmers culling rabbits in a wheat field.

A slew of snow fell across Purity as a figure flashed past her, some of it falling into her open mouth and melting on her tongue. Jackaby Mention! Almost too fast to follow, save for the fact that icy erupting ground trailed the blur of his passage as the globes on top of the defence line spat their evil spark-fire at him. The blur coalesced by one of the poles, Jackaby visible for a second before he took off again, running around the ring of death.

Purity saw what Jackaby was doing. Fire flashed from each pole as he slowed, cutting into the neighbouring rod – and Jackaby was whirling around the beanstalk's perimeter, slowing and speeding up – a brief target for the spheres on top of each black sentry machine. The deadly heads were erupting in flames as neighbours cut at each other with fire, falling like felled trees while Jackaby spun around them like a human whirlwind.

The fence was disabled now. Samuel Lancemaster rose, a titan from the field of death. 'Forward the line! Up from the dirt, warriors of Jackals. Leave the dead behind and make their ghosts proud.'

Picking themselves up from the snow, the surviving raiders lunged past the ruined defence works. Purity was running forward, the thump of the slats' rifles sending bolts of fire sizzling through the falling snowflakes, laying down steam trails that hung in the air pointing back to the defenders' positions. She could hear Ganby running behind her, cursing and moaning, the lee of her shadow as safe as any place in this battle. Shafts of rifle fire were slapped aside by Purity's blade as she ran towards the web of cables anchoring the beanstalk's earthworks to the cold northern rock of the polar wastes. The beanstalk pulsed like a muscle while lifting rooms crawled up and down it on all sides as if they were leaf flies.

Purity tried to close her ears to the beanstalk's song in the wind, a sickening alien sound as the billion carbonized tubes that made this towering monstrosity creaked above her head, pulled by the spin of the world. But Purity's maths-blade showed her how to change its song, right enough, cause enough stress to fracture this hideous construction's hold on the frozen north. Just sever the web of anchor cables on one side of the beanstalk, let the planet's spin pull the roots of the remaining anchors out and send the beanstalk whipping up to cut the iron moon into rusty shards.

Samuel Lancemaster shouted orders to the volunteers to take their defensive positions around the beanstalk. This was Purity's moment. Her task. She came to a mooring point, the first of the beanstalk's white anchor cables as wide as a man and sunk deep into the polar bedrock through a solidified pool of some strange dark substance.

'Swing your blade,' sobbed Ganby from behind her. 'Swing it at the anchor lines and let us quit this frozen hell.'

Purity turned the sword once, willing her blade to cleave a substance so strong that it could clamp the iron moon to their world. Then she yelled and struck down with everything she had. There was a terrible screaming sound as the fibres of the anchor line split apart and the first of the holding cables lashed away to the ground. She ran to the next mooring point and swung her sword in another testing arc. There must have been at least twenty anchor lines on her side of the beanstalk. Already Purity's arm was aching with the effort needed to drive through a million diamond-hard threads bound together more densely than anything the race of man had ever encountered. She hove at the second one, feeling the flash of energy as the maths-blade converted the strength of the carbon into something more brittle and malleable. It went tumbling away. Purity ran to the next line, ignoring the shouts of the raiders calling to each other for more ammunition or screaming as the slats broke through and tore into them with rifle bolts and the force of their talons. Ignoring the blur of Jackaby Mention, darting between the attackers, sending slats spinning away into the snowstorm, and Samuel Lancemaster's spear whirling around like a windmill. Purity forgot even the bite of the cold as the labour of chopping away the anchor lines began to tell. How many lines had she cut now? Half? She was losing count, having to take six or seven lunges at each anchor line to sever it.

'Make speed,' appealed Ganby, shivering from exposure to the freezing winds. 'We don't have long left. Damn this place, I can't feel my fingers.'

But Purity felt the pulse of fire spurting along the ground behind her, accompanied by the screams of the Jackelians sent flying into the air on geysers of exploding rock and snow

389

and blood. It was a flight of the slats' aerial spheres, the leathery crafts' wasp-hum cutting through the storm. Turned back by the destruction of the beanstalk's defence perimeter, the air fleet were dipping in and out of the whiteout, their cannons wreaking destruction among the defending Jackelians. Jigger the beasts! They knew the tough anchor lines would withstand the blasts of their guns, near indestructible compared to the weak, soft bodies of those who had followed her to this place. But they had reckoned without Samuel Lancemaster. He sprinted out of the shadow of the beanstalk, casting his spear forward, his first throw passing through two of the slats' globes, smashing their pilots and the organic machinery inside. Jackaby Mention was out there too, speeding to where the spear had been cast and hurtling it back to Samuel. Allowing him to throw it again and again, as if he had an unlimited supply of deadly javelins by his side.

The attackers' cannons couldn't home in on Jackaby, but they realized who their true enemy was soon enough, avoiding the missiles of their own broken craft falling out of the sky, blazing at Samuel with their guns. His silver cuirass deflected the first of the bursts of fire, then buckled under the continued fusillade, sending him stumbling back. He was on his knees moaning, trying to hold in his shattered living armour with one hand, the other stretched out imploringly for the blur of Jackaby Mention to bring him his spear. The spear appeared in his hand and he used it as a crutch to get to his feet and face the two remaining craft circling him.

'Is that it?' Samuel yelled. 'Is that all you have?'

Both crafts' cannons opened up on him and he cast out the spear at the closest in a chopping motion, driving his missile all the way through the globe and out across the rotating array of blades keeping it suspended, the craft's flight mechanism chewed to pieces as the bandit's projectile smashed across it.

The remaining sphere drifted behind Samuel, almost cutting him in half with its stuttering cannons, creating a gale as it hovered just above the ground, slats jumping down from a hatch in the craft's side. Samuel Lancemaster stumbled forward empty-handed and, ignoring the rifle fire of the dismounting beasts, drove a fist into the front of the globe, lifting the craft up over his head and breaking the whirling array of blades as it dug into the frozen soil behind his back. Purity swore the slat troops actually flinched and stepped back as he roared at them, tossing the broken craft away to detonate across the frozen plain. Then Samuel fell face down to lie still in the snow, burning fluids from the smashed craft leaking across his body.

Jackaby Mention coalesced into solid form in front of Purity. 'Samuel has claimed his fifty corpses, my queen. This is the last anchor line. Sever it, sever it now!'

Purity was dizzy, swaying on her feet. She hacked wildly into the anchor line like a drunken woodsman, dozens of blows needed to break its tightly woven bonds. Purity lined up her final cut, the last cable screeching like fingernails on a blackboard as it subsumed all the stress of the anchor filaments she had already severed.

'Quickly,' begged Ganby. 'There are hardly any of our people left now. The slats are overrunning us.'

'Be quiet, druid.' Jackaby was panting from his exertions. 'Let our queen concentrate.'

Purity let swing at the anchor cable and chipped out perhaps a tenth of it.

'Pick me up,' Ganby pleaded with the only other surviving bandit. 'You can run me out to one of the hills over there. We're almost done here.'

Purity took another fatigued bite out of the anchor line.

Jackaby shook his head, rapping the layer of frost that had formed across his marsh leathers. 'I can't run any more, cramps from the cold. When we've cut the last line I'm going to have to walk out of here.'

Purity was so tired, she almost ignored the sense of confusion coming from her maths-blade as she raised the sword to hack again, but the information came flooding through anyway. It was the blade's stress model. This shouldn't be so much work; with half the anchor lines already severed; this last line should have been half-pulled apart by the drag of the world on the beanstalk. What was going on here?

Purity looked back over their snow tracks. The cables she had already severed were reaching out like snakes to their mooring points, little black threads extending from each sheared line to the stations left embedded in the rock. Tendons of a regrowing muscle.

'Hell's teeth,' howled Ganby. 'It's repairing itself, the beanstalk can repair itself!'

'Strike now!' shouted Jackaby. 'Strike, my queen, while you can.'

'Believe in yourself,' whimpered Ganby, making himself small on the ground as bolts of fire spun past from the dark, splashing against the beanstalk.

Purity swung the maths-blade over her head, trying to use the cold bite of the snow against her bare toes to focus, concentrating on the anchor line's alien material, altering it, allowing her sword to slice deep. She struck. The sword stopped, held tight by the anchor line – the blade was stuck. She tried to yank it out, but the anchor line's material was flowing over it. Repairing itself. Purity's sword was as stuck as it had been before she first drew the blade from the stone circle back in Jackals. But Purity couldn't afford to fail. The entire nation was riding on this. The lives of all the people she had led here sacrificed for . . . nothing?

Ganby was still on his knees, weeping. 'We can come back. If we just escape now. We can come back and mount another attack later, factor in the healing time of the anchors, maybe come up with a way to stop the mooring lines repairing themselves.' Then the terrified druid was on his feet, lunging out of the shadow of the beanstalk, trying to escape.

'Ganby!' bellowed Jackaby Mention. 'Come back here, you craven druid's whore.'

Jackaby tried to grab at the fleeing bandit's back but fell over, the cramps in his muscles toppling him moaning into the snow. As the druid was swallowed by the snowstorm there was a succession of thumps, the volley of slat rifles slapping into a soft human form.

Ganby's smoking corpse appeared a minute later, dragged forward by a line of slats. The Kal at the front of the line looked at his soldiers picking through the slumped bodies of the last of the kingdom's raiders, taking in Purity Drake, shedding cold tears as she lay collapsed over the anchor line, her hand still resting on the grip of the embedded maths-blade. Jackaby Mention lay semi-paralysed on the snow, gazing hatred back at the line of the Army of Shadows' fighters.

Smirking, the Kal went over to Purity and pulled her up by the hair. Then he breathed on her icy cheeks through those monstrous fangs, meeting her eyes. 'When, many generations hence, your ancestors are penned up, soiling themselves in their food cages, the suffering you experience for this day's trespass will still be legendary among them.'

The last legend told by the Jackelians.

CHAPTER TWENTY-ONE

Molly recovered her senses with a start as she was dragged out of the tight confines of the tunnel. There was a clear, pain-free lucidity to her thoughts. The realization that she appeared gloriously free of the burden of Kyorin's memories battled for attention with the fact that it was one of the giant ant's forelimbs currently dragging her out of the dark shaft.

Then she was free on the chamber floor and about to go hell for leather as the ant pulled back, but she heard a familiar voice calling from behind the insect. Sandwalker! The Kal nomad, still in his white sand robes. Molly's eyes danced between the nomad and the insect, and as Sandwalker rested a hand on the ant's thorax, the dim chamber began to lighten. Molly realized that these walls were far too smooth to belong to any ant colony worthy of the name.

'We are deep within one of our mountain shelters,' said Sandwalker. 'And as I promised, the great sage has cured you. Kyorin's memories have been taken out of your mind. It was an operation of great sophistication to unentangle your patterns.'

Molly raised a confused hand to point at the giant ant calmly watching her through its compound eyes.

'Machines shaped in the form of our predators. What better place to hide from the slats' long-range patrols than a false ant colony in the side of a mountain.'

'I thought I was about to be eaten,' said Molly, finding her voice.

'For that I am sorry, although I believe you now know what it has been to live as one of my people for the last couple of thousand years,' said Sandwalker. 'Come, Molly Templar, my tribe's sage is eager to meet you and your friends.'

The nomad led Molly through empty corridors and chambers that had the reek of ages about them. Dusty machinery lay about the place – instruments as large as buildings – most looking scavenged, with plates removed and cables hanging out like torn intestines.

'This was a centre of science, once,' said Sandwalker. 'Built very far from the inhabited lands of my people – to protect against the exotic nature of the experiments that were once conducted underneath our feet.'

Molly was escorted into a large circular room where her friends were waiting and overjoyed to see her recovered, Commodore Black pumping her hand while Coppertracks sped past Keyspierre and Duncan Connor to speak to her. Molly was a little overwhelmed by the greeting so soon after waking. Surreally, bright panels displaying scenes and sounds of Kaliban as it had once existed surrounded them. Lush green forests filled with the familiar blue faces of the Kal, as well as long-extinct creatures she didn't recognize; nothing like the killers that were stalking the wastes now. Images so realistic she might almost have been looking through a window.

'I told you she would be fine again,' said Sandwalker,

proudly. 'The medical devices we still have here date back to before the occupation.'

'So you say, lad,' grinned the commodore. 'And you've lived up to your word right enough. You're blessed lucky to still be with us, Molly. Your heart stopped out there in the desert during your last few minutes. How do you feel now?'

'Clear headed.'

'As you should,' announced a voice behind her. Molly turned. More mind-speech. So, this was *him*! The great sage, Fayris Fastmind, as old a creature as Molly had ever seen. A pale blue body borne along on a floating ceramic carriage, his legs hidden, his face covered in silvery metallic tattoos that glowed with energy pulses as he spoke. 'The magnetic resonance scanner I used to operate on you is the last functioning one we have in this facility. Probably the last one on Kaliban, now.'

Coppertracks looked at the Kal, the energy waves under the steamman's transparent skull circulating in excitement. 'Why, you are a metal-flesher, a man-machine hybrid.'

''Pon my soul,' said the astonished Kal, returning the steamman's gaze. His mind-voice was like the unrolling of an ancient parchment. 'And you are sentient? Self-aware? After all these years, a self-replicating machine entity. I haven't seen such as you for two millennia.'

'People similar to mine once existed on Kaliban?' asked Coppertracks.

'Oh yes,' said the great sage, his carriage gliding around the commodore and Molly. He gestured to the far wall and a panel shifted view to a lightless hall full of black cabinets. Something told Molly she was seeing one of the chambers under the mountain, a view of dust and decay now. Row after row of dead machines.

'Artificial life that was pure intellect, crushed by the Army of Shadows. Burnt out by the machine plagues the masters sent before they invaded in force.' The Kal pointed to the silvery etching glowing around his face. 'It was hard to tell where your kind began and ours ended, once. Now both our races have ended our days on Kaliban. How sad.'

'You are the intellect that was signalling to my world from Kaliban?' asked Coppertracks.

'Not I,' said the great sage. 'We dare not send such messages for fear of being tracked down. We still have a few ancient communication devices in orbit, broadcasting the original warning of the Army of Shadow's invasion out to anyone who might be able to help. You must have heard one of those.'

'We've travelled a long way to reach you,' said Molly. 'I owe you my life for healing my mind, but I have an entire world still to save.'

'You have travelled further than you know, I think,' said the sage. 'And it sounds as if you carry a heavy burden for your people, much as I have done for mine.'

Keyspierre stepped forward. 'We have not come such a distance to trade homilies, compatriot. You have a weapon to destroy the Army of Shadows. To keep my nation safe I must have it.'

'Oh yes,' chuckled the Kal, before he doubled up coughing.

Sandwalker was at the great sage's side, checking the read-outs on the carriage. 'You are tiring him!'

Fayris Fastmind waved the nomad away, irritated. 'Do not fuss so, my friend. I haven't had anyone visit since I dispatched your brother to seek out Kyorin of the city-born. I will lose my reputation as a hermit if you keep on turning up like this, unannounced, with all your associates in tow.' The sage beckoned Molly forward. 'I felt the machine life bubbling inside your body when I unentangled Kyorin's memories from your mind. We are alike, you and I, both the last guardians of our land. But there is a way in which we must not be alike—' he stopped to rummage around inside his floating chair, withdrawing a golden sphere not much bigger than the tip of a finger. 'I have failed my land, so it falls to you to end the sickness of the Army of Shadows.'

Molly took the tiny sphere in her hand, smooth and slippery except where a single tiny black button broke its surface. 'What is it?'

'Why, you hold in your hand the weapon to destroy the masters.'

'Now, I don't mean any disrespect,' said the commodore, 'since it's your genius that's just saved my friend's precious life, but you must be out of your gourd if you think that mortal little marble is going to stop the Army of Shadows.'

'This is surely not the weapon?' said Sandwalker, as astonished as all the others by the sage's revelation.

'One of a pair, in fact. The other was destroyed when your brother's party was ambushed trying to take it to Kyorin. It will stop the Army of Shadows,' said the great sage. 'Starve them to death, in fact.'

Duncan Connor came over to inspect the weapon in Molly's hand. 'We point this at the Army of Shadows, press the wee button, and they all die?'

'More or less. Well, perhaps a little more, when coupled with the truth of the masters' nature. Their little secret.'

'What is it?' asked Molly.

'You have to carry my weapon onto the iron moon, the satellite currently fixed to your home in lunar orbit. The weapon only works inside the iron moon, but if this sphere is activated there, I promise you, the majority of the Army of Shadows will die, and nature will take care of the few that remain.'

'Getting onto the iron moon? That's quite a stipulation,' said Molly.

'The iron moon!' whined Commodore Black, as the shock of what this wizened little man was telling them sunk in. 'It will be full of the wicked slats and their masters and blue-faced vampires.'

'Full is a relative term,' said the great sage. 'There are by my estimate no more than a thousand masters left alive now, half of those biding their time here on Kaliban, half waiting for victory over your people on the iron moon. Perhaps twelve times that number of slats and a handful of Kal carnivores on the moon with the masters.'

'Against a handful of us,' said Molly.

'My plan involves infiltration, not assault,' said the great sage. At a touch of the console on his carriage, a section of floor disappeared and a line of black forms rose into the chamber. They looked like dissected slats hung over a fence post as a warning to any others that might trespass. 'These are slat suits. They will seal around your body when you step into them. Like the soldier ants guarding my mountain they are indistinguishable from the real thing – they smell the same, walk the same, emit sonar screeches from the throat, and will translate the slats' own tongue both ways.'

'An impressive feat, Fayris softbody,' said Coppertracks. 'But not as impressive as a moon-splitting weapon miniaturized down to the size of one of my iron fingers.'

'To understand my weapon you need the truth I talked of,' said the great sage. 'Before you arrived on Kaliban, you passed through a disruptive field of some sort?'

'That terrible wall of energy that nearly burst our craft apart?' whined the commodore. 'The wicked thing nearly did for us.'

'That was because you were passing through it the wrong way,' said the great sage. 'It was only intended to admit causal

399

objects travelling the natural way along the timeline, from the past, forward to the future.'

'Timeline?' said Molly.

Coppertracks' skull blazed with light. 'Of course! All the stars, disappearing, being in the wrong place! Procession . . .'

'Procession? Are we to have a blessed parade now?' said Commodore Black. 'Talk some sense, Aliquot Coppertracks.'

'The field we passed through in the darks of space was no defence field of the Army of Shadows,' said Coppertracks. 'It was a *time* field. When my telescope back at Tock House was looking out onto the sky, the stars had appeared to move because the portion of the sky I was observing was sitting behind a field of time – I was staring at the right stars, but as they were in our past, rotated out of kilter by the dance of galactic procession. No wonder the Steamo Loas have been ignoring my calls, my rituals of Gear-gi-ju . . . it is not physical distance that led them to forsake me: my ancestors haven't even been born yet!'

'Quite correct,' said the great sage. 'The Army of Shadows aren't just invading your world from Kaliban, they are invading you from the Kaliban of *your own past*. As soon as I saw the heavens above Kaliban shifting around your celestial sphere, saw new stars appearing and other stars vanishing, I realized what the masters were doing. From the level of processional movement in the star field, I would estimate that your Kingdom of Jackals lies some five million years in the future of Kaliban as it sits now.'

'How can you be sure of this, man?' asked Duncan Connor.

'Because they plundered the equipment and the fuel source for their time field from a facility very like this one,' said the great sage. 'We only made one, you know. An artificial singularity heavy enough to distort time itself when it rotates, a stillborn star. It was mostly my research into the fifth dimension the masters stole. I had to watch the Army of Shadows plunder my singularity two thousand years ago. Then, a century ago, the masters constructed the iron moon with what was left of our land's mineral wealth, building it around the singularity. They launched it on a comet's trajectory through the solar system, set to pass your world every few millennia. A timer was set to open a gateway back here, a gateway that leads five million years ahead to our future. Our future, but your present.'

'But why did this dead star they stole from you need to be loaded onto the iron moon at all?' Molly asked.

'The only stable time field we found we could project was one that extends backwards, from the present to the past,' explained the great sage. 'We could use our technology to travel back in time, but not forward. Our time machine must already be sitting in our future in order to open up a passage to the present. But that is not a problem. A comet's trajectory keeps the iron moon and its chronological distortion mechanism safe from erosion and geological incident, safe from interference by sentient creatures. You can keep something as hardy as the iron moon spinning around the solar system for millions of years. You could launch the iron moon today, and if you can set the timer on its machinery accurately and it survives long enough, next week you can have the moon open a portal in time above your world, a doorway leading millions of years to the future.'

'But why?' asked Molly, her head spinning. 'Why would the Army of Shadows send their legions forward millions of years into the future, to invade us from our own past? Why not just invade our world as it is now, in your present?'

'You must trust me on that matter, it is better that you do not know,' said the old Kal, avoiding her question. 'I am aware I am asking a lot of you, attacking the iron moon.

Even though your people find violence easier than mine, but there are things that you are far better off not knowing if you are to succeed.'

'They're a strange evil crew,' said the commodore. 'I don't care that they're from our blessed past, it's enough for me that you say that little marble in your hand will stop them.'

'I'm sorry, young Sandwalker,' said Fayris Fastmind looking at the nomad guide, tears in his ancient eyes. 'Do you understand now why this weapon won't help our people? Why I couldn't give it to you when you asked me for it. My little weapon contains the fragment of a cosmic string that can be set vibrating at a frequency that will destabilize the singularity's rotation and collapse the time field, destroying the iron moon in a tide of tremendous violence.'

'You're planning to seal the Army of Shadows off in this age,' said Sandwalker.

'Stranding them in our time, without sustenance,' agreed the old Kal. 'The masters are a cancer and any cancer will die after it has consumed its host. We can give the masters no new bodies to feast on. They have made a graveyard of Kaliban and I shall see them entombed alongside our bones before I die.'

Sandwalker spoke slowly, his mind-speech heavy with remorse. 'This is how the Kals are to fight them? With our own sacrifice.'

'No, *this* is how your people fight!' laughed a familiar voice coming from just outside the chamber's door. Molly spun around. It was the carnivore Tallyle, holding a slat rifle, the black, beetle-armoured bodies of a company of the Army of Shadows' slave soldiers standing behind him. His rifle opened up and a bolt of energy hit Sandwalker square on the chest, burning a smoking hole through his robes. Then the slats were everywhere, their talons flashing menacingly, hissing at Molly, circles of jabbing rifles surrounding the expedition members. Two of the beasts ran to where Fayris Fastmind was hovering and overturned his carriage, spilling the ancient sage onto the floor and smashing his floating chair apart with their rifle butts.

'You fight like a filthy sand-born bean muncher who has never tasted flesh and the kill, who has never sucked the life out of his prey,' laughed the corrupted Kal.

Sandwalker stumbled back, moaning, into Molly's arms and she tried to protect him from the slats coming to seize him, but one slapped her to the floor, leaving a bloody claw gash in her cheek. The other slats howled fanged warnings as the commodore and Duncan bridled. The slats' meaning was clear enough.

Tallyle picked Molly up by her throat and licked at her face. 'So, you're the new breed. Well, more salt in your veins than in the Kals'. Must be your diet.' He tossed her contemptuously against the broken carriage, and turned to grin at Commodore Black and Duncan. 'Yes, I can see you two can fight. Good. Meat eaters. Bring the sand-born to the table.'

Slat soldiers pulled the fatally wounded nomad to a circular table and pinned him down. Tallyle crossed the room, dipped down and unleashed his fangs on Sandwalker's neck and face. The wounded Kal's death throes were thankfully brief as Tallyle tore into him, draining his blood.

Carnivore Tallyle rolled the body off the table and imperiously clicked his fingers, prompting his personal retinue of slats to fall upon the corpse and tear it to pieces. Tallyle turned to Keyspierre. 'Where is it?'

'The woman slipped it into her pocket as you broke in here, compatriot,' said Keyspierre.

Carnivore Tallyle walked over to where Molly was kneeling by the carriage and dipped a hand inside her pocket, triumphantly lifting the great sage's little golden sphere in the air as if it were an eye he had plucked out. Dropping the moon-destroying weapon on the floor he crushed it down under his boot heel into a mound of broken metal filaments.

Commodore Black tried to lunge towards Keyspierre but the slats surrounding the commodore clubbed him to the ground and kept on with their beating until he lay still.

'You filthy jigger,' Molly spat towards the Quatérshiftian. 'How much have you sold us out for? Did they promise to give you a set of blood-sucking fangs?'

'Every land needs collaborators,' laughed Tallyle.

'It seemed such a small thing to buy the survival of the Commonshare,' announced Keyspierre, shrugging his shoulders in that particularly Quatérshiftian way. 'Giving your nomad friend vegetables laced with an isotope that would allow my new compatriots to track us all the way back to the great sage's location.'

'You've been working with the Army of Shadows since the city,' said Molly in disgust, the truth dawning on her. 'They caught you back there, didn't they? You and Jeanne both.'

'I warned you all once that I was here to make sure the Commonshare was preserved at any cost,' said Keyspierre. 'I found no allies in this land capable of resisting the Army of Shadows' legions. Only a dying race of pacifists that wasn't strong enough to cast off the enemy's yoke at the very height of its powers, let alone now. Sometimes, little author, the only way to destroy your enemy is to make them your friend.'

Commodore Black was trying to rise to his feet. 'Kill you, you mortal shiftie piece of—' He was shoved back down.

'Make them your friends, man?' roared Duncan Connor. 'The commodore was right about you all along. You numpty! Your nation will be made into nothing but a stable of wee slaves and pets.'

Keyspierre went red in the face and grabbed Duncan's travel case, smashing it open across the floor. 'I will take no lessons in strategy from a bloated u-boat tar or an asylum inmate!'

Bones scattered across the floor and the nearest slats seized a couple of femurs and started gnawing at them. Connor of Cassarabia screamed abuse and tried to flail past the circle of slats surrounding him, but they beat him to the ground too. The last word on his lips was a girl's name: *Hannah.*

Carnivore Tallyle went over and dragged Duncan's unconscious body to where the great sage was quivering, unseated. Tallyle took the dead nomad's pack and removed the queen ant's pheromone tube, tossing it to his slats. 'Cut the clothes from the sage and this human, spray their skin with the contents of that tube, then toss them outside, naked and with no supplies or water.' Tallyle looked down on the terrified sage, whose ancient body looked shrunken and shrivelled without his floating carriage. 'I liked the false ants, that was uncommonly clever of you, Fayris Fastmind. I had to execute a couple of my slats just to get the others to come near your fake colony. Your ant machines are all destroyed, though. You and your bone-collecting friend can go outside and meet some of the real ones now.'

Molly's stomach heaved as the great sage was dragged out whimpering behind Duncan Connor's dazed form; the smell of what was left of Sandwalker's corpse filling the room.

Tallyle jabbed a finger towards Molly, the commodore and Coppertracks and barked orders at his slat soldiers. 'Take the three Jackelians back to the last city. Then seal this dusty useless place off from the world.'

As the slats pushed Molly past Tallyle, the corrupted Kal leant in and seized her by the face. 'You're the future, are you? The future tastes good.'

* * *

405

Molly was losing the ability to understand the Kal tongue, she realized, now that Kyorin's memories had been erased from her mind. She was forgetting their complex singsong cadences. She became aware of this as the corridor the slats were pushing her along turned into a tight tunnel curving past a series of riveted metal doors. Coppertracks was pushed alone into the first cell, the steamman complaining that the space was too small for him as soon as he saw it. A scowling Commodore Black got the second cell, shouting obscenities at the slat soldiers as they threw him inside. Then Molly was forced into the third compartment. A strange alien voice sounded from a grille in the room's ceiling. What was it saying? But it was no good. Kyorin's burden had passed, taking its blessings with it. As had Molly's mission. She had failed. Failed her friends, failed poor, dead Sandwalker. Failed the Hexmachina and failed all of the Kingdom of Jackals. The poorhouse girl sunk to her natural level, a cell – not for stealing a handkerchief or dipping a wallet. But for conspiring in the murder of her entire world.

Molly didn't know whether to laugh or cry when the first of the transparent pipes pushed out of the wall and began filling her cell with a thick yellow liquid. Soon she was wading though the thick gloop, then it was up to her chest. Was this the traditional method of execution on Kaliban? Drowning in a cell little bigger than a cupboard? You would think Keyspierre could have tipped his new allies off about a nice clinical Gideon's Collar, a quick bolt through the neck from one of his nation's execution machines.

Molly was panicking and smashing on the transparent crystal panel set in the door, but nobody was coming. Finally the liquid flowed into the last inch of air remaining under the cell's ceiling and she was enveloped. She was drowning.

* * *

Duncan Connor turned over in the sand, the raging sun filling the sky and burning his naked body. There was Fayris Fastmind curled up on one of the dunes behind him, the great sage's pale wrinkled body free of robes too. Duncan stifled a gag as he smelled his hand. A right good reek. As if someone had pissed on him after they had beat him to insensibility.

Duncan could just make out the slope of the mountain in the distance, billowing columns of smoke coming from the hidden entrance they had used to enter the great sage's domain. Not so great now, unable to walk and moaning from the aches of age without the medical machinery in his chair to help coddle his ancient, creaking body. So much for the great sage's fake ant colony, too. Sealed shut on them, no doubt blasted away by the explosives of the Army of Shadows.

<*Papa, Papa!*>

Thank the Circle! Hannah lay scattered across the dunes behind him, along with, he discovered, a tauntingly empty water canteen.

'Did the slats gnaw on you, lassie?'

<*They did,*> Hannah cried. <*There were monsters, terrible monsters. Chewing on my legs and arms. Some of them wanted to eat you too, while you were unconscious, but I told them they could bite on me instead.*>

'You're a good lassie. You did the right thing, you saved my life. Brave wee thing, I'm proud of you. Now we can both get out of here.'

He broke the empty canteen's strap and used it as a harness to tie Hannah to his chest. Then he limped across to where the great sage lay.

'Leave me,' begged the ancient Kal, his mind-voice as faint as a whisper.

'Don't be a daftie, man.' Duncan bent down to scoop up the great sage's body, as light as a feather.

407

'We have been sprayed,' said the great sage. 'Sprayed with the pheromone of an ant queen. Leave me here and you might have a chance. They'll come for me first if I'm not moving.'

'Aye, I heard much the same story from Sandwalker when we were trying to reach you,' said Duncan. 'But those ants aren't so hard. I killed one when it tried to fly away with my daughter. Back in Cassarabia, the womb mages grew real kelpies inside the wombs of their slaves. You've never had a shufty at a sandpede or a Cassarabian flying lizard, have you? They're real monsters.'

'Who were you talking to over there, do you have a communications device inside your body?'

'It's called my mouth, man. Do you not have eyes to see? Hannah is coming with us too and I'll thank you to keep a civil tongue in your head when you talk about my lassie. You've been in the sun too long, great sage. But I'll carry you out of here just the same.'

Clicking mandibles interrupted the great sage's bemused reply, a forest of fluttering antennae rising from behind the dune followed by the giant form of an enraged queen ant.

CHAPTER TWENTY-TWO

Molly's journey, nauseous-inducing and timeless in the grasp of the yellow gel, ended much as it had started, with a muffled shuddering, the oblong of light behind the cell door flickering with the violence of the craft's braking. Molly had realized what was going on soon after the gel had filled her nostrils and lungs – a brief sensation of drowning before she registered that the liquid she was suspended in actually allowed her to breathe. After all, this design wasn't so different from Timlar Preston's original plans for a shell to cross the celestial darks. But instead of Quatérshiftian explorers wearing diving suits, insulated from the shock of launch and flight in water-filled chambers, the slats had obviously crossed to Molly's home cosseted in this strange umbilical fluid.

After holes opened in the floor and drained all the gel away, Molly waited, still sopping wet from the sticky protective fluid, shivering and trying to clear the gloop from her hair. She thought she heard the commodore complaining in the corridor outside, then silence as he was removed. Still they didn't come for Molly, but after an hour had passed, two slats unlocked her cell door.

One babbled at Molly in what she thought was the Kal language, and then the second beast stepped forward, towering over her. 'Speak new slave tongue. Come.'

It was disconcerting, no eyes to focus on, fangs sliding up and down as the slat spoke. Molly realized how much of communication came just from looking into another person's eyes.

'Where are you taking me?'

'Food not speak,' hissed the slat, clicking in annoyance. It jabbed her with its rifle barrel, a flared metal pipe with a shaped crystal set inside it. 'Food obey.'

'Food obeys,' sighed Molly.

No sign of her two friends outside. Circle, she hoped they were still alive. The tight corridor of the shell-ship opened up into a vast hangar, walls of rusting red metal rising above lines of capsules, hundreds of shells, some tended by slats with a few blue-skinned Kals overseeing the maintenance. The iron moon! They had sent her to the iron moon. And along-side the capsules they used to cross the darks was Starsprite; the half-steamman craft locked in a vice-like girdle while slats were crawling over her hull. Oh sweet Circle, they had found her ship. Found the looking-glass gate she would have used to jump across to the realm of the steammen. Molly tried to wave to Starsprite, but the slats pushed her brutally past. Failed. The expedition to Kaliban had failed in every way it could have done. She was on the iron moon and she didn't have the great sage's weapon. For the sake of a device the size of a marble she had lost the power to bring down the whole rotten edifice of the Army of Shadows.

As she was marched through the iron moon, Molly saw that its chambers and passages were a bizarre mixture of the advanced and the primitive. She was shoved into a cart pulled by six lizard-like things, the beasts dragging her through the

410

iron corridors of the artificial satellite, past deep halls where legions of slats swung swords at rock posts or trained with their talons. Eventually, Molly reached a more advanced transportation station, a polished black carriage hovering above a rail outside a tunnel mouth. Then the railcar was accelerating her through the iron moon, some tunnels as black and sightless as the Middlesteel atmospheric, others transparent and showing chambers filled with strange glowing machines that swung around each other like the pieces of an orrery.

At one point Molly's tube ran along the outside of the iron moon and the awe-inspiring vista of her world filled the velvet night below. The bone-white cable of the beanstalk Molly had seen in the steammen's observatory pictures stretched all the way down to the surface, like the proboscis of a mosquito impaling its host.

Once back inside the alien satellite, the railcar slowed to a stop alongside a watercourse, a garden waiting on the other side of an ornately carved wooden bridge. It was a surreal juxtaposition: a sculpted green paradise sitting in an ugly rusting chamber. At the far end of the garden, a curving wall of glass displayed the view she had been ogling outside, the gem of her world seen from on high. Precious, fragile. Home. The slats pushed Molly though the garden, butterflies landing on her arm and fluttering away as the gurgle of a nearby fountain startled them.

At the other end of the garden a figure was sitting on a stool in front of a canvas, where the view of the world below was captured almost perfectly. Was this a Kal? The figure turned. He looked like a Jackelian, save that he had to be eight feet tall, a man-mountain rising up from the stool; golden locks curling atop an achingly handsome pink face, his hair bound by a circlet crown bearing a golden helix just above his forehead. Both slats knelt in front of the giant and he spoke to Molly in mind-speech, even though his words were Jackelian. *Jackelian?* Was he a Kal or not?

'So, this is what a slayer of gods looks like?'

'And my,' said Molly, 'haven't you been eating a lot of beans.'

The giant roared with laughter and wiped his brush on a piece of wet cotton by the easel. 'You think me a Kal? No, little animal, I am what the Kals call a master, the master of all masters in fact.'

A master? Molly looked in shock at the ridiculously striking figure. But this was a man, albeit a giant of a man... 'I've seen the Army of Shadows' masters. They look like squids with great big tentacle limbs.'

'Then you have seen how the masters looked in ancient days, when we were adapted for life in the ocean. Form is a fleeting thing, little pet. We cut our flesh to suit our times. You see before you our original form, one that predates even our aquatic existence. I am magnificent, am I not?'

A trick, they were trying to trick her. *But why?*

'No,' insisted Molly. 'I saw the masters' council of war, I saw them planning the invasion of my home. The Army of Shadows' masters are octopus-shaped monsters.'

'Council of war?' said the giant, bemused. 'Ah, those mischievous Kal. Who would have thought that our own sheep would one day try to savage us? I shall be quite glad to leave their kind behind. With the appropriate breeding programme in place your people will make far better slaves.'

'This is a ruse,' said Molly.

'To what end, little animal? If the Kal showed you us in our aquatic form, the memory they shared was ancient indeed. And the only invasion they had to show you was not that of your world, it was of their own, the fall of Kaliban.'

'I saw the Army of Shadows' ships leaving Kaliban to attack us!'

'The Kals' memories are as broken as the machine abominations they were once melded with, or perhaps they have not told you and your little band of explorers the truth, for fear you would not prove as pliable as the so-called great sage obviously hoped you would. You have it the wrong way around. The ships you saw weren't leaving Kaliban to attack your world, they were leaving your world to attack Kaliban.'

To attack Kaliban? What was this mad giant talking about? He was clearly an oversized slave gone mad. 'I'd do it now if I could,' said Molly, 'blow your iron moon to pieces. The great sage wouldn't need to trick me into doing it.'

'I believe you would,' smiled the giant. 'But then in your own primitive way you are as much an abomination as the great sage, a symbiote for that revolting little machine spider we sealed inside the world. The Hexmachina. Very cunning, machines that mimic a blood disease pumping inside your veins. Of course, those that share your heritage can't be allowed to breed on.'

'If you're not just a Kal wearing human skin paint, how are you able to communicate using mind-speech?'

The giant tapped the canvas he had been painting. 'A true artist is never afraid to borrow from others, little animal. We took the ability for mind-speech along with memory sharing from the Kals' own blood code. To the victor, the spoils. You stand in the realm of the masters and I am their emperor, Gabraphrim.'

Molly shook her head. What lies had the great sage told her to bring her to this strange green garden high above the Earth? Had any of what he had said been true?

'Well,' said the giant emperor. 'We're going to cut you apart to see the truth of what makes you tick. You may as well enjoy a little of the same courtesy before your infected blood is flowing around our test tubes.'

The emperor clicked his fingers and the two slats shoved Molly after him as he walked to the far side of the chamber, the walls folding back and forming a corridor for him to stride along. Molly followed and they entered another iron chamber, this one filled with figures just as large as the emperor, giant men and women of prodigious beauty. Carpets and pillows covered the cold iron outlines of the room where slats and Kals worked alongside their masters. And there was a single member of the race of man there too: Keyspierre! The treacherous jigger. Molly had shouted the words before she realized she was crying them aloud. The emperor seemed amused by her outburst.

'I will be hailed as the saviour of all of Quatérshift when I return,' called Keyspierre to Molly, indicating a cage resting under an iron pillar. 'And see what your people's defiance has earnt Jackals . . .'

Molly was hardly able to make out the occupant within the cage, which was surrounded by blue-faced Kal women, prodding at it and hissing laughter through their carnivores' fangs. It was Lord Rooksby! The Lord Commercial was stripped naked and looking emaciated. His throat was bound with a metal collar, and he had two feathery wings rising out of his back. Circle's teeth. They had twisted Rooksby's flesh! Made him into a bird-like chimera.

'You have served me well, Keyspierre,' said the emperor. 'But you have yet to pass the final test. To make a reliable governor of your nation you must first be given the gift of the hunger. As for my fine-feathered songbird here, make it sing, little Kals. Make it tweet its foolishness for us. Let us hear its song of how the race of man and the Kingdom of Jackals is destined for mastery of all your pathetic, flat horizons.'

Rooksby hardly needed the cruel urging of the corrupted

Kal women. His man-beak twitched and he broke into a cracked song, whistling and capering behind the bars while they poked at him.

The emperor grabbed Molly's face and squeezed it painfully, making her meet his burning red eyes. 'Don't you understand why your kind are perfect as slaves, little animal? Five million years ago we discarded your world with only a few exiles, criminals and dissenters remaining behind. Left it as a farmer leaves a field fallow, for the ecos to recover. You people, with your stunted pathetic little lives over in less than a century, are the crippled mongrel descendants of the criminals who wouldn't accept the changes necessary to live under the oceans, who stayed behind on our old home. Those who lacked the courage to conquer Kaliban after our oceans boiled away.'

Molly pulled away from the emperor's grip. 'No!'

'The ecos always recovers,' said the emperor. 'Given enough time. Life begets life. The bacteria at the world's core breed and multiply, the leylines begin to pulse again. Life rallies and grows and spreads across the surface once more.'

It wasn't true. These giants weren't the race of man's ancestors. Her kind's forefathers hadn't invaded Kaliban, hadn't inflicted the miseries she had seen on Kyorin's home.

'Now you see why the great sage wouldn't trust you with the truth,' laughed the emperor. 'We are *you*, but better, our flesh reworked across the ages to perfection. But we are from the same seed. You little pygmies are the stunted offspring of the masters. How could you animals possibly kill such magnificent titans as us when we are your very progenitors?'

At last Molly understood. Why the Army of Shadows couldn't just invade the Earth of their era from Kaliban, a world still left dead and burning from the masters' pillages, its ruined, abandoned dunes as dead as any of Kaliban's wastes; why the emperor's people had to travel five million years into the future to find their new harvest. Why there were lashlites flying wild on Kaliban: the lizard people and other creatures brought from Molly's world to Kaliban when the masters crossed the celestial darks.

'Yes, now you see how it is, little animal. After we've exhausted the bounty of your reborn planet we'll launch the iron moon again on its comet's path. And in two thousand years from now a window to the future will open above what was briefly your land, a passage forward to five million years hence. Kaliban will have healed itself by then, evolved back into life, and something descended from the Kals will look up and see our slat legions falling to their plains anew.'

'You're just a bastard swarm of locusts,' shouted Molly. 'Moving through time, destroying everything.'

'Poor little animal,' said the emperor, sadly. 'It is the law of nature. The strongest prosper and survive.' He pointed to a vast golden helix mounted on the wall of the chamber. A group of his giant kindred were on their knees in front of it, heads bobbing up and down in worship of their own kind's perfection. 'We destroy nothing. We only transform it; we give purpose to that which has none without our presence. Ores become iron. Oils become the fuel to drive a turbine. Flesh becomes sustenance and slaves to serve us. Would you have us weep for your people? Do your farmers weep for the poultry not born when you collect the eggs of your hens? You've had your chance and squandered it. You've had five million years to evolve, to mould yourself into something superior to us. But look at how you've regressed: lives as brief as mayflies, hosts to sickness and parasites. You've even let filthy machine life spread across your land. You can't trust such abominations as your slaves – always changing their parameters and slipping the leash. Flesh, you can trust only flesh.'

'I don't trust steammen as my slaves,' said Molly. 'I trust them as my friends.'

'Spoken like a loyal abomination,' said the emperor. 'No, unlike the Kals I don't think there is much we'll be taking from your revolting kind's bodies to improve our own genetic pattern, but my scholars want to get you under a dissection array anyway.' The emperor clapped his hands in anticipation as one of his giants came striding across the room, a small army of slats following behind her. 'And here is the very chief of the observative sciences who is so eager to analyse your blood.' He turned to his cohort. 'Are you ready to cut up your next test subject?'

The scholar pushed the golden curls of her fringe away from her perfect burnished skin. 'Arrived from Kaliban so soon? Good, then my work can begin. But first, I have brought you the animals that almost succeeded in bringing down the beanstalk.'

Her troops parted, revealing a ragged band of Jackelians, perhaps twenty of them. And Purity Drake! Molly stared in astonishment at the young girl.

'Where is the sword they used to cut the anchor cables? I said I wanted it delivered into my hands!' boomed the emperor.

The scholar bowed, terrified. 'It is rooted in one of the anchor cables, which has healed itself around the blade.'

'Then unembed it!' yelled the emperor.

'I cannot,' said the scholar. 'The anchor cable is a Kal material. We know how to grow it, but we have never possessed a method capable of cutting through it.'

So much for the superiority of the Army of Shadows' masters, thought Molly. They were plunderers, barbarians who for all their protestations of superiority barely understood the trinkets of their stolen Kal superscience.

Molly stared towards Purity. She was swaying from

exhaustion on her bare feet alongside a tall aquiline man in marsh leathers – also wearing no shoes – his black face pocked by frostbite. From their waxed clothes, the others in her party looked as if they might be fishermen. There was a boy about Purity's age with a wooden leg standing behind her, his eyes darting about between their slat guards, as though if only he watched intently enough he might be able to seize the initiative and get them free. Molly really hoped the boy didn't try something foolish. If the slats started firing to protect their emperor, the group wouldn't last a second in the crossfire.

Purity caught sight of Molly and her eyes widened.

'You will find a way to cut it,' hissed the emperor.

Molly shook her head towards the young girl. Best these creatures didn't know she and Purity were friends; they could trust that Keyspierre wouldn't have bothered to acquaint himself with a humble seamstress back at the cannon project.

'Let me examine the new stock,' commanded the emperor.

A single fisherman was separated from the crowd by a slat and sent in front of the emperor. His head was bowed, hardly daring to gaze upon the giant.

'Look at me!'

A cable like a snake-tongue flicked out of the emperor's mouth, lodging itself in the centre of the Jackelian's forehead, the man screaming as the emperor seized him tight. The fisherman's face drained to a powder-white and he was caught in a seizure, crumpling as the giant sucked away his essence, his lifeforce, his very soul. This was the energy the masters craved, stolen from the world and sucked from all its creatures. It took only a second, the husk of a man falling back to the floor. The emperor pointed to one of his corrupted Kals and the female eagerly left off tormenting Rooksby to take the corpse's blood. When she had drained the Jackelian carcass of the last of its juices, she waved forward her favoured slats to feast on the ruin of meat. Nothing wasted, a little something trickling down for everyone in the Army of Shadows.

Molly turned away, sickened. Yes, the masters had higher tastes now. Consuming pure energy, saving the messy inefficient business of digestion for their slaves and pets.

'That one was a little stale,' said the emperor, licking his fingers. 'Take them back to the pens and feed the animals at least one good meal of gruel before you throw them to my wives or I will hear nothing but complaints from the imperial harem.'

'Not these two,' begged the scholar, pointing to Purity and the figure in marsh leathers. 'The male is a mutation and the female cub, I don't even know what she is, but she was the animal wielding the weapon that severed our anchor cables.'

The emperor tutted. 'Well, at least put aside their intestines for the slats when you're done. A little nod towards tradition every now and then would not harm those who work within the observative sciences.'

Molly and Purity were pushed into a railcar, Purity's leather-clad friend in the car behind them, the slat soldiers taking position in cockpits in front, whisking the three prisoners through the tunnels and monstrous chambers of the iron moon.

Molly cleared her throat. 'You look taller.'

'You look thinner,' said Purity.

'Well, a diet of beans can do that,' agreed Molly.

'Did you meet Kyorin's people, find the great sage?'

'All that and more,' said Molly, sadly. She held her thumb and finger out an inch apart. 'I held the weapon Kyorin talked about in my hand, no bigger than a coin. It would have destroyed the iron moon and sealed the Army of Shadows off for eternity, but it is gone now, smashed to pieces. Did they capture Oliver with you?'

Purity shook her head. 'He's gone, too. I think there's part of him inside a sword I left embedded below in the beanstalk. Maybe I could draw the blade out again when I recover my strength?'

'So you became a sword-saint after all,' smiled Molly. 'Just like the legends in Coppertracks' book said.'

'Legends won't save us now,' Purity said. 'I've failed us all, Molly. The Bandits of the Marsh came from legend and followed me, just like the book said, but I believed in myself too little. All my friends died for nothing. The iron moon shouldn't be here now, I should have destroyed it. But I couldn't believe in myself.'

'Well, I think I believed in myself just a little too much,' said Molly, squeezing the young girl's hand. 'No, I'm just a writer of penny dreadfuls now, not any protector of the land worthy of the name. As for this rusting palace of mad gods and their slaves, none of them should be here, not the slats or the Kals or the giant masters that command them. They should have died five million years ago. They've twisted nature to stay alive beyond their means, broken time itself to crawl across to us. Back when I was in the poorhouse, when we were really hungry, we would take a dishcloth and suck it dry, suck it for the juices that were left from the plates. That's what we found the Army of Shadows had done to Kyorin's home, and what they're going to do to Jackals.'

Purity raised a laugh. 'We did the same thing back in the royal breeding house when we were put on short rations. Sucking the dishcloth.'

Molly looked at the tunnel hurtling past. 'What a pair we make, Purity Drake. The princess and the pauper. Well, at least we're not going to live to see them do that to Jackals.'

'No,' said Purity, the force of her voice surprising Molly. 'We're not going to give up. You and I. There's a way, there's

420

always a way. The people of the kingdom will not crawl into the eternal night as slaves of these beasts. I failed once, but I'm never going to fail again.'

Molly was about to say she admired Purity's spirit, but then they came to it, a vast circular cavern that was so immense – many miles across – that it could only be the hollow core of the iron moon. In the middle something black and terrible rotated, twisting under the blazing red fire whipping from a series of vast magnetic guns that emerged from the chamber's curved walls. A titanic hoop-like walkway surrounded the rotating spider of darkness, the tiny figures of masters walking around and ministering to the monster's needs through their consoles and machines. Oh sweet Circle, this was it. The Kals' artificial singularity that the great sage had talked about. A demon more terrible than anything the Army of Shadows could have created on their own, caged and tamed by the Kals' plundered superscience. A comet moon given the power to punch a window five million years into the past. A rift to allow the Army of Shadows to farm worlds across the passage of eternity itself, feeding their dark, fierce hungers. If the great sage had been telling the truth, then the Kals had only created one of these monstrous singularities, but one was all the Army of Shadows had required.

Molly couldn't help it now, she was weeping. 'There it is. I'm sorry, Purity. This is what I should have destroyed. The Army of Shadows consumed everything in their age and now their armada are sailing through the seas of time to claim us.'

Purity turned her face away from the blaze as the magnetic cannons burned at her eyes. The giant masters on the walkway wore brass goggles to protect them from the glare. Molly noticed the determined look on Purity's face. She really didn't know when it was time to give up.

'Time. Yes, I know time. Time is our ally,' said Purity. 'The

421

Bandits of the Marsh have rested in its halls. The bones of our land endure it, are shaped and healed by its flow. I'll save us, I'll save us all.'

'Will you? We've been royally betrayed by time now,' said Molly. 'They're us, Purity. That's the worst secret of them all. The Army of Shadows' masters are *us*. And they're coming home.'

The two of them fell to silence as the railcar bore them along the surface of the iron moon's core, painted by the violence of the energies of time itself being torn asunder.

It wasn't exactly a cell where Purity, Molly and Jackaby Mention were tossed, more the smallest of the feeding pens available. Only Commodore Black stood inside, no sign of Coppertracks, but Molly barely had time to say hello before she was hauled out again and separated from the group.

Purity's face pressed against the pen's bars, shouting at the slats and the giant woman leading her friend away. It was the scholar who had stood in the emperor's throne room, enraging the master of masters by her failure to retrieve the sword.

'Where are you taking Molly?' yelled Purity.

'Quiet, animal,' ordered the scholar, her beautiful features not improved by being twisted in contempt as she glanced back towards the feeding pen. 'Your turn will come soon enough. For *dissection*.'

The first thing Molly noticed about the scholar's laboratory was the large slab with a metal spider hanging above it, all blades, drills and crystal-tipped tubes dangling on iron arms. The second thing was poor Coppertracks, trapped in a vice-like machine, plates opened all over his body and leeched by cables running into the scholar's devices.

'Coppertracks!'

The steamman said nothing, locked into silence by the vice, his voicebox covered up.

'Save your distress for yourself,' advised the scholar.

'What are you doing to him?'

'Peeling its memories like an onionskin. Breaking the encryption on them, then storing them for analysis. This abomination you count as a friend is very clever. It might even be able to contribute to our own natural sciences. But that is of secondary interest to me. My primary concern is that this abomination doubtless controls the key to opening the looking-glass gate inside the craft you used to cross to Kaliban.'

The looking-glass gate! Their way home.

'Yes, we have your gate too,' laughed the scholar, seeing Molly's face. 'It will be most fortunate if, as I suspect, the gate opens out into the realm of the abominations. I have a very special bomb I would like to push through into the deep mountain stronghold of King Steam's palace. How ironic if the mountain walls the abominations think protect them instead become the walls of their tomb.'

'Why do you fear the steammen?' said Molly. 'They've never harmed you.'

'Harmed?' said the scholar, motioning her slats to secure Molly to the dissection slab. 'We once fought a bloody war against the abominations. It is not just your stunted little race that our kind acted as progenitors for. There is a reason why we create no machines able to think for themselves, why it is a capital crime to even manufacture machines with the ability to network with each other. Abominations such as your friend over there are that reason.' She tapped her head. 'Trust only the flesh. That which can be controlled, shaped by other flesh.'

Molly tried to break free of the slats' grip as they pinned her down on the dissection slab, but the monsters were too strong.

423

'You're the perfect example of why their kind can't be trusted,' said the scholar to Molly, walking to her console behind the dissection slab. 'You've been infected by the abominations, made a monster, nothing but a puppet of contaminated meat to advance their schemes.'

Molly kicked futilely at the slats. 'You use your machines to give birth to beasts like this and you dare call me a monster!'

'Oh, I'm exceptionally proud of my slats,' said the scholar. 'My grandmother created the slave labour assault troop pattern during our last wars on what is now your world, securing my family's high position in the observative sciences. The slats are the perfect soldiers, a blend of human, rodent, wolf and insect flesh. They fall out of their birthing tanks ready to function on instinct only. A superannuation date of five years ensures they are retired before the accumulation of memories and experiences outside the tank leads them to question their loyalty, and even if a few become separated from the pack, they can't breed without us. Obedient, hardy, deadly, controlled. Would that everything we made was such a success.'

Molly swore as the slats tightened leather straps around her limbs, cutting off her circulation.

'I don't expect much from you,' said the scholar, a forlorn look crossing her face. 'But I should at least be able to design a plague that will target those with your machine symbiote bloodline. I can't risk your kind polluting the farms' breeding stock.'

Molly yelled as a blade arm came falling down and skimmed above her belly and breasts; but the scholar was only starting by slicing Molly's clothes away.

'Your kind have almost been mongrelized beyond use,' continued the giant, pointing to the far wall of the lab where a transparent pane showed figures floating like pickled sweetmeats in a jar. Craynarbians, graspers, the race of man, their bodies skinned and muscles exposed. 'Look how many subspecies your stunted strain has branched into. You have surrendered your breeding to nature rather than science. This *filth* is the result. To think, there were those who argued that the timer on our comet should have been set to add an extra million years to the clock, to allow the ecos on our old world time to fully recover. I dread to think what we would have had to feed on if we had left your kind feral to jig each other stupid in the dirt down there for another million years.'

As Molly thrashed against her restraints she heard a hooting noise and stretched her neck around to place it. There, to Molly's side, was a cage. Lord Rooksby danced inside, one of his wings torn and bloodied, exposing the flesh underneath.

'You see how little my labours are appreciated,' said the scholar, scowling at the agitated form battering the cage's bars. 'The Kals that pervert the emperor takes to his bed have damaged the animal's wings, and now it is the directorate of observative sciences that must act as vet. Even a child knows not to play with their food, but not the emperor and his disgusting little pets.'

Molly gritted her teeth as one of the medical machine's syringe needles plunged into her newly bared arm.

'This really is such a waste of my time,' muttered the scholar, then she turned to scream angrily at her slats, the pair of soldiers hungrily clicking as they watched the operation. Molly's thrashing was exciting their feeding instinct. 'Shut up and get *out*! Get out, both of you, you'll have what's left here when I'm finished and not before.'

What would be left of *Molly*? A platter of slops for the masters' beasts.

CHAPTER TWENTY-THREE

Purity and Commodore Black watched Jackaby Mention pacing the small feeding pen, the bandit stopping every few seconds to stretch his heavily muscled legs, working out the frost cramps. Purity stood by the door and gave a sad little wave to Watt, who had been imprisoned in the cell opposite along with the rest of the Jackelians who had survived the raid on the beanstalk. The cobbler lad held up a paper-wrapped parcel behind the bars. Her shoes? Sweet Circle. Of all the stupid things to have survived the raid. But there wasn't enough room between the bars for Watt to squeeze them through and toss them across the corridor to her. Purity tried to suppress a sad laugh. When the masters came to the cell to cut her up like Molly, it looked like she wasn't going to be able to die with her boots on after all.

The commodore rubbed angrily at his beard, 'Ah, poor Molly and Coppertracks, is this how it is to end for us? All the tenants of Tock House to be murdered by a race of perfect wicked giants, cut up like anatomy show cadavers under the spotlights of a Lump Street theatre.'

'Where's Duncan? Did he not make it?' asked Purity.

Commodore Black shook his head. 'The brave, luckless lad. I watched the slats toss him out of one of their wicked flying globes, lobbed down onto the sands of Kaliban, naked and smeared with the scent of terrible ants as tall as the trees back in my orchard. His fate was no kinder than the one the Army of Shadows has in store for us.'

'I will not go quietly,' said Jackaby. 'Not when the wind itself envies my heels.'

'The wind may envy them, lad,' said the commodore. 'But it's the slats and their giant masters that'll have them off you before the day is out. And I've seen the slat guards coming by here, eying my grand belly and arguing over which of them is going to have me for their roasting spit.'

'Our cell door,' said Purity. 'You showed me how to pick locks back at the house. All the stories, Jared, the ones you told me about how you broke your friends out from the prison on the lost land of Camlantis. Can you not get us out of here?'

'I've tried, lass,' sobbed the commodore, 'but poor old Blacky's genius with locks has met its match in what the Army of Shadows have done to this doorway's seals. Break us out? I don't even understand the basic principles of what they have running on this mortal clever lock. There are no moving parts, nothing to pick, no transaction-engine drums rotating inside it with codes to break. I'm like a fish drifting through the engine room of a wrecked u-boat, gazing at the expansion-engine scrubbers and wondering what manner of marvel it is that lies before me.'

'Then we are dead,' said Jackaby.

'That we are, lad. But I have one last story for you, Purity, before I move along the Circle,' said the commodore. 'And it's one that I should have told you when we first met at Tock House. A tale I spent every day walking across the hot

427

merciless sands of Kaliban begging the gods of fate for the chance to recount to you. It seems that fickle fate has thrown me that chance, in return for my brave old bones being given to the slats to chew on.'

Purity listened as the commodore explained about his involvement in the royalist rebels' plot to free a prince from the Royal Breeding House, her mother's part in the scheme, and how the man who had worn the title of the Duke of Ferniethian had left a lover he thought was dead behind in the escape attempt. Left her with a child swelling her belly.

'Your father was no fortress guard,' finished the commodore. 'He was a fat fool of a royalist u-boat commander who went back to Porto Principe before its fall, went back not knowing he had a darling daughter alive and in the hands of parliament's dogs.'

Purity was rocked by the news.

All these years, treated like dirt by the other prisoners at the breeding house, called a prison guard's bastard. And she had been the daughter of the Duke of Ferniethian all along. *She had a father!*

'I would have done anything for your blessed mother and I would do anything for you.'

'She is our queen,' said Jackaby, not quite approving as the commodore and Purity embraced.

'She always was mine,' said the commodore. 'But here we are. I have been given my chance to make amends, but it is to be cut short by a crew of monsters strutting about their mortal iron moon, monsters who intend to make us as dead as their land.'

Purity stepped back. 'I am the land and the land is eternal.'

The two men in the pen rushed forward as Purity doubled up in pain.

'Lass!'

'The sword,' said Purity, pushing them back. 'I can feel it at the foot of the beanstalk.'

And she could. It was burning, embedded inside the near indestructible anchor cable securing the beanstalk to the ground; showing her a possible way to destroy the iron moon, destroy the Army of Shadows once and for all.

Purity turned to Jackaby Mention. 'We must get out of here.'

'But how, my queen? Your sword is lost to us, your power with it.'

Purity looked at Commodore Black, looked at her *father*. 'There is more power in the human heart and the imagination of a child than there is in any stone circle or blade.'

'You sound like Ganby,' said the bandit. 'But words have no magic to release us from these four thick walls.'

'Four walls, containing the first queen of Jackals,' growled Purity, 'and the last queen of Jackals. I am no longer a prisoner of parliament to be beaten to silence. I have the blood of Alicia Drake and the House of Ferniethian in my veins; the lineage of Elizica of the Jackeni, knighted by the touch of the Hexmachina. What is the Army of Shadows compared to that? Shadows are banished by any light strong enough to shine.'

'Lass!' shouted Commodore Black. 'Your hands!'

They were glowing, with the same glow as her mathsblade. Purity sliced at the air, experimentally at first, then faster, leaving scratches in the ether. Jackaby and the commodore fell back, the heat growing intense, furnace light cutting the confines of the cell.

'And I have the Bandits of the Marsh sworn to awaken in my land's hour of need!'

Hotter, hotter. The commodore yelped as Purity sculpted a gate of fire across the air. Slat guards were howling in the corridor, attracted by the light of a sun burning inside one of their food pens. Purity pushed up with both hands and the blazing gate she was making slid back into the cell door, killing the slats outside in a spray of molten metal as the door and walls disintegrated. Her gate kept on going, disintergrating the cell door of the feeding pens opposite. Then it stopped. It was another door now, a portal into the hall of ages where the Bandits of the Marsh slept.

Jackaby barked in surprise as the first figures began to emerge from the gate. 'Jed Highaxe, Vela Hisstongue, Burnhand Luke!'

They came. Over a hundred and ninety Bandits of the Marsh, dipping their heads to Purity, recognizing their queen as she recognized them. A sea of spears, tridents, swords, armour and mist-twisted flesh. She knew them this time. The worst of the Kingdom of Jackals and the best of the Kingdom of Jackals. Purity gasped for breath as she let the gate dwindle into a spark dancing on the screen of her eyes. She hadn't been strong enough before. But she had been looking in the wrong place. She had been looking out into the world, not into her heart.

Purity turned to one of the bandits, a blonde woman with an eye patch. 'Emmaline Leap. I have two friends in peril but not enough time to save them and play havoc against those who have invaded Jackals.'

'With your permission.' The bandit placed her hand on Purity's forehead and closed her one good eye. 'Yes, I see them within your memories, a creature of steam and a woman and they are – *I have them*. An ogre of a woman is holding your two friends fettered. She tortures them in . . . inside a moon of iron?'

Purity's eyes narrowed. No, torture at least had a point. To the Army of Shadows, Molly and Coppertracks were unwanted butterflies with wings that needed tearing off. 'You know what you must do, Emmaline.'

'I do not have the strength to jump more than thrice within an hour,' said the bandit. 'You may yet need me . . .'

'My friends need you more than I.' Purity looked at Commodore Black. 'Please go with her. I can spare two.'

'Don't make me leave you again, lass.'

Purity touched her father's outstretched hand. 'Time has betrayed us, in every sense of the word. I need to close the rift into the past and they'll send every slat they have to try to stop me. You can still save Molly and Coppertracks.'

'Please, now, Purity, don't make me choose between them and you.'

'Many years ago, when you were trying to spirit a prince out of a cold fortress, what would my mother have said to you about duty if you had faltered?'

'Duty,' wheezed the commodore. 'Always the hard weight of duty for our cursed family. Oh my poor Alicia, dead in parliament's hands. And now you, I can't . . .'

'I have my people to protect me,' said Purity, indicating the Bandits of the Marsh. She took a spare sabre from one of her followers and pressed it gently into the commodore's hand. 'And you have no choice at all.' She nodded at Emmaline Leap and the woman grabbed Commodore Black.

'Say it once, lass. Just let my poor mortal ears hear it.'

'Good luck,' said Purity, 'Father . . .'

With a sulphur flash the bandit woman disappeared, the commodore winking out of the feeding pen alongside her. Only a small cloud of red smoke was left behind to show he had ever stood there.

'It is always hard,' said Jackaby Mention, seeing the tear in Purity's eye, 'leaving your family when you go to war.'

'I fear the hardest part is yet to come,' said Purity. She

addressed the Bandits of the Marsh who now filled the corridors around the feeding pens, giants mingling with the surviving Jackelians from her raid on the beanstalk. 'I wish I had more time to speak with you. You all left your families for me, some of you have left your age. But now you have stepped into a new age and face an enemy who has also crossed the halls of time. You are in an iron moon filled with wonders and horrors. There are soldiers that are blind walking blades wearing their dark bones on the outside of their hides, giants with a beauty matched only by the fierce emptiness of their souls, blue-skinned beasts that would suck on your veins. They have violated Jackals and there are more of them than we can possibly fight and best in any battle today.'

One of the bandits raised a fist. 'It wouldn't make a good tale for the fireside if it were otherwise and my axe has woken up with quite a thirst!'

'Then it's time for me to warm my hands on a still-born star,' shouted Purity. 'And time for your axe to drink its fill.'

Purity looked at them, a handful of free Jackelians and the wild cheering fey bandits.

Two ancient powers were about to clash.

A new legend for the world to forget across the ages, whichever side won.

An arm swung down from the dissection array, printing a cold ink outline above Molly Templar's heart, a grid of numbered lines. A smaller arm capped with a flower of rotating scalpels was about to strike down into her chest when a buzzing from a console close to Coppertracks' trapped form interrupted the scholar.

Tutting, the giant woman raised the cutting arm and walked across to look at the readout. 'Finally!' She twisted a lever on the console and summoned a Kal wearing a white toga

432

decorated with a golden helix on his chest. 'I have just relayed the key that will activate the looking-glass gate up to the hangar where the abomination ship is held. Ensure my bomb is signed out of the armoury and transported safely to the hangar. If there is even a dent on the bomb's casing when it gets there, I will flush your miserable life into the vacuum.'

The scholar's assistant left to do her bidding and she turned and twisted a knob, the vice around Coppertracks' skull flowering open but leaving the rest of his body still locked down. 'I told you I would tear your secrets out of you, abomination, one memory at a time.'

'You are a sentient race,' begged Coppertracks, his voicebox uncovered enough to speak. 'Consider the morality of what you are doing.'

'Your people are nothing but a virus replicating in metal,' said the scholar. 'But I will let you survive long enough to see our bomb make a tomb of your people's home. It is the least I owe you for your assistance in their extermination.'

Coppertracks emitted a sob.

'Simulated emotions,' sneered the scholar, going back to the dissection slab. 'Let us see what you make of this animal's screams when I open her up. Do you have a simulacrum of pity for your so-called friend?'

The rotating blades were dipping towards Molly's heart when sirens in the laboratory began to clang, a strident sound. There was a flash of light and sulphur in the room, the commodore and a blonde woman in marsh leathers appearing as if they had been borne into existence by the lightning clap.

Commodore Black was near enough to the dissection slab for him to grab the scalpel-tipped arm about to slice Molly apart, struggling against the strength of the device. The giant scholar abandoned the controls and pulled a pistol out of her belt, stumbling back and dropping the gun as the bandit slammed into her. There was another flash and they both disappeared, the giant's legs reappearing embedded in the iron wall of the laboratory, briefly flailing as the scholar impossibly tried to coexist with the matter of the wall, then kicking towards stillness as she expired. The Bandit of the Marsh stood panting just underneath the giant's gently trembling feet.

It took only a second for the commodore to open Molly's restraints and then she twisted the knob to free Coppertracks from the vice.

'They've been giving you a mortal terrible poking about, old steamer,' said Commodore Black, pulling Coppertracks free of the floor clamps and helped him close his exposed panels.

'My people!' said Coppertracks. 'The Army of Shadows is going to detonate something terrible in the heart of Mechancia using the gate we brought.'

'I saw the hangar,' said Molly. 'They have Starsprite up there. That's where the bomb's being taken.'

'Let me have your memory,' requested the female bandit, coming towards Molly. 'I can jump you there.' Molly flinched back.

'Please Molly softbody,' begged Coppertracks. 'My people's survival hangs in the balance.'

'It won't hurt,' said the bandit.

'The last time I believed that I ended up with an extra soul floating inside my head.' But Molly let the bandit woman press a finger against her forehead.

'I have it. A great chamber looking out onto the heavens – and, well take me for a fancy piece, we really are inside an iron moon!' The look of wonder on the Bandit of the Marsh's face turned to surprise as she looked down at the steel tip of a sabre rising up out of her stomach.

'Oh!'

Keyspierre pushed the bandit's murdered body off his sword and flashed the new pair of fangs hanging out of his mouth. 'I thought it must be you when I heard the sirens go off. You Jackelians are so predictable.'

Commodore Black pulled Molly back and raised the sabre his daughter had given to him. 'They haven't changed you so much, shiftie. You were a filthy beast before and your dirty friends have only formalized things with your wicked new set of teeth.'

'The masters trust only the hunger, as they should. I was coming down here to retrieve the little author's slops so I could toss them as gravy into your cage. Then I was going to discover what a doltish fat Jackelian sailor tastes like.'

Commodore Black danced back as their sabres met. 'You'll be finding it a lot like biting on cold steel, you shiftie scum.'

'Please, my people!' shouted Coppertracks from the sidelines as the commodore met the full force of Keyspierre's swinging sword. There was little subtlety in this duel. It was murder being done here. The commodore's hatred of the secret policeman matched with the Army of Shadows' hunger for human veins to rip into. Steel cracking as they smashed at each other, each trying to find a weakness in the other's guard.

'Go,' spat the commodore through gritted teeth as he turned a sabre thrust. 'I'll take this filthy wheatman down. Get to the ship and stop the blessed bomb being pushed through into King Steam's palace.'

Molly and Coppertracks tried to slip past, but the ballet of steel between Commodore Black and Keyspierre was impeding the only exit to the laboratory. Keyspierre hissed in derision at them. They were stuck fast.

'Always choosing the side of the underdog,' laughed

Keyspierre. 'How typically Jackelian. The Army of Shadows will take your land however you choose to die, and it will be my people feasting on your descendants.'

Molly cast around desperately. There had to be something, some weapon she could use. The duelling pair blocked her way to the scholar's pistol, but there . . . *the dissection slab*. She slipped behind the console, trying to work its arms.

'The feast at the revolution's table is coming to an end,' called the commodore over the noise of the sirens, stamping down and turning aside another thrust. But for all his bravado the old u-boat man was weakening. Keyspierre was younger, faster and had all the strength of the hunger, not to mention the training of expert duellists in the Quatérshiftian secret police behind him.

'We shall see.'

'You'll find out what those sirens are sounding for, and it's not for us. It'll be the House of Ferniethian that brings your revolution to an end,' wheezed the commodore, falling back. '*My* house. *My* daughter.'

One of the dissection array's arms lashed out to the end of its reach as Molly struggled with its controls. Not far enough to touch Keyspierre, but the rotating head of blades sliced into Lord Rooksby's cage door. With an eagle-like cry, the twisted Lord Commercial pushed free of the cage and snapped open his wings, gliding forward into Keyspierre, sending both of them sprawling across the laboratory floor.

Commodore Black was on top of them, trying to work out who was who in the struggle as they all rolled across the floor, the clawed fingers of the birdman matched against Keyspierre's fangs.

'You're so proud of your hunger, you dirty wheatman, let me feed it for you!' shouted the commodore as he thrust his sabre down into the shiftie's mouth, sliding the sword out and then slashing back and forth across the body.

Molly grabbed the u-boat man as he cut down furiously at the corpse. 'Jared! He's dead.'

Sense returned slowly to the commodore's eyes.

Molly looked to the open door of the laboratory. 'They're going to kill everyone in the Steammen Free State, Jared.'

Lord Rooksby pulled at his metal collar and made a croaking noise like a parrot, trying to form the words inside his mangled throat.

Molly listened intently to what Lord Rooksby was trying to say.

'*Show. Ship. Way.*'

'Thank you, Rooksby softbody,' said Coppertracks.

It had taken the loss of Rooksby's humanity for him to find it.

A twirling axe impaled the last slat defending the gantry and Purity ran out to stand underneath the dark rotating monster at the heart of the satellite. Half the Bandits of the Marsh had fallen fighting through waves of slats spilling out of the iron moon's halls, barracks and breeding chambers to get her this far. Those remaining began barricading the corridor leading to the vast chamber. It would not take long for the slat legions to arrive in their thousands to protect their most precious piece of plundered Kal technology.

Purity stepped over a master's body, the giant woman's perfect eyes staring lifelessly across at the white-hot barrel of the pistol that had fallen from her hand.

Jackaby Mention was behind Purity, wiping the blood from a knife onto his trousers. Jackaby looked up at the immense monster twisting in the hollow heart of the iron moon, using a broken set of brass goggles taken from one of the dead masters to stare at its malfeasance. A stillborn star, crushed beyond collapse and folding time with its corpse. A horror.

'That is it, my queen?'

'Yes,' said Purity. 'It's creating a window of time, punched through existence back into the past. The rift the Army of Shadows crawled out of.'

'I understand,' said Jackaby. 'Destroy this and we seal the Army of Shadows in the past.'

'It's not quite as easy as destroying it,' said Purity. 'The maths-blade showed me that. It's a dead star. Anything we throw at this thing will only feed it, make it stronger. Energy, matter, it will consume everything.'

Jackaby lowered his goggles. 'Then how?'

Purity stamped on the gantry running like a hoop around the rotating beast. 'There is a field of distorted time being created by this monster. We need to create another one in close opposition to it. One that will destabilize the first. The tides created by the two fields interacting with each other will rip apart the iron moon and allow the torn skin of time to heal itself.'

There were shouts coming out of the narrow corridor leading into the core of the moon, the thump of slat weapons and the cry of men and women dying to protect the entrance.

'I believe I know what you will ask next.'

'Know that I do not ask it lightly,' said Purity.

'I have never run that fast,' said Jackaby.

'The wind envies your heels, Jackaby Mention. Whisk me up a storm inside here, stir up the metre of time itself with your bare feet.'

'There is a reason my body freezes when I run,' said Jackaby. 'It is how I stay alive at such speeds. But for this I will need to run far beyond the cold, the cramps, run straight into the fire.'

'Fire behind us and fire in front,' said Purity.

'And ever was it thus.' Jackaby lowered himself into a sprinter's starting position, and then shouted at the other bandits protecting the gantry. 'Roll all the bodies off the path. I will need a clear run.'

'Thank you, Jackaby.'

'No,' said the bandit. 'Thank you, my queen. It has been my honour to serve you a second time.'

Purity spilled one of her dead fighters off the walkway, taking the corpse's trident first. 'How much time will you need?'

Jackaby stared up at the dark rotating singularity. 'About five million years' worth.'

'I'll buy it in the blood of our enemies.'

'Sell it dear,' one of the Bandits of the Marsh was yelling. 'Sell it dear!'

Purity hardly heard as she jabbed back at the snarling, hissing horde of slats breaking against the torrent of her fighters. This was violence in its rawest, dirtiest, most brutal form, curses and screams, spittle and wounds being given and received. Purity wept as she slashed and thrust her way through the melee. Here was war.

And through this channel of carnage the emperor came striding, surrounded by his personal guard of giants, all wearing the same armour – glistening black shells with massive rippling muscles – as if they had skinned slats alive to make it. The armour gave its wearers incredible strength, adding force to the giants' already perfect flesh. The masters tore into the front ranks of the Bandits of the Marsh, shredding their own slat soldiers to get to the intruders, to protect the dark star ripping time to sate their race's appetites.

Behind Purity a blur was whirling around the gantry,

439

becoming a wall of fire underneath of the Army of Shadows' dark rotating ball; the agonized doppler-shifted scream of Jackaby Mention a shocking drone echoing around the moon's core.

Here was war.

Commodore Black knocked the side of his stolen slat pistol against the hangar door, as if that would do any good. He had discovered that the weapon took three seconds to recharge between shots the hard way, and now he was limping where a wounded slat had torn at his leg.

'They're loading the bomb inside Starsprite,' said Coppertracks, the sharp sight of his vision plate magnifying the scene inside. 'If the slats have activated the gate...'

Then they only had mere seconds left to stop the slaughter of all the steammen.

Molly looked at the crystal rotating inside her pistol barrel, the air steaming around it. The Army of Shadows' damn heat agitation guns were intended to be handled by something of a slat's weight; she needed both hands to lift and point hers. Oh, for a good honest Jackelian purse pistol. Still, at least she was capable of holding one. Poor Lord Rooksby, with his broken, corrupted flesh, could only attack like a beast.

Molly pulled her heavy pistol up, looking at the force moving about their ship. 'So many slats.'

And so much for surprise.

Coppertracks was powering through into the hangar, desperation and panic adding speed to his treads. Molly stepped out of cover and sent one of the slats tumbling off its feet with her first shot, counting the seconds to her next one.

The last desperate charge of humanity and its allies had begun.

Molly was halfway through the hangar, racing through a hail of fire-bolts with Commodore Black by her side, cursing, when a stray shaft of energy severed the stays tying a steep rise of crates to a wall. An avalanche of heavy cases came crashing down towards the four of them.

One of the Bandits of the Marsh seized the lever to seal the door into the core of the iron moon – whether to buy more time for Jackaby Mention or to shut out the final terrible screams of his death rattle was not certain. The man needn't have bothered. The bandit Purity had released from a stone circle had gone beyond a blur, beyond a circling wall of flame, beyond the beat of time . . . and as two time fields that should never have co-existed collided, the rotating monster at the moon's core was compressed, tentacles of dead star-stuff stretching far outside the range of the magnetic guns beating it into submission. Time tore in two competing directions at once, the passage to the past punched by the Army of Shadows' singularity storming against the time field Jackaby's streaking form was whipping up, both bleeding together in the present – a paradox too far for the poor mangled fabric of reality – and the passage's door was sucked off into the core, walls of relativity and matter twisted beyond endurance.

Bandits, slats and their masters in the passage were drawn screaming into the raging maw at the moon's core, hands and talons flailing and digging at the corridor walls, the field of war turned into a mad solitary scramble for survival in a single instant. They tried to hold on despite the terrible quaking as the iron moon's orbit shifted. A flying body bounced off the opposite side of the passage, hitting the wall just above Purity's head and scrabbled onto the same instrument panel she was trying not to lose her grip on. The force of the dead star dragged the figure fumbling down alongside her. It was Watt, the young cobbler's face bleeding badly from a gash on his forehead.

'I told you that you would have been better off staying on the u-boat,' Purity called.

'I bet they sunk it,' Watt yelled back.

A struggling hissing slat flew past Purity and Watt; Purity's fingers clinging desperately onto that instrument panel on the red rusted wall.

Sliding through the broken melee fell the emperor, his giant's frame still enclosed by his slimy living armour. It wouldn't buy him even an extra second in the maelstrom being worked inside the core, not now the deadly singularity his people had looted had been unseated. He was skating down the floor, his hands digging desperately into bandits and his own followers, only succeeding in loosening their holds and sending slats and men toppling towards hideous termination.

The emperor flailed past Purity and Watt, grabbing hold of the edge of a side corridor just down from their position, trying to scramble up into it, but the draw of the singularity was too great even for the emperor's might; the incredible pressure drawing him back down. His bellow sounded over the roar of the singularity. 'Is this how it ends?'

'Every plague burns itself out in the end,' called Purity. She reached out to Watt's back and tore off the wax-paper wrapped parcel hanging there. Her shoes. And she hadn't even got to see them. She held her hand out, aiming the parcel at the emperor. 'Given *time*.'

As she opened her fingers, the parcel was torn out of her hand by the energies below, arrowing down the corridor, hitting the emperor's hands and dislodging him. Screaming, the emperor was sent spinning away into the Kals' creation. His people had consumed the ancient civilization of Kaliban whole; now it was the turn of their slave race's creation to consume him. The emperor's body buckled and bent, becoming a red brume as every molecule burst asunder and merged with the temporal rage of the singularity.

'A bit of a bloody waste,' shouted Watt. 'I could have unstrapped my wooden leg and given it to you for that . . .'

Purity shook her head. 'No, they were the best pair of shoes I ever had.'

'You got the best I ever made,' Watt yelled back.

Purity felt the increasing pressure of the singularity bearing down on her; sweat rolling off her and Watt's palms and pulled into the chaos of the core. She and Watt were going to last only seconds before they joined the emperor in his death beyond time. Purity tried to ignore the screams of the fighters and the surviving Jackelians being dislodged and sucked away, the deaths of her brave fey boys and girls.

The emperor's last words mocked her. *Is this how it ends?*

Purity and Watt exchanged glances and both lost their grip at the same time, falling into the light together.

Becoming the light.

Coppertracks' voicebox gave vent to his anguish as he saw what the slats had done to Starsprite, the half-steamman craft's innards lying spilled across her cabin. 'Vandals! Wreckers!'

The looking-glass gate was fused with the inner hull of the craft. No way to cut it out without risking the mirror's destruction. Poor Starsprite, she had been defying the Army of Shadows to the end. Trying to protect her half-brother Coppertracks and the people of the metal.

Following the steamman inside the craft, Lord Rooksby and Molly manhandled the commodore's unconscious form into the protection of the ship's cabin. They laid him down next to the corpses of the slats that had died defending the craft. He had taken quite a bang on the back of his head when that stray shot had severed the ties holding the supply crates. But Commodore Jared Black was a tough old bird. If any of them survived, surely it would be him.

'The bomb,' Molly shouted, indicating the masters' explosive, a large black egg resting on the two iron rails the slats had used to carry it inside the ship. 'Can it be defused?'

The chattering of the slats' sound-sight was growing loud in the hangar outside ran towards the battle. Lord Rooksby said something to Molly but she couldn't understand his mangled words.

Then the first quake hit, all the shell-like craft inside the hangar toppling over with an immense crash as the iron moon bounced in its orbit. A long, violent oscillation followed as the shockwave passed down the beanstalk connecting them to the world below. It only took seconds for the impact to pass through to the ground station and be reflected back up at them, followed by exploding machinery and a second quake.

'Purity must have made it to the core of the moon,' shouted Molly. 'She's striking at the great sage's dead star and bringing down the house.'

But the steamman had other things on his mind, his metal fingers flickering with urgency across the Army of Shadows' weapon. 'This bomb can't be defused in the little time we have, Molly softbody,' said Coppertracks, inspecting the weapon's panel. 'Its timer indicates a three-minute countdown. They must have armed it just as we attacked.'

'Activate the looking-glass,' ordered Molly. 'You told me that the gate only has enough power to stay open for a few seconds; we can be through and let the iron moon take the bomb's explosion when it goes off.' She dragged Commodore Black's unconscious body close to the mirrored surface. 'Enter the code to unlock the gate, old steamer.'

'Wait,' said the steamman. He was rooting through the components scattered about the floor. 'Starsprite's soul board, it must be here.'

'Coppertracks!'

There was another quake, even worse than the previous two. The moon was tearing itself apart around their murdered ship. Slat weapon-fire hailed against Starsprite's outer hull.

'I have it!' Coppertracks scooped up a black board in his iron fingers, setting his tracks to full reverse. The oily mirrored surface lit up and then faded into transparency as he tapped his activation key into the gate. The hazy outlines of a room were now visible on the other side, centaur-like steammen knights running towards the membrane. From the looks of it, the portal led directly to the steammen's mountain stronghold, King Steam's palace.

Molly and Lord Rooksby passed Commodore Black's body through to the steammen knights, the u-boat man moaning as he began to recover his senses. Coppertracks went next, great iron arms belonging to his kin appearing through the quivering membrane to help lift the venerable scientist through.

Molly turned to Lord Rooksby, tugging at him, a handful of moulting feathers from his wing-like arm coming away in her hand. 'Come on!'

The birdman tapped the black sphere of the bomb. 'Protect.'

'There are womb mages back in Jackals, worldsingers, they might be able to help you—'

Shaking his head, Lord Rooksby opened his man-beak again. '*Protect.*'

As Molly launched herself through the looking glass, she experienced a vertigous feeling, like falling. Her last sight before passing through the membrane was of Lord Rooksby going to the door of the craft and screeching defiance at the attacking slats. It wasn't the cry of a bird. It was the roar of a lion. Molly hit a cold stone floor, scattering the feathers from Rooksby's wing. The mirror cracked, fizzing sparks above her, its oily surfacing growing dark and hard. Their gate had sealed them off, sealed them in the mountain fastness of the steammen.

Commodore Black was on his feet, banging at the mirror, trying to get back to the other side, but it was too late. 'Purity!'

'It's no good, Jared softbody,' said Coppertracks. 'There's a large-yield neutron bomb about to be detonated on the iron moon.'

'About to be detonated?' called one of the steammen guarding the looking-glass gate. 'Have you not seen the moon, brother slipthinker?' He pointed to a door opening out onto a mountain terrace. The baleful iron moon was growing smaller, the white tentacle of the dislodged beanstalk whipping behind it like the flagellum of a bacterium, explosions flowering out from underneath the rusted surface.

'My girl, oh my lovely brave girl!'

'The star field,' said Coppertracks. 'By my ancestors' cogs, look at the heavens. The stars are returning to normal. The time field projected by the iron moon is diminishing. The moon is being sucked into the collapsing field, back towards Kaliban, back along its own original timeline.'

'I told her, Aliquot Coppertracks, I told my beautiful little lass who she was, just like you said I should have done all along.'

'She saved us all,' said Molly, shocked. The sight of the crumbling moon was mesmerizing. 'Purity, she told me that she would.'

A halo of fierce purple light suddenly surrounded the iron moon as the weapon that would have destroyed King Steam's realm briefly lit the heavens. Then the terrible eye winked out, the last of the stars returning to their true positions. The iron moon was gone forever.

'I don't care,' whispered the commodore. He fell to his knees and began to cry.

EPILOGUE

Five million years ago

The four Kal bearers carrying Fayris Fastmind's stretcher-style chair placed him carefully down on the cliff. Not so close to the edge that he might fall off, but near enough that the great sage could see the siege works raised around the last city.

'You should be more careful,' advised the sage's chief bearer, opening a sunshade for his ancient mentor. The thump of slat rifles, dimmed by distance, and the cries of lashlites floated in the furnace-like air above the giant face of Kaliban. All the faint clatter of their siege. 'We could move back a little.' He pointed towards the tent that the others in the nomad caravan had set up behind them, its memory silk already a crimson rock-like haze as it matched the pattern of the mountain.

'We are far enough away from the siege works, I think,' said the great sage.

His people were nervous. The nomads didn't want to lose even one among the few that still understood the old science. Every tribe held fiercely tight to its sages, although they were little more than court sorcerers now.

The great sage's chief bearer pointed down the cliff face they were perched above. One of the giant weather machines the Kals had tampered with was shuffling across the plains on its nest of steel tentacles, coming towards the cliff face, ready to rip out more rocks to hurl towards the masters' domes. 'The machines sometimes cause landslides when they pull rocks out of the mountain.'

'I will take the risk. I'm as old as these mountains,' said the great sage. 'And I like the view.'

Yes, the view. Fayris Fastmind lifted up his set of binoculars and focused on the plain below. He could see trains of lizards pulling canal barges across the dunes towards catapults, the barges converted into fused bombs after their self-destruct sensors had been disabled and the craft pulled out of the canal's sludge. But that wasn't what he was looking for. There! There was the man, riding up and down the trenches, shouting encouragement towards the Kals below and the lashlites above.

Connor of Cassarabia, still mounted on the thorax saddle of his tamed queen ant, a god of war thundering up and down the lines, the proud insect steed rearing and flashing its mandibles.

Who would have thought such things possible? That a queen ant could be broken. Or that a lion could lead a flock of sheep to inherit the world?

A baby's cry came from the direction of the tent, the young female swaddled in white robes and being wet-nursed by the chief bearer's wife.

'We could show him the child now.'

The great sage shook his head. 'Wait for the fall of the city to show him the girl. It will come soon enough.'

After all, it was the least the sages could do. Reactivating a few cells scraped off Duncan Connor's bag of bones had been the easy part. Adapting a stolen slat birthing tank to accommodate the pattern of the race of man as it would be in the distant future, that had stretched the ingenuity and the depleted resources of all of the hidden sages.

Down below, Duncan Connor's upland battle cry roared across the plain.

Connor of Kaliban.

Some time later

The farm boy brushed the snow settling on his woollen breeches off across the rubble of what had once been the base of the Army of Shadows' beanstalk, then pointed to the sword embedded in the hillside. Left rooted just as it might have been if a flailing anchor cable had thrown it against the stone with all the force of a moon being pulled away.

Grunting, the shaman of the tribe of polar barbarians followed the farm boy. So, the sword was there after all, although the shaman didn't believe for a moment that the young farmer hadn't touched the blade before coming to tell the tribe's elders. Such a sword begged for men to come and attempt to pull it out of the side of the hill. And of course, the farm boy had failed in his striving to free the blade.

The shaman inspected the ground and the hillside and the sword and the figure sprawled beside it. It was a man, dressed in the same clothes as the southern traders who sometimes ventured to the polar realm in their steam-driven iron boats. What were their people called again? Jackelians, that was it. This one was a Jackelian, no doubt about it. 'This one is a herald who has stayed to sing of the victory of the gods over the blood drinkers and their black-bone trolls.'

'He's alive? I thought—'

'You are a young fool, there is life here.' The shaman touched the man's neck then ran his hand over the hard frozen soil. 'Just as there is life under here, also. Go back to the caves, fetch my case of herbs and tell the people to hide no more. Tell the ungrateful non-believers they have a great stone circle to raise in the shadow of a sword as thanks to the gods they foolishly thought had forsaken them.'

The shaman shook his head as the farm boy ran off. His people had believed too little and suffered as a consequence. He laid a finger on the man's neck again. The pulse was still there. The shaman shivered – but not from the cold – and unclipped his dragon brooch, laying his cloak over the herald to warm the man up. There was a dark power inside this stranger, he could feel it. Shadows seemed to move around the rocks of this place, shadows given life. Standing up, the shaman stared into the clear night sky, empty of the monsters' red chariot now. A woman's sibilant voice seemed to whisper through the gently blowing snow. *Hood. Hood-o'the-marsh.*

Pulling out a glass tube of golden filings, the shaman scattered the most precious of commodities, star metal, around the ruins of the beanstalk so it would not grow up to the heavens again, blessing the most sacred of grounds.

'There are no marshes here, goddess.'

It seemed fitting to hold their private ceremony on Nagcross Bridge, Molly and Coppertracks anonymous again after the parade through the capital's newly renamed Highhorn Square. After all, with so few surviving workers and scientists from the cannon project the parade's focus had been on the sailors and officers of the *JNS Spartiate*, the fleet sea arm much the fashion among the public again, after centuries spent hero-worshipping the Royal Aerostatical Navy and its jack cloudies.

Molly stopped to look out across the River Gambleflowers,

standing in a break between the shops that rose up on either side of the bridge. 'At least the commodore had managed to keep his mouth shut about Keyspierre during the ceremony.'

'Peace with Quatérshift, dear mammal, is well worth the price of a small lie,' said Coppertracks. 'Who would have thought we would see peace in our time? I read in the *Illustrated* yesterday that parliament is going to repeal the Corn Law and allow grain shipments east again. Mark my words, there will be statues of Keyspierre being chipped out across the border before the end of the month.'

'And a statue to Lord Rooksby here in Jackals,' said Molly. 'Although the House of Guardians is still arguing about who should go on top of the second plinth in Highhorn Square.'

Indeed, Molly had seen the cartoon in the newspaper the steamman had bought. A statueless towering column with a gaggle of parliamentarians trying to push each other off the top, their trousers half-pulled down, a speech bubble rising from a crew of u-boat sailors below trying to dodge the faeces falling out of the politicians' overlarge buttocks, saying, '*Gads, you jolly tars, now it is each other they attempt to give the shaft.*'

'If I had a vote in parliament I would cast it in favour of a statue of you,' said Coppertracks.

'Then let us both be glad that you've never stood for election as a guardian,' smiled Molly.

Coppertracks' transparent dome of a skull flared with energy. 'I am quite sincere, Molly softbody. You risked your life on the iron moon to save my people from the Army of Shadows.'

'I think I risked it to save your people from *my* people.'

'The Army of Shadows were not you,' insisted Coppertracks. 'It is not the composition of our form that defines us, it is our actions on the great pattern. My heart pulses with steam, your heart beats with blood, yet when your people had to choose, you – even that rascal Lord Rooksby – chose to act with the humanity your race wears as its title.'

Molly nodded. Yes, let poor dead Lord Rooksby have his place up on the plinth, as a scientist and the official leader of the expedition, rather than the twisted avian monster he had been transformed into. He had earned it, in the end.

'Then what are we, old steamer?'

Coppertracks changed his treads' configuration to raise him up and stared out across the capital's fast-flowing river. 'Molly softbody, you are my friend.' The steamman reached down into a satchel, bringing out the porcelain canister containing the ashes from the handful of Lord Rooksby's feathers Molly had seized. 'And speaking of friends, shall we wait for Jared before we scatter these in the river?'

Molly shook her head. Commodore Black wouldn't be coming onto the bridge any time soon. 'The hero of Highhorn is in one of those taverns down on the embankment drinking it up with the *Spartiate*'s crew. One of the officers mentioned he had a brother in the State Office of Shipwrights who might be able to put a decommissioned u-boat Jared's way for the right price.'

'By the beard of Zaka of the Cylinders,' said the startled steamman. 'Please tell me you are making a jest?'

'Would that I were,' said Molly.

'He is too old to go jaunting about the world in a u-boat,' said Coppertracks, passing the jar of ashes for Molly to scatter. 'As am I for such foolishness.'

'Oh, I don't know. Now that your tower's been taken down, a gentle voyage of scientific discovery might be just the thing.'

'The last time I followed Jared softbody on a seadrinker vessel, the only discovery I made was how much treasure and death lay hiding on the Isla Needless. I shall talk him out of this folly after we are finished here. My arguments coupled with the attractions of a warm house and a full pantry will win the day, I am sure, with winter coming.'

Molly shrugged. Good luck to that. Opening the jar, she tipped the ashes from Lord Rooksby's feathers away, a shroud of dark dust falling into the wind and drifting above the surface of the river's green waters.

Molly bowed her head and said a quiet meditation to the Circle for Rooksby's soul to be cupped out of the one sea of consciousness and refilled into a happier life. 'To all the friends we have lost.'

Below, Lord Rooksby's ashes joined the water and were borne away by the frothing course of the Gambleflowers. The river took everything, in Middlesteel.